Lost Letters

Lost Letters

— *A Civil War Love Story* —

Lori Roberts

iUniverse, Inc.
Bloomington

Lost Letters
A Civil War Love Story

Copyright © 2012 by Lori Roberts.

All rights reserved. No part of this book may be used or reproduced by any means, graphic, electronic, or mechanical, including photocopying, recording, taping or by any information storage retrieval system without the written permission of the publisher except in the case of brief quotations embodied in critical articles and reviews.

This is a work of fiction. All of the characters, names, incidents, organizations, and dialogue in this novel are either the products of the author's imagination or are used fictitiously.

iUniverse books may be ordered through booksellers or by contacting:

iUniverse
1663 Liberty Drive
Bloomington, IN 47403
www.iuniverse.com
1-800-Authors (1-800-288-4677)

Because of the dynamic nature of the Internet, any web addresses or links contained in this book may have changed since publication and may no longer be valid. The views expressed in this work are solely those of the author and do not necessarily reflect the views of the publisher, and the publisher hereby disclaims any responsibility for them.

Any people depicted in stock imagery provided by Thinkstock are models, and such images are being used for illustrative purposes only.
Certain stock imagery © Thinkstock.

ISBN: 978-1-4759-1336-1 (sc)
ISBN: 978-1-4759-1335-4 (hc)
ISBN: 978-1-4759-1334-7 (ebk)

Library of Congress Control Number: 2012906999

Printed in the United States of America

iUniverse rev. date: 05/12/2012

To Haden & Hadley ~ my precious grandchildren.

For Blaire, Blake & Annie ~ my greatest accomplishments.

For my parents ~ the first to teach me about my ancestors and introduce me to what would become a passion~ the Civil War.

For Doug ~ my answered prayer, who makes me believe that I can do anything.

Special thanks and deep appreciation to my mentor and dearest friend, Charlotte.
Proverbs 17:17

Lost letters . . .
Ellie Morgan has just inherited an old house: musty, and full of other people's memories. Hidden inside forgotten letters, she discovers a story of lost love and the soldier who draws her into his world. Ellie uncovers a love that was lost. Will she find love for herself in its unveiling?

January 1, 1863
Martha Elkins listens carefully to the young soldier beginning to tell her what she should write. *Poor boy, he could not be any older than my own boy, Thomas. So many boys; so young and full of promise.*

Listening to the wounded soldier mumble his final words, her pencil scrabbles hurriedly as she struggles to hear over the moans and cries of the wounded soldiers being carried in from the battle in nearby Murfreesboro.

"Soldier, what is your name?" she softly inquires.
"Raford Collins, Ma'am, but my folks call me Rafe."

Offering a weak smile, he succumbs to pain and surrenders to the abyss of unconsciousness.

The measure of a woman's character is not what she gets from her ancestors, but what she leaves her descendants.
~ Unknown

Chapter 1

Ellie Morgan closed the door to her classroom and walked slowly down the hall. *Now what am I going to do for the next three months?* Ellie thought to herself as she dug through her large bag for her car keys. In truth, she couldn't imagine how she would fill her summer. With her divorce final and her only child, Cassie, working her first job in another state, life would certainly be quiet. There was that fellow from the technical department that had asked her to have dinner sometime, but she felt uncertain about him. He seemed interesting, but going on a date was another matter. Ellie had ended twenty-two years of marriage in a not-so-friendly divorce. She was just glad the whole experience was now in the rearview mirror. The marriage had ended for Ellie when her husband decided to visit his old ways. Ellie tried to ignore the signs, but Brad Morgan was unfaithful, before and after their wedding. He promised it would never happen again. That was just one of many vows he broke. It actually was a blessing; it was Ellie's way out. Now, here she was, at forty-three years old, starting over again.

Ellie's nightly ritual had involved picking up the mail from the row of mailboxes, shoving bills and junk mail into her school bag, and then driving into the condominium garage. Once inside, she usually made a snack and got on her laptop to check her emails, talk to friends on a couple of social media sites, then sort through the pile of mail. Tonight, she decided to change her habits and call her best friend, Charlotte Hobbs, to have a dinner out for a change. Charlotte had never married, saying that no man could make her happy, so she would just date them all instead! Charlotte would have made someone a great wife; she was funny, pretty, and would have been a great mother, but didn't seem to regret being childless. Charlotte had been a real estate agent for years, making good investments and surviving the recent market crash fairly well. She was always taking a cruise, going on weekend getaways with a friend, and the one Ellie called when she needed advice or just a shoulder on which to cry.

Ellie drove her father's pickup into the parking lot of *N'Kahoots*, the local bar and grill in Newburgh, Indiana. The truck was one of Ellie's dearest connections to her father, Frank Camden, who had lost his battle with cancer much too early in life. Everyone loved Frank. He was the high school basketball coach and church deacon. The red Silverado still smelled of her father's pipe, a habit he promised Ellie's mother to relinquish. Ellie breathed in deeply as the smell of English Leather cologne and Captain Black pipe tobacco filled her nostrils and brought a smile to her face.

"Hey you, are you going to sit in that truck all night? It's happy hour, ya know," Charlotte laughed as she tossed her long brown locks over her shoulder.

Ellie followed Charlotte into the dimly lit bar. After her eyes adjusted to the low lighting, she noticed her former husband sitting at a table with a very shapely young blonde.

"Good lord, the one night I decided to get out of my house, do I honestly have to see *him?*" (Ellie had gone several delightful weeks with no contact.)

Charlotte, fearful the carefree mood was ruined, offered, "We don't have to stay, ya know."

Ellie didn't intend to let her ex run her out of a public place. After all, they were no longer married. She could ignore him, or acknowledge him. Either way, he was sitting right in the path where the server would be taking them. *Take the high road, Ellie.*

Before the pair could reach their booth, Brad Morgan turned, "Hello, Ellie," he said sardonically.

"Hey, Brad," Ellie countered as she moved right through the crowd, never glancing back.

As the two friends slid into their booth, Charlotte rejoiced, "Now that's the Ellie I remember!"

Ellie looked flustered, but tried to appear nonplused.

"Char, you know that he was hoping to draw my attention to the blonde. I wasn't going to give him the satisfaction! Besides, I have had a change of heart since we talked last."

Charlotte's eyebrows lifted, leaning in as if to hear a long-lost secret. "And just what epiphany did you have since Monday? Do tell!"

Ellie paused, as the waitress placed their drinks on the table, and then asked for their order.

"How about giving us a minute; we haven't decided yet."

The pretty young college student had plenty of other patrons waiting for service, so she smiled and promised to return in a few moments.

"Okay, Char, I am three hours into my summer vacation; my first summer vacation as a single woman, mind you! I don't want this summer to be like all the others. I need to move on with the rest of my life."

Charlotte, listening approvingly, added, "Ellie, you know I have been preaching that sermon to you for months. It's high time you stopped living for everyone else."

Ellie knew her best friend was correct. She had been staying in an unhappy marriage for Cassie, helping with the college expenses for the last four years. They had been close, but now Cassie was spreading her wings thirteen hours away. She would always need her mom, but Ellie was beginning to realize that she was the needy one. The grief that remained when her dad died had escalated into a void of loneliness. After that realization, Ellie had her *Come to Jesus Meeting*. She was still young, and it was time to start living again!

"Char, I'm thinking about going out with Sean Barrow, the computer technician at school," Ellie confided. "He's asked me a few times, and I am leaning towards accepting."

She held her breath in anticipation of Charlotte's response, "Sean, the metro-sexual computer nerd from the high school?" (Charlotte had a way of making everyone have a title.)

"Metro-sexual, honestly, Char!" Ellie laughed at Charlotte's assessment, but she could visualize Sean pulling off a sexy look.

Sipping her tea, Charlotte leaned in closer, continuing, "You've got three months to enjoy being a lady of leisure. You teachers have it made."

With that comment, Charlotte dodged the rolled up napkin Ellie sailed passed her head.

Ellie slept in that first Saturday of her summer vacation. Walking down the hall to the sunny kitchen, she rubbed her eyes, not used to the brightness. As she poured her coffee and began to eat her bowl of cereal, she began to leaf through the pile of mail that she had flopped down on the counter the night before. Evidently, credit card companies loved her. Each day, a new one appeared in the mail. She knew she had good credit, but she didn't need any debt. The insurance bill for the truck was in the pile. Its tires needed changing, as her dad had been the last to do that. *Dad, you weren't supposed to die. It wasn't fair!* Ellie sometimes felt real anger for losing her parents. If her mother had been living, she doubted she would have married Brad, but then she wouldn't have her precious Cassie.

The next piece of mail was unfamiliar to her. She had seen enough letters from *Billings, McDonough and Pratt* to last her a lifetime, but this letter was from an unfamiliar law firm.

The envelope was addressed to Ms. Ella Camden. In pen, the local postmistress had penned in her last name, *Morgan*. Ellie cringed. *I wish I had dropped Morgan; I miss being a Camden.* Ellie wasn't sure whom the letter was from, but it was someone who knew her from her younger days, as only her family and very close friends knew her given name was Ella. Her mother had loved Ella Fitzgerald, and had vowed that if her child were to be a daughter; her name would be *Ella*. Frank had started calling her Ellie right after they brought her home from the hospital. It was Ellie from then on.

The envelope was from *The Law Offices of Langley & Murdock*, Hendersonville, Tennessee. *Who in the world?*

"Oh for Pete's sake, I won't know if I don't open it!" Ellie chastised herself, and began to rip open the envelope.

The letter looked official, with the letterhead matching the names on the envelope's return address. Ellie reached for the pair of cheaters she kept in the basket on the table, trying to focus on the letters that seemed to blur. *Note to self: make sure to get that eye doctor appointment this summer!* The letter was addressed to Ms. Camden, so obviously the person who was trying to sue her didn't realize she was married and now divorced. As Ellie began to read the letter, it became clear that no one wanted to sue her, quite the contrary!

> *Dear Ms. Camden,*
> *It is with much sadness that I must write to inform you of your great aunt's recent passing at the age of 101. Mrs. Lavina George had been living in the Bridges Retirement Village in Hendersonville, Tennessee, for the past ten years. She had*

recently suffered a stroke, and within a few weeks passed away. Your great aunt had been a client of my father's for over fifty years, and I was present when her final will and testament were rewritten ten years ago. We will be reading the will on Friday, June 3. Your aunt named you the executor of the will, and you are required to be present for the reading. Mrs. George had no children and Mr. George passed away over forty-five years ago. My father has retired from the firm, but continued to offer Mrs. George assistance until her passing.
Please contact me at your earliest convenience.

Respectfully yours,
Riley F. Langley
cc Carol Pennington

Ellie sat with the spoon still in her mouth, dumbstruck from the contents of the letter.

Who was Lavina George? Surely, this was a clerical error. Someone had made a terrible mistake. Ellie knew all of her father's family. The Camden's were a close-knit family who met yearly for reunions. She knew of no Lavina in the family. However, her mother's side of the family was not close. Her parents had died before Ellie was in elementary school. She didn't even remember hearing about her mother's distant relatives, as they had lived in Tennessee and North Carolina. Liz Camden, Ellie's mom, had been Elizabeth Caroline Ridgeway. Her father and mother had moved to Indiana after World War II, when her father had taken a job with the railroad. Liz and her brother, Loren, didn't see much of their mother's family after that. Maybe it was a relative of her mother's.

Her uncle Loren had been in a nursing home since his wife passed away. His mind was good, but he suffered from a heart ailment that had confined him to his wheelchair or bed. Maybe she should drive over to visit him. He would remember her, even though it had been two years, and perhaps be able to fill in the blanks of the family's history. The letter went into the wooden bowl that sat on the dining room table. Ellie would take care of that next week. *I will see Uncle Loren and put an end to the mistaken identity.* In the meantime, she decided to give Sean a call. It was time to start her new life!

Newburgh, Indiana isn't what most people would call a big city. Ellie had lived in this small town since she was born. She had found her job right out of college, even with a small baby. Brad had been fortunate to have a job with his father's construction company. Playing basketball at Bellarmine College in Louisville, Kentucky gave him a business degree, and his father's business ensured a career until he wanted to retire. Brad and she weren't wealthy, but they lived in comfort. Cassie always thought they were the tightest parents who ever lived, but they wanted her to appreciate her things, not expect them. Ellie felt that she was part of Newburgh, and couldn't imagine living in a big city. When Cassie announced she would be moving across the country to work near the large city of Baltimore, Maryland, Ellie had cringed.

Having lived in the condo a year, it was time to think about getting her things out of storage, and selling what wasn't sentimental or donating it to charity. Sean Barrow had offered to help her with the heavy things, even hauling it to wherever she decided. She had forgotten about his offer until now. Maybe that would be a good excuse to have him come over, and then fix him dinner. As her mind began to race from first one thought to another, she had to laugh at herself and the little flutter that was in her stomach at the thought of a date. *Goodness, how long had it been since she had actually had a date? Twenty-five years? Well, no sense putting the cart before the horse.* She would have to call Sean first.

Before she could find the staff directory from school, her cell phone began to ring. Ellie answered the phone and heard Cassie's voice on the other end.

"Hey! I thought while I had a minute, I'd give you a buzz."

As the mother and daughter began to talk, it was clear that Cassie needed and missed her mother, no matter how she acted three weeks before!

"Mom, there is so much to do at work, so much to learn! I just don't know if I can do it!"

Ellie wasn't sure what Cassie was expected to do, but knew that her first job as a television reporter had to be overwhelming! She accepted a job working in the newsroom, with an opportunity to work some weekends on air, once she proved herself capable. Cassie had taken the job at the television station after an interview four weeks before. Her move resembled a whirlwind. Cassie understood Ellie wasn't able to help her move due to end-of-year responsibilities, including graduation ceremonies. Brad had rented a van and driven the thirteen hours to the apartment complex near

Hagerstown, Maryland. Ellie would be flying out to visit her daughter in two weeks.

"Cassie, what's wrong?" Ellie asked, hearing the anxiousness in Cassie's voice.

Cassie explained how the newsroom producer was irritated with the soft-spoken mannerisms she used interviewing subjects.

"Things are paced so much faster than they were at the station in Evansville," she said. (Cassie had interned at the Evansville station for three years while attending the University of Evansville. She felt she was prepared to take on this role.)

"You know, Cassie, all jobs take some getting used to. I think things will start to settle down once the producer appreciates your style. We're all different!"

Cassie could hear her mother's support through the phone, but added, "Mom, you have to say that. You're my mom. Besides, I don't know a soul here, and I am really tired of having no one to talk to besides my friends online!"

Ellie could tell she and her daughter were both experiencing loneliness.

"Why don't you ask someone to go to dinner? Are there any single girls or guys who have just been hired?"

Ellie could tell that suggestion didn't go over well when Cassie fired back, "Mom, it isn't like living in Newburgh. People are, well, friendly, but not welcoming. It just isn't like I thought it would be."

Ellie felt her mothering defenses start to kick in, and she wanted to walk down the hall to her daughter's room, hug her, and tell her it would eventually all work out. She realized even though Cassie was a woman, she would always be *her little girl. Ellie smiled as she remembered that her father had always referred to her as his little girl too.*

"Well, you know I'm coming out there in a couple of weeks! I'm really looking forward to seeing your new home, Cassie."

Cassie's tone changed, "Did Daddy tell you about my apartment?"

"No, I have only seen your dad once since your move, and we really didn't have a conversation, but I saw your pictures that you posted online. It is just lovely, Honey!"

"It's really nice, Mom. I think I need some advice on decorating though. Your visit is just what I need! I'm really looking forward to you coming. I hope you won't be bored while I'm at work though."

The days wouldn't be boring to Ellie. She had already decided to hit the historical sites in and around Baltimore. First on the list was the battlefield of Antietam, then drive to Gettysburg for a day. Cassie had never been interested in history, even though Ellie had hoped her love of the subject would rub off on her only child. Cassie took after her father, in that her loves were sports and television. The two agreed that she would spend the days sightseeing and the nights helping Cassie settle into her new home. Cassie then changed the topic of conversation by asking her mom about her social life.

"Mom, are you going to start dating now that I'm not living in Newburgh?"

To say Ellie was surprised was an understatement!

"Cassie, is that what you think? That I was waiting until you moved to have a social life. That couldn't be further from the truth."

Cassie rolled her eyes. "Mom, I didn't mean anything bad by it, I just figured you were trying to just make things easier on me."

There was no sense beating around the bush since Cassie opened the door.

"So, you'd be okay with me dating someone?"

Excitement was evident in Cassie's voice, "Are you thinking about it then?"

"Well, there is someone with whom I might go to dinner. It would be nice to have some adult conversation after teaching kids all year!"

Cassie laughed at her mom's sudden defensive tone.

"Back off of the ledge, Mom. I am perfectly fine with you having a life. I've been doing a lot better with the divorce. I'm still angry with Daddy, don't get me wrong, but he's my dad. I love you both, and I want you to be happy, Mom."

Ellie knew she had raised her daughter to honor her commitments, and she felt that she had let her down by divorcing her father. Hearing Cassie sounding more supportive than ever, she decided to wait until their time together to tell her about her date, *if* there was one.

"Well, I'll call you in the middle of the week to see how things are going, so be sure and keep your phone charged. Also, remember that you're not living in Newburgh, Cassie. I hope you are taking our advice and being cautious."

Cassie rolled her eyes at the sound of her mother's admonitions.

"Mom, I am living in freaking Fort Knox here. I don't think you and Dad could have chosen a more secure location for me to move. I can't believe Daddy paid my first year's rent."

Ellie was glad that Brad had thought ahead to do that.

"Cassie, he just wanted you to have a safe place to live until you could find something more to your liking once you were established."

"I know, Mom, but I feel like most of the people here are senior citizens! Everyone is old!" Ellie had to laugh at her daughter.

"Cassie, it is better this way for now. You'll meet so many new people once you're settled. I promise! Maybe you should think about getting a kitten!"

Ellie knew how much Cassie missed her cat, Miss Kitty, who had to be put down just two months before her graduation from the university.

"I'm thinking about getting a dog," Ellie confessed. "It is so quiet here at night, and I am living around *old* people!"

They both laughed at that, and then Cassie continued, "Mom, I'm getting another call. It's Daddy."

Ellie remembered Brad's expression the night before at *N'Kahoots* with the blonde. *Ugh.*

"Well, it's okay, go ahead and take his call. We'll talk later in the week. You be careful, honey. Remember what I said."

"I will, Mom. It was so good to hear your voice. I love you!"

"And I love you, Cassie."

The conversation left Ellie thinking about her daughter being all alone in a strange city. Ellie was lonely, but she had Charlotte. Cassie's best friend had gotten married the week that Cassie moved. Her wedding was the last time she had seen her friends all together. Ellie walked out to get her newspaper thinking about looking in the classifieds for a puppy. After entering the condominium, Ellie relaxed in the large leather recliner that had once belonged to her father. *I guess I really should call Sean while I have my nerve up!* Ellie sat the paper down and reached for the cell phone lying on the table. As the phone was ringing, she thought to herself, *He really wasn't a computer geek, but metro-sexual? Well, maybe.*

The phone call didn't last more than a few minutes. Ellie was not nervous, but she did find herself having a hard time forming her thoughts into words.

"Hullo," Sean sounded like he had been asleep. *Was it that early?*

Ellie looked at her watch as she said, "Sean, its Ellie. Did I get you at a bad time?"

Sean Barrow immediately perked up when he heard her name.

"Ellie, how are you? Have you already crashed your laptop in the twenty-four hours since we left school?" Sean laughed.

Ellie swallowed, wondering why her throat felt so dry.

"Well, I was hoping you weren't too busy this weekend. I want to move some furniture of Dad's out, and bring some of mine over to the condominium. But if you're busy . . ."

Sean interrupted her in mid sentence, "Sure, I'd be glad to. And to think I was just gonna have a fly-by-the-seat-of-my-pants day!"

They both laughed, and Ellie exclaimed, "Well, thank you! How about you come over whenever you're ready, and I'll put you to work!"

"Sounds great! I'm going to mow my folks' yard, but I can be there around 4:30. Is that too late?"

Ellie smiled. *What a great son he is*!

"No, that would be just fine. What sounds good for supper? I haven't been cooking much lately, but I think I still remember how to fire up the grill!"

Ellie couldn't believe she'd just invited him to dinner!

"I'd love it. I'm tired of the frozen entrées I have here. Whatever you fix would be great!"

Ellie had to get in gear! She wasn't sure she even had steaks in the freezer.

"Okay then, I will feed you first, but then you have to work it off!"

Ellie was surprised at the ease with which the two of them conversed, having not said more than a dozen words throughout the school year to one another.

"Good deal! I'll see you around 4:30 then!" Sean ended.

Ellie thanked him, and put the cell phone on the counter.

She would have to go to the grocery and get some food. Ellie had forgotten to ask him if he drank beer or wine. She had a good supply of soft drinks and iced tea, so to cover all her bases, she added beer and wine to the list. *Now where did I put my keys last night when I came inside?* Ellie rummaged through her purse, but couldn't find the key ring that seemed to get bigger by the year. As a creature of habit, she usually left the keys on the front flap of her purse, held on with a purse hook.

As she began to retrace her steps, she remembered sitting them on the table along with the mail. *The mail. The letter. She would have to let the attorney know that he had made an error, but first needed to visit her uncle Loren.* It was only half past twelve; she could drive over to Hampton House, talk with her uncle, and still make it back from the store by three o'clock. Ellie quickly put her hair up in the ponytail and grabbed the keys to her dad's truck.

When she arrived at Hampton House, her uncle Loren was sitting in the dining hall. At first, he didn't notice her. He was watching another resident having dinner with his daughter and granddaughter.

"Hello, Uncle Loren." Ellie smiled and touched her uncle's broad shoulder.

Even having aged, he still had quite the large build. His heart may have been giving out, but he still had the upper body of a much younger man.

"Ellie! How are you, Kid?"

From her earliest memory, Uncle Loren had always called her 'kid'. Being his only niece, he enjoyed spoiling and teasing her. It had been two years since she had seen him, and suddenly she felt ashamed she'd let the time lapse.

"How are you feeling, Uncle Loren? You look great!"

Ellie tried to sound upbeat, but Loren bluntly countered, "Oh come on, I feel like I've been road hard and hung up wet, Ellie. You can see that."

Loren didn't mince words, and Ellie stopped pretending.

"I'm sorry. How bad is it? Does your doctor come to check on you often?"

Loren became engulfed in deep coughing, and the fit clearly took a great deal out of the elderly man.

"Well, Doc says I have congestive heart failure. Just a matter of time until the old ticker quits. I guess I already knew that, but it still kicks ya in the gut, ya know?"

Yes, she knew. She was still having a hard time accepting the death of her father, and now it seemed she would lose her only uncle before long.

"Uncle Loren, do you remember having an aunt named Lavina George? She lived down South." Ellie hoped the name struck a chord.

"Lavina George? Well, sure I remember her. She was quite the spitfire!" Uncle Loren snickered.

Ellie suddenly didn't know if hearing the bad news of her passing would be the best thing to tell her uncle.

"Why didn't Mom ever talk about her? I think I would have remembered her."

A smile spread over his face.

"Well, your mom probably didn't talk much about her because Lavina didn't like your daddy."

Ellie couldn't believe there was a soul on the face of the earth that didn't like Frank Camden!

"Lavina only met him one time when the family went with Mother and Father to a family reunion down in Tennessee. Your daddy and mother had only been married a short time, and they took you along. Aunt Vinnie loved children. She couldn't have her own, so all the babies had to be plopped down on her lap first thing to be kissed and petted! Your daddy felt like you needed to warm up to her first, and that didn't set well with Aunt Vinnie. Besides, she felt like your momma could do better than a teacher and coach. She thought the girls in the family should marry doctors or lawyers. But the worst of it was that she married *a Yankee*. I think she was still having a hard time believing that the South lost the war!"

Loren began laughing, which was promptly followed by another fit of coughing. *So there was a great aunt named Lavina.* Once the coughing had passed, Loren took a drink of the large glass of tea on the table.

"What made you ask about Aunt Vinnie, Kid?"

Ellie wasn't sure if telling Uncle Loren about his aunt's death would unduly upset him, but she felt she couldn't lie.

"Well, I received a letter from Tennessee today from her lawyer."

"I thought she was getting on in years, but why would her lawyer need to contact you?"

Loren seemed confused.

Ellie explained, "It seems that Aunt Lavina had a stroke some time back and never fully recovered. She passed away a few weeks ago."

Loren seemed saddened, but not upset.

"A stroke, you say? Well, she lived a long, good life."

Ellie continued, "The lawyer says that she was one hundred and one years old and died peacefully. He also said that she changed her will, naming me her executor."

Loren seemed interested, but not overly so.

"Is that so? You'd think someone on Uncle Shelby's side would have done that. How'd Vinnie find out where you were? She hadn't seen you in over 40 years."

Ellie wondered that very same thing.

"I don't know, Uncle Loren, but I have to go for the reading of the will. I don't know any more than that."

Loren thought a moment then said, "I remember going to see her and Uncle Shelby back in the early seventies when your aunt Becky and I went to Florida. At that time, they lived around Nashville. He was a banker as I recollect. Mother always said her family had money, but I don't think she ever saw any of it. Aunt Vinnie was southern, that's for sure. I remember she had that accent that just floated off her tongue like a mist. She wasn't bigger than a minute, but she could hold her own against the most cantankerous of characters."

With that, Loren began to cough again.

Not wanting to wear him out further, Ellie said, "Thank you for telling me all that you did. I had no idea I had an aunt named Lavina, but I will honor her wishes, make a trip to Hendersonville, and see to whom she left all her riches! Like most wealthy women, she probably left all her worldly belongings to her French poodle named Claude!"

She quickly pecked her uncle on the cheek and promised that she wouldn't wait so long to return. Loren asked her to let him know how the visit went, and commented that it was so good to seeing her again. He told her that she looked so much like Liz. She hadn't thought of her mom in a while, and the mention of her brought tears to Ellie's eyes, even after all these years.

"I miss her just as much as I did the day she died, Kid. It never goes away."

"I miss her too, Uncle Loren."

And with that, Ellie bent down and kissed her uncle on his whiskered cheek, and said goodbye. She turned and walked out of the facility with many questions running through her mind.

By the time Ellie made it home from the store, it was already half past three, and she hadn't even started the meal! The afternoon was beginning to look like a storm could blow in. The cotton candy clouds had quickly turned into a swirling mass of bubbling charcoal, offering a rumbling of thunder now and again that signaled something ominous. Living in the Ohio Valley, Ellie was used to sudden changes in the weather, and

Indiana in the late springtime offered up a variety to those living within its borders. While she fired up the grill and skewered the veggies, the weather radio began to go off. *Oh great, a storm brewing and me wanting to move furniture.* Ellie wasn't sure that part of the evening would work out, since her furniture was across town in a storage facility. She wasn't sure she had a tarp in her dad's things. *Maybe she should put that on hold.* Sean would be finished cutting his parents' lawn, probably just getting ready to head over to her house.

While she was changing into a comfortable shirt and jeans, the doorbell rang. To Ellie's surprise, she felt a flutter in her heart. She remembered getting that same feeling when the phone would ring in the middle of the night when Cassie was out with friends. It was a sudden panic, the thought that something could be wrong. *But why would she have that feeling with Sean?* It was just dinner, period. As she came down the hall, she could see him standing outside the window. He was actually looking over her pitiful landscaping, which was nothing to brag about.

As she opened the door, he turned, smiling, "Hi Ellie! Did you order this weather so you don't have to grill?" Sean laughed and stepped inside.

He seemed to be taller than she remembered, and Ellie took a whiff of his cologne as he brushed passed her. *Nice, but I'm not so sure about the metro-sexual part.* She let a chuckle escape.

"What's so funny? Do I need to have my mom check out my choice of clothes for the day?" Sean asked.

"Actually, I was thinking how nice you look, Sean, pleasantly different from work."

A big grin spread across his face. "I like the way you look too, Ellie."

Ellie suddenly seemed embarrassed at their compliments. She smiled as she asked Sean to make himself comfortable. He looked very casual in his jeans and T-shirt. In the thirteen years since they met, Ellie had never been with Sean in a social situation outside of work. He always wore a tie and dress slacks at work. She didn't know him beyond their connection with school, but she felt that she could be at ease tonight.

"What can I get you to drink? I wasn't sure if you were a tea or beer drinker."

Sean walked over to the bar that separated the kitchen and dining area, bringing him closer, and Ellie surprisingly liked it.

"I think a beer would be great!" Sean said.

Ellie handed the bottle of Miller Lite to Sean, and then put a slice of lemon in her tea.

"I never acquired a taste for beer, but I do like a Captain Morgan with pineapple on occasion!"

Sean took his beer over to the recliner in the living room, Ellie following. The two began to talk about their plans for the summer, to which Ellie volunteered her upcoming trip to Baltimore to see Cassie.

"That is really great that she found a job right out of college. With so many out of work, her qualifications must be excellent to get hired so fast!" Sean complimented, as he took a drink from the bottle.

"And what a relief too," replied Ellie, as she excused herself to check on the steaks and veggie kabobs on the patio.

"Is there anything I can do to help?" Sean hollered from the living room.

"Sure, I need the potato salad out of the fridge."

Ellie started setting out plates and silverware and then Sean helped her to carry the steaks.

"I'll grab the kabobs and then we're ready."

"This is really nice, thanks for dinner, Ellie." Sean was speaking softer now, but still keeping to a casual distance.

"You're welcome, but don't get too excited, I haven't cooked in awhile," Ellie replied.

During dinner, the two discussed the plans for which pieces of furniture to put into storage and where the storage barn was located. It was decided that they would take the items that were being sold to the storage facility that she still had from her divorce. Brad had agreed to pay a year's lease for her, during the civil days of their divorce. She had taken over the last few months' payments, and it was evident this was a bill she could do without. Thus, the sale . . .

After the dinner dishes were put away, Sean excused himself to bring in some moving straps and gloves from his car.

"Wow, you look like you've done this before!" Ellie exclaimed.

"Well, I got divorced a few years back, and at the time didn't know anyone. It was just my dad and me doing all the heavy lifting."

Ellie could tell that it wasn't something Sean was proud of, but sensed he didn't dwell on it. *I have worked with him thirteen years, and I didn't even know he had gone through a divorce!*

Ellie put her hand on his shoulder, "I'm sorry, I can't believe we work together and I didn't know!"

Sean seemed unemotional about her comment, but smiled and said, "It's okay, I didn't broadcast it. My ex decided that the grass was greener where the city cop lived across the street."

"That's horrible. I'm sorry. I know how hard it is when you find out you've been played for the fool. I was for most of my married life."

Ellie found herself feeling sympathetic to Sean, but more than that, finding out that she really didn't know what her coworkers were going through made her feel uncaring.

"Well, let's stop feeling sorry for ourselves and get your condo cleaned out!" Sean grinned and made a gesture for Ellie to show him where to start.

"I really appreciate you helping me, Sean. I have to get this place updated, and the first place is to start with this stuff!"

After Ellie and Sean got the bedroom suit and dining room furniture moved, they finished their date with a trip to Dairy Queen for ice cream.

"Now this is my kind of date, Sean!" Ellie laughed delightedly.

"Anytime. I'm all about showing a girl a good time!" Sean flashed Ellie a sexy smile and wink.

It was obvious that the two were hitting it off, and Ellie was glad that she decided to have Sean come over. He was just what she needed after being rejected.

After Ellie parked the truck, Sean walked over to unlock his door, saying, "I really enjoyed tonight. Even though you used and abused me, it was fun!"

Sean had an upbeat personality that Ellie found refreshing.

"Even though I'm whipped, I enjoyed myself too, and thanks again for all the help moving the furniture. I really appreciated it."

Now was the awkward part; they had done so well all night. The conversation and time together had been surprisingly easy. *Now was the time when the guy usually made a move, wasn't it? Good lord, it's been so long since I've been on a date, I don't know what to expect.*

"You get a good night's sleep, and call me when you get back from Cassie's. I'd like to take you out--my treat!"

They both wanted to make it easy, so they hugged. Ellie hadn't been in someone's arms, even for a friendly male hug, in a long time. His hug was quick, but Ellie could tell there would always be an option for more.

"I'll call you, and dinner would be great. Drive safe, and I'll talk to you later!"

"You too! Night, Ellie!" Sean said as he backed his car out of her driveway.

Ellie closed the door and locked the deadbolt. She had made it though her first date. In record time, Charlotte was calling to get the update, just like when the two were in high school.

"Hello Char. What's up?" Ellie liked teasing her best friend.

"What do you mean, what's up? How did it go? Was Mr. metro-sexual worth the steak?"

Charlotte was not one to beat around the bush, and the two had always been able to tease one another and understand the meaning.

"Yes, actually he was worth the steak! (Knowing that Charlotte would assume, Ellie didn't let her mind run for long).

"I got two rooms moved out to the storage shed. He even popped for ice-cream afterwards," Ellie laughed.

"Well honestly, what is Sean Barrow all about, Ellie? Are you going out again?"

Ellie wasn't sure Sean meant to keep the date, but she told Charlotte about their plans to go out when she returned from her Maryland trip.

Ellie wanted to tell Charlotte about the letter, about discovering she had an aunt who had passed away leaving her as executor of her will. Charlotte would love this . . .she was always interested in a story! But Ellie decided she would wait until she made contact with the attorney, Riley Langley. The idea of having to drive to Tennessee alone wasn't too appealing, so she might just ask Charlotte to take a few days off and come along. It would be fun; a long awaited road trip that the two had wanted to take since the divorce. Ellie would fill her in tomorrow.

"We are who we are because they were who they were."
- Author unknown

Chapter 2

On Monday morning, Ellie began to organize the week ahead. She dropped the bills off in the mail and arranged for the auctioneer to come by and load up her father's belongings. As she started crossing off items in her mind of the things she must accomplish, one item kept invading her thoughts throughout the day: Lavina George, her long lost great aunt. *Now where did I put the letter?*

Ellie began tracing her steps back to the dining room table where she had placed the letter and envelope Friday evening. Being executor of a will was still a recent memory because she was the executor of her father's will, besides being his sole heir. She had already been through the reading of a will, but this time should be much easier. She didn't even know the lady. Besides, if Lavina had money, one could be sure every relative who had any claim would be there. Ellie began to wonder why Aunt Lavina didn't choose Uncle Loren as executor. More questions filled her mind. *Now what where is the number for Mr. Riley Langley?* Ellie found a pen and tablet, and after copying the telephone number for the Law Office of Langley and Murdock, decided to get it over with and call. The sooner she made contact, the better. She would fulfill her obligation to the aunt she didn't know.

The receptionist answered the telephone in the Southern drawl that Ellie had always found poetic, almost as smooth as melted butter dripping off an ear of sweet corn.

"Langley and Murdock, this is Carol Pennington, how may I direct your call?"

Ellie swallowed and began, "Hello, Carol. My name is Ellie Morgan. I received a letter from Mr. Langley in regards to my great aunt's estate and the reading of her will. Do you think it would be possible for me to speak to Mr. Langley?"

Ellie could feel her pulse race as she suddenly felt nervous about speaking to the lawyer.

"Please hold a moment; I'll let Mr. Langley know you are calling," Carol answered.

Ellie smiled through the phone, "Okay, thank you."

As she waited, the music that she heard was a familiar tune, although she couldn't place it.

Just as she was trying to sing the words in a low voice, a very deep and Southern voice began, "Ms. Morgan, how good to hear from you! I must again offer my deepest condolences on behalf of my father and myself in the passing of such a dear lady."

Ellie felt obliged to thank him for such a heartfelt sentiment.

"Mr. Langley, I must tell you that I was very surprised to receive your letter last week. I didn't even know Mrs. George was my aunt."

"I knew that you were unaware of your aunt, Ms. Morgan," Riley said, "that is why I had hoped you would call me so that we could speak at greater lengths. You see, she was quite the business lady, even though your great uncle was the one who worked for many years as the president of the local bank here in Hendersonville."

Until then, Ellie hadn't given much thought to her great uncle.

"Ms. Morgan, would there be a time in the near future, say within the next week, that we could schedule the reading of the will?" Riley asked. "As the executor, I need you to be present."

Ellie was prepared to settle the arrangements while she had the lawyer on the phone.

"I was thinking about driving down this weekend. I could meet you Monday morning, if that works with your schedule."

After pausing a moment, Mr. Langley answered, "Ms. Morgan, I have to be in court early Monday morning, but I would be happy to clear the rest of my schedule for the day if you could be here, say, around eleven o'clock?"

"That will be fine," Ellie agreed.

In less than a second, Mr. Langley's Southern hospitality kicked in, "Just give me a call Monday morning and we will give you directions to the office. My cell is *615-555-0189*. Please don't hesitate to call if you have any problems, and my secretary, Mrs. Pennington, will be happy to offer suggestions for lodging while you are here."

"Thank you for rearranging your schedule, Mr. Langley. I'll see you on Monday," Ellie replied.

"You're welcome, Ms. Morgan. I'm looking forward to our meeting. Good day."

Riley Langley seemed like a very kind, Southern gentleman. Ellie had had a preconceived notion about Southern men, probably from the yearly rituals of watching *Gone with the Wind* with her mother. Ellie was suddenly reminded of how much she wished her mother had told her about her life and family. *If only they had been more time, time to grow older together. Okay, enough of the pity party, Ella!* Ellie laughed for calling herself by her given name. To think that her now deceased great aunt knew her by this special name only made her want to know more. After writing her appointment time and Mr. Langley's phone number on a post-it note, she went about the rest of her day. The call was quick, and much to Ellie's dismay, Charlotte couldn't get away for the weekend. She was committed to a real estate closing on that Monday, but was intrigued by the whole matter.

"You have to promise to call me right after you have the reading. That is so exciting!" Charlotte bubbled.

"Char, I'll be sure and give you all the details about how many of my long-lost relatives show up with their hands out!" Ellie laughed.

For the rest of the week, Ellie made plans for her trip. Char would come by and check on the plants. She also called Sean, to thank him again for helping her over the weekend. Ellie thought pleasantly of the time she and Sean had spent together just hanging out. She liked her life at the moment.

For the past year, she had learned what it was like to live totally on her own, without the help of her father or a husband. Granted, when her father passed away, he had left everything to Ellie. He had seen two wives pass on before him. Mary Lou had come into his life after Ellie's mom had been gone ten years. Ellie thought very highly of her new stepmother, and was so thankful that her father had found someone to share his life. Their marriage was only to last five years, as she was diagnosed with breast cancer and died within a year. When Frank passed, he was financially sound. He left to Ellie a home and a truck that he owned outright. *Who was this long-lost aunt, and why hadn't she tried to contact me before her death?*

Ellie filled the car with gas and headed out of town, making a quick stop at the cemetery. The dew was thick that morning, and she felt the moisture immediately as her feet slid sideways in the flip-flops she had donned that morning. The squishing sound seemed to be amplified by the quiet, peaceful setting of the cemetery.

She walked straight back through the generations of headstones to the dark granite stone with the grass just starting to grow again. She took a tissue out of her purse and wiped the headstone to remove the grass clippings that had been recently thrown against it during the lawn service's trimming. She bent to pull the stubborn weeds that were snaking around the two urns that flanked either side of the headstone.

She put two bouquets of flowers into the urns; then, in a whisper said, "Mom, I am going to be the executor for your aunt Lavina. I wish you'd said something about her or some of the other people in your family."

Ellie then touched the stone and added softly, "Dad, I know you and Lavina didn't quite hit it off, so please don't be upset if you aren't mentioned in her will--not that it matters to either of you now."

With a quick, 'I love you both', she stood and brushed the dried grass off her knees.

The sun was shining brightly through the trees, reaching down to the ground like a beacon from heaven. Ellie felt the warmth on her face as she made her way back to the car. *It's just too pretty outside to be all cooped up inside this car.* Ellie rolled down the windows and headed south towards Hendersonville, Tennessee.

The drive to Tennessee was relaxing for Ellie. Since Char couldn't join her, she listened to several of her favorite CD's. She enjoyed the feel of the warm breeze coming through the window as she made her way through Kentucky. By three o'clock, she was crossing into Tennessee. It was around five o'clock when Ellie came upon the exit for Hendersonville. As she made her way down the off ramp, she noticed how the city had a modern flair as well as Southern charm.

The downtown area was divided by the Cumberland River. Ellie should have done her homework before making the trip. It would have been the perfect opportunity to learn some of the history about the town.

The town was larger than she had imagined, and the first item on her list was to find the hotel. Having already programmed the GPS, she shouldn't have any trouble finding the Hampton Inn on the east side of town. The timing for Ellie's arrival wasn't well planned, however, and Ellie found herself in the middle of rush hour. Traffic was bumper to bumper as she made her way down Main Street.

While she sat waiting at a light, she scanned both sides of the street. She noticed the Civil War marker beside the street, but she wasn't able to make out the contents. Traveling further down the road, she noticed a sign that read *Civil War Trail. I love this place already!*

Sighting the Hampton Inn ahead, she pulled into the lot and parked her truck under the portico. Stretching her legs, which had become stiff from sitting in the truck all day, she caught a glimpse of herself in the window of the entrance to the hotel. Her hair had started to fall out of the ponytail that had been keeping her thick tresses confined during the open-air ride from Indiana. Before approaching the front desk, she quickly fixed her unruly mane.

The gentleman behind the desk was very friendly, and made small talk as he registered her for the next few nights. Ellie inquired about the location of the courthouse and public library, hoping to visit both.

"I'm excited to get out and explore the town!" Ellie chimed as the guest attendant wrote out the number of her room on the key packet.

"I hope you find Hendersonville to your liking. Please let us know if we can be of any help to you while you're here."

Ellie read the man's name from a small, gold nameplate on the counter.

"Thank you, Robert. I'm sure I will be back for directions or something during my stay." Ellie smiled and took the key and receipt from Robert.

Southern hospitality isn't a dying art. I hope my meeting with Mr. Langley goes as smoothly. Ellie felt a jolt of excitement as she made her way back to her truck. In just a couple of days, she would be meeting her aunt Lavina for the first time, albeit through her last wishes. She would be able to put another piece of her family history in place.

Ellie drove around to the front side of the hotel to park her car and unload her baggage. The room was very clean, and she was excited to begin her search for answers. First, she took a long, hot shower. The drive had been longer than expected, and she still wasn't used to taking long trips alone. It had been quite awhile since she had taken a trip anywhere.

Her thoughts changed to home and Sean. He had asked her to call him, which she would do when she returned home. Her impression of him prior to Saturday and been wrong. The erroneous vibe she experienced prior to their evening together was something she chalked up to a bad marriage. She liked Sean, and felt that whether they continued to date or just remain co-workers wasn't that big of an issue. She enjoyed the laid-back style that Sean had with her.

The shower worked wonders, and soon she had dressed in a pair of flannel pajama pants and a University of Evansville sweatshirt. Digging through the large bag for her notebook, she began to think about what her meeting on Monday would be like with the attorney. Ellie wasn't even sure who else would be attending the reading of the will. *I wonder why Uncle Loren wasn't mentioned in the will and I was chosen to be her executor?* It just didn't make sense to Ellie that someone she didn't remember would entrust her with such importance.

It also bothered her that Mr. Langley mentioned Lavina changed her will ten years prior to her death. *Who changes her will at ninety-one years of age, and why?* Ellie guessed those questions would be answered on Monday. In the meantime, she set off to find some place to grab a quick bite for dinner.

The GPS listed a variety of establishments in town, but Ellie really didn't like dining alone. She was used to being in a group or with Brad; that is, when they actually went places as a couple. She decided to go to the local sub shop where she ordered a sandwich and drink; she was too excited to eat a large supper.

Ellie made her way to the back of the restaurant. Her nervous energy caused her to finish quickly. Instead of returning to her hotel, she took a trial run to the Law Offices of Langley and Murdock.

The drive from the *Sub Hut* on East Main to the office of Mr. Langley only took Ellie a few minutes. Enjoying the scenery as she drove, she arrived at the intersection of Main and Poplar Streets. Many of the buildings had once been private residences, and these businesses welcomed their visitors in from the street with Southern charm. The large gas street lamps long ago had been converted to modern streetlights, and parking now claimed the once green expanse of lawn.

Mr. Langley's law office was situated at the end of Poplar Street. The offices took up two floors in an old, antebellum style home. Ellie couldn't help but wonder if this had been a home of a relative of his.

Driving slowly passed the converted home; Ellie noticed the large porch with beautiful bougainvilleas hanging from long, metal hooks. Two large wooden rockers were placed at the side of the porch, giving the impression of a much simpler time. Ellie could see a large chandelier that was lit in what she expected was the entry hall. The sun was now setting, and the beam of light coming through the Palladian window above the massive oak door reminded Ellie of the homes she had toured in Charleston years before. *Oh, how lovely. It must be beautiful on the inside*, Ellie thought to herself.

After she had taken a good five minutes admiring Mr. Langley's office building, she turned her truck towards East Main Street. Since the drive from the Hampton Inn to the law office wouldn't take more than ten minutes, Ellie would be able to eat a leisurely breakfast, head to the library, and try to find out about Lavina George.

Ellie awoke around eight, having slept soundly throughout the night. Showered and dressed, she made her way down to the lobby to the hotel's deluxe continental breakfast. The buffet offered a variety of Southern delights, including bacon, one of her favorite breakfast foods. Ellie chose a spot near the back of the dining area and began to watch the people who came and went as she ate. Long ago, she and Char decided the art of people watching was a talent they both shared and enjoyed.

Now that she didn't have her best friend along for the ritual, she decided to give Cassie a call, since it was the weekend. Cassie answered on the first ring.

"Mom, is everything okay?" Cassie asked. Ellie's mood suddenly lifted.

"Hi Cassie, how did your week go?"

Ellie missed her terribly, and it wasn't hard to distinguish it in her voice.

"Actually, it has gone better than last week. I met a girl about my age in the laundry area who works in one of the buildings near the station. We decided to carpool!"

Ellie and Cassie continued to catch up on the week's events. She shared her 'date' with Sean, and then began to tell her about her adventure to Tennessee.

"Mom, why didn't you ask Charlotte to go with you? That is a long way for you to be traveling alone!" Cassie was suddenly sounding like the mother.

"Cass, I think I am old enough make a trek out of state alone! Besides, I'm just fulfilling the last wishes of my great aunt."

Well, it just seems odd to me that someone you never knew picked you to handle her estate!"

It was even more strange to Ellie, especially knowing that Lavina felt animosity toward her father.

"If she didn't like Yankees, why would she ask one to carry out one of her last wishes?" Cassie continued.

"Well, Cassie, I guess I'll find out on Monday. In the meantime, I'm just going to do a little sightseeing, maybe try to see something historical--you know me!"

They both laughed, and then Cassie asked, "Mom, you're still coming next week, right?"

Ellie was looking forward to flying out to see Cassie's new apartment. It had been a month since she had seen her daughter.

"Of course, I have my plane ticket and rental car all taken care of. It will be so good to see you again!"

After chatting a few more moments about the latest happenings in both Newburgh and Hagerstown, Cassie ended the call. Ellie finished her meal and headed back to her hotel for the night.

Ellie awoke early the following morning, eager to get started on the day's activities. She hurriedly dressed in her most comfortable T-shirt and jeans, putting on her makeup in record time.

Walking into the lobby Ellie voiced a cheery 'Good Morning!' to the young lady working the front desk. More interested in the text message she was sending, she barely lifted her head when Ellie spoke. *Doesn't anyone under thirty communicate verbally anymore?*

Ellie moved passed the girl, going straight to the dining area where she filled her plate with a small helping of sausage gravy and a biscuit and her travel mug with coffee. Making her way to one of the small tables, she glanced at the clock on the wall: 8:30 A.M. *The library will open in 30 minutes. I have plenty of time.*

Ellie had been concerned with time for as long as she could remember. In fact, Char had reminded her that she was OCD (Obsessive-Compulsive Disorder) with time. Ellie couldn't understand how anyone could be late. Her breakfast finished, and in typical 'Ellie time' wanting to make sure she was at the library when its doors opened, she headed for her truck.

Finding the coordinates on her GPS, she headed to Magnolia Street. Within a few minutes she arrived at the library, discovering it was very reminiscent of the library in Newburg. Part of it looked to be the original turn-of-the-century Carnegie library building, with a modern addition attached. *Where do I begin? I would love to know more about Aunt Vinnie and her husband, along with any other family history I might find.*

As Ellie walked from the parking lot, she began thinking about her mother. Ellie hadn't had enough time with her mother to learn family stories and the family history that most parents pass along to their children. She thought it was sad that she didn't have any real connection to her mother's family. Without her uncle Loren, she would have had no information whatsoever about this great aunt she was about to meet!

Ellie walked through the two large oak front doors. It smelled of old books, but looked very bright and cheery, having lots of natural light to brighten the dark wood accents around the rooms. At the entrance sat a receptionist behind a large mahogany desk, typing away on a computer. When Ellie approached the desk, the lady looked up from her work.

"Good morning! What can I help you with, Ma'am?"

"Good morning," Ellie replied pleasantly, "I'm trying to find some information about a relative who recently passed away. Would there be records on file that might include obituaries and other newsprint documents?"

The receptionist pulled out a map of the library, and explained to Ellie where she could find the genealogy section as well as the records section.

"We sometimes have someone here from the UDC and the genealogy department to help locate lost relatives. I believe someone is working in the genealogy section this afternoon if you'd like to question them."

Ellie wasn't quite sure what the UDC was, and was feeling suddenly like one of her students that hadn't read the notes before the test.

"I know I'm sounding ignorant, but what is the UDC?"

Smiling, the receptionist explained, "The United Daughters of the Confederacy; they help people much like the DAR, Daughters of the American Revolution. It's a very old and respected organization dating to the War Between the States."

Ellie now knew that southerners held their heritage very near and dear to their hearts. It wasn't the Civil War once the Mason-Dixon Line was crossed. It was the War Between the States.

Ellie must remember that to many a Southerner, the North was the invader. She would tread lightly on those who still felt a bit of the Rebel yell yearning to be set free!

"Thank you for the information. I might have to ask for their assistance."

Locating the records room first, Ellie went to the computer to type in the name of her aunt, Lavina George. Glancing through the obituaries on file, it only took a moment for the online account to appear on the screen. Ellie grabbed her reading glasses and began scanning the newspaper. *Mrs. Lavina Stone George, 101, Hendersonville, passed away Monday, March 25, 2011, after an illness.* The account reported that Mrs. George had no surviving relatives, aside from nieces and nephews, describing her as genteel, compassionate soul who never tired of doing good. *It sounds as if she is being recommended for sainthood.* Her husband, Ellie's great uncle, had died in 1990, and both were buried in the Resthaven cemetery.

Ellie printed out the account listing family members including Ellie's grandmother, who had passed away when Ellie was only six years old. There was also a photograph in the account, but it appeared to be of Lavina when she was much younger. Ellie studied the photo closely: the lady was of middle age with a pretty smile and large eyes.

Ellie closed her eyes, trying to remember her grandmother's face to compare to Lavina's. Sadly, for as long as she could remember, she only knew her father's family. With the exception of Uncle Loren and Aunt Becky, her mother's family tree was just a misshapen bush.

Ellie sat at the table, pondering what to look for next. She'd only just learned her grandmother's maiden name today in the obituary. Now that she had a piece of her history, she would definitely want to find out more.

Ellie went to the back of the room to the copy machine and deposited twenty-five cents to copy the obituary. She placed the sheet inside her bag and made her way out of the room. As Ellie approached the genealogy room, she was disappointed the room seemed to be unoccupied. However, as she entered, an older gentleman who appeared to be in his late seventies sat at one of the large tables with books piled high like a beehive around his head. He peered over the mound of reading materials in front of him.

"Don't expect Miss Ethel to be back today, Ma'am; she took sick yesterday and isn't feeling quite up to snuff today. There isn't anyone to help with searches today, I'm afraid."

Smiling, Ellie said, "Thank you. I'm new to this, so I really don't have a lot of information to go on. I'm just looking around more than anything."

The man smiled and mumbled something else, then went on with his search. Ellie turned and walked out of the musty-smelling basement.

Well, nothing ventured, nothing gained! Ellie decided to go back upstairs to find the cemetery listings and maybe find where her aunt was buried. That would be her final jaunt for the day, as she was feeling tired from the long drive the day before. As she scrolled through the listing for the Resthaven Cemetery, the address popped up. She quickly copied it in her notebook, and then walked out to her car.

It was noon, and hunger pains were starting to distract her. Ellie found the local burger joint, went through the drive through, and headed back to find the cemetery.

After entering the location into her GPS, the trek for the cemetery was on. Only a few short blocks from the library, the large cemetery spanned almost two city blocks. As she parked her truck, she took a quick inventory of the massive task that was set before her. How in the world was she going to find her great aunt?

Ellie began walking toward a small block building that sat adjacent to her truck. An older lady with her back toward Ellie was locking the door as she left the building. As she turned, she noticed Ellie walking towards her.

"Hello, may I ask you a quick question, please?" Ellie began with a smile, "I'm trying to find the grave site of my great aunt and uncle who are buried here. Could you tell me where I might be able to find a record of the graves?"

The lady raised her head, using her hand to block the sun.

"Hello, I would be the person to help you. Whom are you trying to find? I know most of the people in here, either by name, face, or through the files."

The lady seemed very warm and receptive to Ellie, and it sounded as if she would have no problem helping her find the graves.

"My aunt was Lavina George. Do you remember her?"

The lady smiled, as if she had just remembered a dear old friend.

"Land sakes, I remember Mrs. George very well. She is a recent resident here. I remember the day of her funeral. The poor soul lived to a ripe old age of one hundred and one! She was as spry as any one of us right up until her stroke last summer. It seems to me she went downhill quickly after that. By the way, I am Helen Eubanks. I work for the cemetery association; it's nice to meet you."

They both smiled, and Ellie took her outstretched hand and shook it softly.

"It is nice to meet you too, Ms. Eubanks. I'm only here for a short time, and wanted to pay my respects."

Helen looked at Ellie as if she was trying to find a resemblance to her aunt.

"Now who is your mama, honey? I don't remember Mrs. George ever talking about any family who were living. Mrs. George had more to say about those who had already gone on."

"It's odd to be saying it, but I only saw my great aunt one time, and that was when I was an infant. My parents drove down from Indiana to see her and my great uncle, along with my parents. My mother was Elizabeth Ridgeway, and my father was Frank Camden. They're both gone now."

Helen Eubanks' round face had eyes almost too small for her face. When she smiled, they seemed to disappear into two small slits.

Her large grin suddenly turned upside down in sympathy, "Oh, I'm so sorry. I can take you to Mrs. George's grave now, if you'd like. Let me set my book down and we can go."

Ellie began to feel many emotions rising up from a place she tried to keep at bay: grief was one she hid from others. She had done so when her mother died, and more recently when her father passed away. However, having a similar feeling for a person she never knew surprised Ellie.

"Did you know my aunt well, Mrs. Eubanks?"

"Oh yes, dear. Everyone who knew your aunt loved her. She was the epitome of Southern grace and charm, a past President of the UDC, and such a wonderful cook!"

Ellie wished she could have met her aunt Lavina when she was younger and in good health.

As the two made their way down a winding sidewalk, Ellie couldn't help but notice the different headstones. Some were covered with the dark, black stain that comes from modern pollution in the air, others time worn from years of weathering. Taking a moment to admire the beautiful stone carvings that marked many of the graves with precious lambs and chubby-faced cherubs, she realized sadly that these graves belonged to children who had been taken far too soon from their families. There were gravestones that showed the honor of military service for the sleeping ones below.

Ellie noticed a particular grave as they passed with a beautiful bronze cross, now the familiar color of aged bronze. On the headstone, she could barely make out the soldier's name: *COLLINS. Pvt. Raford Isaac.* Below the dates of birth and death was the name of a Civil War regiment, *11th TENN VOL. INFTRY.*

Ellie read the headstone carefully and asked, "Helen, what does the star mean on this grave?"

As if she were teaching a class on Civil War history, Helen Eubanks began to explain the placing of the Southern Cross on each of the graves belonging to a soldier in the Confederate army.

"Sadly, he was just one of thousands who lost his life in the War Between the States."

Ellie could see how moved the lady was when talking about the soldiers and the War. She also noticed that she referred to the Civil War as the *War Between the States.*

"Well, I appreciate your taking time to tell me. I've seen similar markers in the cemetery where my father and mother are buried. They have GAR on them, and Dad told me that meant the Grand Army of the Republic."

Ellie stopped, feeling she was about to teach a history lesson.

"I'm sorry; I teach U.S. history at our high school. I get carried away with my subject sometimes!"

They both laughed and Helen Eubanks added, "You know, history isn't just what they write in books. It is about real people and the lives they lived."

Ellie nodded, "I think we are on the same page, Helen."

The two continued walking down the path until Helen stopped upon reaching the final resting place of Shelby and Lavina George.

"Here is Mrs. George's grave," said Helen almost in a whisper.

Ellie saw it long before she mentioned it, as it was one of the largest stones in the section. The headstone was cut from a large slab of black granite, polished to a high shine. In the center of the stone, was a carving of both Lavina and Shelby George.

The picture used for the carving had been done many years prior to the death of Mr. George. Ellie felt very sad suddenly, not sure why this sudden burst of emotion fell upon her. Ellie hurriedly wiped away the tears, but Helen Eubanks saw the grief that Ellie was experiencing.

She said, "I'll just leave you here to visit with your aunt and uncle. If you need anything, please don't hesitate to stop by on your way out because I'll stay a bit longer. It was very nice to meet you."

Ellie reached in her bag for a waded up tissue and wiped her eyes.

"I'm sorry; I didn't even tell you my name. I'm Ellie Morgan, and it is so nice to meet you. I won't be much longer. Thank you for taking the time to show me the grave site."

Helen smiled, "You're welcome and please take all the time you need."

With that, Helen Eubanks made her way back up the path to the small concrete building at the front of the cemetery. Ellie wasn't sure why the sudden flood of tears came, but she let them flow freely.

After she had composed herself, she sat looking at the headstone. *Why have you brought me here, Aunt Lavina? I don't even know you.* Ellie felt that this trip wasn't just about reading a will. In only a few hours, she would find out. In the meantime, she took a picture of the headstone to show Uncle Loren when she returned. At least he remembered her.

As she made her way out of the cemetery, she stopped once again in front of the soldier's headstone. The Southern Cross was something she could show on Power Point when she taught Civil War next year. This was something she hadn't talked about, so she could actually have a great example with this photograph. *Raford Collins, I'm sorry you died so young, and so sorry for all the others who went before and after you.*

Frank Camden loved the Civil War, and after Ellie was old enough to travel, the family went on many excursions touring Civil War battlefields and taking pictures of monuments. She felt a connection somehow with her father whenever she visited sites that related to the War. She would have to tell him about this when she visited his grave after her return home. Ellie stopped by the small block building to let Helen Eubanks know she was leaving. Helen followed her out through the large metal gate.

That evening, Ellie dreamed the most unusual dreams. The cemetery was suddenly a place for much activity filled with mourners in long black gowns and veiled faces. Ellie watched the women in their Victorian attire, weeping and wiping their tears on long black handkerchiefs. A coffin was being lowered in the ground, and Ellie could see from her vantage point near the gravesite two young women standing near the open grave, each holding a single rose in their hands. Ellie felt as though she were a specter flying over the gravestones, seeing the faces of those who were sleeping below. When the mourners were gone, only Ellie was left to sit beside the newly covered grave.

As she sat in the closing hours of daylight, the only sound that she heard was *'you have to help me!'* Not knowing from where the whisper came, she moved closer, and the voice became louder, "*Ellie, you have to help me!*"

Frightened, Ellie asked, "How do you know my name? Help you? You're dead!" Her heart pounding as though it would explode, she suddenly awoke from the dream.

She sat upright in the bed, the room still bathed in darkness, and the dark motel curtains closed, not allowing the illumination from the security lamps outside to filter in. *What in the world was THAT all about?* Ellie tried to remember the details of her dream, but only could remember the mourners and the words *'help me'*.

She looked at the clock on the nightstand. It was only 3:45. *Good grief. I have to get some sleep before I go to the reading of the will.* She lay there for hours, listening to the air conditioner unit make the hissing sound for exactly thirty-five seconds when the unit kicked on, and gurgled for twenty-nine seconds when the unit shut off. Hearing the sound of a couple talking in low tones in the room next to her, she tried to go back to sleep by thinking about Sean. That was pleasant. But it didn't bring the deep sleep she longed for.

At six o'clock, she finally gave up, making her way to the restroom, walking past the mirror. Red, swollen eyes stared back. *Have I been crying in my sleep?* She vaguely remembered something about crying in her sleep, but didn't realize that she actually had. After taking her shower, she dried and flat ironed her hair, then took out the pale pink linen suit from the plastic garment bag.

Gazing into the mirror, she tried to remember what her dream meant. Her memory was void of who and what was written on the headstone.

Remembering the sadness of the dream was easy as she equated it to her grief at her mother's funeral. Her poor father looking like he had lost twenty pounds caused her to do her best to be strong for him, and not grieve publicly. Charlotte told her that wasn't normal as her sorrow overflowed in Charlotte's presence only. Ellie wanted to be brave for a young Frank who now would assume dual roles as both her father and mother.

As she began to pull the flat iron down through her shoulder length hair, she let her thoughts wander to where Sean would be taking her for dinner when she returned. Thoughts of her flight to Baltimore at the end of the week were also on her mind. She had so much to do! This trip would be over today, and she would return to the sleepy town of Newburgh and her boring life as a teacher on summer vacation. There wasn't much adventure waiting for Ellie in Newburgh.

After finishing the final touches of her makeup, she grabbed her purse and the motel key. It was half past eight, and she had plenty of time to enjoy a leisurely breakfast. Afterward, she would come back to the room and freshen up before travelling to Mr. Langley's office.

When she got down to the dining area, she noticed a group of re-enactors. She smiled, as did they, and exchanged pleasantries.

"Where are you re-enacting today?" Ellie asked. One of the men dressed in a Confederate Frock coat spoke first.

"We have a living history display today at Hendersonville High School's Civil War Day. The history department is having a timeline event for the community. We have a small camp set up as a walk-through for the school kids. You ought to come down if you're interested in the Civil War."

The second re-enactor volunteered, "It's their last week of school, so the teacher thought they'd like to get out for awhile."

Ellie smiled, thinking how glad she was her school had ended the week before!

"Well, I just might do that later today. Do you mind to give me the directions to the school?"

The older of the re-enactors offered, "Let me get my directions since I'm not from here either!"

Taking a paper and pen from his haversack, he quickly jotted down the name of the school and directions.

"Hope to see you there!"

Ellie thanked him, "I appreciate it!"

With her final cup of coffee, Ellie read the paper placed on the tables for the patrons, and then made her way back to her room to reapply her makeup and brush her teeth. Grabbing her purse, she headed out the door.

When she arrived at the law offices at 2011 Poplar Street, it was only 10:30. With thirty minutes to spare, she began to collect her thoughts. As she was checking herself in the visor mirror, a sporty black Lexus pulled into the parking lot in one of the two spots marked *Reserved*. A young, dark haired man, very tall and nicely built, wearing a dress shirt and tie, emerged from the car. Distractedly looking at his watch and talking on his cell phone, he rushed to the front door. *I wonder if that is the lawyer or someone coming to the reading of the will. I imagine there will be many people wanting to get some of the inheritance, especially in these hard financial times.* Glancing at the dainty silver watch on her wrist, she noticed it was only 10:43. Early, but not too early to arrive in the reception area.

Retrieving her things from the truck, she smoothed down her skirt and walked through the large wooden doors into the antebellum style office. Entering the door on the left of the hall, she was enthralled with the beauty of the entry. The stairway before her looked like something out of *Gone with the Wind*. She could only imagine the lovely décor above her, as she peered up the stairs from below. Hearing the slight cough and voice behind her, she jumped.

"May I help you, Ma'am?"

Ellie turned, embarrassed to be caught snooping, "Yes, I have an appointment with Mr. Langley at eleven. I was just admiring the beautiful staircase."

The lady held out her arm as if to guide her, "You can come this way. I'll show you to our offices."

Ellie followed meekly like a child caught with her hand in the cookie jar.

"Thank you," she said softly.

Turning, the receptionist asked, "May I get you something to drink, a soda or coffee?"

"No, thank you. I'm fine," Ellie replied.

Entering the offices of Langley and Murdock, Ellie noticed several large paintings hanging from what appeared to be gold threads attached to a thin strip of mahogany lining the perimeter of the wall, but several inches below the top. The furniture appeared to be from the antebellum period, but she guessed it was reproduction. The pattern on the high back chairs and settee were a floral motif of pastel pink, green and deep rose. She had seen a similar pattern when visiting another plantation home some years back in Georgia.

On the polished wood floor, rugs in pink, green and deep rose were placed at various points around the room, very reticent of the way the homes would have been furnished during the mid 1800's. Across the room, Ellie noticed two doors situated on either side of hall. Ellie assumed those were the law offices of Mr. Murdock and Mr. Langley, as well as other necessary rooms for filing, meeting rooms and the like.

The receptionist busily typed away on the computer that sat on her beautiful desk. Ellie imagined this desk had once belonged to the owner of the house, as it seemed too wide to fit through the entry into the offices. Nervously she checked her watch, a habit she had acquired during her youth. The time was 10:55. Surely, the people mentioned in her aunt's will would be arriving by now. Perhaps they were assembled in another room. She took a quick glance outside to see if there were any stragglers arriving in the parking lot. To her surprise, there weren't any more vehicles in the parking lot than when she arrived.

Ellie quickly inspected herself, making sure she looked professional. Wondering what sorts of things would be bequeathed to her great aunt's family and friends, her mind began racing between thoughts. In the midst of her imaginings, the receptionist stood and walked back through the long hall. Ellie sat up straight, feeling as if she was about to be called to the principal's office.

In less than a minute, the receptionist walked back into the room, offering Ellie a smile and saying, "Mr. Langley will see you now. If you'll just follow me."

Picking up her purse, Ellie followed the pretty receptionist through the archway and down the hall. Looking to her left, she saw a huge, sunny room with a large conference table surrounded by burgundy leather chairs. To her right, she saw another room, which appeared to be a records room with a large copy machine and cabinets lining the walls. As they passed by those rooms, she saw there were only three more doors to go. Only three doors left. One door was closed, and that was the office of Mr. Sheldon Murdock. The door opposite his was a powder room, which Ellie now wished she could use. At the end of the hall, in a large room with a bay window facing the back of the establishment was the office of Riley Langley.

"You may go in, Ms. Morgan." Smiling, Ellie thanked the receptionist, and walked in.

Riley Langley, seated behind his desk with his back to Ellie, turned upon hearing the two at his doorway. He stood to greet Ellie as she came towards the large desk and two wingback chairs facing it. Extending his hand across the desk, he welcomed her.

"Ms. Morgan, thank you for coming; it's a pleasure to meet you. I know it is an inconvenience making such a long drive."

Since Ellie had seen Riley in the parking lot, he had changed into suit and tie, looking very handsome and tanned. His voice was deep, but had a Southern drawl that Ellie found charming.

"I'm pleased to meet you as well, Mr. Langley."

Riley motioned for Ellie to be seated, saying, "Please, have a seat and we'll get started."

Ellie turned to look to the back of the room, and then to the door, as if there were more people to be ushered in.

"Am I early, Mr. Langley? I thought you said eleven o'clock."

Ellie seemed confused, and she wasn't sure why she was being singled out from the rest of the people for the reading.

"Where are the others?"

Riley placed the file folder containing the will down on his desk.

"Ms. Morgan, you're the only person required to be here today. If you'll just bear with me, I will explain everything."

Ellie suddenly felt as though she had been misled by Mr. Langley, and her expression must have been one of dismay.

"I don't understand, and please call me Ellie."

Riley smiled, backpedaling to the start of their conversation.

"Ellie, your aunt changed her will in 2001. Her husband and she had made their will together, but when he passed away in 1990, all of the assets were given to her. They had no children, and all of Mrs. George's surviving siblings were deceased. The only living relatives are you and your uncle Loren."

Ellie remained silent, waiting for the rest of Mr. Langley's speech to continue.

"When your aunt went to the nursing facility ten years ago, she wanted to change the wording in the will to include the name of her only surviving female relative. Sometime after the death of your mother, she had contacted your uncle Loren to see if there was anything financially she could do for you. Your father refused her offer of assistance. In the spring of 2001, she decided to move into assisted living since she was having difficulty climbing stairs and driving. It was then she came to my father to revise her will. She wanted you to be her sole heir, Ellie."

Ellie looked as if she might faint, not yet fully comprehending.

"There are no other people for whom she made provisions? I mean, she was 101 years old. Was there no sale after she went into the nursing facility?"

Riley smiled, "No, she specifically asked that her possessions be put in a storage facility, and her home on East Forrest Drive has been rented to a client of my father's for the past ten years. The tenants are retired and pay a small amount in rent for the property's upkeep."

Ellie rubbed her temples hoping this would help the words sink in.

"Are you telling me I have inherited her home and all her belongings?"

Riley affirmed this. Feeling her heart racing, Ellie was sure Riley heard it too.

"After the death of Shelby George, all of the family heirlooms from the George family were given to family members per Shelby George's last wishes. The rest remained with your great aunt for the rest of her life. Let's open the will and do this properly. I have a copy for you, and I will be reading from the original copy that my father wrote in May of 2001."

Dumbfounded, Ellie nodded as she received her copy. As she opened the folder, she read the words, *The Last Will and Testament of Lavina Stone George, deceased.*

Placing a pair of stylish glasses from his jacket pocket on the bridge of his nose, Riley began reading the will.

"*Item 1. My home on 175 East Forrest Drive, including its contents, will be given to Ms. Ella Camden upon my death to do with as she wishes. These shall be sold or distributed as Ella Camden deems fitting and proper. Item 2. The amount of $5,000 will be given to Loren Ridgeway to do with as he sees fitting and proper, along with $1000 to be given to each of his heirs.*" Ellie knew she only had one cousin, Todd, who was married with four children, only one still living at home. *Item 3. To Ella Camden, I leave the remainder of my estate, to do with as she sees fit, with the exception* *of the following: Ella Camden will regularly attend the seventeen graves of the Confederate veterans that are buried in Resthaven Cemetery and will decorate the graves on the following days: Memorial Day, Confederate Memorial Day, and Veterans' Day. Graves of the seventeen Confederate soldiers will be decorated with a single red rose, just as I have done for the past ninety years. This tradition has been passed down from mother to daughter since the end of the War Between the States. Since I have no daughter of my own, this duty will be passed to Ella Camden."*

As the will was being read, Ellie wondered about the remainder of the estate and what was included. Riley moved to the next item in the will.

"*Item 4. In addition to the tending of the Confederate graves, from this day forward, Ella Camden will be sole owner of Mimosa Grove, and all its contents and outbuildings.*

Ellie had been reading along with the lawyer until she heard this and immediately looked up from the will.

"Mimosa Grove? What, pray tell, is that?" Ellie sarcastically asked.

Riley Langley sent Ellie a look that made her suddenly feel ungrateful.

"Mimosa Grove was your aunt's ancestral home, the plantation home where her great-grandparents settled in the early 1800's. The home is quite interesting, Ellie."

Riley smiled as peered over the top of his glasses.

"You are now the owner of a plantation. After we finish here, I would be happy to show you the homes you now own. I'm sure you're probably hungry as well," Riley said.

Ellie's mind was racing in a thousand different directions. In a matter of thirty minutes, she learned that she was not only the executor of her aunt's will, but also the primary heir of her estate. Just how much that was worth, she didn't know. It was all very overwhelming, and Ellie felt as though she might have a panic attack.

"Ellie, are you all right? Would you like some water?"

Ellie composed herself.

"No, thank you. I'll be okay; I just need to catch my breath. This is all such a surprise to me. I didn't even know Lavina George!"

Smiling, Riley adjusted his reading glasses.

"Let's go ahead and finish reading your great aunt's wishes, then we'll talk over the business end later. Shall we continue?"

Ellie couldn't imagine anything being left, but she sat up in her seat, nodded, and turned to the next page in the will.

"Item 5. The balance of my estate shall be liquidated and given in a lump sum to Ella Camden to do with as she sees fitting and proper."

Ellie wasn't ready for what Riley shared next.

"My father and I have a copy of Mrs. George's net worth. If you'll look at the bottom of the last column, you will see that after her funeral expenses were paid, her net worth was a little over $500,000."

Riley glanced at Ellie who was still staring at the amount on the paper.

"Is there anything you would like to ask, or do you have any questions about any of the items on the will?"

Ellie swallowed, but no words came out. She couldn't quite believe what she was hearing.

Within a matter of moments, Riley finished reading Lavina George's last wishes. Carol Pennington, the receptionist, appeared in the doorway with a large legal folder.

"Mr. Langley, are you ready for the papers now?"

Riley stood to walk and take the folder.

"Yes, Carol, thank you. Ms. Camden and I are just finishing the reading of the will and we're ready for signatures."

Needing time to evaluate the situation, Ellie asked, "I would really like to go over all the particulars with you at length before I sign anything. I can't quite wrap my head around all of it."

Riley reached across the desk and patted Ellie's arm.

"I'd be happy to walk you through all of the particulars again, Ellie."

Perhaps because Riley's tone reminded her of her father and his way of making her feel like everything would be all right, Ellie felt more at ease. She signed the legal documents, and they were taken from the office.

"I'll be sure you have your copy as well, Ellie. And as I said, we can go over each part again so that you understand all that pertains to you."

Smiling, Ellie thanked him.

"I would like that."

"Okay then, let's go grab a bite to eat. I am about to eat the legs off my desk, and I know you've got to be anxious to see all the real estate you now own in Hendersonville."

Ellie laughed, noticing the devilish twinkle in his eyes.

"That sounds good to me. I'm ready for some lunch too."

With that, Ellie picked up her purse and bag, hoping her legs would be able to support her to the car.

"So, as you go into battle, remember your ancestors and remember your descendants"
- Publius Cornelius Tacitus

Chapter 3

Ellie and Riley left the offices of Langley and Murdock and walked down the sidewalk toward their cars.

Wishing to avoid any awkward feelings, Riley spoke up quickly, "Why don't you put your bag in your truck and jump in with me. I promise no more surprises today!"

Riley had a dimple in his right cheek, something Ellie had missed when they were sitting in the office.

"That makes sense because I don't know where we're headed anyway."

Riley held the door open to his Lexus as Ellie walked around to the passenger side.

"I'd like you to call me Riley. Mr. Langley is my father."

"The habit of speaking properly in front of my teenage students stays with me," Ellie explained.

Raising his eyebrows, Riley exclaimed, "It's great you're a teacher, I don't see how you manage! I think teachers get such a bad rap; my mom was a teacher. I'd say that's the reason I had the determination to become a lawyer."

"Not because your father was a lawyer?" Ellie questioned.

"Actually, I started out wanting to teach myself. I have my undergrad in history. I guess I decided I would take my chances in the court room instead of the class room."

Feeling a special bond with Riley, Ellie shared, "Believe it or not, I teach high school history. I've been teaching for twenty years, and my first love is history."

Laughing, Riley said, "Then you were the right choice."

Seeing Ellie's puzzled look, he added, "Your great aunt . . . she picked a history buff to handle her estate."

Riley pulled the Lexus onto the divided highway that ran through the center of the downtown area.

"Do you like bar-b-que? Miss Nell makes THE best north of Memphis!"

"I would love to try it; I haven't had a good barbeque sandwich in ages," Ellie replied.

He pulled into the only parking spot left on the street in front of the *Filllin' Station,* a popular restaurant for the downtown business crowd. The establishment had been in the same location for almost forty-five years. A large chalkboard with the daily specials sat facing the street. Two large window planters full of pansies guarded each side of the entrance. Ellie especially enjoyed the entry: an old-fashioned screen door.

Riley opened the door for Ellie. She was trying to remember the last time she had eaten out with anyone besides Char. Char would want an update, so Ellie quickly sent her a text message so she wouldn't call during the meal. *I need to call you later tonight. Too much to text.* She was certain that would get her attention, but she didn't want to go into detail at the moment.

A short, dark-skinned, older woman, whose round face had jowls that hung down to her chubby neck, greeted the couple. Wearing a red-checked apron over a white knit dress, her short bowed legs made her look like a mug with double handles.

"Mr. Riley, you ain't been here in ages, ah thought you was avoiding me."

Riley was transformed into the sheepish boy that used to pick up lunches for his father when he'd hang out at his law office.

"Now Miss Nell, you know I have to work at the court house most days. I can't get in here as often as I'd like. Come here and give me some sugar."

With that, Riley grabbed the woman and gave her a big hug. She laughed and swatted him on the back with her towel.

"Your mama would whip your hide clean off if she saw you forgettin' your manners. Who is this pretty gal you got with you?"

Miss Nell looked at Ellie with a look of approval. Smiling, Riley introduced the two.

"Miss Nell, this is Ms. Ellie Morgan. She is Mrs. Lavina George's great niece."

Miss Nell looked back at Riley and every tooth gleamed like light on a crystal.

"It's a pleasure, Miss Ellie. Mrs. George was a fine lady. It's nice meet'n you."

Ellie immediately liked Nell for making her feel welcome and at ease.

"Thank you. I didn't know her, but I am finding out she was quite popular."

Nell took Ellie's hand in her dark, wrinkled one.

She patted it, and commanded, "Come on you two. I have just the table for ya."

Turning, she walked through the restaurant leading Ellie and Riley to the booth in the back.

"Is this okay, Mr. Riley?" Nell asked.

"It's perfect, Miss Nell."

From the large, front pocket of her apron, Nell extracted a small pad of paper and pencil.

"What will the two of ya be drinking today?"

Riley looked at Ellie, who asked for a glass of sweet tea, remembering how delicious the tea at dinner had been the night before. Riley ordered lemonade. Nell was back with the drinks before the two had time to start a conversation.

As Nell placed the tall glasses on the table, she gave Ellie a quick glance and asked, "Have you decided what you want to eat, Miss?"

Ellie guessed that whatever Miss Nell brought back from the kitchen would be wonderful, as the smell emanating from the kitchen was pure heaven.

"Well, I think the barbeque sandwich with steak fries sounds good."

Ellie smiled and handed Miss Nell the paper menu. Riley was holding his menu in readiness, although his order was already being written down.

"You know what I'll have, Miss Nell. Just bring me plenty of napkins."

The arthritic hands had scribbled something down only Nell could decipher.

"I known's what you wanted, been ordering the same thing since you was knee high to a grasshopper."

Nell cackled as she took the menus, stuffing them under her arm.

"You two enjoy the drinks and I'll have your lunch back in a jiffy."

Approving of his choice for lunch, Ellie gushed, "Mr. Langley, the food smells delicious!"

Riley looked pleased.

"I think we can dispense with the formalities. I would really like it if you'd call me Riley."

"All right then, Riley. Thank you for introducing me to a hometown favorite."

Riley Langley was an attractive man; obviously interested in keeping himself fit, and was impeccably groomed. Ellie appreciated his neatly trimmed mustache and the goatee that formed down to his chin, framing his lips. It was difficult for Ellie not to stare at his eyes: the deepest shade of blue, almost azure. Ellie continued to appraise his features as Riley filled her in on the restaurant and Miss Nell.

Although Ellie was careful with her words, he noticed how she spoke with natural ease. Assessing her round face that showed no overuse of tanning beds, but a natural, wholesome, complexion, he liked what he saw. The lines appearing around her eyes when she smiled told him she was someone who smiled often. He didn't see a wedding ring, nor did he assume she was single. A woman in this day and age didn't have to wear a ring to be in a relationship. Watching earlier as her trim figure walked to the table, he enjoyed the view of her long, shapely legs in her sleek, pink linen suit.

After a few minutes of discussing the years of knowing Miss Nell, she soon appeared pulling a cart with their lunch.

"Here you are! Miss Ellie, here is your sandwich and fries, and Mr. Riley, your usual, ribs and onion rings."

Ellie, surveying his plate, laughed, "You're the first person I know to eat onion rings with ribs!"

She watched his hand as it reached to take a napkin from the dispenser. *No wedding ring. The long, tanned fingers must mean he's a golfer.*

Nell, having finished placing the side dishes on the table, asked, "Can I get ya two anything else?"

Riley looked over at Ellie, and replied, "No, I think we're fine. Thanks, Miss Nell."

The room began filling with lunch patrons, and Nell was off to welcome them.

"This looks fabulous, Riley. I don't know how you could eat here all these years and not be as wide as a barn door!"

Riley chuckled at her comment, thinking how much he could see Lavina George in her great niece.

"Well, I do have to work at it."

During their lunch, Riley tried not to ask questions that would make Ellie uncomfortable.

Ellie kept the conversation at surface level, not wanting to discuss too much of her personal life with a total stranger. Nevertheless, Riley didn't seem like a stranger, even though she had just met him two hours before.

"So, tell me more about what I am in for, Riley. How much, exactly, will I inherit from my great aunt?"

Riley wiped his mouth with the paper napkin, and moved in closer to Ellie.

"Ellie, you are going to be very pleased to know that your great aunt was quite wealthy, even after being in a retirement facility for ten years. Your uncle Shelby had made sure that he invested well, and both had been rumored to have made quite a tidy sum at the River Boat Casino several years before your great uncle passed. As I mentioned in my office, even after taxes and expenses, you're looking at six figures."

Ellie almost choked on the French fry, not expecting the amount of her inheritance to be any larger than that of her uncle Loren.

"You see, she and Shelby were worth nearly two million dollars at his death. They had made sound real estate investments, and sold when it was profitable. My father always said that Shelby was *old money*, and there is no end to it. Your aunt Lavina inherited her mother's family estate when her folks passed on. I heard rumors that the family had invested in the railroad prior to the War, so you can imagine they left her quite a nice nest egg."

Ellie heard what Riley was saying, but the realization was far from sinking in.

"It is so overwhelming to me, Riley. I'm a schoolteacher; I live modestly. It's not that I'm hurting financially; I just live within my means."

Riley gave Ellie that devilish smile.

"Well, now you will be able to live a little *more* comfortably. Don't forget, you have two homes as well as the money you've inherited. You will be quite a wealthy lady, Ellie."

Having fixed her thoughts on the home in tow, Ellie had almost forgotten about the other home. *How would she handle the renters who had made it their home?*

"Where exactly is the *other home* you mentioned, Riley? I almost forgot about it!"

Riley wondered if she wasn't sure about the prospect of owning this other home, or just still trying to absorb all that she had learned today.

"The large plantation home, *Mimosa Grove*, is about ten miles outside of town and is prime real estate. It backs up to the Cumberland River. If the home sold today, it would be worth a few million. It originally had about five hundred acres, but over the years was sold off in large farm tracts. In the early eighties, Shelby was getting frail and Lavina was encouraged to sell off some of the property so that they could buy the home in town. Those three hundred acres or so were sold to a developer. Today, the home and all outbuildings entail about two hundred acres of pasture and wooded ground. It hasn't been farmed for about fifty years, just left fallow. Mrs. George maintained the care of the home, and one of her husband's cousins lived in the home until his death five years ago. Since then, no one has lived there. My father promised Mrs. George, at the time she changed her will, he would be sure the home was taken care of until her death."

Ellie was fascinated with the story, anything having to do with history peeked her attention.

"So I am the new owner of Mimosa Grove, lock, stock and barrel?" Ellie drawled in her best mid-western accent.

"It appears so, my lady. Would you like to see it today?"

Riley's eyebrow rose with anticipation. Expecting to head back to Indiana after the reading of the will a few short hours before, Ellie realized her plans had just been changed.

"I'd love to, but I would want to get out of this suit. Do you mind if I head back to the motel and put on something more suited to exploring plantations?"

Reaching for his wallet to pay for the meal, Riley answered, "I think that would be great. I can run back to the office and change as well.

He must have living quarters in the law office building, or perhaps just keeps clothes on hand.

"Why don't you meet me back at my office in about an hour? Would that give you enough time?"

Excitedly Ellie countered, "That would be great! I'm ready if you are!"

Riley pushed his chair in, stepping aside, to let Ellie walk in front. As the two walked through the restaurant, several of the lunch crowd waved or spoke to Riley, obviously popular in town. She could understand why: easy to talk to, and easy on the eye. Miss Nell came from behind the counter to give Riley a hug.

"Now don't you go be'n a stranger, Mr. Riley. And it was nice meet'n you, Miss Ellie."

"It was nice meeting you too, Miss Nell. The barbeque was to die for, and I have been waiting a long time to have sweet tea like that."

Miss Nell was pleased with the comments on her establishment, and she patted Ellie on her back.

In a lower tone, she said, "It's nice to see Mr. Riley out and about. We've missed him in here."

Ellie wasn't sure what that comment was about, but Riley heard it and quickly changed the subject.

"Well, it was good seeing you, Nell. I'll be back again soon. In the meantime, you try to stay out of trouble."

Nell's chubby face beamed with adoration for Riley Langley. She felt like he was one of her own, having known him and his family since he was born.

Riley held the door for Ellie, and the two walked back to his car. He walked around to the passenger door, and opened it for Ellie, who was about to get in before he could reach for the handle.

"Thank you," Ellie said, impressed with his politeness, as she watched Riley walk around to the driver's side.

Suddenly aware of how exciting the day had been, Ellie wanted to hurry and change so she could visit her Mimosa Grove.

It only took five minutes to get from the restaurant to the law offices. As Ellie dug into her bag for her keys, she thanked Riley again for his hospitality. They agreed to meet back at the office within the hour when Riley would take Ellie to the house on East Forest Drive, then drive out to Mimosa Grove.

As soon as Ellie had the keys in the ignition, her phone began to ring. *I forgot to call Char. She must be going crazy after the text I sent her!* Ellie answered her phone as she pulled out of the parking lot.

"Hey Char!" Ellie said cheerily.

Charlotte was quick to ask, "Hey yourself. What's going on? You've had me on pins and needles all morning. How'd the reading go?"

Ellie took a deep breath, letting the air out in a long, drawn-out exhale. "Char, you aren't going to believe the day I have had so far, and it isn't over yet."

"Well, are you going to tell me, or am I going to have to drag it out of you?" Charlotte implored.

"I was wrong about the number of people who were at the reading. I was the only one!" exclaimed Ellie.

"You mean you are the *only heir?*" Charlotte asked.

"Yes, other than my uncle Loren. He was bequeathed five thousand dollars with five thousand dollars distributed among his son and grandchildren. The rest was left to me."

Charlotte sounded enthusiastic about the news.

"So how much did your great aunt Lavina leave you?" she asked.

"I am now the owner of a home on Forest Drive, a two hundred acre plantation home, including contents, and about $500,000 dollars," announced Ellie.

The phone went silent. No sound.

"Char; did you hear what I said?"

After a pause that seemed like an eternity, Char finally breathed.

"I don't think I heard you, I could have sworn you said $500,000 dollars!" Charlotte laughed.

Ellie could tell her friend thought it was a very good joke.

"I'm completely serious, Char. I've inherited ALL her worldly goods. In addition, I have to take care of some Confederate graves in a local cemetery. I'm not sure what that entails, but of course I will do what she has asked."

Charlotte let out a squeal.

"I can't believe your luck, girl. You are financially set. When are you going to quit work?"

Ellie had no intention of that, but she did see that money wouldn't be an issue with a nest egg that size.

"No, I'm not resigning! I'm so glad I will be able to help Cassie with a down payment on a house. Both she and I would love that. Listen to me! I have only had the knowledge of this money for two hours, and I am already spending it. I need to keep my wits about me."

Charlotte advised, "Well, the first thing you need to do is get a good financial consultant. Invest that money! Be sure and call me later after you see your plantation, Scarlett."

Ellie and Char shared delights of joy!

"I'm meeting Riley in an hour, and we're going out there to explore."

Char asked, "Riley? Who is Riley?"

Ellie hadn't meant to let that slip.

"I mean Mr. Langley, the lawyer who is handling the estate. He's very nice."

Charlotte was already thinking ahead of Ellie.

"It sounds like you and I need to get together once you get back, Girlfriend. I want all the details on this lawyer. Oh, before I forget, I watered your plants today. I also saw your computer geek friend."

Ellie felt a bit defensive, "He isn't a geek, Char."

"Oh settle down, I was just teasing. He actually looked cute in his shorts and T-shirt."

Ellie had a flash of her evening out with Sean earlier in the week.

"What was he doing, and where'd you see him?"

Char wasn't lost on Ellie's sudden interest.

"I was eating with a client at Golden Corral, and he came in with a group of people. I assumed it was family."

Ellie didn't have time to talk about Sean, but she did want to hear more about him.

"Hey, I'm at my hotel, so I am going to head inside to change. I'll call you tonight, okay?"

Char wanted to know more about this Riley Langley, but knew Ellie was pressed for time.

"Okay, be careful. Keep your cell phone on, just in case. He may seem like a good ol' boy, but remember, he's still a man."

Ellie suddenly felt like a daughter being lectured.

"You remember how to defend yourself, right?"

Charlotte and Ellie had taken a self-defense class together some ten years earlier after a teacher had been attacked on her way to her car after working late at school. Brad had insisted Ellie be able to defend herself should she ever be put in that situation.

"Yes, I remember, Char. I'm a big girl. Thanks for being concerned."

Charlotte always seemed like the mother her to Ellie, but she loved her for being there throughout all her crises.

"Okay, go have fun. Call me!"

Ellie laughed, "I will *Mom*."

The comment made Charlotte giggle. "Talk to you later."

Ellie quickly made her way to her room and began to change for the next adventure. Expecting to walk through tall grass and chiggers, she decided to dress accordingly: jeans and a long sleeved T-shirt. As she slipped her shoes on, she decided that the dream must have been her overactive imagination. After all, it had been quite an overwhelming twenty-four hours. *I still can't believe I inherited $500,000 and two homes. It's nuts!*

Ellie grabbed her purse and keys and took a last look in dresser mirror. As she gave herself the once over, she was pleased that she had taken time to reapply her makeup, wanting to look attractive for Riley Langley because he looked so attractive.

After closing the door behind her, Ellie remembered her camera was still inside her bag on the bed. She hurriedly unlocked the door and went to retrieve it. Heading back out, she had a strange feeling she wasn't alone. Quickly, she turned to look behind her, only to see her own reflection in the bathroom mirror. *Silly overactive imagination. I can't believe I'm getting this freaked out from a dream, for heaven's sake.*

Ellie closed and locked the door, and headed down the walkway to her car. Putting her bag on the front seat, she slipped on the seat belt, and began to drive out of the motel lot, glancing at her watch a second time. The thought of being late always made her nervous. The well-manicured lawns that lined Magnolia Avenue washed away her hurriedness.

Most of the homes, she suspected, had been there since the nineteenth century. Obviously, the present owners had treasured the historical aspect when restoring their homes. A couple of the houses were painted in the colors that were typical of the late Victorian era, reminding her of Southern belles, extending their colorful fans in a flirtatious gesture. They beckoned her to fall in love with their grace and charm. *I'm already hooked.* As she turned towards the older section of town, Ellie noticed the homes were even larger, defined with wide front porches and ornate columns.

Everywhere Ellie looked history enveloped the town, largely brought on by the closeness of the historical Cumberland River. As she made her way to Poplar Avenue, the large antebellum house that was now the law offices of Langley and Murdock came into view. Ellie saw the black Lexus in the spot where Riley had parked earlier, and checked to see she was right on time. Taking the key out of the ignition, she saw Riley Langley come onto the porch still looking impeccable in cargo pants and a bright orange University of Tennessee T-shirt and ball cap. If she hadn't seen him only an hour before, she would have sworn he was just a dad waiting to take his kids to a little league game. Waving as she exited the truck, she hurried to join him.

"You made good time, Ellie! I wasn't sure if an hour meant an hour," Riley said with a sarcastic smile.

"My timing is just fine, thank you very much, and I'm not one to be late, *ever!*" Ellie stressed.

"Well, you dressed appropriately because we'll have to wade through some tall weeds once we are out at Mimosa Grove. I would say no one has ventured out to mow in a good while."

Walking around the car to open the door for Ellie, he took out a small aerosol can and waved it in front of her.

"I found this can of bug spray in the office. It might not hurt to give your legs a once over."

Ellie was glad Riley had thought of that. She always had to spray herself whenever she went outside in the summer because ticks seemed to love her.

"I'm excited to see what Aunt Lavina left me. I still haven't quite wrapped my head around being an heiress just yet! I grew up on *Gone with the Wind*, and I can't help but imagine I am going to see *Tara* when we get there!"

Riley was happy for Ellie and her newfound wealth.

Closing her door and walking around to the driver's seat, he ventured, "I hope you're not too disappointed when you see what you own. As best I remember, it's no *Tara*."

Ellie countered, "I'm certainly no Scarlett."

They both laughed, with Riley continuing, "If you don't mind, I thought I would drive you past the house where Shelby and Lavina George lived prior to her going to the assisted living home. Then I thought since you're a history buff, you'd like to see the cemetery that you've been charged to visit."

"I'd like that, Riley. Thank you. Aunt Lavina must have been very much the history lover, making sure the Confederate soldiers' graves wouldn't be forgotten."

Riley nodded, "I think most Southern ladies still hold the memory of some lost rebel near and dear to their hearts. I believe most of the townsfolk have Confederate soldiers in their family tree. It's our heritage, you know?"

Ellie was beginning to understand that the War Between the States wasn't buried and forgotten. As they drove down the back streets of downtown Hendersonville, Ellie relaxed and enjoyed the scenery. The older neighborhoods were still maintained, and Ellie could see why it was one of the fastest growing cities in Tennessee, according to the Chamber of Commerce's website. With the windows down, the smell of fresh cut grass filled their nostrils.

"How old are the homes in this section of town?" Ellie asked.

"I'm going to say this part of town dates back to the mid 1800's. I know Derrick Jameson's house was built before the War. He found the original owner's war pension papers inside a drawer in the built-in buffet in his dining room. Can you image that?" Riley said.

"Wow. How cool is that to find such a unique piece of history in your home!" Ellie replied excitedly.

Riley pointed out the sign that told of a plantation built right after the Revolutionary War.

"We can drive out to Rock Castle some time if you'd like. The lake has taken up most of the property, but it's a real neat place to tour."

"I'd like that," Ellie agreed.

Someone was mowing the lawn at her great aunt's home. The gentleman on the Cub Cadet riding lawn mower, appearing to be in his late sixties, wore a long sleeved, light blue work shirt with well-worn Dickeys work slacks. His straw hat reminded Ellie of the one her grandfather had worn around his farm. Parking the lawnmower, he took a red bandana out of his back pocket and wiped the sweat from his forehead. Waving at Bobby Ray, Riley drove up the driveway and put the car in park.

"I'll introduce you to Bobby Ray Parker. He and Louise have lived in Miss Lavina's house for the last ten years. Have you any thoughts about what you are going to do, now that you own the house?"

Ellie hadn't given any consideration about the house until now.

"Are Bobby Ray and Louise retired, Riley?"

"Yes. Bobby Ray and Louise retired to Florida a few years back. Bobby Ray and my father grew up together. He worked for the gas company reading meters; she worked for the phone company. When Mrs. George wanted to rent her home rather than selling it, Dad thought of Bobby Ray and Louise. They had decided to sell their home and just rent this house from Mrs. George, still wintering in Florida." They've lived in Hendersonville all their lives."

Ellie wasn't sure what to do, but there was plenty of time to decide, and she did not intend to boot the couple from their home.

Riley turned off the car as Bobby Ray made his way over to the driveway.

"Riley! How are you?" Bobby Ray greeted with a huge grin across his suntanned face.

"Bobby Ray, it's been too long. How have you been?" Riley extended his hand and the two shook hands and patted one another on the back.

It took Bobby Ray a couple of seconds before he noticed the attractive woman standing to the rear of the car.

"Well who'd you bring along with you, Riley?"

Riley held out his hand to gesture for Ellie to come closer to be formally introduced.

"Bobby Ray, this is Ellie Morgan. Ellie is the great niece of Mrs. George."

Bobby Ray extended his hand towards Ellie.

"It is very nice to meet you, Ellie. I'm sorry about your loss. Mrs. George was a dear, old soul."

Bobby Ray had the same slow, deliberate Southern drawl that Riley had.

Ellie smiled, saying, "Thank you, Bobby Ray. I have heard how kind and generous she was from everyone I've met. I'm sorry I never had the chance to know her."

Bobby Ray wasn't sure why Riley had brought Ellie to meet them, but he was about to discover the nature of their visit.

"Bobby Ray, would it be all right for Ellie and me to talk with you and Louise for a moment?"

Bobby Ray took off his straw hat, wiping his forehead once again.

"Of course, where are my manners? Please, come on in the house. Louise is probably watching her Stories. She doesn't miss an episode of that *Young and Restless* show. Been watching it as long as it's been running."

Ellie smiled at that, as she was also a fan of the soap opera.

As they walked into the house, Bobby Ray called out for Louise. Coming through the archway separating the living room from the entry hall, was a petite woman with short stylish gray hair, wearing clothes displaying a woman very much concerned with her appearance, even while at home. She smiled sweetly, looking at Bobby Ray to make the introductions.

"Louise, you remember Donovan Langley's son, Riley, don't you?"

Louise extended her hand to Riley, "Of course I do, but it has been ages since I saw you. It is good to see you again."

Riley returned the warm greeting, adding, "Louise, I'd like to introduce you to Ellie Morgan, great niece of Lavina George."

"Pleased to meet you, Ellie," Louise returned smiling.

Ellie immediately liked her. The years had been very kind to Louise Reedy Parker: she had a pretty, heart-shaped face that lit up when she smiled. Spying a large collection of dolls housed in curio cabinets in the formal living room, and seeing no photographs of children, Ellie wondered if this collection was from Louise's childhood. She didn't see any photographs of children or grandchildren. *Was this delightful couple childless?*

"Come in and have seat. Can I get you some tea to drink?" Louise welcomed.

Thanking Louise for her hospitality, both Riley and Ellie declined. Entering the living room, which was liberally decorated in lovely furnishings that could have been showcased in *Southern Living*, Ellie's eye caught a pianoforte.

"That is a beautiful instrument, Louise. Do you play?" Ellie asked.

"Oh no, not a note. It belonged to Bobby Ray's great-grandmother. We inherited it when no one wanted to pay to have it moved after she passed on. It is the oldest piece of furniture we own. Bobby Ray's grandmother told me it was transported on a flat boat all the way from Chicago before the War Between the States. I wish I'd taken lessons when I was younger!"

After a few more moments of small talk, Riley changed the course of conversation to explain the nature of their visit.

"Ellie and I have come to talk to you about the reading of her great aunt Lavina's will today. In the will, Ellie was named sole heir of Mrs. George's estate. Now I don't want you to think that we are here to tell you that you now have to move."

Bobby Ray and Louise looked unsure where the conversation was heading.

Ellie spoke up, "I am in no hurry to do anything with the house. There is plenty of time to decide what is best for everyone."

Bobby Ray spoke next, "Well, truth be told, Louise and I are ready to move to our winter home full time. Driving back and forth is starting to get to us. We aren't getting any younger, and our kids have all moved out of the area as well."

So they do have children.

"It might help us get going if you had a time frame to sell the house, or whatever you had planned to do with it. We could be out within the month, if you need us to be."

Louise looked at Ellie to see if that would be agreeable with her. Ellie was suddenly becoming aware of the decisions impelled of a landlord.

"Well, I haven't had time to process everything yet. I'll be happy to work with you on getting things settled so that you a can make arrangements for the move. I'm sure Riley will be advising me as to what would be the best course to take."

Riley added, "I'd be happy to help in whatever capacity, Ellie."

Louise smiled, wondering if Riley could be smitten with this pretty woman.

After a few more moments of discussing the house and what work would need to be done, Riley and Ellie promised to keep in touch. Bobby Ray and Louise stood to walk the couple out to their car.

Walking with Ellie to the car, Louise commented, "Bobby Ray and I appreciate you coming to meet us. We have enjoyed living in the house for the past ten years."

Ellie wanted to give the Parker's all the time they needed to arrange for movers to come.

"Louise, you and Bobby Ray take all the time you need. I really have no plans to do anything with the house right now."

She still had another home to see. It was about two o'clock, and Riley wanted to make it out to Mimosa Grove before it got too late, unsure what he would find. As the two got back in the car, Riley spoke.

"Well, I think that went well. They seem to be ready to move on to Florida, even relieved that Lavina didn't leave the house to them."

Ellie nodded, "I was thinking that very same thing. I don't want them to think I am going to make them move though."

Riley added, "Maybe we can get together soon to talk about what you want to do with the house."

Ellie looked at the house, then back to Riley, "Well, if I can sell it, I think that would be my best option. I have a job in Indiana, and I don't foresee moving to Tennessee just yet."

Riley hid his disappointment at that, not wanting to influence Ellie one way or another.

"As you said, you have plenty of time to decide. Now let's go see what's behind door number two."

Ellie chuckled, "It does seem like I am on the winning end of a game show today."

"Okay then. Let's hit it."

He pulled the car out of the driveway, and headed east out of town towards Mimosa Grove.

Riley took the car onto the interstate, heading east on Highway 31. The afternoon temperatures had thankfully remained in the upper seventies, making it possible to have the windows down to enjoy the breeze. Ellie noticed the farmland as they drove along and wondered what they would find when they reached Mimosa Grove. Noticing that the houses in the subdivisions were starting to look more expensive, she assumed the Cumberland River was close by. Riley seemed to be in deep thought so they remained silent for a time.

Finally, Ellie queried, "Do you think the house will be worth saving? I mean, has it sat empty for years?"

Riley hadn't been out to the house for many years, but he knew that it had a caretaker who was responsible for looking after it.

"I don't think the house was left to run into rack and ruin since my father promised Mrs. George that Mimosa Grove would remain just as she left it. I know that someone is responsible for taking care of the property, and as far as I know, he has checked on the house daily, keeping his word. Besides, my father has also gone out and checked on the place. I remember a few years back, he had to go out after someone reported seeing a strange truck backing down the driveway."

Ellie's eyes widened.

"Did they break into the house?" she asked.

"No, it was just a couple of teens wanting to get off the beaten path to be alone."

Ellie grinned, getting his drift.

"Well, I'm glad that the house is not falling in around itself, knowing how much it must have meant to Aunt Lavina."

After they had been on Highway 31 for ten minutes, Riley slowed down to a snail's pace.

"Now where is that road? I remember Dad saying to look for two cedar tree posts and an iron gate. Oh, there it is."

He turned off the highway onto a gravel road, actually a driveway, with a gate barring intruders from entry. Ellie noticed that there were gated communities on both sides of the highway. She assumed this land was the original farmland of Mimosa Grove before it was sold to developers.

Ellie began to feel the butterflies fluttering in her stomach, anticipating the excitement of what was to come. Riley got out of the car, reached into his pocket and removed a small key ring. As he turned the lock on the padlock, Ellie scanned the area around the gate.

The field to the right was once used for crops, but now had grown tall with a variety of weeds. On the left, there were stray, withered corn stalks standing as silent sentinels to the property that lay beyond.

Riley slid back into the driver's seat and looked at Ellie, "Well, are you ready to see your new plantation, Miss Scarlett?"

Ellie let out a sigh and said, "I am so excited, I want to take pictures of everything the way it looks right now."

With that, she pulled out her digital camera and began to snap pictures as Riley slowly drove up the driveway. At one time, the driveway had been lined with large cedar trees, but over the years, many had suffered the effects of blight and weather.

As they drove into what was evidently the yard area of the property, Ellie began clicking away. To the right of the car, was a large, slightly slanted barn, which Riley explained, had been used to house hay to feed the cattle in the winter. Behind this barn, Ellie could see a dilapidated chicken coup, once well stocked with hens that kept the inhabitants in fresh eggs each day.

Riley parked the car, Ellie grabbing her purse from the backseat. She set off to take pictures of the two outbuildings.

"There's a tobacco barn over the hill down there; I remember it being in better shape. Behind the house is the springhouse and smokehouse. I remember my dad saying that when he came out to see the George's, there was still the smell of smoking ham coming from it. Seems to me there is also a building that was once the kitchen."

Directly in front of her, some twenty-five yards from the drive, stood Mimosa Grove, ancestral home of Lavina George. The home was still beautiful to Ellie, but the house was in need of a tender touch. From where she stood, the house seemed to be waiting to let out a breath, as if waiting for Ellie's approval. Ellie took picture after picture of the outside of the house. The exterior of the plantation house was brick. When standing in front of the house, the visitor could see two identical porches supported by four large columns and two identical doors, one above the other, with a Palladian window above and sidelights beside the door. The porch railing was in need of fresh paint. All the windowpanes appeared to shimmer in the light. *Were they original to the house?*

The shutters were a pale shade of gray now, having once possibly been dark green or black. The front door seemed to be beckoning Ellie to come inside, appearing to have been the site of many happy returns as well as sad farewells in the years it breathed life.

"I'd like to walk around before we go inside, if that's okay," Ellie asked.

"Of course it is. This is your day, Ellie. I want you to see it all."

Ellie appreciated how easy-going Riley was, or was *trying* to be. She wasn't sure if this was the *real* Riley, or if he were just appeasing a client. Either way, she was enjoying whatever caused his genial mood.

Ellie walked from the porch to the side of the house. She noticed there were two chimneys on both sides of the house. Attic windows jutted out from the dark slate roof, and for a split second, Ellie was sure a shadow appeared in one of the windows. Shading her eyes with her hand, she tried for a better view. The shadow was no longer there. *That's odd. I know I saw a shadow in that window!* Ellie continued walking to the back of the house, Riley, unaware as he checked the foundation for any signs of cracks or issues that needed attention.

Ellie stepped back from the house to assess the view. Across the back were two large porches that spanned the length of the house. The summer porch across the second floor was reminiscent of the piazzas on the homes in Charleston that she had visited. Ellie assumed whoever built the home had brought architectural designs from the Deep South. The slate roof had been very expensive when the home was built, and Ellie was thankful she didn't notice any missing tiles. Anxious to get inside the house, she hurriedly pressed on to inspect the rest of the exterior.

As Ellie scanned the area behind the house, she could see a grove of mimosa trees giving an abundance of shade to the rear of the home. Then she saw it, the reason for the large, wide piazzas on the back. Down the sloping field, behind the smokehouse and springhouse, was the river, it's winding, snaking shape carving out the landscape below. Across the river, on the opposite bank, were several docks. There were also several very expensive-looking homes with private docks. Ellie credited little merit to the progress that had taken place since Mimosa Grove had been built.

Riley caught up to Ellie.

"You own prime river property, Ellie. Back in the day, the folks who lived here would have been able to watch steamboats and keelboats going up and down the Cumberland River. They also could have deliveries made to the dock down there."

Ellie noticed an ancient wooden dock jutting into the water.

"I had no idea, Riley. It's beautiful!"

Riley felt that perhaps Ellie might keep the property; after all, that's why she was brought here in the first place!

Vines had begun to climb up the opposite side of the house, giving the appearance of a veil trailing down from the top of the home.

"Would you like to take the tour inside? I'm not the greatest of tour guides, but I think I can at least find my way around."

Riley searched in his pocket again for the mass of keys. Some were very old, but others appeared to be modern dead-bolt keys.

"I'm ready, Riley!"

Ellie snapped a few more photographs before following him back around to the front of the house.

Riley and Ellie walked up the large stone steps that led to the massive front door. The paint was beginning to chip off, and Ellie noticed that the knocker was engraved, but too dirty and worn to read. *I'll have it taken off and cleaned.* Riley fiddled with the lock trying to get the key to go in. Finally, the key turned and he walked in first, looking for a light switch.

The two stood in a large foyer with a large stairway leading up to another floor above. The entry hall narrowed to a smaller hallway that led to the back door of the house.

Riley began, "Before the George's lived here, there was no electricity. Shelby spared no expense to make sure plumbing and electric lights were added. From what I understand, the home has all the original fixtures and woodwork. Bathrooms were added, as was a 'modern' kitchen. I believe that work was done in the early fifties, and, as you might have guessed, is in need of updating."

Ellie hadn't noticed; she was in awe of what lay before her.

"For the most part, it's a diamond in the rough," Riley said enthusiastically.

Ellie was busily snapping pictures of the entryway and stairway before her. "I love it already!" she squealed. And with that, the house let out a sigh of relief. Ellie's senses on overload, she felt a draft blow past her. *Probably the rush of air as the door was closed.* She shivered and rubbed her hands over her arms. The entry way wasn't by any means large, but it was adequate for a home of its size. On either side of the entry hall were two doorways that led to other rooms. The floor beneath her feet was poplar smoothed to a shine, and apparently protected by a large rug.

Glimpsing several cobwebs drooping down from the beautiful chandelier hanging in the entry hall, Ellie guessed the house had not been cleaned in a while. At first, it seemed as if the walls in the foyer were papered. However, upon closer inspection Ellie saw that the walls were actually painted. Large limbs appeared to be branches from mimosa trees with their pink pom sprays of flowers. No doubt, the owner wanted to show the connection to the name of the home. Walking closer, Ellie inspected the artwork.

"This is absolutely beautiful, Riley. All it needs is a little cleaning to bring it back to life!"

Riley was so glad she approved. Ellie took more pictures, making sure to note every detail. The smell of the home reminded her of Grandmother Camden's where she stayed summers, growing up. A mixture of kitchen smells and old house, Ellie found the smell to be oddly comforting. Ellie chose to start her exploration of the downstairs first, beginning with the room on her left. Upon entering the room, her eyes had trouble adjusting to the darkness.

"Let me find the light switch, Ellie. Don't want you bumping into something and getting hurt."

Riley began feeling his way around the perimeter of the wall, looking for a light switch.

"Here it is."

When he flipped the switch, nothing happened.

"I guess the light bulbs are toast. Remind me when we leave to jot that down. I can spring for a new light bulb. Call it a housewarming gift!"

Ellie chuckled at Riley's comment. As he was searching for the light, she had felt her way to the middle of the room, suddenly feeling another presence. Something was so close to her that she felt claustrophobic. She was getting ready to let out a scream, which she muffled, when Riley drew back the curtains, allowing daylight to stream through the tall window. To her astonishment, the whole room was covered in white sheets and old blankets. It was as if the owners had just vacated.

"Did the caretaker cover all of this, Riley?"

Riley hadn't been to the house in such a long time, he had forgotten about the contents.

"I thought the belongings were in storage. Dad never mentioned everything being just as it was."

"So there has been heat in here during the winter, for ten years?" Ellie asked.

Riley replied, "As far as I know, the caretaker was told to keep heat in the house. I remember the furnace failing a couple of years ago, and my father had Junior Wallace come out and put in a new one. Mrs. George had cashed in several savings bonds that had reached maturity, and paid the bill in full. This house was very important to Mrs. George. She wanted to make sure it remained in the same condition as when she lived in it."

Ellie interjected, "Was this her mother and father's home?"

Riley gazed at the ceiling, as if trying to recite a memorized script.

"I was told this home has never left the hand of Mrs. George's ancestors. Dad told me that the house has been in the family for about seven generations. I guess that is why she wanted to be sure another relative would own it after her."

Ellie began lifting sheets to inspect what was underneath.

"This must have been the parlor. The furniture under the sheets seems to be very expensive, very old, possibly early Victorian."

To Ellie's joy, in the far right corner of the room, covered with a large white sheet, was a very old piano. Large, thick wooden piano legs were exposed when the sheet was lifted. It appeared to be a pianoforte, a popular version of the parlor piano. Ellie touched the ivory keys. She sat down to play a quick song, checking for loose keys and finding it kept tune fairly well.

Riley complimented, "You sound accomplished."

"I was required to take lessons all through school; my mother's dream was that I be a concert pianist someday. I had other plans!" Ellie said, displaying her independent nature.

Riley walked over to the fireplace, admiring the antique figurines on the mantel.

"I can't believe all of this is here and no one has stolen Mrs. George blind," Ellie commented.

"As I said, Dad paid the caretaker well to come and check on this house daily. For awhile, he stayed in the downstairs to be sure no one bothered the home."

Ellie's brow furrowed in thought.

"Why didn't he sleep in one of the rooms upstairs? I would assume there are plenty of bedrooms up there?" Ellie asked.

"He told my father he didn't feel comfortable being up there, so he just stayed on the first floor."

Ellie thought that was odd, but didn't comment further. A large round table sat in the middle of room in front of the fireplace. Under the sheet was a silver liquor service that had long ago turned black from tarnish. Beside the empty serving set was an ancient looking Bible.

"Riley, look! It's a family Bible. I've always heard that a family in the 1800's kept all of their history inside the Bible. What a treasure to find! I can't believe no one has taken it."

Ellie picked up of the large Bible, removed the sheet from one of the high back Victorian chairs that flanked either side of the table, and sat down. Seeing the copyright date was 1830, she was afraid to go further for fear pages would crumble. A name, almost too faint to decipher, appeared in the front: *Camille Townes*.

"Riley, would it be okay if I took this with me tonight?" Ellie asked.

"It's all yours, Ellie. You can take whatever you like."

Ellie couldn't wait to get the Bible back to her motel room to see what treasures and family history could be inside.

"Do you want to go across the hall to see what we can find there?"

Ellie was now even more curious as to what treasures lay waiting to be discovered. Riley led the way out of the room, waiting for Ellie to bring the Bible, and then shut the large sliding wooden parlor doors. Ellie was already heading into the next room.

"I'm assuming this was a gentleman's room or possibly the library," Riley offered.

From Ellie's vantage point, she was able to scan the room in the partial light that came in from the hallway. Riley found his way to the large window that was covered with a dark blanket. As he removed the blanket, Ellie felt a chill run up her spine. She had felt the same way earlier when she walked into the house.

"Do you feel that draft, Riley?" Ellie asked quietly.

It was as if the two were not alone in the big house, even though they knew they were the first people to be in the house for quite some time. The cobwebs had made a series of traps that Ellie had to go through before she could uncover the sheets that donned furniture and collectables. Directly in front of the large fireplace was a small sofa that was covered in dark brown upholstery. A plaid coverlet lay thrown across the back, just as if someone had carelessly tossed it there earlier.

Above the fireplace mantle, another portrait was covered with a sheet. Ellie started to take the sheet down, but Riley moved in to help. Riley took a sturdy wooden chair that was sitting beside the fireplace and stood on it to take the rest of the sheet off.

"It does feel a bit cool in here, but that's probably due to the house being closed up for so long without the heat running."

Riley tried to sound sure of himself, but even he felt uneasy. Ellie was busy staring at the portrait Riley had uncovered. It was of a gentleman, perhaps in his early twenties. Ellie imagined that this was one of Aunt Lavina's ancestors. He was handsome, with dark brown eyes that seemed to look through Ellie, but his gaze was comforting, not something to fear. Admiring the portrait, Ellie decided that she would have to find out who the young man was.

Still feeling the chill as she scanned the rest of the small, but finely decorated room, Ellie uncovered a large secretary in the corner, filled with old books. The desk was something she would have to come back and explore.

"I know my imagination is just running wild today, but I felt a presence when I first arrived. Let's keep looking. There's a lot of house to see before we check out the grounds!"

"I don't have a black belt, but I think I can protect you against your wild imagination," Riley offered.

The more Ellie was around Riley, the more she felt they had a common bond. Call it kismet or karma, whatever the correct vernacular was. Ellie felt a kinship to Riley she couldn't explain. Whatever it was, she felt completely at ease with this stranger. She was enjoying having this exploration with him.

Ellie found herself standing in the entry hall once again. She stared up the stairway to the second floor above. *Stop it, Ellie! There's no such thing as ghosts! Stop being so childish. It's just an old, drafty house.*

"I wonder if I should make plans to have the house checked out. Since I can afford to hire someone, it might not be a bad idea. What do you think, Riley?"

Riley was busy looking around for signs of leaks and came back into the hallway.

"I don't think it could hurt. I'd say the wiring needs to be checked. One good thing is the heating system was put in a few years back. Might not hurt to have someone check the chimneys either. You plan on living here?"

Riley didn't wait for Ellie to comment.

"The roof seems in good shape, no sign of any water damage down here. We'll have to look around upstairs for the real signs of water damage."

Ellie was chomping at the bit to get a look at what was up there, but the rest of the downstairs still needed to be explored. Riley was walking in front of her.

"Okay, let's see what lies behind door number two!"

The two walked beyond the entry and started down the narrow hallway that led to two more rooms. To the left of the hallway were two large pocket doors. Ellie assumed this room had not been used in many years when the musty smell assailed her nostrils as he parted the doors. The feeling of walking into a tomb came to mind as Ellie hesitantly peered into the dark.

"Hold on, I need to get a flash light, Ellie."

Riley walked back down the hallway and out to his car. Inside the trunk, he had placed a tool kit and flashlight. While he was gone, Ellie listened. *I know old houses are notorious for creaks and groans, but footsteps? Maybe it is just the house settling, or possibly a limb hitting the roof.* Ellie was ashamed of herself for even letting such thoughts enter her mind. She jumped at the sound of Riley, who was already back in the hallway.

"Lucky for me the flashlight actually had a battery in it. I think it has been in the car since I bought it!"

He turned on the light, illuminating the dining room of Mimosa Grove. The sheets that hung over the large pieces of furniture gave the illusion of ghostly apparitions in the semi darkness. Ellie scanned the room from side to side. It appeared that this room was identical in size to the first two rooms in the front of the house.

Ellie began tossing sheets from the furniture. Under the sheets the room was finely decorated Victorian furniture. In the center of the room was a large table that appeared to be solid cherry. Eight high back chairs were placed around the table. Ellie touched the chair pads, marveling at the delicate embroidery stitching of the design on each of the seats. Even though some of the threads were starting to unravel, the pads were still lovely and well preserved.

Ellie marveled at the carving on the large sideboard. Someone had taken great pride in the furniture, as it appeared to have been lovingly preserved through many generations. In fact, of all the pieces that Ellie had uncovered, these appeared to be museum quality, and she felt unworthy to be touching any of them. Riley was admiring the furniture as well.

"It probably would be a good idea to have an insurance agent come by and give you some idea of what the contents are worth. You want to be sure these antiques are protected."

Ellie nodded, "I can't imagine what all of this is worth, and I haven't even seen the upstairs!"

Above the large fireplace mantel was a portrait of a pretty young girl. On another wall in the room was a portrait of yet another young woman. It appeared that the two young women were from the same family, as there was a definite resemblance between them. Directly across the room from one of these was the painting of a much older woman with haunting eyes, seeming to stare straight into Ellie's soul. This portrait was possibly an earlier ancestor, and Ellie assumed the three were related.

"Do you suppose these paintings were relatives of Aunt Lavina? They seem to be in exceptional condition. Everything is," Ellie marveled, looking around the beautiful room.

Riley was admiring the furniture, taking sheets off the chairs.

"I had no idea all of this stuff was left in the house. I can't believe it has remained in such great condition after all these years!"

The next room had obviously been renovated since the home was built. Riley wasn't sure what the original room was meant to be, but this room had been converted to a kitchen. At the back of this room was a small powder room.

"Well this looks out of place. I'll bet Aunt Lavina had this room re-decorated. No woman wants to use an outhouse when there are ways to incorporate plumbing!" Ellie chuckled.

"It doesn't look like it has been updated in a long time, Ellie. You might want to think about redoing it. I know it's a big expense, but if you find the right designer, you can take the house back to more historically accurate features, even if you go modern. There's a lot of ways to make a new room look old."

Contemplating, Ellie agreed, "I might do that. I just don't know right now what I am doing."

Ellie took a quick mental check of the room. The cabinets were few, and looked to be formica. The counter tops were also formica, something that she had been accustomed to when she visited her grandparent's 1950's style home growing up. The bathroom was simple in its furnishings, containing a commode, pedestal sink, and small closet. It was functional, and that would do.

As Ellie looked out the back window, she was aware that at one time this room must have been a porch. She saw the brick kitchen that was placed directly behind the house, and it was connected to the main house by a once manicured pebble or stone walkway. Now it was overgrown with weeds. Ellie was thankful for the converted kitchen. It would help the resale value having a kitchen and small bath on the ground floor, if she put the home on the market. *The home can't be sold; Aunt Lavina wanted it to stay within the family. Now that she was gone, would it matter?*

Riley had walked outside to inspect the structural aspects of the back of the house. Ellie left the heavy wooden door open, and closed the old screen door behind her. As she peered out at the expanse behind the house, she was immediately drawn to the old grove of mimosa trees that dotted the back yard of the home. Two very large trees flanked the sides, giving great shade in the evening.

"These trees are just beautiful. How old do you think they are, Riley?" Ellie asked.

Riley had moved farther back away from the back porch to get a better view of the roof: slate shingles, very expensive for the time, and only one looked like it had cracked and chipped off. Finding one to replace it would be a problem.

"I would think the trees were planted sometime after the house was built. I'll check on the date again, but I thought I saw somewhere that the original house was built around 1830. There was another house standing here before that, but it burned. I don't think the trees were here before that. I would say they're the shoots from the original trees. Those were here before the War."

"They are amazingly beautiful," Ellie said softly.

Ellie was drawn to the windows on the third floor. This was most likely the attic in the home. The last rays of daylight were shining in the windows as the sun began to set. She couldn't help but wonder about all the families who had lived within the walls of Mimosa Grove.

"Do you think we have time to walk down to the river today?" Ellie asked.

Riley looked at his watch, "I think maybe we should go back and finish the tour. By the time we get done there, it will be getting dark. I'd like to lock up and have the alarm system set before too late."

Ellie was glad to keep exploring. She was most anxious to see what treasures lay in the upstairs rooms. Riley opened the door, and Ellie thanked him as she walked through. He made sure the doors were locked and the lights were off as they walked back to the front of the house. The entry hall's main focus was the stairway that sat directly in front as the visitor entered the front door. The poplar wood throughout the house gave the woodwork a lighter look than a Victorian-era home.

The newel post at the bottom of the stairway contained a large disc that caught Ellie's eye right off.

Riley could see her interest and asked, "Did anyone ever tell you why homes had this newel post on the stairway?"

Ellie shook her head as Riley continued.

"The homeowner placed this on the bottom of the stairway to signify the home was paid for: his way to boast of wealth."

Ellie followed Riley as he began to climb the stairs. At some point, a runner had been tacked to the stairway, similar in pattern to the mimosa leaves and flowers that covered the walls in the entryway. Over time, the pattern had faded, but considering the age of the home and families who inhabited the house, it was in remarkable condition. Again, this home had been lovingly preserved.

As Ellie ascended the stairway, her shadow was cast on the wall, climbing to the second floor. Riley was leading the way with his flashlight. The chandelier was missing several of its bulbs.

"I'll pick up some bulbs for you and have them put in before you come back. No sense taking a header down the stairs," joked Riley.

"Thank you, kind sir," Ellie countered, "that's so gallant of you to do that."

Reaching the top of the stairs, they were once again in a large central hallway. The upstairs was much brighter than the downstairs, and Ellie noticed immediately when she reached the landing. Sunlight streamed from a large window, causing the hallway to be warm and inviting. The upstairs had five rooms, which at one time were all bedrooms Riley assumed. Directly to the right of the landing was the smallest of rooms with two large windows from ceiling to floor. One could see the large porch that extended the length of the back of the home. There was no closet, but standing in the corner was a large chifferobe.

The furniture was covered, but Ellie assumed the original bed covers had long since been removed. At one time, this room, the color of lilac, must have belonged to a girl. Riley, busy checking for leaks in the ceiling, noticed a spot above the chifferobe.

"I would say that is an old stain, since it doesn't appear to be damp, but it would be best if I have someone come and check it. We can set something up today, if you want."

Ellie was in full agreement. The next room was on the same side of the hall that faced the drive. Appearing to be another child's room, although larger, it had a small bed and was decorated in more masculine in nature. Its window was the one Ellie noticed when they drove up to the house. The two rooms on the other side of the hall were empty. Only boxes and crates littered the floor. Ellie would have to explore the contents later.

The large back windows were used as a way out to the large piazza that lined the back of the house. Upon being raised, a cool breeze from the river was allowed to filter through the muggy upstairs rooms. The view was spectacular from this vantage point. The river's bend was just to the left of the window. To the middle of the two front rooms was a smaller room. It contained a door that led to a porch identical to the one below, but it was now made to look like a window instead. This room was directly above the entry below and Riley assumed this could have been the trunk room or closet room. Someone had converted it to a modern bath some time ago. The tile appeared to be from the 1950's, and thankfully it boasted a shower /tub combo, large vanity, closet, and commode.

Coming out of the bathroom, Riley said, "Well, looks like we've seen it all. I think you have a nice house here, Ellie!"

Ellie's eyes were searching the hallway.

"Where's the entry into the attic? I would love to see what's up there."

Looking to see if Riley could be persuaded to search for the stairs, she noticed that the stairway had been enclosed. With a little work though, the stairway could once again be brought to floor level.

"Are you sure you want to go up there? I'm sure there are bats, mice, maybe even snakes."

Ellie was determined.

"I'm sure. If you don't want to go, let me have the flashlight!"

Riley's manliness, threatened, joined in, "No, it's okay. You don't need to go alone. Let me go first, just in case."

In case of what? Had he heard the sounds too? When the door was opened, a rush of warm air struck their faces. Ellie thought she heard the house say, 'Aah', as if letting out a deep breath.

As the two climbed the small attic stairs, Ellie got that feeling again. She didn't share that she thought someone was waiting for them in the attic. More heat escaped from the attic as they climbed each narrow step. At the top of the stairs, Ellie and Riley felt a rush of air that passed through them both.

"Wow! Did you feel that?" Riley asked.

Even in the heat, Ellie shivered.

"I sure did. That was phenomenal!"

The stairs creaked loudly, and below the house became still, almost as if it was keeping a dark secret. Ellie tried to cast off the feeling she had earlier, but it was tangible as they reached the attic floor.

The sunlight from the windows wasn't enough to offer a good amount of illumination to explore, so Riley reached in his back pocket to turn on the flashlight.

"It looks like no one has been up here in a long time."

Ellie, walking through a large spider's web, let out a scream. Riley turned to see what was wrong.

"I'm okay . . .I have this arachnophobia issue."

"Well, mine is snakes. Don't feel bad. Let's stay close, just in case the floorboards are rotten. We can fall through together!"

"Ha! I'd like to stick close; you have the flashlight!" Ellie laughed.

They started with the side of the attic that was near the stairs. There were boxes that were misshapen from the heat and cold of the attic over the years. These boxes mostly contained old dishes, magazines and books. Riley was surprised by an ancient-looking wooden box. He lifted the lid and saw several slates shingles.

"Well I'll be! Here are the shingles from the roof! These have to be over one hundred and fifty years old!"

In another box were odds and ends from the remodeling jobs of the kitchen and bathrooms. Ellie found a couple of old trunks and suitcases. She immediately wanted to explore the contents. Treasuring antiques, she immediately wanted to explore the contents.

"Riley, could you hold the light down here. I'm going to try and open this trunk."

"Sure, here . . . ." Riley said, illuminating the inside of the trunk.

The contents had been placed with loving hands, as each item was folded and wrapped in decades-old tissue paper. The items were mostly feminine in nature, and whomever the articles of clothing belonged to was small in stature. The dresses were formal attire, and Ellie imagined they were from the 1800's. None of the dresses were bustled, so that helped to date them. There were shawls made of pale ivory lace, a pair of small slippers made of satin with tiny rosettes on the toes, and three christening gowns.

Ellie lifted the shoes out carefully. Marveling at the delicate workmanship, she carefully placed them back inside the trunk. She moved one of the dresses aside to see what was underneath. Lying in the bottom of the trunk was a small wooden box. Ellie sat it on the floor, lifting the lid to discover small black cases. Upon opening them, she found they held tin types.

"Oh look, Riley. Pictures!" Ellie gasped.

"How about we take the trunks with us, and you can look through them back at the motel. I hate to cut our fun short, but it is getting dark," Riley said.

Ellie was disappointed, but knew they should go while they could still see without the flashlight.

"Okay, I'll help you carry these two trunks."

After two trips downstairs, the two went back through the house to check for lights and doors to be locked. As Ellie walked out the door, she turned back to take one last look at the attic. For a second, she thought she saw a face in the window. She tried to focus her eyes on the window, but the sun had already set, and all that was visible were the shadows from the mimosa tree in the front yard.

"Okay Miss Ellie, your trunks are wedged into the back seat. Are you ready?" Riley asked.

"Yeah, I think I have had enough excitement for one day. Thanks for taking time out of your day to cart me all over creation," Ellie said.

"You're welcome. It's been my pleasure."

Riley gave Ellie a look that she hadn't received for a long time. She suddenly felt a rush of heat that caused her to feel flushed. Hoping Riley hadn't noticed the effect he had on her, she gazed out the window. The sun had set, and dusk was quickly setting in. Riley drove the car down the dusty drive to the entry gate.

"I'll just be a minute," Riley said, jumping out to close the gate.

Grabbing the old iron gate, he pulled it toward the post. It made a mournful sound as it closed.

Ellie rolled the window down, drawing in the aroma of honeysuckle as it wafted into the car.

"I remember honeysuckle at my grandparents' house when I would stay with them in the summer. In fact, that is one of the things I think of when I hear the word, summer."

Riley was having similar thoughts as he sniffed the sweetness coming through the open windows.

"My grandparents had a house in town, and my father and mother would leave my sister and me with them for a couple of weeks during the summer. I remember going out to the back yard, pulling the ends out of the flowers, and sucking the honey into my mouth. I used to make myself sick on that stuff."

Ellie laughed at the mental image she had. Riley was so different from the first impression she had formed. He had similar memories, which united them. As they drove down the highway towards the office, they didn't say more than a few words. Ellie was trying to remember all that she had seen and heard that day. It was truly overwhelming.

As they pulled into the parking lot, Ellie began looking for her keys. The key ring always ended up in the bottom of her purse, and it became an inside joke with Char. Retrieving her keys, she walked over to unlock the covered topper of her truck.

"Do you think one of the steamer trunks will fit under the topper of my truck?" Ellie asked as she moved her things from the back seat.

Riley took the smaller of the two trunks and placed it in front of the truck. Then he carried the large steamer trunk and placed it inside the bed of her truck. He made sure to test the lid before closing it all the way.

"I think you'll be fine with this one back here. I'll be glad to follow you back to your motel and carry them in for you."

Ellie hadn't thought of that. Even if she got the trunks into the motel room, how would she get them loaded back into the truck to go home?

"I'll tell you what. If you would feel more comfortable, I would be happy to meet you tomorrow to finish settling the estate. I also want to give you some papers Mrs. George had; it will give you the numbers for contacting the representative from the UDC and the matron of the cemetery here in town."

"Oh, I think I met Mrs. Eubanks already," Ellie chimed in, "when I went to visit Aunt Lavina's grave."

Riley took out his pocket calendar from his car and came back over to her.

"I would imagine you will want to go back to Indiana within the next couple of days. I'll give you the keys to Mimosa Grove and all the documentation you'll need for the transfer of funds tomorrow."

Ellie still couldn't quite wrap her head around that.

"I can meet you early, if you have an opening."

Riley thought for a moment and decided, "I can meet you around nine, before my appointments begin for the day. I'll let Carol know you are coming in. We should be able to conduct our business in about an hour."

Ellie was glad she could meet with him before the day got away from her. She wanted to make a trip to Mimosa Grove by herself. She wanted to go back to the attic.

"I'll see you first thing tomorrow, Riley. Thank you again for today. It was really fun AND eventful!"

Riley smiled, "It was my pleasure. I haven't had a day like today in quite a while. Thank YOU!"

Riley waited as Ellie backed her truck out and pulled away. As she looked in her rearview mirror, she mulled over his words wondering what he meant by them.

On her drive back to the motel, Ellie began to wonder what she would find inside the two trunks. She glanced over at the small trunk that was sitting on the seat beside her. All sorts of thoughts went through her mind. She had had her appetite whetted with the dainty dresses and shoes that were wrapped up just as they were packed over a century before.

She could hardly keep to the speed limit as she made her way down Main Street to her motel. As she pulled into the parking lot, she remembered she'd promised to call Char as soon as she got back to the motel. She decided that she would need to bring in the larger trunk from the back, but could safely leave the smaller trunk inside the cab of her truck. Ellie looked around outside of the motel entry doors to see if anyone had left a luggage cart. Not seeing one, she decided to go inside and inquire. Making sure the car doors were locked, she walked across the parking lot to the office. The gentleman behind the desk appeared not to notice her as he played a game of *Solitaire* on the computer. He turned when she cleared her throat.

"Can I help you, Ma'am?"

Ellie smiled as she asked, "Well, I need to bring in a trunk to my room, and I wondered if you had any luggage carriers around that I could use?"

He looked outside, and then back to the lobby.

"I swear, if people would bring the darned carts back where they find them . . ." His voice trailed off to murmurs under his breath. "Hang on; let me see if I can find you one."

With that, the desk clerk went to check the walkways. Within a couple of minutes, he was back again, obviously angered by the fact that patrons hadn't returned the carts.

"Well, I thought at least one of the three carts would be out or about, but I guess the guests have left them in their rooms for the night. Let me put the machine on, and I'll be more than happy to help you carry in your trunk."

Ellie was grateful for the chivalrous gesture. She thought the clerk looked like someone's grandfather. He told her he had retired from working in the insurance business, and was helping his daughter and son-in-law run their motel.

"Thank you so much for your help. I wasn't thinking when I brought these back with me. They are a little too much for one person to carry."

She walked around to the back of the truck. The clerk saw the age of the trunk, and very carefully put his hand under the bottom to scoot it out from the tailgate.

"You been to the antique mall today, Miss?" the clerk asked.

"Yes, something like that," Ellie remarked.

After the two loaded the trunk carefully on the cart, Ellie went to her room and opened the door, allowing the clerk to wheel in the cart.

"Would you like me to help you unload the trunk?"

It was obvious he didn't want to come in to her room, with her being alone. *Thank heavens* he is worried about appearances.

"I think I can unload it, but thank you so much for helping."

Ellie cautiously took the trunk one end at a time off the low cart. Taking the trunk off the cart took a little more ump than she thought it would! *What in the world did they store in this, a lead ball?* She wheeled the cart back to the clerk.

"Tomorrow I will be leaving. I don't think I can lift the trunk to put it back in the pickup by myself."

The clerk smiled, and said, "Of course, it's no trouble. Just call down to the front desk and someone will be happy to assist you."

Ellie smiled at the clerk and said, "Thank you again for being so kind and helpful."

"You're welcome, Ma'am. Have a good evening."

It was already nine o'clock, and she hadn't eaten dinner yet. She didn't have any food in the motel room, so decided she would go down to the vending machines and get a small bag of chips and a soft drink. It wasn't nutritious, but she was really too excited to eat. She went to her purse to get her dollar bills for the machine, and it was then that she remembered the Bible she had found in the parlor. *Oh no, I forgot the Bible! I must have sat it down on the floor in the attic when I was looking inside the trunk.*

Ellie was disappointed in herself for being so scatterbrained. She would have to make another trip to Mimosa Grove. The Bible could be a treasure trove of history; *her history.* She would be able to explore the contents of the trunks tonight, but first she needed to call Char and tell her all about her exciting day. She munched on the chips, as she dialed Charlotte. She could hear the television in the room next to her and decided to turn hers on as well, to drown out her conversation. The familiar phone message came on telling Ellie to wait while the party was being reached. *I'm too excited to wait! I have so much to tell Char.*

"Hey Ellie, I have been on pins and needles here waiting for you to call! What in the world have you been doing for the last nine hours?"

"Char, you are going to have to sit down for this one! I own two houses in Hendersonville. One of the homes is in town, but the other is on a plantation!"

She could hear Charlotte gasp.

"Riley and I went to see the house that Aunt Lavina lived in prior to her going into the nursing home. The couple who live there are so nice."

Charlotte interrupted the flow of Ellie's explanation.

"So how did they take it, about you being the new landlord?"

"Oh they are ready to move, just have to get packed. They are itching to move back to Florida. After we met them, Riley drove me out to Mimosa Grove. Char, it is right out of a Civil War novel."

Char was suddenly full of questions.

"Is it like Ashley Wilkes' plantation? What's it like?" Charlotte's excitement had finally started to show.

"I was in total shock when Riley unlocked the door. It is like walking into a museum. I own a house full of period antiques, well worth a small fortune! I haven't even started to look under all the sheets," Ellie squealed.

Ellie's love of history was well known to Charlotte.

"Well if anyone knows about antiques and history, it's you. How in the world did it stay in that house all this time without someone stealing everything?"

Ellie explained the situation with the caretaker and Riley's father.

"Oh, well, that makes sense then. I still can't believe you had all this just dropped in your lap. Girl, you need to come to Vegas with me while you're still hot!"

Ellie added, "That isn't all, Char. I inherited her financial estate as well."

Ellie tried to remain perfectly calm as she told Charlotte the dollar amount that she inherited.

"I'm sure $500,000 will last me a while. It will go a long way helping me keep up the property and retain a good nest egg for retirement. I won't be worrying about bills anymore!"

Charlotte could scarcely believe the amount of money that Ellie had just inherited.

"Do you plan on coming home? I mean, what are you going to do with two homes in Tennessee, and a job and life in Indiana?"

Charlotte posed a good question, and the amount that she had inherited was still quite overwhelming to Ellie.

"Char, I have to come back home this week. I have to get my thoughts together, and I promised Cassie I would fly out at the end of the week to spend a few days with her. I know I'll have to come back and get things finalized."

"Well, call me before you leave so I can have an idea when you'll be home. I'll drive over and help you unpack."

Ellie smiled, as she knew Charlotte missed her and the daily talks they shared each day.

"I'll be sure to call you. I'm bringing home a few things, just to show you I'm not making it up!"

Charlotte laughed, adding, "Oh, I believe you. I can't wait to see them. You be careful."

Ellie smiled at her best friend's concern.

"I will. Talk to you soon!" Ellie and Char said their goodbyes, and Ellie turned her attention to the large trunk that sat on the floor.

Confederate Memorial Day
Author Unknown

The marching armies of the past
Along our Southern plains,
Are sleeping now in quiet rest
Beneath the Southern rains.
The bugle call is now in vain
To rouse them from their bed;
To arms they'll never march again-
They are sleeping with the dead
No more will Shiloh's plains be stained
With blood our heroes shed,
Nor Chancellorsville resound again
To our noble warriors' tread.
For them no more shall reveille
Sound at the break of dawn,
But may their sleep peaceful be
Till God's great judgment morn.
We bow our heads in solemn prayer
For those who wore the gray,
And clasp again their unseen hands
On our Memorial Day

Chapter 4

Ellie sat down on the floor in the front of the trunk. It was in amazingly good condition even though it had been sitting undisturbed in the attic for over one hundred years. The leather handles were starting to show signs of dry rot, but Ellie was careful when she turned the trunk towards her. As she opened the lid, she noticed again that someone had lovingly wrapped each item in tissue or cloth. The pretty dress that Ellie had unwrapped earlier in the attic showed some damage, she assumed from moths, but was still in good condition for its age.

Carefully removing the satin slippers, which were enveloped individually in cloth, she placed them gingerly beside the dress. *Such tiny, dainty shoes. I wonder whose feet were the last to wear these to a dance or to walk down the stairs to meet her groom. The dress appears to be a wedding dress, but whose?*

Next, she took out two items that were placed between two pieces of cardstock and wrapped in tissue. Immediately she recognized the first article. During the seventeenth through nineteenth centuries, young girls practiced their sewing talents by stitching a sampler on a piece of muslin or cotton material. It was a trial practice of the skills that would be expected of a young wife or mother. Appearing to have been sewn by young hands, the verse had been stitched in faded thread.

For God so loved the world that he gave his only begotten Son, that whosoever believeth in Him shall have life everlasting. John 3:16. Caroline Townes - 12 years

The second item was a sampler made by Harriet Townes, similar in design to the first one, but of a different verse and of less quality.

A good man leaveth an inheritance to his children's children- and the wealth of the sinner is laid up for the just. Proverbs 13:22 Harriett Townes - 8 years

For a moment, Ellie thought of the verse as related to an inheritance. *How odd. Talk about coincidence.* Enclosing the artwork once again in the thin material, she laid them on the bed. Leaning over the side of the trunk, she found a diploma placed between two pieces of yellowed paper. Harriett Colbert Townes was written neatly across the certificate acknowledging completion of time at the Female Academy in Gallatin, Tennessee, October 15, 1860. *Now I have a name to start my research. Who were you, Harriett, and how do you fit into the puzzle of my inheritance?*

Ellie felt as though she was invading someone's privacy by gazing upon the treasures. Even feeling such, her desire to continue exploring the contents of the trunk won out. Under the next thin piece of material was revealed a small wooden box. The box was about the size of an 8 x 10 photograph, and its satin purple lining had begun to separate from the inside.

Over the years, the lid had apparently been lost or damaged, and now all that remained was the bottom portion. Lying neatly within were several tin type photographs. Each was placed in a case with gold braiding surrounding the photograph. On the opposite side of the image was a piece of material. Sliding her finger over the faded velvet and wondering who last touched these heirlooms, Ellie inspected the pictures. Each was exceptional in quality, and Ellie had seen similar ones sell for over a hundred dollars at antique malls. The first picture was of two young women who appeared to be reading letters. Even though the gold trim was tarnished around the edge, it still held its shape against the deep rose velvet that lined the inside of the frame. Ellie stared at the faces, long dead and forgotten, wondering if they were Harriett and Caroline.

The next photograph was that of a man and woman who appeared to be middle aged. The woman was dressed similarly to the young girls, but the man was dressed in an officer's frock coat, resembling a Union soldier. Even though the frame was worn, the image on the tin type was clear. Ellie decided she would scan the photos later and give copies to Uncle Loren and his family, as well as Cassie. The next photograph took Ellie by surprise because she sensed the beautiful lady in the photograph was calling out across time to her. *I definitely have to find out who these people are. Could this be Harriett? She does resemble one of the women in the first picture.* The outside of the last picture was beautifully carved, with a military insignia on the front of the case.

When Ellie took this frame out of the box, she found a handsome soldier staring back at her. The uniform was that of a Confederate soldier, which made sense with Aunt Lavina so tied to the Confederacy. *But who were the Union couple? How odd that both Union and Confederate soldier photographs were placed together in the box.*

Having spent nearly two hours mulling over the contents of the first trunk, Ellie still hadn't reached the bottom. Underneath the box of photographs, almost as if purposely hidden, was a diary. The front almost being torn away from the rest of the book, which was about eight inches long by five inches wide, Ellie was extremely careful opening it, so as not to inflict more damage. Smelling old and musty from years of being tucked away, the old script so faded Ellie could hardly decipher it: *Camille Burnell-1830.* Ellie lovingly placed the diary, once more cocooned in its protective tissue, on the bed with the other treasures.

Peering inside the trunk to observe the last of the contents, she glimpsed the two yellowed christening gowns, each about the same size, with matching bonnets. Lifting them up for closer inspection, Ellie wasn't sure cleaning the delicate stained lace would be advisable. She held them up to get a closer inspection. *What child or children had worn the tiny gowns and how had they looked?* A small box lay under the gowns, causing Ellie to imagine what treasure came next.

Lifting the small wooden lid slowly off the box, smelling of cedar, Ellie found two precious treasures: two dark brown curls. Obviously, from a small child, each curl was tied with a thin, white ribbon around its end. Ellie suddenly felt a wave of sadness come over her. She wondered if this was a remembrance, the last physical memento from a lost child. A small frame, enclosed in tissue, lay beneath the locks. It was part of a broche that held a tin type of a very small child. Across the top of the broche was a black mourning ribbon. Ellie touched the delicate frame, feeling another wave of sadness. *Who are these people, and how do they connect to me? Maybe the answers are in the family Bible that I forgot at Mimosa Grove.*

Slowly, she put each item carefully back in the trunk, trying to arrange them in the order they were originally found. Glancing at her watch, she saw it was almost midnight! Her curiosity got the better of her, and she went outside to retrieve the second trunk. The security light illuminated the area outside her door, so she quickly went to the truck. *Well, let's see what surprises lie within you, little fella.*

The trunk was quite a bit smaller and much lighter than the steamer trunk. She easily carried it inside her room and locked the door. Ellie grabbed the latch and tried to open it as she had the first trunk. To her disappointment, this trunk wasn't willing to share its secrets. Afraid she might damage the trunk, Ellie decided to leave well enough alone for now. It was after midnight, and she wanted to make one last trip to Mimosa Grove after her meeting with Riley Langley in the morning. She carefully moved the trunk to the luggage rack and began to prepare for bed. Too tired to read, she put the journal back in the larger trunk. As she lay in the darkness, her mind worked overtime with thoughts and questions concerning the people and things she'd discovered in the attic. *Who can answer my questions? Everyone is gone.*

Ellie awoke at some point during the night, not sure of the time. The clock on the nightstand flashed twelve o'clock in bright red. Ellie wasn't sure what had caused her to awake, but her senses were suddenly on high alert, in the darkness, and she felt she wasn't alone. Her heart beat to such a cadence she thought she'd have a heart attack. Afraid to open her eyes, she lay in the darkness, listening. When she no longer felt the presence, she quickly reached over and pushed on the lamp switch. Sitting upright, she surveyed the room. Both trunks were placed exactly in the same spots before she turned off the lights. She reached for her cell phone. *2 A.M. I have to get some sleep. I won't be worth two cents when I meet Riley!*

Ellie turned off the light and tried to calm herself. Considering the past twenty-four hours, it was no wonder sleep evaded her. There was so much to think about. *All in good time,* as her father said. How she missed her dad! He would have loved all the antiques and history involved in her inheritance. As she settled into thoughts of her father, she slowly drifted into a peaceful state.

The alarm on Ellie's cell phone woke her from a sound sleep. She had promised to be at the office early, before hours. Relishing her shower as the hot water cascaded over her tired body, she suddenly remembered Sean. He would want to have that dinner with her as soon as she got home. Even though she had enjoyed spending a nice evening with him, she wasn't sure if she felt like developing a relationship just now. She was still trying to get over a disappointing marriage, but she would call him, as promised. Knowing he would get a kick out hearing her news, it would be interesting to see how another date would go.

After finishing her shower, she wrapped a towel around her head and quickly laid out a pair of shorts and tee shirt that was befitting for attic exploration. She didn't feel the need to dress to the level of yesterday's meeting with Riley. After all, this meeting was just an informal settling of her aunt's estate. Excited to be getting the keys to Mimosa Grove today, she was sure she could find it on her own.

It didn't take her long to get ready and put her hair in a ponytail. Deciding to go ahead and pack the two trunks, she would put them both in the back of the truck. She didn't think she could hoist the larger one up and onto the tailgate. After much effort, she loaded first one, then the other, onto the luggage carrier. Making her way to the front desk to ask for help loading the larger of the two trunks, she found a young man attending the guest registry. He was all too happy to help Ellie with her trunk.

Seeing that she had time to spare, she decided to drive through the McDonald's on the way to Langley and Murdock's. The sausage and egg biscuit and small coffee would taste good after the bag of chips the night before. The sun was up and shining brightly and Ellie loved the feel of the warmth coming through the cab of the truck. She couldn't wait to get the meeting over with Riley, so that she could hurry out to the house, *her house.*

Parking the car, she grabbed her purse, and as she was locking her doors, noticed the black Lexus parked in the same spot as yesterday. *Does he ever go home?* Making her way into the office, she saw Carol Pennington sitting behind the large mahogany desk, talking on the telephone. Smiling as she caught sight of Ellie, she mouthed, *I'll be right with you.* Ellie returned the smile and sat down. Ellie suddenly felt underdressed as she saw an attractive woman walking down the stairs. The woman looked to be in her early thirties, and her long slender body was dressed in the latest fashion. *Ugh, I really need to join a gym or something to lose weight!* In reality, Ellie was still in good physical shape, never being more than five pounds over her goal weight, and blessed with good skin and thick hair. Brad had always made her feel she wasn't pretty enough, at least for him. *Is that why he cheated so often?*

Ellie snapped out of her self-assessment, and watched as the pretty woman laid a key on the desk, smiled at Carol, and said goodbye. Ellie wondered if this might be Riley's wife. She hadn't even thought about him as a married man, and suddenly felt as if she had done something improper by keeping him out with her all day yesterday.

"*Miss Morgan, Miss Morgan* . . . ." Ellie hadn't been listening, and suddenly realized Carol was trying to get her attention. "Mr. Langley will see you now."

Ellie followed Carol down the hall, remembering the way from yesterday. As the two approached the doorway to Riley's office, he was already coming from behind the desk.

"Good morning, Ellie," Riley greeted with a genuine smile. "Did you sleep well last night?"

Ellie took a seat.

"As good as can be expected, after the day I had yesterday."

Riley turned to Carol and thanked her, and she closed the door on her way out.

"Well, Ellie, there are just a few more things I need to go over with you. It should only take about thirty minutes, and then we can have you sign some papers. I'll have your cashiers' check when the accountant has the final amount after taxes. I'd like for you to look at this page, *item number 3.*"

Riley sat down next to Ellie and began to go over the items on the page. She could smell the cologne he was wearing. The scent was very appealing, not overly strong like many masculine scents. She had forgotten the dimple in his cheek and his dark blue eyes.

"When you receive your check, all of the taxes for inheritance purposes will have been taken out. I'll take the liberty, if you prefer, in having that amount placed in another check that can be separate for payment at the end of the year."

He doesn't have a wedding ring on. Surely he has a wife or a significant other. Ellie nodded as she listened to Riley go over the payment of her inheritance.

Finally, she spoke, "It's all really overwhelming. I have so much to think about."

Riley could see the weariness in Ellie's expression. He hoped his explanation and suggestions would help to ease that. Next, Riley explained that he would need to write up a legal document for the house on Forest Drive. Ellie had already decided that she would keep the house for now. She asked if Riley might know of a potential renter after Bobby Ray and Louise moved to Florida.

"I'll keep that in mind; there is always someone looking to rent these days. I think that's a wise decision, Ellie. In this day and age, holding on to real estate makes more sense. I don't think houses are moving too fast here."

Ellie was writing notes to herself to keep Riley's suggestions in mind. Riley moved to the next page in his folder.

"Ellie, this is a list of soldiers in the Resthaven Cemetery that you will be responsible for when it comes time for Decoration Day and Confederate Memorial Day. Mrs. George wanted you to carry on her family's dedication to this task. Mrs. Helen Eubank's number is here."

Riley pointed to the telephone number highlighted in yellow.

"You'll need to contact her for dates, if you're unfamiliar with them."

Ellie took the sheet and saw there were 17 names; she would look more closely at the list when she was home. Right now she wanted to move through the meeting as quickly as possible. Riley removed another sheet from his folder to share with Ellie.

Actually, it was a large manila envelope with her name scrawled in very small script across the front. Obviously, the penmanship was of someone who did not have a steady hand.

"Lavina asked that this be given to you at the reading of the will," Riley shared, as he handed the envelope to Ellie. "I don't know the contents. She gave it to my father about a year before her death. She asked that you read it after her death."

Ellie sat staring at the envelope.

"Do I have to read it now, here? I would rather read it later, alone, if that is acceptable?"

She would like to be alone as she met her aunt for the first time, through the reading of this, perhaps, personal letter.

"Of course, she didn't specify that you read it in my presence, or that it had to be read during the reading of the will. It's entirely up to you when or if you read it," Riley smiled.

He continued, "There will be papers you'll need to sign, and of course it will require you coming to the Court House to make it legal. I'm sorry you have to make another trip from Indiana."

Riley didn't show it, but he wasn't being entirely truthful. He wouldn't mind at all having the opportunity to spend more time with Ellie Morgan.

"I don't see that being a problem. I'd love to come down and spend some time at the house," Ellie declared.

"Okay then, let's go ahead and sign what we can today, and I'll give you the keys to Mimosa; then, I'll Fed-Ex you the keys to the house on Forest Drive. The rest of the documents will also come to you through Fed-Ex when all the ducks are in a row," finished Riley.

Ellie was relieved this could all be handled rather easily.

She continued, "Thank you for everything, Riley. I have your number, and if you don't mind, I might call you if I have any questions about anything."

"I'm here whenever you need me; I know it's a lot to digest. Feel free to call if you need anything."

As he spoke, Riley was looking into Ellie's eyes, and for a moment, both were mesmerized until something caused Riley to look away.

"Let me get you those keys," Riley offered as he walked around to the drawer in his desk.

He came back with a large key ring and a small envelope that he sat on the table.

"These are the original skeleton keys to the front and back doors of Mimosa Grove. They have been with Mrs. George for decades. The keys here, on the key ring, are for the outbuildings and the new locks on all the doors in the house. The numbers on the keys correspond to the numbers on the paper in your folder. I wrote down each key and number as well as what each unlocks," Riley added.

"Thank you so much, I would have been lost on which key opened which door!" Ellie gasped.

They both laughed, and Ellie started to stand.

Riley said, "It has really been a pleasure meeting you, Ellie."

Ellie smiled, "It's been my pleasure as well, Riley."

Walking with Ellie towards the door, Riley ended, "Remember, if there is anything you need, don't hesitate to call. I'll be happy to help."

He held out the envelope and files that he'd had underneath his arm. Receiving all the papers and items from Riley, Ellie placed them inside her bag.

"I'll remember! Take care."

They embraced, and Riley surprised himself by enjoying the closeness. Ellie wasn't sure why she felt so at ease with someone she had only met twenty-four hours before. She walked down the hall, telling Carol goodbye.

When she got to her truck, she pressed the button to unlock the door and slid in, laying her bag in the seat. Before she could put the key in the ignition, Riley startled her. Shading her eyes from the bright sun, she rolled her window down to hear him.

"It dawned on me that you might not remember how to get to Mimosa Grove."

Ellie smiled, both inside and out, feeling special that he was so concerned.

Laughing, she said, "I think I can find it, but I have your cell number just in case!"

Riley scratched his head and ventured, "Are you sure you don't want me to go with you?"

Ellie felt as if he didn't want her going there alone. However, this is just what Ellie wanted: to explore alone.

"I think I'll be just fine. But I appreciate your willingness; I'm confident I can find it."

Riley surrendered.

"Okay then, you be careful. I'll be in touch."

"Okay. Thanks again." Ellie replied.

Riley patted the door, then turned and walked back to the office. Ellie watched as he walked inside. *I feel as if he really doesn't want me to go alone for reason, but I'm too excited to wait.*

As Ellie drove on Highway 31, out of town, she delighted in the scenery. Remembering that she would need to stop by the cemetery to catch Mrs. Eubanks to get the date of Confederate Memorial Day, as well as get a map or legend of the Civil War soldiers' graves in the cemetery, she decided to visit her in the morning. Right now, she was on a mission to see her plantation.

The weather had been beautiful during Ellie's stay in Hendersonville. The temperatures were in the upper seventies, perfect as far as Ellie was concerned . . . She loved the smell of the flowers that were blooming everywhere around the city. The large flowerbeds that were placed between the divided highway were in full bloom. Day lilies and pansies were two of Ellie's favorites, and there was an abundance of both throughout the town.

Driving out of the city, the landscape reminded Ellie very much of the farmland and rolling hills that were part of Newburg and the surrounding area where she lived. The land was important to the families who lived in and around Hendersonville. Ellie wondered if the large farms had been in the families of the owners for generations as Mimosa Grove had been in hers. She noticed that there were several large housing additions on the outskirts of town. *Maybe these were part of the original plantation during the early 1800's.*

Ellie passed a large horse barn and remembered to slow down for the driveway into Mimosa Grove. Sure enough, on the left side of the road, she saw the familiar iron gate that was attached to the fence surrounding the perimeter of the property. Pulling off into the drive, she put the car in park and reached into her bag to find the key ring with keys for the doors and outbuildings. *Thank you, Riley, for labeling all of these!*

Quickly locating the key with the plastic tag marked "gate", she put the key in the padlock and gazed up the long driveway. The leaves of the trees formed a natural canopy, giving the visitor a glimpse of the view.

Ellie was sure in time she would remember which key went with which lock, even getting colored keys, if necessary.

Ellie was seeing Mimosa Grove through new eyes this morning. The sunlight was brilliant through the trees, and the shade that the trees provided in the late afternoon was not yet visible in the early morning light. Ellie got back in the car and pulled through the gate. She hesitated for a moment, but remembered that she was alone and had to practice "safety first". She put the car in park, jumped out, and pulled the gate back to lock it once again. As she drove the car slowly up the drive, she took time to take in the scenery that flanked both sides.

The field to the right housed a large barn, and Ellie could see that it had two stories. The whitewash had begun to wear off, and Ellie noticed the gray wood showing from beneath the paint. Over the years, repairs had been made to both the roof and the siding. There were still remnants of round bales of hay resting against the walls inside. The pasture had long since been without horses, and Ellie imagined that when Mimosa Grove was at her height of glory, it would have been a very impressive home. To the left of the drive were now fallow fields that once possibly yielded corn or tobacco. Ellie would have to find out what was grown here, as she might want to rent out the fields once again to use the land as it was meant.

She pulled the car in front of the house and got out. She noticed that the Mimosa trees that surrounded the house were just starting to bloom with pink pompons. The fronds on the tree swayed gracefully in the breeze, as if they were reaching out arms to welcome her back. She glanced towards the front of the house, now fully bathed in light.

The glass in the windows shimmered and gave the appearance of heat that one sees coming off the highway in the hot temperatures. She was pleased that this house was hers. *I'm already thinking as a homeowner. Am I seriously considering keeping the house and living in it myself?* She wasn't sure just what her plans were, but she knew what the plan for the day was. Ellie walked up the large stone steps, noticing the post and large block that was situated to the right of the porch. Jerking the mass of keys from her purse, it took a moment to find the key labeled *Front Door*.

The front door would need to be sanded and refinished. Years of weathering had taken its toll on the wood. The sidelights and window above the door were still in good shape, but it was evident neither had been cleaned for at least a decade. There were actually two keys for the door. Ellie put the ancient-looking skeleton key in the bottom lock, and then put the modern key into the deadbolt. Twisting the knob, she cautiously entered the house.

Having forgotten the flashlight, she began silently reprimanding herself for her absentmindedness. Coming into the large foyer, she could see sunlight coming down the stairs from the second floor. *I love the light. The house is so much homier with the light streaming in.* There, right on the large round table that sat at the foot of the stairs, sat the old Bible. Ellie put her purse on top of it so that she would be sure to get it on the way out, and turning to the door, she locked the deadbolt.

She had an uneasy feeling being in the large house alone. She'd have to get over that. She quickly went from room to room, opening the shades and curtains that were on each window. The furniture in the rooms made her feel as though she were an intruder trespassing. Taking a quick walk through the downstairs, she checked to be sure that everything was as it had been the night before. Making the rounds took less than five minutes, and she was back in the entry hall where she started. Ellie looked up to the second floor from below.

As she started up the stairway, she began to wonder if the lovely portraits that hung in the dining room were the women who were in the photographs in the trunk. When she reached the small landing where the stairway curved to the left, she looked back down at the entry. It must have been beautifully decorated when the plantation was in its prime. The mimosa tree motif on the walls must have been impressive as the large chandelier highlighted it.

As she stepped onto the foyer, she imagined what it would have been like when the house was full of life. She peered into the rooms, slowly wandering from first one room then the next, but heard nothing. The house was an antique dealer's delight, and it was all hers! She couldn't imagine selling it now or ever. Turning to the attic door, she remembered the unusual feeling she had the night before as she and Riley made their way up in the dark. Ellie hoped that there would be enough light from the morning sun to give her enough illumination to see what else was being stored in the attic.

When she opened the door, no draft or cool breeze flowed through this time. Just the smell of old, musty things long ago forgotten beckoned her up the steps. Creak after creak echoed as she climbed from step to step. Just as she was about to reach the top step, her phone rang, almost causing her to lose her balance. *For heavens' sake. I am really getting jumpy.*

"Hello," Ellie answered, noting the call was from an "unknown" number.

"Ellie, this is Riley Langley. I'm sorry to bother you, but I just wanted to make sure you were able to get in the house okay."

Ellie rolled her eyes, she suddenly felt as though her father was checking on her.

"Hi Riley, I made it in just fine. I'm in the attic right now, just got up here when you called."

Riley was relieved to know that she had no trouble getting back to the house.

"It sounds like you have it all under control, so I won't keep you."

He suddenly felt as though he were a parent checking up on his child.

"It's okay, I appreciate the concern. I'll call you when I leave, if that would make you feel better, Dad," Ellie teased.

She didn't know it, but a smile clothed Riley's face, as the ends of his mustache turned upward.

"Okay, point made, Miss Ellie. Have a good time exploring. Bye now."

She put her cell phone back in her pocket and proceeded to walk back to where she and Riley had ended their search the night before. In the daylight, Ellie could see the whole attic in clear view. Besides the contents of stacked boxes, she could tell that anything owners tired of had been relegated to the attic. A dressmaker dummy was standing as if to guard the secrets that lay within the walls. Ellie would love to have that back home to display the antique dress.

Ellie counted two sleds, suitcases, and an old iron baby bed that appeared to be from the late 1800's. She would have someone come out and give her an appraisal on it to be sure. Walking between crates of books and old magazines from the 1930's, she found a pair of oars and a cache of fishing poles. *Well that makes sense; we are on the river. I wonder what it was like to see steamboats and keel boats coming up and down the river.*

Then Ellie spied something back behind one of the chests that lined the wall. She thought it was a hatbox and she was very excited at the thought. She loved old hats; she had bought a few from an estate sale years ago. As she cleared a path towards the dresser, she noticed that the mirror showed the reflection across the room into another mirror that was hanging forlornly on the opposite wall.

She caught a glimpse of her backside.

Typical of her self-assessment, said aloud, "Well that is one view I would rather not have today. *I really need to work on my weight!*"

Ellie turned her thoughts back to the mission at hand; she assumed that the hatbox must have fallen behind the large dresser when the furniture was moved around over the years. Ellie wedged herself between the wall and another old table in order to see it better. Sure enough, it was a very old hatbox, and from Ellie's estimation, one that was from the 19th century. She hoped that a bonnet or hat from the era would be her prize for being so persistent in her quest.

As she reached down to lift the box, she was careful to avoid putting pressure on the sides. She placed her hand under the delicate box and lifted it up and out of its hiding place. Ellie could hardly believe her luck. The hatbox had escaped any real damage, just a bit of discoloration and staining from condensation over the years.

She sat the box on top of the table and slowly lifted the lid up and off the box. To her utter disappointment, the box did not contain the prized bonnet or hat that Ellie had imagined. Instead, just a pile of old papers, with something red wrapped around them, greeted her. Removing the contents of the hatbox, she quickly saw that she had made another interesting find: letters. It appeared there were close to ten letters, and they were bound together with a very old, satin red ribbon. *Well, what do we have here? Someone must have treasured these to put them in this box all these years.*

Ellie once again felt she was not alone. She quickly glanced over her shoulder, but all she saw was the shadow of the mimosa tree's limbs swaying in the gentle breeze outside the window. *I really need to stop being so paranoid!* Ellie went back to the task at hand, carefully untying the delicate ribbon. As she did so, she couldn't help but realize her hands were the first to touch the ribbon since it was tied. Putting the ribbon aside, she saw that the first envelope was a military one with CSA embossed on the front. The handwriting was light, but legible, typical of the 1800's. Ellie almost jumped up and down when she saw the name in the center was Miss Hattie Townes. *Hattie Townes? So she did live here!* Delicately opening the envelope, she saw it was a letter from a soldier dated May 1861, Camp Cheatham, Tennessee. Ellie couldn't believe what she held in her hands!

She loved anything to do with the Civil War, and this was her Christmas and birthday all rolled into one. She began to read the letter, which was from Rafe Collins to Hattie Townes. *Rafe Collins. Where have I seen that name?* She tried to think back to all the things she had seen and done since Friday evening when she arrived. *It will come to me!* Trying to read the letter was difficult because over time the penmanship had faded.

> *Dear Hattie,*
> *I hope these lines find you well. I havent stopped thinking about our pleasant evening two weeks ago, and found my thoughts being posessed by yor face and the sound of yor voice. I carry the lace hanky that you gave me in my breast pocket. It will be a constant companon, but I fear that the knoledge of it would cause me a great deal of harrassmint by my pards. Hattie, we will be moving out soon, and it would give me great comfort and calm in my soul to know that you would remember a line to Providence each day on my behalf. I trust that He will keep you safe and watch over you night and day. I had hoped your father would change his disposition on Lincoln's invading our homeland. I hope we don't meet on a battlefield somewhere in the future. I am part of Vaughan's Brigade, and we are in the Tennessee 11th Infantry Regiment. I will contenu to write. Could you send me a line when you can? It would be a joy and delite in my times of lonleyness to read a letter from you. I will be forever yours, Rafe.*

Ellie sat staring at the letter, starting to piece together the puzzle of the letter's meaning. Hattie's father supported the Union, and Rafe was the enemy. The pictures in the trunk were Hattie and her family. The small, Confederate soldier's picture had to be that of Rafe Collins. Aside from the occasional spelling errors, the letter was touching and romantic. She sat holding the letter, envisioning the face of the woman in the picture in the trunk.

Checking the window at the end of the attic, she didn't see any cracks. The two windows facing the front of the house were also closed. Twisting around to look at the window across the room, her breath caught in her throat. In the reflection of the mirror, she saw a face.

For a moment, she froze. The face slowly became a torso and that became a filmy figure of a man. Ellie was too afraid to move, she tried to blink, but couldn't move a muscle. "Who . . ." was all she could whisper. The figure appeared to be transparent, as she could see the chest behind him. His face appeared pale, but she could see his hair was dark. She couldn't hear a sound, but the apparition appeared to be saying, *Will you help me?* Ellie backed away from the figure, suddenly feeling a rush of panic overtaking her. She had never seen a ghost, but she knew this was not her imagination, and she wanted to scream, but no sound came. As suddenly as it appeared, the vision began to fade.

Ellie looked all around her, afraid there was more of whatever she'd seen. She had seen it. Of that, she had no doubt. Ellie quickly put the letters inside the box and made her way out of the center of the room. She made her way to the stairs, taking one last look to the dresser. She tried to keep her wits about her as she closed the door and walked down the stairs to the second floor foyer. Her legs were shaking so badly, that she had to sit in the floor to calm her nerves. *What is happening to me? I have to get it together! It's just my imagination. I can't tell anyone, they'd think I was crazy.*

Feeling her strength returning, she decided that she would close the window coverings before going back downstairs. No sense denying it, she was afraid. She had seen something, and it was clear the feeling of someone being in the house was not her imagination. Ellie went back down the stairs, traveling from room to room closing curtains. While in the dining room, she felt as though the portrait faces were staring at her as she moved about the room. Going into the hall, she felt the chill go through her again. Afraid to turn around she heard it and was terrified. The sound was muffled, but loud enough to be considered audible.

"Please, will you help me?" the voice uttered again.

Ellie shuddered, feeling the panic bubble within her.

She couldn't explain this away. The voice was talking to her. *Help you? Help you HOW?* Ellie closed her eyes, deciding to answer the voice.

"Who are you?" She waited, hoping she wouldn't hear a reply.

In a soft, Southern drawl came, "Rafe Collins, Ma'am."

Ellie felt her knees go weak again as she turned to see who was standing behind her. In the semi-dark room, she glimpsed the figure of a Confederate soldier. He was standing near the doorway, and Ellie could see the piano through him. Clearly an apparition, he didn't seem harmful. Ellie took hold of her fears and faced the soldier.

"I heard you in my dream the other night."

The soldier repeated, "Can you help me?"

Ellie couldn't believe she was standing in the house talking to a ghost. Perhaps she wasn't, after all, she hadn't eaten lunch yet, and the light-headedness could have overtaken her.

Flippantly she replied, "I don't know how I can help you. You need to go back to wherever you came from; you don't live here."

The soldier, looking crestfallen, replied, "She said you could help."

With that, the soldier began to fade before her eyes. As suddenly as he had appeared, he was gone. Ellie looked all around, afraid that he could appear again. Quickly grabbing the Bible and her purse, she hurried out of the house. After locking the door, she practically ran to her car. As she got inside, she put the Bible on the seat and locked her doors. Closing her eyes, she tried to gather her wits about her. *What in the world? I've inherited a haunted house. Great!* Ellie suddenly felt a panic attack coming on, but she practiced the technique she had learned after the death of her mother: take slow, deep breaths, and visualize filling a jar with air; then imagine slowly blowing out a candle.

After a few moments, her breathing returned to normal. Rationalizing what had just happened, she concluded the letters had clearly been the open door through which Rafe Collins walked into her time. *With what did he want her help? And what did he mean, "She said you would help?" To whom was he referring? I have to make sense out of this. Maybe after I read the letter from Aunt Lavina, I'll feel better.* Ellie quickly turned the car toward the road and made her way back to Hendersonville to make a stop at Resthaven Cemetery.

Riley had to be in court shortly, but took a minute to think about Ellie Morgan. He wasn't accustomed to calling his clients, and couldn't believe he had made the call earlier. The call had lasted all of two minutes. In some ways, Riley was indifferent to his clients once they left the confines of his office. Yes, he was a kind, compassionate lawyer; his father had instilled that in him since he began helping out during summers, doing odd jobs around the office. Having clients pass through his thoughts during the day was quite another thing. What was it about Ellie that intrigued him so?

Obviously, she was pretty, but it wasn't so much her good looks that had peeked Riley's interest. The two had clicked, even in the short time he had spent with her. It had almost been ten years since Riley had thought about someone instead of his work. He sat in his office, staring down at his desk, remembering his appointment with Ellie this morning and had been preoccupied with the reading of Mrs. George's will. He'd let his thoughts drift from the special anniversary which was fast approaching. The day he spent with Ellie had triggered a memory or feeling that he had tried to repress over time: a feeling of caring for someone. He had tried to bury those feelings when he buried his young wife and daughter ten years before.

Kate Langley was only thirty-five years old, a physical therapist who worked at the hospital in Henderson. She and Riley had been married for seven years, and were the doting parents of pretty brown-eyed Taylor, who was three. Riley had decided to take the family on what would be Taylor's first vacation. Not far from the intersection of Poplar and Main, an elderly driver suffered a fatal heart attack, running through the intersection and hitting the passenger side of Riley's SUV. The EMT who responded to the scene later remarked that Taylor didn't suffer, but that didn't take away the pain that ripped the very heart and soul out of Riley. The force with which the car had slammed into the passenger side had caused Riley to be ejected from the driver's side door. He still couldn't remember how he came to be lying in the middle of the road, with a broken leg and arm and a gash to his head. The paramedics tried to save Kate, who was pinned against the dash and door. Later he would learn that both his girls had massive head and internal injuries. His recovery was slow, and many thought he would die of a broken heart. Miss Nell came to his house faithfully, every Friday night, to bring him carryout from the restaurant. His father and mother tried to take care of him as his physical wounds healed. Six months later, he was back working with his father. He buried his grief, and for the most part, it worked each year---until the anniversary of the accident.

He would want to make a call to the florist today, for special arrangements at the cemetery. Maybe he would just go after work; it was too soon to go on the actual date. Now he couldn't stop thinking about Ellie. How odd.

As Ellie drove into Henderson, traffic was heavier than it had been all week. It was Tuesday, and she would need to leave first thing in the morning. At the rate she was going, it might be midnight before she could head north. She still had two more stops to make before going back to the motel. She looked at her watch; it was one o'clock. Purposely not thinking about the encounter she had had earlier in the day, she busied her thoughts with Mrs. Eubanks at the cemetery. She would swing by Resthaven and see if she could get a copy of the grave registry. Somewhere she had that list, and would try to map out the graves she would be responsible for decorating. Her stomach reminded her that it had been quite some time since her trip through McDonald's earlier in the morning. Not wanting more fast food, she tried to remember where the restaurant was that Riley had taken her yesterday. *What was the name of that place? Gas Station, no, that wasn't it, thankfully! Oh yes, the Fillin' Station. Now how do I get back to Magnolia from here?* Ellie was getting used to talking to herself; no sooner had she asked the question than she found the answer.

When she rounded the corner from Main Street, there in the middle of the row of buildings was The Fillin' Station. The lunch crowd had cleared out, she guessed. She pulled her truck into the angled space and inside. Miss Nell was behind the counter, as she was before. At first, she didn't recognize her, but when Ellie took off her sunglasses, the round faced woman sported a smile from ear to ear.

"Well ah was wonderin' when you'd make it back in to see Miss Nell. Where's Mr. Riley?"

Ellie smiled, "Hi Miss Nell. I'm all alone today, and I would sure love some of that delicious barbeque you made for me yesterday!"

Seeming disappointed that Riley hadn't joined her, Nell grabbed a menu and led her to a nice table by the front window.

"Is this here seat okay, baby girl?"

Ellie nodded and said, "Oh yes, this is just fine, thank you."

Nell took her drink order and disappeared to the kitchen. While waiting for her sweet tea, Ellie watched patrons come and go.

When Nell returned a few moments later, Ellie nonchalantly asked, "Do Mr. and Mrs. Langley come in often?"

Nell looked puzzled, "You mean Riley's folks? No, since his daddy retired, he don't come in much."

"No, I mean Riley and his wife."

Ellie paused, waiting for a reaction from Miss Nell. Her question caught Nell off guard, and the look she gave Ellie was one of sorrow.

"Miss, you don't know Mr. Riley too well now, do you?"

Ellie sensed something was wrong, and she quickly backtracked, "Oh, I'm sorry; I didn't mean to pry into his personal life, I just . . ."

Before she could finish her sentence, Nell pulled out the chair next to her and sat down.

"Miss, I want to tell you so's you don't go asking Mr. Riley something that would just upset him. He lost his wife some time back. I hadn't seen him in here for a few years, and when he came in with you, I thought he was feeling better."

"I had no idea, Miss Nell. I saw a women coming from the office yesterday, and I assumed he was married. I feel awful now. I'm sorry for intruding."

Nell softened, "It ain't your fault, Miss. Riley lost a pretty wife and a little baby girl, just rips your heart out to think about it."

Ellie knew about death and the unfairness of a young life lost. *But both his wife and daughter? How could anyone survive the pain from such a blow?*

"Thank you for telling me, Nell. I won't say a word. I feel so sad."

Nell stretched her hand over Ellie's and said, "It's all right, Miss. I was so happy to see him smiling and laughing with you. It did him good to be around you. I hope you will be around a lot more."

Ellie smiled, "Well, I don't know how much I'll be around, but I will have to make a couple of trips back down this way before summer's end."

Nell stood and winked, "Well, I'll go get your order since I'd already figured on ya orderin' what ya had yesterday!"

Ellie laughed, and Nell hobbled back towards the kitchen with her order.

Waiting for her food to arrive, Ellie had time to digest what Nell had shared with her. *So he was married, now a widower. Poor Riley.... if the pretty woman wasn't his wife, then maybe he had a lover that visited on a regular basis, or perhaps she was simply a client, just like me. He was a very attractive man, and after all, even a widower has needs. I'm relieved I wasn't being seen around town with a married man. From now on, I'll mind my words carefully.*

The food was delicious, and Ellie thanked Miss Nell as she paid her bill and said goodbye. Checking her watch and seeing it was almost two-thirty, Ellie decided to swing by the office quickly, and then on to the cemetery. As she made the drive to Poplar Street, she wondered what Riley would think if she told him what had happened after his call this morning? She thought better of sharing that with him. Ellie didn't want him to think she was mentally unstable. She pulled in to the parking lot at Langley and Murdock, wishing she'd worn something a little cooler since the air was much warmer now.

Once inside the office, Ellie immediately noticed Carol wasn't at her desk. She sat down on the settee that faced the offices in the rear of the suite. From her vantage point, she could see into Riley's office. The door was open, and she could faintly hear him talking.

"Yes, I can pick them up this afternoon. Thank you. Bye now."

Trying not to look obvious, Ellie bent down to look inside her bag, and was drawn to the letter Riley had given her earlier. She would read it later, after she had returned for the night. Ellie heard his voice before she saw him.

"Ellie? Is everything okay?"

Ellie noticed he was wearing a pair of jeans and a button-down shirt.

"Hi, Riley! I just wanted to see if you needed the keys back to Mimosa Grove. I'm going back home tomorrow morning, and wasn't sure what to do about them."

Ellie held out the key ring and the envelope with the old keys.

"I really don't need them, since Dad still has a set. If I were you, I would think about changing the locks after you decide what to do with the place. Safety first, you know."

It was coming up on Memorial Day weekend, and she had the whole summer to decide.

"I'll be looking for the Fed-ex truck to bring the rest of the papers, and I locked up when I left earlier today."

Ellie felt her heart beat a little faster when she remembered her earlier encounter at the house.

"How'd your exploring go today? See any ghosts floating around in the attic?" Riley laughed.

Ellie's face must have gone white when he said that, because Riley sensed something amiss.

"Did something happen out there? You're okay, right?"

Keeping the morning happenings to herself, she answered, "Oh, I just heard some noises, you know, creaky old house . . .nothing to be worried about though. It's all good."

Riley looked satisfied with her explanation.

"Well, it has really been a pleasure, Ellie. I hope you found your time in Hendersonville enjoyable. Just call me and let me know a date when you can come back to run over to the court house. By then, you should be getting your inheritance check."

Ellie still couldn't wrap her head around the amount that would soon be coming her way.

Extending her hand, Ellie offered, "I appreciate everything you've done, Riley. Thank you so much. I'll be back the first of the month, after I've had a chance to see my daughter and my uncle. They will want to know about the trip. I'll call you. I'm off all summer!"

Riley teased, "Yeah, you teachers have it made."

"And you, the son of a teacher . . .what would your mother say?" Ellie laughed, heading out of the office.

She looked back and found Riley watching her. Suddenly feeling a flush of heat rise up her neck, she was embarrassed to be blushing at the thought of Riley *checking her out.*

Riley flashed a wide grin and said, "You have a safe trip back, Ellie. Bye now."

And with that, she almost skipped to her car.

It was three o'clock, and Ellie hurried to the cemetery, wanting to catch Mrs. Eubanks before she left for the day. Riley was close behind her, planning a stop at the florist and then on to spend time with his girls.

As Ellie pulled into the parking area at Resthaven Cemetery, the sun was starting to make its descent through the large oak trees that flanked the perimeter of the cemetery. Ellie hadn't noticed the first time she visited the cemetery, but the large iron gate that marked the entrance into the cemetery was quite lovely. The iron had a scrollwork design that had the name of the cemetery woven inside. To either side of the iron archway was a stone pillar. A large plaque was inserted inside one of the stone pillars that listed the year 1830. Ellie assumed this was the date the first burial.

She walked up through the archway and headed for the small stone structure that housed the cemetery office. The office door had the hours of the attendant on duty, and thankfully, Ellie made it thirty minutes before. Mrs. Helen Eubanks was sitting behind small desk writing on an index card. The local radio station was playing a country tune, and Ellie saw that she was in deep thought.

"Hello, Mrs. Eubanks," Ellie said softly.

Helen looked up from her work, obviously not aware that Ellie had even passed through the front door.

"Hello, how are you today? I was so busy writing myself a note, I didn't hear you come in."

Helen Eubanks had a lovely Southern accent, and a very warm, inviting smile.

"I don't know if you remember me, but I stopped in last week to find my great aunt Lavina George's grave."

Helen nodded and said, "Of course, I remember you! What can I help you with today?"

Ellie took out the notebook that she kept inside her bag, bringing out the paper from Riley consisting of directions for maintaining graves of Confederate Soldiers.

"I'll be tending to several graves now that Aunt Lavina's will has been read. I'll be taking over her UDC and family duties as far as decorating the headstones of the Civil War soldiers."

Helen smiled and said, "Yes, Lavina and her mother before her took care of that. I remember seeing Mrs. George in her later years carrying those flags from headstone to headstone, laying a red rose on each. I believe that tradition was passed down from the mother to daughters in your family. It's a noble thing that you do. Most folks around here who had a relative in the war have either died off or moved away. Some just don't know their family history. It's sad."

Helen was proud of her heritage, and felt others should be as well.

"It will be my pleasure carrying on such a long tradition of Townes' women. First, I need to know where each soldier is buried. I have the list of seventeen names here, given to me in Aunt Lavina's handwriting."

Looking over the list again, a name suddenly jumped from the page at Ellie: *Raford Collins*. Helen noticed the expression on Ellie's face.

"Is something the matter, Ms. Morgan?"

Ellie tried not to show her shock.

"Uh, no, I just saw a name that I recognized."

"Oh really? Which one is that?" Helen asked.

Ellie showed her the paper.

"This one, Raford Collins. I have seen that somewhere."

Helen remarked that on Ellie's last visit, she had asked about his grave and the Southern Cross that was placed on it. Ellie remembered now, and it was beginning to make sense: how she happened upon his grave that first day, the dream about his funeral procession in the cemetery, and now meeting him face to face at Mimosa Grove.

Helen looked at the list, then went her filing cabinet and pulled out an ancient looking binder.

"We used to keep everything in pencil and paper filing, you know, how they did it years back. I will check the hard copy and then go print out the online version."

Smiling, Helen added, "You know, technology is great, but I trust the pencil-paper version almost as much."

Within a few moments, Helen had printed out several sheets and was in the process of scotch taping them together.

"Now, I've put the sheets in an order as if you were walking in from the front iron gate. The older headstones will be found in the earlier portion of the cemetery, here."

Helen tried to orientate Ellie to where this section was on the paper.

"Oh, I see," Ellie said, "this is the section I walked through to get to Aunt Lavina's grave last week."

Helen continued, "Well, I'm pretty sure this is the most updated list. I have all the last names listed according to the plot. If you need any help, just ask."

Ellie took the lists, thanked Mrs. Eubanks again, and reached inside her purse to get one of her business cards containing her school and home emails, as well as her cell phone.

Giving Helen the card, Ellie asked, "I'd appreciate it if you would let me know of any special ceremonies involving the Civil War graves. That way I can be sure to have them appropriately decorated."

Helen took her card, glanced at it, and said, "I sure will, Ellie, and thank you again for carrying on this important tradition."

Ellie smiled and walked out of the office. It was four o'clock, and Mrs. Eubanks was readying the office to be closed. *I have a few minutes, I think I'll walk back over to Raford Collins' grave, maybe take a picture. Now as I specifically notice headstones with soldier names, they take on a different meaning.* She began to notice the different graves that belonged to soldiers, something she had overlooked the first time down the path. *There's the tiny headstone with the lamb sitting on top, so I know I'm close to Raford Collins' headstone.* Raford Isaac Collins, born July 31, 1839, died, January 7, 1863.

Ellie still couldn't believe that the apparition she saw, talked to, was Raford Collins. Recollection of her encounter earlier in the day caused her to take a few more pictures from different angles. *Well, that should do it. I don't know why I need pictures, but maybe they will remind me that this is where the REAL Raford Collins is, not in my house!*

Ellie felt a chill go up her spine as she said the words to herself. Grabbing her purse, she began to walk down the path when someone moving across the way caught her eye. She stopped, strained her eyes to see the figure of a man, standing over a grave with two bouquets of roses. As her eyes acclimated to the distance, she saw that person was Riley! Ellie felt as though she were invading his privacy, as he was clearly in a grieving state. Wiping tears from her own eyes, she watched his shoulders sag, his hand wiping his eyes in sudden jerks. Losing her parents had been difficult enough, but her child? Cassie was the love of Ellie's life, and the thought of losing her caused a great wave of panic to overtake her. Desiring to keep her presence unknown to Riley, she quickly and silently made her way back to her car.

As she unlocked the car door, she glanced back to see if she was alone. Thankfully, she was. She drove back to her motel room for the evening. After taking a long, hot shower, she had the urge to call Cassie and check on her. Later, she would open the letter from her great aunt.

Ellie dwelled more on her daughter being so far away because of the tragedy with which Riley had to live. Sitting in the middle of the bed, she dialed Cassie's number. Usually Cassie answered on the first ring, but this time she wasn't picking up. Ellie got her voice mail, and while she hated leaving messages, she wanted her to know that she called.

"Hi Cass, it's Mom. I'm heading home in the morning, but wanted to see how your week was going. Give me a call when you have a minute. I love you! Bye!"

Ellie sat for a moment, disappointed that she couldn't talk to Cassie. Realizing she had plenty to occupy her time, she picked up the bag with the papers from Riley, cemetery records from Mrs. Eubanks, and the letter from Aunt Lavina. Flopping on the bed, she took out the envelope that was sealed and tied shut with the little strip of cord. On the outside of the envelope was her name, Ella Camden. *What secrets do have to tell me, Aunt Vinnie?*

The letter looked to be a couple of pages, handwritten, naturally. Ellie stared down at her great aunt's aged, yet neat and articulate penmanship. She took a deep breath and began to read silently.

> *Dear Ella,*
>
> *I suppose if you are reading this, I have gone on to my heavenly reward. I'm quite certain that the news of me and my passing has been quite overwhelming for you, Ella. I hope that what I have left in your care will be of help financially to you, as well as a link to the heritage that your Mother was unaware. It is my hope that a Townes descendent remains sole heir of Mimosa Grove. You were but a tiny little thing when I*

saw you last. Your green eyes and dark hair were unmistakably Townes traits. Your mother would have been my heir, but after learning of her death, I chose you, her only heir, to take charge of my earthly possessions. I am confident you have grown into a beautiful woman, much like your mother, Elizabeth. To this day, I regret that I didn't send for you. Your heritage was something of which you should have been proudly aware. Upon your visit to Mimosa Grove, please find the large family Bible I have placed on the sideboard in the dining room. It will be of great help and a wealth of information in your quest for answers. Ella, I pray that you will keep our Mimosa Grove within the family. You have a special task, one that will be evident once the home is yours. I trust you will soon find the treasures in the attic, all of which were meant for you. Every item in the home is original to your ancestors, Ella. These are your people, and you are part of them. I do hope you appreciate the care in which their belongings have been preserved over the decades, and will continue to do so yourself.

Please remember to care for the soldiers buried near my dear Shelby and me. Honor their memory and remember to carry on the Townes' tradition of decorating the graves. Your great-great-great-great-grandfather, Captain Daniel Townes, is buried behind the grove of Mimosa trees beyond the house. You will find his grave, along with your great-great-great-great-grandmother, Camille, and other family members buried in the small cemetery. You are to tend their graves, Ella. I am sure you will make contact with the cemetery matron at Resthaven. She will help you locate the Confederate dead, along with Shelby and my headstone. I wish I could have known you, Ella Caroline. I can rest knowing that you will be watching over those which have no earthly home.

Your loving great aunt
Lavina

Ellie was still sitting motionless on the bed after finishing the last lines of the letter. Re-reading the letter, she tried imagining her Aunt Lavina writing the lines to her ten years before. *If she knew about the items in the attic, why didn't she bring them out of that attic years ago? I would bet she had to know about Raford Collins as well.* Ellie had no idea there was a graveyard behind the house. She hadn't seen it when she and Riley were outside exploring around the back of the house. Now she had to go back.

She would return to Newburg, get her affairs in order, and come back to Mimosa Grove. Telling Uncle Loren of the money he had inherited was important, but the knowledge of Mimosa Grove would be even more so. Feeling very tired, and knowing she would have to get an early start the following morning, Ellie prepared for bed.

The Blue and the Gray

By the flow of the inland river
Whence the fleets of iron have fled,
Where the blades of grave-grass quiver,
Asleep are the ranks of the dead,
Under the sod and the dew
Waiting the judgment day;
Under the roses, the Blue
Under the lilies, the Gray.

Francis M. Finch, G. Avery Reeder

Chapter 5

Ellie didn't hear her radio alarm ringing at six o'clock. She assumed the radio alarm had been going off quite awhile when she finally rolled over to hit the snooze button at seven a.m. Quickly setting her feet on the floor, she tried to steady herself as she walked to the bathroom. She had wanted to be on the road by now, but clearly, she needed the rest more. Hard to believe after the previous day, but she couldn't recall dreaming. Showered, she rapidly applied makeup and brushed her teeth. *Better go down and settle the bill, then grab some breakfast and get on the road.*

Ellie carried out her luggage and makeup bag, then did a once over of the room. The desk clerk was busy taking a call as Ellie approached.

Finally, when the clerk's phone call ended, he asked, "Ready to check out this morning?"

Ellie smiled and said, "Yes, I am heading home."

"I hope you had a good stay with us. Was everything okay?"

He gave Ellie the bill amount.

"Oh yes, it was just fine. I'm sure I'll be back soon."

Taking her a credit card, the clerk commented, "Good, thank you!"

Replacing the card back in her wallet, Ellie walked out the door. Her mind raced with the events of the last few days as she walked to her car.

Locking her door, Ellie clicked the GPS, already programmed for home, and let out a sigh as she pulled out of the motel parking lot. *Well, Aunt Lavina, I have no idea what you have gotten me into, but I guess I have a mission now. What will everyone think when I tell them my plans? It's Memorial Day weekend, and I have the whole summer ahead of me.*

The drive home seemed to take much longer. Eight hours later, Ellie was pulling into her driveway. It was still daylight outside, and she wanted to carry in all her possessions and put them safely inside the house. First, she called Char to let her know that she had arrived safely home, and then she called Sean to tell him that she was back from Tennessee. He was sitting outside drinking a beer when he got the call.

"Ellie! How did your trip go?" Sean sounded excited to hear from her.

"It was beyond amazing, Sean. I was blown away by the whole experience. If you're not busy, maybe you could come over one night this week for dinner, and I'll fill you in."

Sean didn't hesitate, "I'd love it. When?"

Ellie smiled at the obvious interest he was still displaying.

"Well, I was hoping you'd be free tomorrow. I have a few things I have to get done before I fly out this weekend to see Cassie. I am leaving Friday and won't be back for a week."

Sean thought for a moment about his week's agenda.

"Tomorrow night should be good. I can swing by and pick you up around five, if that works. I want to take you out, so don't plan on cooking."

Ellie thought it would be nice to have a quiet evening at home, but she appreciated someone wanting to take her out too.

"Thanks, Sean. See you around five."

Sean added, "Well, I'm glad you had a good trip, Ellie, and it will be good to see you again."

Ellie blushed, a little giddy about having a date.

"I am looking forward to seeing you too, Sean."

"Have a good night, Ellie."

"Bye, Sean."

Ellie put her phone on the table. *Well it looks like I have a date. Now to carry in all my treasures.*

Ellie went outside and opened the back of the truck. Down inside were her luggage and the larger of the two trunks. She went into the garage and brought out the little wagon that her dad used to haul things in around the yard. It was a little lower than she would have liked, but it would work to carry the trunk to the house. Making one trip into the house with her luggage, she was back, trying to lift the trunk off the tailgate. Maneuvering the heavy trunk to one side didn't work; she was too weak to lift it alone.

She tried once more to get under the bottom of the trunk, but it was too heavy to pull out. Her neighbor, Tom Schmidt, starting out to his truck, saw Ellie's predicament.

"Hey, you need some help, Ellie?"

Startled, having not seen Tom come outside, she turned in his direction.

"If you have a minute, I would sure appreciate some help. Thank you."

Tom walked across the yard that separated their condominiums.

"What have you got here? Looks like you've been to the antique mall."

Ellie smiled, "Well, it's actually from my great aunt. I inherited a few things from her estate."

Tom put his hand under the trunk and lifted the corner. The two were then able to lift the trunk up and out, onto the wagon.

"Oh, thank you, Tom. I got it in here by myself, but I think it grew on the drive home."

"I'd be glad to help you unload it," Tom offered.

Ellie looked apologetic, "Would you mind?"

She planned to display it in the living room, near the fireplace.

"No, not at all. It's a neat old piece, I'm sure Courtney would love this in our living room."

Ellie went to open the door, while Tom pulled the wagon in to the condo. They were able to lift the trunk out and set it on the floor with little trouble.

"Thanks so much. I wasn't sure I'd be able to get it out by myself. I owe ya!" Ellie patted Tom on the back.

"No problem, Ellie. You can just bake some of that zucchini bread and send it over."

Tom laughed as he walked back out to the yard.

"Do you have anything else you need carried in while I'm here?"

"No, thank you, I think I can get the rest. That was the biggie!"

Tom turned and walked across the yard.

"Thanks, Tom."

He waved and got in his truck.

"You're welcome, Ellie! Anytime!"

Ellie went back to her truck, reaching in to hoist the hatbox, smaller trunk and Bible. Placing them down in the wagon, she started back toward the door. Attempting to reason away the experiences she had while inside Mimosa Grove, she was unable to make herself believe that both experiences were a figment of her overactive imagination. Raford Collins was in her mind!

After one last trip to her truck to get the papers from the front seat, she closed and locked the front door. It was only eight o'clock, but her body felt like it was much later. After her short time inside Mimosa Grove, her condo suddenly seemed small. She sat down in the recliner beside the trunk. *What in the world am I going to do? I can't research the family history and find out how to help Raford Collins do if I stay here all summer. There is so much to consider in spending the summer away from home and in a place that I have a ghost roaming.*

Ellie shocked herself by saying it aloud: *ghost* now had a different connotation. Raford sounded real enough. Ellie quickly changed her clothes and put on a pair of nylon running shorts and a T-shirt. Retrieving the letter that her aunt had written, she placed it on the hearth of the fireplace. Next, she unwrapped the Bible from the sheet in which she had placed it for protection. The hatbox sat on the floor, its contents waiting patiently to be read.

At one point during her drive home, Ellie contemplated not reading the letters. In fact, she even thought that it might be best if she put the hatbox back in the attic, not going back to Tennessee again. That option didn't get much consideration because Ellie loved Mimosa Grove, and she didn't intend to let a ghost run her off her property. Deciding she would ask Charlotte to watch her condo for the summer, she picked up the family Bible.

The cover had been quite lovely in its younger years and had been well preserved, but was showing signs of deterioration. Ellie slowly opened the Bible's cover and discovered the words, Daniel and Camille Townes, April 16, 1835. *The pretty penmanship is beginning to fade.* Ellie assumed this was the couple's wedding date. The Bible appeared to have many things inserted into the pages; the copyright date was 1830, The American Bible Society, New York.

Ellie turned the page to find another hand-written note placed at the top of the page:

Christmas 1835 from General Adam Burnell and Mrs. Isabelle Burnell. So they were most likely the parents of Camille Townes and this had been a Christmas gift or even a wedding gift to the couple. Ellie wondered what year brought the young couple to Tennessee. She had learned that her mother's family originally settled in Kentucky from North Carolina. Information on Adam Burnell of Kentucky would surely be recorded in the library.

Ellie continued turning the page, and saw several ancient pressed flowers lying between the pages . . . They appeared to be daisies, but the third flower she couldn't quite distinguish. The fronds or leaves were so brittle that Ellie decided not to remove them for closer inspection. The flower was practically dust, but the leaves' shape helped her to determine that this could possibly be a mimosa flower. Ellie smiled at the connection to Mimosa Grove. On the next page, was a sheet that had been inserted between the pages. On this sheet were the birth and death dates of the four children of Daniel and Camille Townes. It was a family tree of sorts, and the style of writing changed slightly from one group of names to another.

Ellie assumed the Bible had been passed down from one generation to other, hence the change in penmanship and information listed. The names and dates began with Camille Burnell and Daniel Townes' births and wedding date. Below their names were four children: *Daniel Adam Townes, January 1, 1836-March 11, 1836; Caroline Isabelle Townes, February 13, 1838, Jacob Washington Townes, August 17, 1840-June 15 1844, Harriett Colbert Townes, May 9, 1842,* Joseph Burnell Townes, February 7, 1850-July 1864.

She wondered if the two little boys were buried in the plot behind the grove of mimosa trees that Aunt Lavina spoke about in her letter. The youngest brother, Joseph, was much older when he passed away. There were so many questions that she wanted answered, as she leafed through the rest of the Bible, finding more pressed flowers and passages marked with strips of ribbon. Inserted toward the middle of the Bible, between the books of Matthew and Mark, was another faded sheet of paper containing another generation of names and dates.

Caroline Isabelle Townes-James Thomas Corbin, June 19, 1860. The names of Caroline and James Corbin's children were listed with only birthdates. Next on the page were the names *Harriett Colbert Townes-Randolph Cooper Lankford, November 27, 1865.*

Their children were listed with names and dates of births: Amelia Caroline Lankford, July 3, 1867-August 11, 1869, Eugenia Camille Lankford, December 23, 1869, Edward Thomas Lankford, March 17, 1871, Lucy Burnell Lankford, June 6, 1873.

Ellie placed her hand over the names of Harriett and Caroline. The samplers inside the big trunk were made by these two women, mothers and wives who carried on the bloodline of Daniel and Camille Townes. Ellie wasn't sure what became of the romance between Hattie and Raford, since she was clearly the wife of Randolph Lankford. Her bloodline would be from one of these two women.

She decided to put the Bible back on the fireplace hearth and look inside the hatbox. The letters numbered seven, much less than she previously estimated. Beneath the letters was an old bonnet, wrapped in ancient tissue paper. Ellie chuckled, since she had hoped when first seeing the box that she would find a bonnet to display. The bonnet was small, more of a hat, dark green with black and green silk appliqués on the sides. Only a hint of the ostrich feathers graced a small portion of the appliqué now.

Ellie carefully removed the bonnet and sat it on the hearth. She held the letter she had read while in the attic at Mimosa Grove, feeling a chill go up her spine as she remembered the ghostly apparition that appeared. Retracting the next letter out of the hatbox, she removed it from the envelope. It appeared to have been from another camp, but Ellie recognized the handwriting, and knew immediately she was holding another letter from Raford Collins.

> *My dearest Hattie,*
>
> *I hope these few lines find you well. I wanted to write you sooner, but I got the fever two weeks back. Me and Jesse, my friend, caught sick with it the same time. Our regiment pulld out on the Friday last, leaving us in the camp to get fit for marching. We plan to head out with another company tomorrow. I haven't herd any news from you and hope yor family and you are good. I think about you all the time, Hattie. It greevs me to be away from you. I will write again when we are with Vaughn's brigade.*
>
> *I love you,*
> *Raford*

Ellie spoke aloud, "How sad. Poor Raford, all he wanted was for Hattie to know how much he loves her."

She noticed the next four letters had not been taken out of their envelopes. All four were still sealed, and Ellie was baffled as to why Hattie would have placed the letters in the box unread, and obviously hidden from view. She sat looking at the pile of unopened letters, deciding keep them sealed for now. Something kept her from invading Hattie's privacy. Besides, Ellie knew they were hers, and she was the only person who knew about them or the people in them.

As she was sitting in the middle of her floor looking over the letters, her doorbell rang. She quickly put the letters back in the hat box and wrapped the bonnet back as she found it, laying it on top of the letters. Ellie walked to the front door and peered through the peephole. Char was standing on the porch, holding a grocery bag.

"Hey you, I wondered how long it would take you to get over here. Come on in!"

Ellie hugged Char, as she was saying, "I figured you were out of food, so I brought you some groceries. I hope you like Lean Cuisine. I figured you were on yourself to lose a few pounds having eaten out most of the week."

"You are so good, girlfriend!" Ellie said with a giggle.

She added, "Come to think of it, I haven't eaten dinner. I've been going through some of the things I brought home."

Char followed her into the kitchen where she began unloading the contents onto the counter.

"So, how was your trip to Dixie, Miss Ellie?"

Char plopped herself down on one of the bar stools that lined the counter.

"It was better than I had imagined, Char. I can't believe Aunt Lavina had so much money, just lying in a bank. I don't know anyone who even has that much money!"

"You do now, sweetie. You own that much money, and you are going to have to meet with a financial advisor to help you invest it wisely."

Char was always thinking in terms of investing and saving. Brad always handled the financial end of their marriage, and the only money she ever had above her salary was from her father, after his death.

"Char, I have given some thought to that, and I want to make sure Cassie has a nest egg for herself. I also am thinking about taking a sabbatical from school this year, just to get my affairs in order."

Char looked puzzled, not sure what affairs she was talking about.

"What's going on, Ellie? Are you sure you want to take time off from school, knowing how quickly they would throw you under the bus to save their school corporation a few dollars? I mean, you are one of the "old guard", earning the experienced salary. If you leave, would you have a job to come back to?"

Ellie looked at Char, then out the kitchen window.

"I hear what you're saying, but I have had two years of stress that has about done me in. I'm tired of trying to keep everything together emotionally. I buried Dad and a bad marriage, all within just a couple of years. I have only been on my own a little over a year. I love teaching history, but I have a chance to LIVE history."

Ellie seemed to be arguing her case before Char.

"Well, you know that I'll do whatever I can to help you. Do you have a plan?"

Ellie smiled, relieved, saying, "I own two homes in Tennessee. I want to rent out the one where my aunt and uncle lived before their deaths, but I am going to keep the plantation home, Char. I have to."

Char seemed a bit taken aback by Ellie's sudden resolve to do this.

"What on earth do you know about running a farm, much less why would you want to?"

"If you could just see it, Char, you'd understand. I actually own a museum," exclaimed Ellie, "all of the furnishings are from my family, my ancestors."

Ellie's tone changed, "Besides, my great aunt wrote me a letter asking me to do it."

Char's eyebrows lifted when she heard this.

"I thought you'd never heard of this relative before. When did you get a letter from her?"

Ellie went around the corner to the living room, retrieving the letter.

"Here, see for yourself. I got it yesterday from Riley."

"Oh yeah, Riley. The lawyer?" Char asked, her voice taking on a higher, playful pitch.

"Yes, he handled the reading of the will and went with me to visit the two homes."

Char read the letter slowly, taking much longer than Ellie thought necessary.

"So, now do you see what I mean? I have to go."

Ellie had made her case.

Char lay the letter down on the counter, becoming the voice of reason Ellie had come to respect.

"I still think it is a bad idea to leave your job, without pay, for a year. *But*, if you're determined to stay in the house and fix it up, I think you should buy a gun and get a dog."

Char turned her head, looking smugly towards her best friend.

"Besides, I've already taken care of the dog part. You can take care of the gun part."

Ellie wasn't following Char on her comment, but smiled.

"Thanks for supporting me. It's scary for me to do this. All I know is *here*. I think I can survive on some of the inheritance for the year and decide what I want to do for the future."

Char asked, "What about Sean? Do you think the two of you might have something?"

Ellie sighed, "Oh Char, I don't know how I feel about him. He's taking me out on a date tomorrow. I'm really looking forward to seeing him again. Who knows?"

Char knew Ellie all too well; she wasn't making a very convincing argument for wanting something more with Sean. Ellie ran her hands through her hair, pulling the long strands away from her furrowed brow.

"I just know that I need the time to spend in Tennessee to get myself together."

Char could see Ellie was worn out, so when the dinner was heated in the microwave, she asked if Ellie would like to eat in peace.

"No, stay awhile. I'd love the company. Besides, you haven't seen some of the treasures I brought home with me!"

"Oh yeah, I want to see all the antiques for sure. First things first though. I found you a dog."

Ellie grimaced, "A dog? You know I don't want a huge dog, I live in a condo. And I can't stand little yappy ankle biters."

Char laughed, "I know exactly what you need. One of my clients had a litter of cocker spaniel puppies six weeks ago, and they're just beautiful. In fact, I suckered myself into buying one. I can get her this weekend."

Ellie had always liked the size of the cocker spaniel, and she thought they had the sweetest little face.

"You know, I am thinking I'd like a dog for the company. I miss Cassie so much, and I think I would enjoy having someone who needs me!"

Char was thrilled to hear that.

"Then it sounds like you can go with me to get your new friend, I'll call them and tell them we'll come by on Thursday so you can pick one out."

"I'm leaving Friday for Baltimore, Char. Do you think they'd wait till I got back before I took the puppy?" Ellie asked.

Char said she'd make a call to set things up, and then call her with the final word.

Ellie was excited to be getting a pet, and it seemed the two would be making a road trip very soon together.

"Char, would you mind checking on the condo this summer while I'm gone? I'll take my plants, and I am going to drive the truck down instead of my car."

Char nodded, "I'd be glad to, Ellie. I'll have my friend Rick make a few passes by your house on his evening shift, and I'll let him know you are going to be away. I'm glad your dad had the security system installed."

Char and Ellie went into the living room, Ellie carrying a tray with her supper on it.

"I want you to see what I have. It's beyond amazing."

Char excitedly peered down into the contents of the trunk. She marveled at the preservation quality of each, right down to the tiny satin slippers and gown. The pictures were a favorite of hers, and when she saw the picture with the lock of hair, the effect was similar to what Ellie had experienced. She saw the Bible and hatbox, and she inquired about them both.

Ellie took the items and put them back into the trunk, then moved over to the hearth.

"This is the Bible that my 4th great-grandmother received from her parents on her wedding day. The names are all in there, and there are paintings in the house of most of them. Oh, I have pictures that I took on my digital camera too. You won't believe it."

Char was in total disbelief at the wonderful treasure trove Ellie had been bestowed.

"It blows my mind to think you own all of this! Have you thought about selling it, or seeing if museums around the area would want to buy some of the items?"

Ellie looked chagrinned at the suggestion.

"I have no intention of selling anything; it will stay in our family."

Noticing the hatbox again, Char was curious.

"Oh girl, what do we have here?" Char moved towards the hatbox, and Ellie suddenly thought of the letters.

"Oh, it's just a hatbox."

She tried to sound less than excited about it.

"I can see that, but what treasure did you find inside?"

Ellie couldn't lie to her best friend.

"There's a beautiful bonnet inside, see?" Ellie opened the box gingerly, taking out the delicate bonnet.

"Ellie! It is absolutely exquisite!" Char exploded, "you need to display this under a glass dome, you know, like they put silk flowers under?"

Ellie agreed, "Yes, I plan to display it. I think I'll put it in the back bedroom on the dresser, along with the other hats I have collected."

Char saw them before Ellie could say anything.

"What's this? Letters? Who are these to?" Char was intrigued.

"They are to my great-great-great-grandmother from a beau she had during the war."

Char, being a romantic, said, "Love letters. How precious! Have you read them all yet?"

Ellie wasn't sure if this would be the time to tell her about Raford Collins or not. She was afraid her best friend would think all the excitement of the last couple of days had challenged her mental capacity.

"Yes, it is a love story, but there's a mystery involved I haven't quite figured out."

Char smiled, "It sounds like something out of the movies. You are so stinkin' lucky. So what are you going to name your pup?"

Ellie laughed, "You whiplash the most of anyone I know! I don't know, maybe I'll pick a good Southern name."

The two finished their discussion about Ellie's plans for the summer, and then Char stood.

"I need to be going, Ellie. I have another closing at nine in the morning, so I had better get myself home and tucked in. What time do I need to run you to the airport on Friday?"

"Oh, I have an early flight, around nine. I'll be waiting around seven."

Char hugged her and said, "Okay, I'll be here bright and early. Tell Cassie that Aunt Char says 'hey'."

"I will, and thank you for everything. I know I am not making much sense right now, but once I get back to Tennessee and immerse myself in my family history, I will know more of my future."

Ellie turned on the porch light for Char to see her way to the car. She locked the door, and went back to the living room where the smaller trunk was still sitting on the hearth, unopened. Ellie thought she would try to get the small lock to open; having gotten out the keys Riley had given her. To her dismay, the trunk was hopelessly secured. None of the keys fit, so if she wanted to get the trunk open, she would have to find a locksmith. Disappointed that the contents inside the little trunk would have to remain a mystery for a while, Ellie put it back on the hearth.

Bushed, and feeling a good night's sleep in her own bed would do wonders, Ellie snapped the lights off and made her way back to the bathroom. After taking a long, steamy bubble bath, and quickly donning a pair of satiny pajamas, she crawled into bed. Remembering she'd wanted to read some of Camille Townes' diary before bed, she decided to put that task off until tomorrow; her eyes were just too heavy. Before she gave way to slumber, she said a prayer of thanks for the many blessings she had received over the past few days. She also gave thanks for the protection and safety of her precious Cassie. Before she could say '*amen*', she was in a deep sleep.

The morning light streaming through the bedroom window woke Ellie from a night of complete rest. She arose and went about doing her morning rituals. As the coffee began to brew, she looked up in the cabinet to find a box of cereal. She sat on the barstool eating her cereal and drinking a cup of coffee. She would do her laundry, and then pack another suitcase to take on her trip to see Cassie. Cassie was excited to have her mom come and see her apartment for the first time. Ellie was excited to be seeing Cassie after a month of separation, and would call her in a little while, making sure everything was a go.

Ellie busied herself with the trunk's contents for most of the morning. Taking out the shawls, shoes and dresses, she held them up against her body as she stood before the full-length mirror in her bedroom. Remembering to call Cassie, she clicked on speed dial. Cassie answered on the first ring.

"Hi, Mom!"

"Hi, Cassie, I hope your week is going well. I just wanted to touch base and make sure we were still a go for Friday."

Hesitating, Cassie said, "Oh, Mom, I have to work all week. The schedule got changed last night after one of the other writers had a family emergency. They have asked that I work her shift."

Ellie felt as though she would cry, she had been looking forward to seeing Cassie for almost two months.

Hoping her voice didn't give her away, and trying to sound supportive, Ellie encouraged, "I understand, Cassie. I'll try and call the airline today and see if I can get the flight changed."

Cassie added, "Mom, I'm not sure how long I'll be working her shift. Let me find out today what the producer wants me to do, and I'll call you back tonight after work."

Ellie wasn't sure if Cassie would understand her decision to spend the summer in Hendersonville, Tennessee, but she decided to tell her while she had the chance.

"Cassie, I might not be able to come up there next week. I am going to be going back to Tennessee to spend the summer at Mimosa Grove."

There, I said it.

"Mom, you never did tell me about the reading of the will. What is Mimosa Grove?"

Ellie began to tell Cassie all about the reading of the will. Between her screams of excitement and squeals of delight at her mother's amazing sudden fortune, she was able to catch her up to speed on her plans. She decided not to share *all* of her experiences in Hendersonville, mainly because she knew Cassie would find talk of ghosts to be a figment of her mother's imagination. There would time later for sharing about Raford Collins, if she wanted.

"Cassie, when I get the final check, after Uncle Sam dips his fingers into the till, I would like to give you some of the money. I want you to have a nest egg, even if you just left the nest."

Cassie was trying to keep her emotions in check, "Mom that is your money. Your great aunt wanted you to have it."

Cassie was Frank Camden's granddaughter through and through.

"Cassandra Elizabeth, you listen and listen good. I am giving you this money so that you will always have security."

"Okay, Mom, I'm sorry I sounded ungrateful. If you are determined to give me some of the money, then I accept and thank you. It will be nice to know that I have a backup plan."

"You're very welcome, Cassie, I love you so much! I want to show you all the antiques I brought home. This is your family history too, Cassie. I hope you'll come and stay a weekend with me while I'm in Tennessee," Ellie added.

"Of course, I will! And I am so sorry about the plane tickets. I wish you could still come. I really miss you, Mom."

Cassie sounded as though she were about to cry.

"I miss you too, Honey. I'm sorry it won't work out this time, but we'll get together."

"Thanks, Mom. You're the best. Well, I need to get ready for work. I'll call you later this weekend. I love you!"

Ellie beamed picturing her daughter.

"I love you too, Honey. Bye."

"Bye, Mom."

Well, it looks like I will be heading back to Tennessee sooner than I thought. Stop feeling sorry for yourself, Ellie Morgan.

Ellie grabbed the delicate journal belonging to Camille Burnell Townes. Bringing her cup of coffee into the living room, she curled up in the recliner. Ellie was concerned about the journal being left out in the humidity. After all, it had been wrapped and placed inside the trunk for over one hundred years. Opening the cover page, she saw in dainty script: *Camille Burnell Townes, May 1835.* Camille Burnell, of Lexington, Kentucky, had met her future husband, Daniel Townes, when he and his father came to her father's horse farm to purchase a mare in May of 1832. Eighteen-year-old Daniel caught seventeen-year-old Camille's eye that very day. She wrote only a few lines about meeting Daniel Townes.

> *11, May, 1832—*
> *Today I met such a handsome boy. He came with his father all the way from North Carolina. No other boys in all this fine state compare to him, so as I have seen.*

Ellie enjoyed reading the small, dainty penmanship of her ancestor. Unable to read the next few pages, as the ink had almost disappeared from the page, she did find an entry some pages back to April of 1835. Daniel's father made several trips to the Burnell home, and Camille's family enjoyed having the Townes' family of North Carolina as extended guests. After many visitations, it was confirmed that the two should marry. To the delight and approval of both Camille's mother and father, the two would marry upon Camille's eighteenth birthday in Lexington. The entry on Camille's wedding day gave quite the account of gifts and guests that converged on the family plantation in Lexington.

16, April, 1835~
I will very shortly become the bride of Mr. Daniel Townes. For my eighteenth birthday, Daniel brought me a lovely cameo broach that his grandmother wore on her wedding day. Such a delicate little piece, I shall treasure it always. The wedding gifts have been arriving since Tuesday last, and Aunt Sally and Old Jack have been helping Mother with the preparations. The muslin and lace gown that Mother stitched herself is of rare beauty. I trust I will be all Daniel sees today at our wedding.

Carriages bringing family members of Daniel Townes from North Carolina began arriving the week prior to the nuptials. Camille's parents spared no expense on their only daughter's wedding, and both sets of parents made sure they young couple would begin their married life in comfort. Ellie was able to read from an entry the following day that Daniel's father and mother had given him land in Tennessee on the Cumberland River. Daniel's father had been given five hundred acres in trade for a fine mare from his stable. This land was promised to Daniel upon his marriage when he would move into the sparsely populated area. Camille's father gave them two beautiful horses from his stable, to start their own horse farm if desired. Along with this gift, Camille's mother had given her a table, chairs and sideboard, and a lovely pianoforte. All would be sent by flatboat to Hendersonville.

So the furniture in the dining room at Mimosa Grove had been the wedding present to Camille and Daniel from her parents. Camille must have jotted these details in her journal on her honeymoon! Who has time to write in her journal on her honeymoon?

The couple set off for their new home the day following the wedding. They loaded two wagons and headed out for the first leg of their journey, which would entail a few days on a flatboat traveling down the Cumberland River. Soon after their engagement, Daniel had taken a trip to his homestead, along with a brother and several slaves. He built a small cabin and the barn before starting on Camille's home. During their stay, the cabin had caught fire, burning to the ground. It was then that Daniel hired a team of craftsmen to construct a home for his future bride. The home was to be similar to the large home in which Daniel grew up, with the rear of the home facing the Cumberland River. Across the first and second floors would be large open porches, similar to piazzas.

It took almost a year for the home to be finished, as well as the kitchen, smoke house, chicken coop and horse barn. The other buildings would come later. Camille would come to the new home as a young bride, setting up housekeeping for the first time. There would be several deliveries from Kentucky and North Carolina. These would include family heirlooms and gifts being showered upon the young couple. When Daniel chose the site for his new home, he cleared a grove of poplar and oak trees that had been damaged during a tornado the previous season. The only trees that had remained intact were three mimosa trees that appeared to have weathered the storm without damage.

As the flatboat made its way around the curve of the river, Daniel called for Camille to come out of the little makeshift hut for a view. The sun was starting to set over the hill, but she was able to see the dock jutting out from the bank. "That's our dock, Camille." Daniel happily proclaimed. Camille saw the house sitting as a sentinel on the rise of the hill. The boatman threw the rope over to the dock, waiting for the two slaves on the bank to retrieve it.

Once the boat could be pulled close enough for a safe departure, Daniel stepped down to the dock and held out his hand to help his young bride. Camille, falling in love with the sight of her new home, gave Daniel her hand and let him lead her up the path from the dock. Coming up the slope of the back lawn, Camille's eyes were immediately drawn to the three large mimosa trees.

"They are so pretty, Daniel. We have to plant more of them, all around the house if possible."

He walked her around to the front of the house.

"Oh, Daniel, it is just beautiful!" Camille squealed with delight.

"I hope the inside meets your approval, Camille. The furniture is still arriving, and I would like for us to take a trip to Louisville or Nashville to purchase the rest. You can select what appeals most to your taste," Daniel promised.

Camille was used to being given preferential treatment as the only daughter to survive into adulthood. Her brother, Robert, would someday inherit his parents' home and horse farm.

"Have you given though to what you would like to name the house?" Daniel inquired of his new bride.

"Indeed I have. I want the house to be called Mimosa Grove. I love it, Daniel, and I love you," Camille answered.

It would continue to be called such by the next five generations of Townes' descendants to occupy the homestead. The couple shared a passionate kiss under the shade of the trees, and Daniel led Camille up the large stone steps to the front porch.

"Come, let's go inside. I want to show you the house, Mrs. Townes."

Camille loved her new home, and once inside showered her husband with hugs of approval as he showed her the four rooms and large entry hall in the downstairs. The stairway that led to the floor above was a work of art, having been designed to appear as if it were suspended without support, a relatively new design in homes of the early 1830's. Daniel spared no expense on his plantation home, and wanted to gain the respect of the older, more established families who had homes in the surrounding counties.

Within the year, Camille would be bringing a child into the nursery at Mimosa Grove. This child, a son, would be the apple of his mother's eye. Ellie put the diary down, laying her head back on the recliner. She began to think about all she had read. *What excitement there was in the young couple's lives. Camille was mistress of a new home and had a husband who loved her. Now she was writing about a baby, and how his coming had brought a new dimension to the love she felt for Daniel.*

Ellie read the next entry, announcing the birth of her first child.

> *1, January, 1836–*
> *From the valley of the shadow of death, God has delivered me. Only Lucy and Mrs. Flynn were here to aide in my time of pain, but what joy beyond measure has the good Lord heaped upon me. Not more than seven pounds, such an angel in my arms. A new year today has brought a new life in our home. Daniel Adam, named after his papa and my father, Adam Burnell, has the dark eyes of his father. Mrs. Flynn says she has seen many babes come, but not a mite prettier than he.*

Ellie went to the page in the Bible that recorded the births and deaths of all the Townes' children. *This was the baby who was to die; I wonder if this young son was the baby in the picture with the lock of hair and mourning ribbon?* The next entry answered the question about the child.

> 5, March, 1836–
>
> My heart breaks for the tiny babe lying in the parlor below me. Little Daniel breathed his last Tuesday morning. Mr. Flynn helped Mose make the burial coffin for our sleeping angel. I feel as though I have nothing left in me to go on. We dressed Daniel in the christening gown and wrapped his tiny form into the rabbit fur blanket Lucy had made for him. The ground is frozen, but Daniel keeps digging. As soon as he is able, he will bury our little lamb beneath the mimosa trees beyond the house.

Ellie felt tears falling down her cheeks. Brushing them away, she bent down to see inside the large trunk. Ellie carefully reached down into the box and brought out the tintype of the young child. The child appeared to be a toddler, maybe three or four years of age. The child had dark curls that framed his round, cherub-like face. This couldn't be the baby of only two months that Camille wrote in her journal about. Ellie wondered if this child was a different child who had passed away. *Who knew what treasures were inside the small trunk?*

She would look behind the house for the cemetery, maybe some of her questions could be answered there. Ellie had spent a good portion of the day trying to decipher the pages of the diary, and decided to put it back in its covering and give her eyes a rest. The script was difficult to read and also faded with time, which added to Ellie's discomfort in straining to read it.

She had lost track of time, and saw that it was early afternoon. She was to meet Char to go look at the puppy this afternoon! In less than thirty minutes, Char was calling Ellie.

"Hey, I'm on my way. Are you ready to go meet your new furry baby?"

Ellie smiled, and was suddenly excited about the prospect of having a new pet to have around the house.

"Yes, I'm ready and waiting! I need to be back before five though. Sean is coming to pick me up for a date."

Char was glad that her friend was getting out with Sean again.

"Okay, no need to panic. It's not that far from your house to the McNeal's, and it shouldn't take long to pick out your darlin'."

Char was glad that Ellie had this adventure to counter her disappointment in not getting to visit Cassie.

Char arrived soon after the phone call ended, and the two drove out of town towards Evansville. The two talked about Char's day and the closing she had finished. Her business was going well, having made Broker in the real estate company. Ellie was proud of her best friend and all the hard work she had done to build a successful clientele. Ellie changed the subject of work and began to tell Char about her disappointing phone call.

"Well, my trip to Maryland is off."

Char turned toward Ellie, "Off? What do you mean? What happened?"

Ellie let out a sigh.

"I called Cass today to find out if we were a go, ya know, just to make sure she'd be there in case I needed directions. She told me that her boss changed her work schedule, and she would be working her shift plus that of a coworker who had a family emergency."

Ellie sounded deflated, "So she wouldn't be able to see me while I was supposed to be there."

Char put her hand over on Ellie's arm, patting it sympathetically.

"Oh Ellie, I'm sorry. I know how much you've missed Cassie. Were you able to get your tickets changed?"

Ellie shook her head, "No, I got busy today and didn't call. I will first thing in the morning. I need to find out about getting an open-ended date on my ticket."

"I'm sure Cassie feels bad too, Ellie. So are you going to leave earlier for Tennessee?"

Char was going to miss Ellie; the two of them had seen each other every weekend since her divorce, either hanging out or trying to do something one night out of the weekend. It was going to be hard for Char not being able to just pop in and visit Ellie.

"I think I'll drive down this weekend. If I can pick up the puppy tomorrow, I can take him or her to the vet and get what shots it needs. Later, I'll find a vet in Hendersonville after I am settled. I'm sure it will all work out. So, what are you getting, a male or female?"

Char smiled, "I chose a female since I don't have good luck with males."

They both laughed, and Ellie added, "Well I don't have much of a track record in that department either, Char. But I think I am going to get a male."

They pulled into the driveway of a nice ranch style home. The long asphalt driveway led up to the front of the house. Ellie saw a young woman look out the front window.

"I guess they are expecting us. I saw Mrs. O'Neal look out the window," Char said.

They parked, and as they both got out of the car, heard two dogs bark. Ellie saw two cocker spaniels come to the front glass storm door, wagging their tales and barking.

"I hope they aren't biters."

Angie McNeal came to the door, shooing the dogs back.

"Hi, Charlotte. Molly and Ben won't bother you; they're just a little protective of their brood. They have eight puppies!"

Char introduced Ellie to Angie.

"So you want a puppy too, huh? We've just put the ad in the paper, so you and Charlotte get first picks!" Angie announced.

Ellie and Char smiled, and followed Angie to the back of the house, into a room that once had been a garage and was now converted into a family room.

"I'll put Molly and Ben outside in the back yard so you can have a chance to play with the puppies. They tend to get in the way."

Angie took the adult dogs and put them outside in the fenced yard to roam. When she returned, she removed the baby gate so Char and Ellie could enter the room. In the corner of the room was a large playpen. Eight puppies greeted them with tails wagging. Each looked very healthy, jumping and nipping at one another. There were three black, three blonde, and two brown with black coloring. Ellie went to the brown and black puppy, while Char went to the Blonde.

"Char, are you sure you want a blonde female?" Ellie laughed.

Char thought about it, and said, "True. Maybe I should go with the brunette with black roots!"

Angie laughed at the two, adding, "If you are interested in a male, I have two.

Ellie looked at the black male; his silky coat was almost ebony, except for one white patch under his neck. She had an urge to choose him. So she did.

"I think I am going with this little fella," Ellie said.

Char chose a black female.

"I think I am going with this little lady."

Angie asked, "Do you ladies want to take your babies tonight, or do you want to come back another time to get them?"

Char spoke first, "I think we decided that I would take mine tonight, but Ellie needs to get her supplies yet."

Ellie chimed in, "If possible, I'd like to come by tomorrow and pick him up."

Angie McNeal was glad to accommodate the two. Now Ellie would start thinking of a name for her new puppy.

Ellie returned to the house in record time, hurried to change her clothes, and gave herself the once over before walking into the living room. *Not too bad, for an old gal.* Watching television, she waited for Sean. Promptly at five o'clock, Sean's car pulled into the driveway. Trying to catch a glimpse of him before he made it to the front door, Ellie went to the window.

Sean was wearing a nice pair of jeans with a button-down oxford shirt. With the sleeves rolled up fashionably, and he looked, well, 'metro-sexual', to put it on Char's vernacular. Ellie remembered he played softball, and the sun had started to give him a nice tan. He gave a couple of quick knocks on the door, and Ellie opened it with a smile.

"Hey stranger, come on in."

Sean gave her a hug as he came in, which surprised Ellie. She led the way into the kitchen.

"If you're ready, I can grab my purse and we can be off."

Sean didn't seem to be in any big hurry, but said, "Sure, I'm ready if you are. If you don't mind, I thought we'd grab a bite down on the riverfront."

Ellie hadn't been on the riverfront for ages.

"I'd enjoy that; I haven't eaten there in such a long time. Oh, I'm getting a puppy tomorrow. Wanna help me pick out some things at Pet Smart after dinner?"

Ellie hoped it wasn't in bad taste to go shopping on a date.

"Sure, I have a dog myself and I need to pick up some more biscuits. Hank loves the gourmet variety; he's spoiled," Sean said.

Ellie was glad Sean was so easy-going.

"Okay, thanks. I still have to name him."

Sean held the door open for Ellie, and then she turned to lock it. Sean politely walked before her to open the car door. It was still hard seeing him as a date; he had always been a nice guy to talk to, but Ellie had never thought much about him as a romantic interest.

They talked about Ellie's new puppy, and then the topic changed to her week in Tennessee. All through dinner, Ellie filled Sean in about the will and owning two homes. He was floored by her good fortune.

"Surely you aren't going to come back to school, now that you are loaded. You can finally tell the powers that be what you really think of them!"

Ellie chuckled and said, "Well, I don't know how much I can count on once good ol' Uncle Sam grabs his take. I do know that I'm going to spend the summer down there, working on my new plantation."

Sean looked surprised. "You mean you're staying there all summer?"

Puzzled by the tone in his voice, Ellie wondered if he was upset with her.

"Well, yes. I gave it some thought, and that is the only way I can get things in order. I can't do that living seven hours away. You know, I would love to have company, and I have prime river property. Maybe I'll buy a boat!"

Ellie tried to sound upbeat, but Sean wasn't so excited.

"I'm really happy for you, Ellie. I just thought that we might spend time getting to know one another better this summer."

Ellie didn't know what to say. She liked Sean, but she wasn't going to let a man run her life any more. She liked her independence, and if that meant losing the possibility of a relationship with Sean, then so be it.

"Sean, I have enjoyed getting to know you too. I have the summer months to find out what I will be doing. Even if I decide to take a leave of absence, you are more than welcome to come to Tennessee to hang out."

Ellie wasn't sure that was appropriate, so early in the game to offer extended visits.

"Hey, I'm sorry I am sounding like a wuss. I want you to have this time to enjoy your summer and your adventure with the house. I didn't mean to sound like you couldn't leave because of me. It isn't like we're exclusive."

Wow. Where did that come from?

"Sean, I would love to be exclusive, or at least give it a try. I haven't dated anyone since my divorce. I just got my sea legs, ya know?" Ellie explained.

Sean did know. He had been divorced two years now.

"Well, I know a little about that. My ex and I have been history for a couple of years. I wasn't ready to date anyone for a while, mainly because I wasn't too trusting. Her leaving me for a neighbor, and so-called friend, was a little hard on my ego."

Ellie reached across the table and touched Sean's arm.

"Sean, let's just take a chance and see where it goes, no guilt trips or pressure. I enjoy being with you, and if you want to come down this summer and visit, you will always have a place to stay. I have plenty of room in either house!"

Sean smiled, "I think that sounds like a good way to proceed. I just don't like the idea of maybe someone else taking my chances!"

Ellie laughed at Sean's jab. *Who else did he think might take his chances?*

After dinner, they walked out to the riverfront. There were barges going up and down the river, and Ellie couldn't help but think about the Cumberland River, and Mimosa Grove. As she and Sean walked along the pathway, he reached to take her hand in his.

Ellie felt a sudden charge in her body when Sean leaned close and asked, "Are you okay with this?"

Ellie smiled, "Of course. Thank you for tonight. It has been just what I needed."

They walked over to the railing that overlooked the river. The sun had started to set, and the streetlights would be coming on at any moment. Sean let go of Ellie's hand and put one hand on the railing, and the other behind her back. Ellie liked the feeling of him near her. It had been a long time since she had felt any romantic feelings, but whatever the reason, she was letting the good feelings carrying her along. Sean turned to her.

"Thank you for tonight, Ellie."

He bent down to touch his lips softly to hers, pulling her into to his arms. Ellie returned the kiss, feeling a warm, delicious feeling spread throughout her body. When they moved apart, neither made an effort to talk. They just stood, still with his arm around her waist, watching the sunset.

Before it got too dark, they walked back to the parking lot. Sean opened her door, and then walked around to start the car.

"You still up for a trip to Pet Smart?" Sean asked.

"Of course I am! I have to get a doggie bed, puppy chow, and toys," Ellie said.

When they arrived at her condo, he opened her car door, grabbed her purchases, and then held her hand as they walked to the house.

"I had a great evening, Sean," Ellie softly said.

"Me too, Ellie."

He leaned down to take her in his arms.

"I could get used to this." Sean said as he kissed her long and passionately.

This time, he was making a statement: he would like to be exclusive.

"Ellie, when are you leaving for Tennessee?" Sean asked as Ellie searched for her keys.

She told him that she would be leaving Friday, maybe Saturday morning. Sean looked disappointed.

"I have to play a double-header Saturday, but if you need me to help, just holler."

Ellie thanked him, and said he was welcome to come over tomorrow to see her puppy.

"Sure, I'll come by for a quick visit; don't want to be in the way. If you're going to be packing for the summer, you don't need me hanging around."

Ellie smiled, "I don't mind. Thanks again, Sean, for the good time."

Sean gave her a quick peck on the forehead, waited for her to go inside.

Ellie stood inside the door for a moment before going into the kitchen to put her purse on the counter. *What in the world was I thinking tonight? Letting him kiss me, and encouraging it? I can't start something now . . .*

The rest of the evening was spent packing. Ellie wanted to get her two largest suitcases filled with her summer clothes and shoes, and then pack all of the necessary toiletries. There was so much to think about, since she would be stocking the house with everything. She decided to wait and buy the majority once she got there. She would have both months, June and July, to spend in Tennessee, only planning to come home once each month to be sure bills were paid and the condo was still standing. She would have to come home in August to decide what to do about school. That was going to be the hardest part. Then there was Sean. Ellie finished putting her luggage in the spare bedroom, and, as she started out the door gave a glance at the items on the bed that had been brought from Mimosa Grove.

Ellie decided not to leave the items in the house while she was gone to get the puppy. She would load everything tomorrow in the back of the truck, and then take the truck over to the McNeal's house. Trying to concentrate on names, the thought of a Yankee being in the South made her think of Sherman. That didn't seem to work for her. She had always loved General Stonewall Jackson. Naming him Jackson, and calling him Jack for short, was growing on her.

As the mantle clock in the living room struck twelve, Ellie began to feel the butterflies in her stomach: taking on a little puppy and moving into a new home for the summer. Thinking about seeing Riley again, his comment about the day that they had spent together was running through her mind. The loss of his wife and little girl weighed on her mind as well. A restless soul that June evening, Ellie tossed and turned throughout the night, dreaming about her encounter with Sean.

She briefly awoke, sometime during the night, and was surprised at having such explicit thoughts about Sean. When she finally dozed off again, her dream changed to another time, a place she had never been. She walked through a dark grove of trees, trying to find her way out to the light. She was lost, and couldn't find her way out. She began running, feeling that someone was chasing her. The branches that hung down into the path slapped at her arms and leaves brushed her face. She caught the hem of her long skirt on a log that had fallen near the pathway, ripping a hole into the fine material. Her heart began to beat faster in her chest, as if she would faint from exhaustion. Who was behind her? The sound of twigs snapping and leaves rustling were getting closer. Ellie was having a hard time breathing, her lungs burning from trying to gulp air into mouth as she ran faster. Ahead of her, she saw a faint light coming through the branches of the trees. The edge of the woods loomed ahead, if she could only make it without losing her footing on the uneven path.

Just as she reached the edge, a hand reached out to grab her arm, and Ellie was jerked around to face her unseen follower, the face of the Confederate soldier was inches from hers. She could see the panic in his eyes, and could feel his warm breath on her face. His eyes implored her to listen to him.

"Why are you running from me? Please, you're the only one who can help me."

Ellie tried to pull free, to wriggle her arm from his grasp.

"Why me? I can't help you," she gasped, out of breath.

Ellie sat upright in the bed, the cover clenched in her fists, her breathing irregular. Her eyes searched the room, which was bathed in darkness except for the moonlight streaming into the room through the blinds. *What in heavens' name is going on with me? Am I losing my mind?* Ellie tried to slow her breathing. Would this aparation haunt her for the rest of her life? She wouldn't let this silliness drive her away from a wonderful opportunity this summer. Now she was more determined than ever to find out what Raford Collins wanted of her. The sooner she moved into Mimosa Grove, the sooner she could put this ghost to rest.

Ellie fell asleep after what seemed an eternity. By the time she awoke the next morning, the sun had been shining for a couple of hours. She couldn't believe the clock on the nightstand displayed 9:00. *Good grief! I have slept half the day away. I have so much to get done, plus I want to have everything loaded for when I leave in the morning.* Ellie was chastising herself, as she moved from bathroom to the kitchen.

Walking into the bright, sunny kitchen, she remembered her dream from earlier that morning. She felt herself blush at the thought of what she had remembered doing with Sean. What if he was thinking similar thoughts, after their passionate kiss by the river? She still found the memory pleasant, and half heartedly wondered if leaving now was such a good idea. Not having felt passionate with Brad for several years prior to divorcing him, she'd almost given up on ever experiencing it again. Sean had given her reason to hope for a loving relationship. She waited for the coffee to finish brewing, grabbing her favorite mug, one she had acquired from her grandmother, from the cupboard.

As a child, she would drink coffee with her grandmother during her morning rest. Of course, Ellie would mostly have milk in her cup, but what a grown up privilege her Grandmother Camden had shared with her. Eating a granola bar and enjoying her coffee, she began to sit out the items for the puppy. Ellie was glad Sean had suggested puppy pads that encourage potty training. The food and water bowls were cereamic, and Ellie would later paint his name on the front. She really liked Jackson, and that would be his name. Ellie reached for the two chew toys, washed and dried them, and laid them in the kennel crate she had bought.

She went to the closet and brought out a rug that had been in the bath at her home with Brad. She brought it, thinking it would go in one of the condo's bathrooms. Now it would be a nice, warm bed for Jack. She made a quick call to Angie McNeal, asking if it would be all right to come get the puppy. When she told her a good time, being around noon, Ellie busied herself with getting all the suitcases and bags carried out to the truck. She also put the hatbox, Bible, photographs, and diary back into the trunk. Wrapping each of the items from the large trunk, she placed them into a tote, leaving the antique trunk inside the back bedroom. She would throw a blanket over it, and take the smallest trunk back to Hendersonville. After two more trips to the truck, she was ready to go pick up her puppy.

Making sure the check was inside her purse for the McNeals, she drove from Newburg to Evansville. In an hour, she was heading back to her house with Jack. He was absolutely precious. Thankfully, Angie had given her a whole bag of puppy food that he had been eating, so his tummy wouldn't have to adjust to a new food. Ellie put him on her lap as she drove down the highway, chatting to him as if he were a child.

Arriving at her condo, she pulled the truck into the bay, and locked all the doors. Jackson's deep, brown eyes would surely melt butter.

"You are just too stinkin' cute, you know that?"

Jack chewed on her finger, and Ellie could feel the razor sharp puppy teeth that gnawed on her nuckle.

"I'm going to introduce you to your chew toys, Jack!"

Ellie carried the pup into the house, after he did his business in the grass.

Jack climbed onto Ellie's legs and fell fast asleep. Their bond was forged, and Ellie had found an outlet for her sadness over not seeing her child. The puppy was placed in the crate and Ellie went about getting her packing finished for the next morning's trip. Having written instructions for Char, she made sure all the windows had their protective bars placed in the sills, trusting Char's police friend to check on her home.

Char was on her way with her puppy, Bella, so that she and Jack could play for a while. Ellie was on the back porch when she heard the doorbell. Standing in the door were Char and Bella, and of course, Bella already had on a little studded collar. Char brought her new pup into the house, and the two carried their newest family members out to the back patio where they could play within the fenced yard.

Ellie and Char went over the plan for watching the condo the next two months.

"I want to come and see your plantation home, so I'll call and see when a good time would be for Bella and me to make a house call! I don't think we have ever been apart more than a few weeks, Ellie. Even during college, we made sure to visit one another. What are we gonna do for two months?"

Ellie hugged her best friend, "I don't know what I would do without you. I have to do this though: it's more than just keeping my part of the inheritance agreement."

Char looked puzzled.

"What else is going on?"

Char knew her best friend better than anyone else, and keeping a secret from her was almost next to impossible.

"Char, I want to tell you everything, and I will, when the time is right. Trust me. I don't know if even I believe everything at this point."

Char was concerned, and voiced her opinion.

"Ellie, are you in some kind of trouble?"

Ellie looked surprised at Char's statement.

"Heaven's no! There are just things I don't know the answer to yet, and that is why I need to spend time at Mimosa Grove and Hendersonville. Really, Char, it is okay. I promise!" Ellie exclaimed.

Ellie wasn't sure she believed her own pleadings, but she didn't want her friend worrying about her.

"If you say so, I'll let it go, for now."

"I want you to come and visit as soon as I get settled. I'm anxious to show off my ancestral home," Ellie beamed.

"So what time are you leaving tomorrow?" Char asked.

"I need to make a stop in the morning, but I want to be on the road before lunch," Ellie said.

Ellie went to see what Jack and Bella were chewing on, and pulled a part of a bird's nest that had fallen down out of the tree between her property and the neighbor's.

"I hope these two aren't part billygoat!" Ellie chided.

Char picked up Bella and walked back into the house with Ellie.

"I need to be heading home, Girlfriend. I bought Bella a pink puffy pillow to sleep on. I guess this is my only shot at being a mom, so I am going to indulge my little princess!" Char laughed.

Ellie gave Char a hug, and thanked her for being such a good friend. She gave her spare key to the condo, and told her to make a quick trip by the house a couple of times a week, since it was on her way home from the office.

"You be careful, Ellie. Call me when you get there, too!"

Ellie smiled, "Yes, Mom. I will!"

The two hugged again, and Ellie walked Char to the door. Char carried Bella out to her car and drove off down the street.

Ellie took Jack and placed him in his crate.

"Now it's time for your nap, Jack. Mama needs to get some things done, and you have had a big day."

Ellie closed the crate door, and Jack took a few moments to settle down and go to sleep.

"I hope you sleep all night, buddy." Ellie finished her packing, and then grabbed a bite to eat.

As she was finishing her dinner, her cell phone began ringing. She picked up the phone, and saw that Sean was calling her.

"Hey Sean, what's up?" Ellie asked.

"I was just checking on you and the new pup. How's he doing?"

Ellie looked over to the crate, "He is passed out. Char brought Bella over, and they had a big time playing in the back yard. I think they already had separation anxiety."

Sean took a deep breath and asked, "You mind if I swing by on my way over to mow Mom and Dad's yard?"

Ellie smiled, thinking about their kiss, "Sure, that would be great. Have you eaten?"

"Yeah, I grabbed a bite earlier. I won't keep you long, just wanted to tell you goodbye."

He sounded sincere, and Ellie didn't think he would expect more.

"Okay, just stop in whenever. I'll be here!"

Sean was heading out the door as he said, "All right, I'll see you in a few."

Ellie suddenly felt the need to touch up her makeup.

In a few minutes, Sean was standing outside, with one foot propped on the top step of her porch. Ellie looked at him for a minute, admiring his good looks.

"Hey stranger, come on in."

Sean smiled and walked past her into the entry hall. She offered him a glass of tea, which he gladly accepted.

"That sounds good; I had better load up before I start mowing. It is really getting hot out there."

Carrying his glass, he moved over to the crate, peering in to see Jack sleeping peacefully on the furry rug.

"He's a cute little guy. What did you name him?"

"I decided on Jackson, after General Jackson. But I'm calling him Jack," Ellie explained.

"Well, he will make you a good watch dog; I can tell he is going to be ferocious." Sean chuckled as Jack was obviously having a dream, his short little legs jerking in his sleep.

"Yeah, I can tell he is going to be a killer watch dog!"

Ellie moved over to sit on the stool beside Sean.

He turned and said, "You know, I'm really going to miss you; especially after last night."

Ellie blushed and said, "I enjoyed our date too."

Sean leaned in closer, "I didn't just mean the date."

He brushed his finger across her forehead to move a lock of hair that had fallen into her eye.

"I know what you meant, Sean. I'll miss you too, but it won't be forever."

Sean reminded, "I'll be here, so just remember you have someone waiting for you."

Ellie wasn't sure how to take that, but she smiled. Sean finished his drink, and started to get up.

Ellie thought he might stay just a while longer, but he said, "I told the folks I would be there by four, and Dad gets antsy when the grass isn't mowed by Friday night. I would love to stay though."

Ellie walked with him to the front door. Sean put his arm around her waist and pulled her to him for a hug. Ellie put her arms around his waist, and patted his back, in a friendly gesture.

"I hope you don't think I'm moving too fast, but I can't let you leave without another kiss."

With that, he leaned down to gently touch his lips to hers. Ellie moved in to him, and the kiss became more passionate. The room started to spin, giving Ellie a feeling of lightheadedness. If she didn't stop the kiss soon, she felt her legs might buckle. He might give the impression of a computer nerd at work, but he knew something about romance. When Ellie ended the kiss, Sean leaned down and pecked her forehead with one more.

"You be careful now, and call me when you get to your stopping off point."

Ellie gasped, "I will. And thanks again for stopping by."

Sean winked and said, "It was my pleasure."

Walking outside, he waved goodbye.

*"To forget one's ancestors is to be a brook without a source,
a tree without a root."*
- Chinese proverb

Chapter 6

Ellie woke early Saturday morning to the sounds of a puppy wanting out of his crate. She stumbled down the hall into the utility room where the crate was sitting; Jack had not been able to make it through the night.

"Oh no, Jack! You haven't gotten the idea of potty training yet, I see."

Ellie went to the cage and lifted Jack out.

"Come on; let's go outside to do your business, or what you have left in you."

Ellie could see she would have to clean the utility room and the crate before loading it for the trip. Jack's short little legs waddled out through the tall grass while Ellie sat in the chair on the patio.

The air had a fragrant smell, due in part to the honeysuckle vine that grew up the fence behind the condominium. Jack was busy chasing a grasshopper through the grass as Ellie tried to think about the things she needed to do before leaving. She was glad the truck was loaded, and all that was left was a quick trip by the cemetery before she headed south to Tennessee.

Ellie left a note on the bar for Char, and then made sure to double check the house once more. She carried her purse and Jack out to the truck. Backing her truck out of the driveway, her thoughts turned to Sean. She had wished there would have been time for him to come by this morning, but she wanted to make the drive to Tennessee as quickly as she could. She would have to make stops along the way for him. She pulled into Green Hill Cemetery a little after nine, and walked back to the newly mowed gravesite of her parents. As she stood thinking about her parents, she wondered if there could really be such a thing as ghosts. Ellie wished that she could see her father, just one more time, and she had so many questions for her mother. After quietly bidding farewell to her parents, she walked back to the truck. She pulled the truck around the lot and out to the highway. In about nine hours, she'd be pulling into the driveway of Mimosa Grove.

The trip took Ellie a little longer than she had anticipated, due to Jack's frequent need of a walk in the grass. Ellie was glad for his company though. He was content to walk in her footsteps or beside her, still unsure of the world around him. She had bought a small collar and lead, and thought it would be a good idea for him to learn how to walk on a leash. She drove into Hendersonville around seven o'clock. The area was still familiar to her, and she made her way through town quite easily.

She had thought about calling Riley Langley. She wanted to ask him to meet her at the house, just to show her where the fuse box was located. In all their exploring, she had forgotten about the important things. She couldn't even remember if there was a utility room with a washer and dryer. She might need to have a set bought and delivered, since she would be staying at the house all summer. She hated to bother him, but he did tell her to call him if she needed anything. Besides, she would have to call him about coming over to the courthouse to sign paperwork. She'd do that tomorrow.

Tonight, she would make a quick trip to Mimosa Grove, and then come back into town just for the night. She didn't feel comfortable spending the entire night alone there alone without knowing more about the house's utilities. The drive to Mimosa Grove was a pleasant one. The sun would still be up for a few more hours, and Ellie wanted to try to carry in her totes and suitcases, along with the trunk. Jack was becoming restless in his crate, and she figured he was hungry, thirsty, and in need of a bathroom break.

She remembered where to look for the big horse barn, and her driveway came into view very soon. She pulled into the gravel drive, parked, and got out with the keys. The gate was easier to open, now that she had done it before. She pulled her truck through, parked again, and walked back to close the gate and lock it. Jack seemed to know he was going to be able to get out of his crate; no sooner had she pulled up the long drive than the whimpering began. "Okay! I know you are about to spring a leak. Mamma will open up the crate so you can do your business." Ellie put the truck in park, and walked around to take her purse and the crate out on the passenger side. Carrying the crate up to the large porch, she sat it down.

She didn't look up, but felt that eyes were upon her, watching her every move. A cold shiver went up her spine, and her stomach felt as though a multitude of butterflies had been unleashed. Jack walked out of his crate, sniffing the porch. Ellie reached down and picked him up, carrying him out to the grass. She sat on the steps, waiting for his short little legs to take him out in the grass to relieve himself. He came back to Ellie, quite pleased with being out of his virtual prison. She walked over to the camper shell and flipped up the top. Inside was his water dish and bowl, and Ellie had prepared a baggie of food and water bottle full of cold water for him.

As he quickly ate his dish of food, Ellie scanned the area around the house, looking closer than she had before. She thought of the first time Camille Townes had seen Mimosa Grove. How beautiful it must have been, the white of the clapboards, the freshly painted shutters, the slate roof perfect and giving off the reflection of the sun. Ellie tried to imagine the mimosa trees surrounding the house. The diary explained the layout of the outbuildings and trees that surrounded the house. *Aunt Lavina's letter had mentioned the family cemetery beyond the grove of mimosa trees....* Ellie looked closely at the trees to the left of where she was sitting. Jack had come to Ellie's side now, whimpering.

"What's wrong, Jackson? Are you afraid to be away from Mamma?"

Ellie bent down, picking up Jack and carrying him in her arms; she took her purse, with the camera inside, and put the strap over her shoulder. She wanted to take more pictures, for insurance purposes. With that many period antiques, she knew she would need a good policy to cover over and above the value.

Ellie's eyes were drawn to a particular spot in the woods that was to the left of the grove of trees. She had seen this in her dream; she had seen Raford Collins in the woods. *Stop it, Ellie! I have to get a handle on this. He can't hurt me!* Jack snuggled down inside Ellie's arms. The sun had not gone down since she arrived, and Ellie loved the feel of it on her face as she walked around the house. She looked up at the house, wondering if she was truly alone. At one time, a flower garden had been lovingly tended, offering a variety of perennials. To the rear of the house was a grape arbor, long ago forgotten. She made a mental note to work on getting that cleaned out. From the back of the house, down the pebble path was a trellis. It was covered in climbing roses, and around the trellis were a variety of rose bushes, in dire need of tending.

Ellie kept walking towards the grove of trees, which were now nearly twenty feet high. Their branches gave the appearance of a pergola the farther she went. The sun's rays were only barely able to pierce the soft grass. It would have felt good to take off her sandals and walk barefoot through the grass carpet. If her toe hadn't stubbed the corner of a stone, she might not have seen the entrance into the small cemetery.

Ellie's breath stuck in her throat as she looked down to see a marker stone. Thankfully, this stone was not a grave marker, but actually one of the original stones that had been part of a wall that extended the perimeter of the small graveyard. Coming into full view were a small set of stone columns and an iron gate. Over time, the weeds had taken over both the wall and cemetery. *This is so sad, I have to get this cleaned out, but I'll need help.* Her mind centered on the possible ticks crawling up her legs as she walked through the grass. There were several taller monument stones, many weathered from years of being in the elements. She saw many small stones, each with a name and dates. Without her glasses, she wouldn't be able to make out the words.

To the rear of the cemetery was neat row of headstones. Ellie could see the name TOWNES, and there were two other names that she could barely decipher. With a good scrubbing, she might be able to get the moss out of the grooves. She felt sure these were the stones of her great-great-great-great grandparents, Daniel and Camille Burnell Townes. She walked along the row of graves, certain that the two little boys who never grew up were lying near their parents. Sensing a strong sense of duty to find out more about these people, her people, she walked the length of the cemetery, looking at the tiny headstones, and wondering when Townes ancestors began burying their dead in the local church or community cemeteries.

Making a trip to the local library was a necessity. Lavina George was a president in the United Daughters of the Confederacy, and Ellie could claim her heritage as well. Raford Collins also entered into her thoughts, and she wondered what help she could be to a long dead and most likely forgotten Confederate soldier. Having brought her letters and the trunk along, she would have the whole summer to find out information about her home and her family.

She carried Jack to the edge of the grove of trees, and then sat him down to toddle beside her. The house was bathed in the evening sun, starting to set low in the sky. The windows glistened with the orange glow of sunlight, and the breeze coming up from the Cumberland River below the house gave Ellie an air of excitement, knowing *this* was all hers.

"Come on, Jack!" Ellie called.

The little cocker spaniel tried to move his little legs as fast as his master's stride, but ended up tripping on the long ears that hung slightly below his shoulders. Ellie laughed at the sight of Jack, and bent down to nuzzle his soft, silky face. She picked him up and walked to the front door.

Her head was abuzz with decorating ideas. She would make a trip to the attic again, to see if there were any chairs or urns that could be carried down and cleaned up. Keeping the antique look was a definite must in replicating 1800's heyday. She turned the deadbolt key, and the door slightly creaked as she pushed it open. Seeing a paper on the table in the entry hall, she walked over to see what it was. It was a note, left there by Riley Langley. *Hmmm, what could this be about?*

> *Dear Ellie, I hope you don't mind my taking the liberty to come and bring you new light bulbs and fuses. I am known for keeping my promises. My father has listed the names and telephone numbers of the heating and air company that installed the furnace, as well as the utilities that are going to have to be switched over to you name. The water comes from a well, so you will have plenty of water for you needs. When you get this note, feel free to call, and I'll be happy to show you about the fuses and breaker box in the kitchen. Congrats again, and enjoy your new home! Riley*

Ellie had to smile at Riley's comment about keeping his word, and he had said the night they explored the house that her housewarming gift would be a light bulb. She was thankful he was so thoughtful, but she had inherited that hardheaded trait of doing things for herself from her dad, Frank Camden. She took the letter and dropped it inside her purse. She walked over and flipped the wall switch, which brought forth a sudden stream of light from a beautiful, antique, crystal chandelier. Illuminating the entry, it also spread light to the stairway and landing above. Ellie went back to the porch and carried the crate in for Jack to nap.

Before she did anything else, she would keep her promise to call Sean. Ellie sat down on the settee in the entry hall with her cell phone, and after only a couple of rings heard Sean's voice.

"Hey lady, how was the drive to Mimosa Grove?"

Ellie was impressed that Sean got the name right.

"It was a bit longer, with Jack having to pee more than me," Ellie laughed, "it was a nice drive though. We're in the house now."

Sean sat down on his kitchen barstool as the two began to catch up.

"I already miss you, Ellie."

"I miss you too, Sean, but you know you're welcome to come visit anytime."

Ellie wasn't accustomed to having a man miss her, and in some ways, felt uncomfortable.

"I know you'll be back before long, but I . . .we . . .had such a good time the other night."

Sean scratched his head, frustrated that he might not get another chance.

"Well, I haven't forgotten, Sean. I'm sorry that my timing sucks. I have to do this, for me."

Sean tried to sound supportive.

"I know, Ellie. I'll be here. Just keep me in the loop."

Ellie replied, "Okay, I will. You have a good week. I'm going to head back into Hendersonville to stay tonight. I need to clean and put new sheets on the bed before I stay here."

Sean was trying not to sound clingy.

"Please be careful."

Reflecting on his goodnight kiss, Ellie grinned.

"I will. I'll keep you up on everything. Good night, Sean."

"Night, Ellie. I'll talk to you soon."

After working for nearly thirty minutes removing sheets from the furniture and portraits in the gentlemen's parlor, Ellie heard the echo of footsteps across the floor above. Still, suddenly afraid, she stood frozen, as the footsteps began to make their descent down the stairs. It sounded like boots, with studs on the heels, coming down the stairs at a leisurely pace. Ellie could hear her heart beat.

From his crate in the entry hall, Jack began to whimper.

"I'll be right there, Jack!" Ellie said loudly.

No sound came from the stairway. She quickly walked into the entry, and summoning all her courage, gazed up the stairway. Nothing.

Thankful for the yelps of her little watch dog, Ellie decided that she would finish the rooms downstairs before dark, then head to town for the night. Her plan was to leave before dark. The clock in the hallway was no longer working, but Ellie's watch showed it was almost eight o'clock. Another hour and a half of daylight, but she wouldn't stay that long.

She had made her way over to the parlor, removing the sheets that covered the Victorian furniture and paintings. Busy with her thoughts, she took the sheets into the hallway when a movement caught her eye.

The apparition on the stairway appeared to be transparent, seeming to hover between the here and the beyond. Clearly, Raford Collins was making his presence known. Ignoring his form on the landing, she turned to go back in the parlor, her legs shaking. *Lord, please give me the strength to stay strong and do what I can to honor Aunt Lavina's requests. I want to stay in this house, so please give me the courage to do whatever it is I'm supposed to do here. Amen.*

Hearing a loud bang from the room above, and thinking it best she leave while it was daylight, Ellie went into the hallway and gathered her purse and Jack's crate.

Half joking, half defiantly, she looked up to the stairway saying, "I know you're here, but I am not letting you run me off. I'll be back, Raford Collins!"

With that, she walked out of the house, locking the door behind her. She drove back to the gate, which she quickly opened and locked again. The sun was beginning to set behind Mimosa Grove. Ellie would be back early tomorrow, and Raford Collins would have to mind his manners.

The motel, in which Ellie had spent the week previously, still had its vacancy sign lit when she pulled into the lot close to nine o'clock. She was worn out, and having heard the noises in the upstairs earlier, her nerves were on edge. The desk clerk, a young college-aged girl, was busy texting when Ellie walked in. Whether the girl didn't hear her or was rudely finishing her text, Ellie was being ignored.

She cleared her throat in an attempt to politely announce her presence. Obviously, the clerk was unaware of Ellie entering the lobby.

"Excuse me," Ellie softly said, "I would like to get a room for this evening, please."

The girl seemed distracted, but smiled saying, "Hello, just give me a moment, our computers are slow tonight."

She looked up and asked, "Will there just be one tonight?"

Ellie smiled, "Yes, and a puppy in a crate. I know it will be a little more for him."

The clerk figured the extra amount for the pet, and then gave Ellie her room key. She paid her bill, thanked the clerk, and headed back out to her truck.

Ellie hadn't eaten since a snack on the ride down earlier that afternoon. Her stomach was making all sorts of gurgling noises, and she was beginning to feel a bit light-headed from the lack of nourishment. After bringing an overnight bag, Jack and his crate, food bowl and food, and her purse into the room, she closed the door and sat down. Jack looked forlorn as he peered through the metal bars on the crate.

"Would the prisoner like to take yard privileges?" Ellie laughingly asked.

Jack was excited to be out of his crate. Ellie grabbed the room key, taking him out for a quick potty break.

She couldn't shake the feeling that Raford was not going to go away. He was in that house, for whatever reason, and until she figured out why, he wouldn't be leaving.

Ellie brought Jack back inside and left him to eat his food while she got ready for bed. First thing tomorrow morning, she would call Riley and thank him for his note. Then, going back to Mimosa Grove, she would check out the bed situation upstairs to determine what size she needed to buy. There were so many things she needed to think about, or should have thought about, before heading full throttle into this adventure. She took Jack out one last time, and put him inside his crate for the night. She crawled into bed, falling asleep before her head hit the pillow.

The alarm on Ellie's cell phone woke her before the sounds of Jack whimpering. She stumbled to his crate, and found that he hadn't had any accidents. Thankful for that, she attached his collar and leash before taking him out. The morning air was heavy; almost stagnate with the smell of industry hanging in the air. Anxious to get her day started, Ellie took Jack back in and searched in the complimentary packets for the coffee. Once that was brewing, she started to feel human once again.

As she sat eating a banana and munching on a granola bar, she began to plan the day's events. She looked for the number of Langley and Murdock, and then jotted it down on a piece of motel stationery. That would be the first order of business: to contact Riley. Next, she wanted to hurry back to Mimosa Grove to be sure there was a working washing machine. Its first job would be a load of rags she'd dirty from cleaning. Thankfully, she had remembered to bring the supply of cleaning materials from home. At least she remembered something! Ellie could hardly wait to see what treasures rested in the other rooms of the house.

After she dressed, she dialed Riley's office number, and Carol Pennington answered in her usual genial tone.

"Hi Carol, this is Ellie Morgan. Would it be possible to speak to Mr. Langley?"

Carol asked how Ellie was doing, and the two women shared a brief conversation about the recent acquisition of Mimosa Grove.

"Ms. Morgan, I will transfer you to Mr. Langley's office; he's off the other line now."

Ellie was glad that she caught him this early. Riley picked up the call immediately.

"Ellie, it's good to hear from you. How was your week?" Riley asked.

"It was fine, thank you. The reason I'm calling is to schedule a time when we could meet to go to the courthouse. Oh, and to thank you for your note."

Riley paused a moment.

"You saw the note? You're here in town?"

Ellie smiled, "Yes, I got in last night."

Now Riley was confused.

"I thought you were going to your daughter's this week?"

Ellie was impressed that he even remembered where she was supposed to be. That was something else she liked about Mr. Riley Langley: he paid attention.

"Well, it didn't work out. There was a change in her work schedule, so our plans fell through. I decided to just pack up and head down for the summer."

Riley didn't realize he was smiling, but it was quite noticeable.

"I had no idea you had made your decision. That's great! So, did you stay at the house last night?"

Ellie remembered her encounter.

"No, I had to go back to the motel. I need to buy some things before I stay tonight. I really appreciate you taking care of the light bulbs, and the fuses. That was a concern for me."

Riley was looking at his appointment book.

"I'm just working till noon today. I can meet with you on Monday about eleven. We could grab a bite for lunch and head to the courthouse."

Ellie was looking forward to seeing him again.

"That would be just fine, Riley. I'll see you then."

Riley copied the times in his appointment book.

"See you then. Bye now."

"Bye, Riley."

Riley Langley hung up the phone and sat staring out the window of his office. He hated to admit it, but he had been thinking about Ellie Morgan since she left last week. He had thought about Katie and Taylor every day for the last ten years, and last week had finally been able to go to the cemetery without breaking down. Riley pondered that maybe time starts to lessen pain, but it is always present.

Jamie Willard had been flying into Nashville and driving over to Hendersonville the last two years. They would have dinner, hang out for a night, and then she would leave the following day, driving back to the airport to work the flight back to D.C.

Jamie had meet Riley two years earlier when they sat together at the airport bar during a layover. Their relationship was one of convenience. The last time Jamie dropped in for a visit, it was the morning after Ellie had arrived. She stopped in unannounced, having spent the night in the apartment above Riley's office. He wasn't proud of his arrangement with Jamie, but he had no intention of making it more permanent.

Now there was Ellie. He couldn't quite decide what it was about her that he couldn't get out of his mind. He was attracted to her, yes, even though he guarded his emotions. When he buried his girls, he thought he had buried his ability to love another. Desiring to know Ellie better, he had subconsciously wished she would come back to stay at Mimosa Grove.

Ellie drove out to Mimosa Grove with the hopes of getting a list together for supplies and groceries. She wouldn't be able to take Jack to the store, so she would let him have the run of the house while she did her work. She'd start with the kitchen. She would have to clean out the fridge, oven and cupboards. It had been ten years since anyone had lived in the house. Thankfully, Riley's father had made sure the utilities were taken care of, as well as making sure the house was kept in immaculate condition over the course of the time it was in the hands of a caretaker.

When Ellie and Jack began working in the kitchen, she recalled the room that had been converted to the pantry and utility room. Lavina had bought a new washer and dryer some time back. They looked brand new, but had to be over twenty years old! Ellie would use them, until she could bring her set down. *Listen to me! I have already made my decision. How am I going to just quit my job and leave my hometown?* Ellie got to work on the appliances. They were covered in grime, having set for such a long time. Thankfully, she had remembered to load her microwave since she knew cooking might be an issue if there were no working appliances.

She walked from the kitchen to the bathroom, and heard the noise of footsteps walking around on the second floor landing. Not letting the sound frighten her, she decided to go upstairs to choose her bedroom.

"Come on, Jack. Let's go!"

Jack came running, his long ears causing his little short legs to trip. Ellie seeing that the stairs were still a challenge to such a small puppy, bent down to lift him into her arms.

"It's okay, little guy. Pretty soon you'll be beating me up and down the stairs."

Jack nuzzled his face into Ellie's neck, licking her skin with his rough little tongue.

When she got to the second floor landing, she stood, surveying the rooms that lay on each side of the landing, as well as one odd room straight ahead. Ellie wasn't sure why she chose it, but she went to the room that was in the front of the house. It would get the morning sun, which Ellie loved. It also had the large four-poster bed with the canopy, which Ellie would have removed and cleaned. As she started removing the sheets that covered the furniture, she decided that she would eventually make the larger room to the rear of the house her bedroom because it opened onto a sleeping porch.

For this week, she would stay in the front. She began searching inside drawers for sheets. The drawers were empty. The bed appeared to be a full size, but the ropes that had once been used to give the mattress support had long been transformed into a modern bed. Ellie sat on the bed, trying to picture what the different generations of children would have looked like running up the stairs, telling secrets to their siblings at night. Sadder images appeared too: the loss of a child and the death of a spouse. Still, there were images that remained locked away in the darkest corners of the house. Mimosa Grove held its mysteries, but Ellie planned to solve them.

Shaken from her daydreaming by the sound of footsteps, she looked for Jack. He came scurrying in, looking spooked. He turned back to the door, barking at an unseen intruder. The bark broke the silence that Ellie had grown accustomed.

"What now?" Ellie thought aloud.

She didn't have to wait for her answer. In the doorway, the outline of a human form began to materialize before her eyes. Frozen in place, Ellie quickly closed her eyes, wishing the image would disappear as before. Slowly opening her eyes, she viewed the Confederate soldier, his uniform appearing to be new with no effects of battle marring it. The soldier's physical characteristics were becoming clear. Jack backed away from the soldier, and Ellie quickly reached down to lift him into her arms, not sure if the gesture was partly for security or to comfort her little pet. She realized if she were to discover the soldier's purpose for haunting her, a great mystery would be solved.

Advancing toward the figure, which now was completely formed, she recognized him as Raford. He didn't come through the doorway, but stood just outside in the hall.

"Will you help me? I know you came back to help me."

Raford Collins was a real being, standing four feet away from Ellie. His voice was that of a young boy, the Southern drawl something Ellie had grown to love. She walked closer, but Raford didn't move. Jack began to bark again, a high-pitched yelp that broke the silence throughout and echoed into the hallway. Reaching out her hand, she felt the scratchy material of the grey uniform. Raford flinched, almost afraid of the touch. Immediately Ellie jerked her hand back, a look of amazement on her face.

"You're real," Ellie gasped.

Rafe's expression suddenly changed.

"You can see me? Now, can you please help me, Ma'am?"

"I don't understand how you're even here, Raford," Ellie said, shaking her head.

Raford Collins peered into the room, without crossing the threshold.

Ellie looked at Rafe and asked, "How did you get here? You aren't from this time, Rafe."

He looked at Ellie, dressed in her jeans and T-shirt.

"I don't know, Ma'am. You don't look like the girls I know. This is Hattie's room. Where's Hattie?"

Raford seemed almost embarrassed. *I can't believe I am sitting here talking to a ghost. I guess I should find out what he wants.* Ellie walked behind Raford, looking at his form from behind. He was small, maybe only couple of inches taller than her five foot seven inch frame. His dark curls, peeking from beneath his cap and reaching the top of his shell jacket, gave him a boyish look. His eyes were a deep blue, and his lashes were thick and long. The kepi hat that he wore had a unit insignia on the top, and she could make out an eleven.

"Well, I don't know why you decided to pick me to help you, Rafe, but maybe you should tell me why you need help, and how I can give it."

Ellie's breathing had returned to normal, and her legs were no longer shaking.

"You remember my name?" Raford asked.

"I saw your . . . . err, well, yes."

I can't tell him about the cemetery. I don't think he knows that he's dead!

"You aren't in your own time, Raford. I'm Ellie Morgan."

Ellie reached out her hand, not sure what it would feel like shaking hands with a ghost. His hands were not large, but long and tapered. The warmth of his hand surprised Ellie.

"Pleased to meet you, Miss Morgan. I'm Raford Collins. You can call me Rafe."

He smiled a sideways grin, something Ellie had seen before in a photograph.

"Well, you can call me Ellie, Rafe."

The two stood smiling at one another. If Ellie had told this to another living soul, they would have committed her that very day. She laughed out loud, causing Rafe to seem puzzled.

"So, as I said, what exactly is it that you need my help with?"

Rafe sat down on a chair in the hallway, his brogans stretched out before him. Ellie couldn't stop looking at the soldier sitting before her. It was as if she had been transformed back in time. She could only wonder what Rafe was thinking about his situation.

"I need you to find Hattie for me. I have to talk to her, have to see her. It's a matter of honor that is at stake, I have to talk to her."

Ellie felt so badly for Rafe, but didn't know what to say to him that would make him move on 'to the light' or whatever lost souls were supposed to do.

"Rafe, I don't know how to find Hattie. She doesn't live in this time."

Ellie's voice seemed to take on the sound of a compassionate friend that Rafe seemed so desperately to need. She was about to ask him about the letters when the doorbell rang, causing a look of fear to cross Rafe's face. In an instant, Rafe became a filmy vision before her eyes. Before she could tell him to stay, he disappeared from sight.

Ellie made it down the stairs with Jack in record time. She peered out the small window that flanked the side of the large wooden door to see Riley Langley was standing on the porch, looking out towards the fields that now were now fallow. Commanding her heart rate to slow, she opened the door.

"Well I didn't expect to see you out this way today. Please, come in."

Ellie moved back to let Riley come into the house. As she moved to let Riley pass, he caught sight of Jack.

Riley smiled at the pup and said, "Well, who do we have here, a new watch dog?"

Riley patted the pup's head, and Jack immediately began wagging the cropped stub of a tail in affection.

"Riley, meet Jack. Actually, his name is General Stonewall Jackson."

"He's cute. How old is he?"

"He's eight weeks old today, actually. Do you mind if we take him outside; we've been upstairs awhile, and I think he is antsy to go outside."

Riley followed Ellie through the hallway and into the kitchen. She opened the back door, and they stepped onto the porch that ran the length of the backside of the house. As Ellie sat Jack down so that he could toddle off the porch to do his business, she sat on the top granite step. Riley pulled an old metal chair beside her.

"So, what brings you out my direction of a busy work day?" Ellie smiled.

Riley looked down at his feet, suddenly not sure if she was annoyed that he dropped by unannounced, or just being congenial.

"I just wanted to check and make sure everything was okay. The house has been empty for a long time, and my daddy would be shamed if I neglected to check on a lady who had no other male relatives nearby."

Is he serious, or just trying to tease me?

Ellie looked up, shading her eyes from the sun, "Oh, so it's just business. I thought I was special or something!" Ellie chided.

"Well, you are. Not everyone inherits a plantation and the wealth to go with it. I just want to check that no 'long lost relatives' show up to relieve you of your good fortune. Not all people in the south are as neighborly as we Langleys, you know."

Riley was smiling now, enjoying their banter.

"It's okay, Riley. I know you're just keeping your promise to make sure Aunt Lavina's wishes are followed. Whatever your reason, I'm glad to see you again. I was thinking about heading into town after awhile. I have to buy some things to get me through today and the summer."

Riley tried to keep his expression in check.

"You decided to stay the whole summer? I think you'll love it here. It might be a little quieter than you're used to though. Did you realize your nearest neighbor is on the other side of the highway? You do have a passing boat every now and then. I'm sure you've seen the luxury homes on the other side of the river."

Ellie hadn't given a lot of thought to her being so isolated.

"I do have protection, if you're wondering."

Riley's head jerked up, not sure of her meaning. She saw the look in Riley's face and set his mind at ease.

"I mean, I have a gun."

Riley was glad for the clarification.

"Well that's good to know, but you realize you'll have to register it with the police department."

Ellie added, "I carry a concealed weapons license from Indiana. If I'm not making this my permanent residence, wouldn't that be enough? And don't forget I have a ferocious beast to guard me too!"

Riley wanted Ellie to be a permanent resident, and clarified, "Your permit is only good in Indiana; you'll need one for Tennessee as well. You shouldn't broadcast that you have a gun. As your lawyer, I'm offering you free advice."

Ellie raised her eyebrow, "As my lawyer? I thought you were Aunt Lavina's lawyer. I didn't retain you for myself," she bantered, trying to keep a straight face.

Riley continued to take joy in the ease of their conversation.

Jack waddled up, too short to make the large leap up the granite step. Ellie reached down and lifted him up, cuddling him under her chin.

"He is just the sweetest little fella. I think he'll be a good watchdog. He's already barked!" Ellie caught herself.

"I'm sure he'll have lots of critters to bark at out here in the sticks," Riley chuckled. Ellie thought of Rafe.

"Yeah, he has already found a surprise or two in the house. I'm glad he's here with me."

Happy that Riley just wanted to make a friendly visit, whatever his ulterior motives, Ellie was glad to know someone was watching her back. Her new independence, while liberating, was also unsettling at times. She always second-guessed her decisions, and if she messed up, it was only herself that could be blamed.

While Jack busily chewed on her finger, Ellie looked down the sloping backyard, overgrown and in much need of a lawn care service. Gazing beyond the weeds and buckplanton grass to the river below, she knew there had once been a dock here, the very one that brought Camille Burnell Townes to Mimosa Grove.

"You have a million dollar view, Ellie." Riley said.

Ellie turned, shading her eyes with her hand, "I know."

"You could take tours out here. You have a museum on your hands. Have you given much thought on what you're going to do with everything?"

Ellie had contemplated a good deal about it, but now that she had formally met Rafe Collins, her plans had taken a somewhat different turn.

"Yes, I am going to stay on the rest of the summer for sure, and I'm considering taking a year's leave of absence to get my finances in order and repair my home. I still have the house on Forest Drive to rent out, and I have a condo back in Indiana."

Riley didn't want to pry, but he was interested in Ellie's life. Sitting down on the step, he began scratching Jack's chin.

"You have a child, a daughter?"

"Yes, her name is Cassie. She just graduated last spring from the university in Evansville, and now has a job working her way up at the local television station in Baltimore."

Riley often fantasized what Taylor would have been like today had she lived.

"That is pretty impressive for a twenty-two year old. Is she your only child?"

Ellie didn't want to open Riley's wounds from the recent anniversary of the death of his wife and child, so she answered quickly.

"Yeah, Brad and I only had the one child. Sometimes I wish Cassie would have had a brother or sister, but I think I have the number of kids God intended for me to have. I sure do miss her."

Riley looked out towards the river, as if trying not to make eye contact. Her words touched a corner of his heart that he kept locked to those who didn't know about his loss.

"I understand having a child so far away is tough. She'll always be your little girl, no matter how much time passes."

Ellie looked at Riley and patted his knee.

"She's all I have left, Riley. My folks are both gone now, and I'm divorced."

The limbs of the mimosa trees began to sway with the gentle breeze that began to roll across the grove like waves reaching the shore. Riley wasn't sure what to say. He wanted to say something that would show he cared, but he remembered how empty kind words were after the deaths of his girls.

Smiling at Ellie, he said, "I was hoping I wasn't doing anything to raise folks' eyebrows by calling on a married woman."

Jack started chewing on a stick that was lying under one of the small maple trees that had been growing near the summer kitchen.

Ellie smiled and said, "I think Jack is trying to tell me he's hungry. He must know that was once a kitchen."

"I guess I should get back to work. I took a long lunch, and Carol is probably wondering if I got lost."

Riley stood, brushing the puppy hair off his jeans. Ellie walked across the wide porch to the back door, holding it open for Jack to run in.

"There is so much to be done around here. Maybe you could recommend a good lawn service, and I want to get the house painted this summer as well. If Aunt Lavina left me money to keep the house in good condition, I want to have it renovated before it sets through another winter."

Riley smiled, "I think Mimosa Grove has cast its spell on you. I'll make some calls."

Ellie was surprised by his offer.

"I would really appreciate your doing that," she said.

"Maybe you could ride out to see the folks sometime. I know they would love meeting Mrs. George's niece. Dad sure did think a lot of your great aunt and uncle," Riley added.

Ellie went over the cupboard to offer Riley something to drink, but saw that the cupboards were bare. She would need to buy some things to put in those cabinets. She didn't have any food in the house, and she still needed to finish cleaning.

"I would love to meet them, Riley. Sounds like fun. I do think I'll finish cleaning the downstairs as best I can, then head into town. I brought a truckload with me, but if I'm staying all summer, I don't think I can make it on cereal and lunch meat."

Riley walked down the hall and into the entry hall. He started to walk out when he heard what sounded like footsteps above.

"Did you hear that?" Riley asked, alarmed.

Ellie wasn't ready to tell Riley about seeing ghosts and decided to keep quiet for now.

"It's just an old house, makes all sorts of noises. I'm not too worried."

Riley wasn't sure he felt comfortable leaving without taking a walk upstairs, but he didn't want to overstep his welcome.

"Okay, I guess Jack would tear anyone limb from limb anyway. You're in good hands."

They both laughed at the thought of the cute, floppy-eared pup being a vicious watchdog.

"Remember to meet me Monday for our trip to the court house. I know you're ready to have the deed to the two houses and your cashier's check."

Ellie smiled, "I think it will feel good holding it, before it goes in the bank. I need to open an account here."

Riley and Ellie walked to the front porch, and he started down the large granite steps that led down the brick path to his car.

"Take care, Ellie. I'll be in touch. If you need anything, don't hesitate to call.

Ellie waved as he backed his Lexus out of the semi-circle.

Ellie spent the rest of the afternoon cleaning the downstairs. She found a broom and swept the floors, gathering a great amount of dust from the rooms, even with the carpets on the floor. She was so glad she remembered her vacuum cleaner. Putting Jack in his crate after he had eaten and taken his usual stroll through the yard, Ellie headed for town to purchase the supplies needed to get her through the first week or so at the house. She spent over $300 on groceries and things for the house. She would be glad to have clean sheets and a couple of thin blankets on the bed. She even purchased new pillows for the bed she would be sleeping in. Riley was right, she was living in a museum. It would take some getting used to!

Arriving back to Mimosa Grove with her truck loaded from the day's shopping; Ellie pulled in front of the house and turned off the ignition.

She was physically worn out from her morning of cleaning, and she knew she would need to spend the rest of the day dusting furniture and cleaning out the fridge and cabinets, but she was ready to call her cleaning craze quits for the first night. She had all summer, and she had to explore a little more.

Going into the front parlor to admire the furnishings, she placed the diary of Camille Townes on the entry hall table inside the small wooden box she had found in the gentleman's parlor. Ellie decided that was the library, and would call it Captain Townes' room. She had finished dusting the front parlor, and wished she had remembered to bring her radio with her. She had no television, and the silence was unsettling, especially in such a large old house. She was glad for electricity, as the rooms looked much prettier in the full light of the chandelier that hung from the ceiling. The height of the ceiling was at least nine feet, possibly ten.

Ellie imagined that those were once lit with oil or gas. She was looking at the portraits that were hanging in this room: the two girls' portraits were that of Caroline and Hattie Townes; she wasn't sure which was Hattie, but felt very sure that the pretty woman whose portrait hung above the fireplace was that of her great-great-great-great grandmother, Camille Burnell Townes. The family resemblance was unmistakable. Ellie knew that the family had money; it was apparent in the furnishings. She wondered what items throughout the house were Camille's. In the corner was a wreath. Ellie had seen one in the local historical society back in Newburg. It was called a Mourning Wreath, and she knew that the wreath's flowers were formed from human hair.

Peering into the glass box, she marveled at the workmanship. She felt it could be from several adult family members. Her attention presently was averted to the beautiful pianoforte. Ellie had been dying to play the piano since she first saw it. She expected that it would need tuning, but wanted to play it, regardless. Lying on the top of the piano was an old book, full of music from the late 1800's, she assumed. Her fingers almost trembled as she placed them on the ancient ivory keys. She remembered a song that she played on her piano at home, and she started playing from memory, filling the house with the melody. She loved the sound, much richer than her piano back home. She played for another hour, losing track of time, until Jack began to whimper.

Thinking he needed a potty break, Ellie turned herself around on the stool. Her heart sprang into her throat when she saw the image of

Rafe slowly becoming more substantial. He appeared to be listening to the music, not necessarily noticing her. As he stood there, she began to chord the only song she thought he might know: "*Dixie*".

When she had played it through, she turned back to see if he was still standing in the center of the room. He was facing Hattie's portrait, and his hand had moved up to his eye, making a swipe across his cheek.

"Can you help me find Hattie? I need to talk to her; I have to know why she didn't answer my letters."

Ellie walked closer to Rafe, who now was as real as she was. She sat down in one of the floral embroidered high back chairs, Rafe's back to her, still admiring the portraits.

"So you wrote the letters?" Ellie queried.

Rafe turned, looking as if she could see into his soul.

"You know about the letters I wrote?"

Ellie wasn't sure how much to tell him.

"Yes, I found them. Would you like to see them?"

Rafe appeared crestfallen.

"What are you doing with Hattie's letters? I sent them to Hattie."

Ellie walked into the front parlor, and reached into the trunk. Rafe was standing behind her, and Ellie was unnerved that he could move without a sound.

"Here, I found them upstairs. Remember when I saw you in the attic? That was when I found them."

Rafe touched the neatly wrapped stack of letters as if he were touching a hot iron. He looked at them, addressed to Miss Hattie Townes, from Pvt. Raford Collins. He slowly untied the faded red satin ribbon. He looked at each envelope. Only two had been opened.

"Why were they tied together? She didn't even read them."

Rafe was even more distressed after seeing the letters, now lying on the settee.

"Rafe, I only read a couple. I didn't open the others. I didn't even know about you until I had the dreams."

Rafe seemed confused.

"I don't know what you're talking about. I just know that I wrote Hattie all these letters, and I only got one back."

He reached into his jacket pocket, and brought out a yellowed envelope. He held it out.

"This is the only letter she ever sent. I don't understand. I already talked to her daddy, and I planned to marry her when I got furlough."

Ellie knew that Rafe was in love with Hattie, and she decided not to tell him that she had married another man.

Instead, she asked, "So you want me to find out why Hattie didn't answer your letters? Is that all you want?"

Ellie cocked her head to one side, as if to show disbelief.

"It's not really proper to talk about it with a lady. I've gotten myself in a real di-do, Miss Ellie. I have to find Hattie to talk to her."

Ellie was having a conversation with a ghost. She sat staring at her reflection in the mirror. Rafe was sitting right beside her, as real as Riley had been only a few hours before. Ellie had so many questions for Rafe.

"How did you get here, Rafe? I mean, it isn't 1861 any longer. You surely haven't been here for the last one hundred and fifty years."

Rafe seemed even more confused.

"I can't explain it. It is like walking into a fog, it's a mist like what creeps on the water early in the morning. I saw you upstairs, and knew you were who I was supposed to meet."

Ellie was more intrigued.

"So have you been here before?"

Rafe stood and walked back to where he could see the portraits.

"That is Mrs. Townes. That is Caroline."

Rafe pointed out to the portrait of the pretty young girl on the left. She had her hair parted in the middle, but large curls were cascading to her shoulders.

"She was older than Hattie. And that is Hattie."

He pointed to the picture on the right, the one who resembled her mother. Hattie Townes was a lovely girl. Her large green eyes seemed to dance as the portrait showed a playful side. She appeared to be slightly smiling.

"Do you have any photographs of Hattie? I have some pictures in the trunk, maybe you could tell me who they are."

Rafe appeared interested in what she had. Ellie walked over to retrieve the wooden box inside the trunk.

She nonchalantly asked Rafe, "So, could I go back in your time, the way you have come here?"

Rafe didn't answer her. He looked at the tin types from the box. He held up a picture frame that held the tin type of two young women.

"These two are Miss Caroline and Miss Hattie. It was taken when they were in Nashville."

Ellie looked at the picture. She looked up at Rafe.

"She's very pretty, Rafe. They both are."

Rafe smiled, "I wanted to make her my wife. Then the war started, and everything changed."

Ellie knew her Civil War history, being a history teacher. She also knew that the history of Hattie Townes didn't have her marrying Rafe Collins. She wouldn't tell him, because she didn't know what had happened to cause Hattie to keep the letters sealed.

She looked back at Rafe again, "Can I come back with you?"

Rafe scratched his head.

"I reckon you could, but it's not safe. There's a war going on, Ma'am."

Ellie stared at Rafe.

"Can you take me back there? I would be very careful."

Ellie hoped she still had some feminine persuasion.

Rafe looked at Ellie, imploring, "Would it help you find Hattie?"

Ellie lied, "Oh yes, I need to go back to find her. She doesn't live here, now."

Rafe said, "I'll take you. Soon."

Ellie bent down to pick up the letters, and as she turned to tell Rafe about Aunt Lavina, he was gone.

"Rafe? Don't go yet."

But it was too late. Raford Collins had gone back to the dimension in time that held him in limbo. Ellie would need to do some studying. She had letters to read, and a diary to go through as well. If she were going to help Rafe rest in peace, she would have to know more about Hattie Townes.

"But those who came before us will teach you. They will teach you from the wisdom of former generations." Job 8:10

Chapter 7

The house was as quiet as tomb, and Ellie was thankful that she had brought her compact disc player. She missed having the noise of her television on during the evening back at her condominium. With papers to grade of an evening, she rarely had time to just sit and watch TV. Tonight, the sound coming from the compact disc player was a way to mask the quiet. Ellie couldn't stop thinking about Rafe and him telling her that she could go back to his time. Didn't she have to be one of the 'dearly departed' to be able to do such things. It didn't seem possible that she was having conversations with a dead Rebel soldier, and yet she had been doing it for the past two days.

Ellie had made good use of the time after Rafe's appearance. She had completely removed every sheet and covering from the downstairs rooms, and used a good supply of furniture polish to begin the tedious task of dusting the precious heirlooms in the home. A telephone would be installed as soon as possible. Her cell phone was fine, but she felt the need to have another means of communication. A satellite dish would be installed somewhere inconspicuous behind the house, so that she could have a connection to the outside world.

She was finding items that had belonged to other members of the Townes family. On the bookshelves were books that belonged to family members who lived sometime during the late 1800's or early 1900's. The names were unfamiliar to Ellie, but she had the family Bible and could investigate later. Inside the secretary of the gentleman's parlor was a pair of glasses in a very old, brown leather case. The glasses appeared to be from the 1800's. Ellie took the little spectacles, appearing to be from the 1800's, from their case and put them on. Looking in the large mirror that hung on the opposite wall, Ellie had to laugh. She removed them and began exploring further. The contents of the drawers had long been removed, with the exception of a small pocketknife, letter opener, and a small calendar from the Hendersonville Bank and Trust dated 1965.

Ellie peered into the small slots that went across the bottom portion of the large secretary and found nothing. Inspecting the books on the shelves more closely she found one that was different from the others. Similar to the small journal that Ellie had found down inside the trunk, it was larger. The only words across the leather bound book were faded, but the embossed lettering appeared to say *Accounts. Now this is interesting.* Beneath the cover was the musty odor associated with leather and paper that had been in a humid environment over a hundred years or so. The handwriting was beautiful: curls and swirls that were prevalent in Victorian times. This ledger belonged to Daniel Townes. In it was an inventory of the supplies bought over the course of several years. Ellie flipped the pages carefully to see details of life on the plantation. There were horses being sold to different gentleman from around the state, as well as a few from Kentucky. There were entries showing repairs being done due to a tornado that damaged the roof of the horse barn. Another page, one that seemed to jump out at Ellie, listed the name Isaac Collins of Nashville, Tennessee. In April of 1860, Isaac Collins purchased a mare from Daniel Townes for $250.

Ellie wondered if that is when Rafe was introduced to Hattie. The ledger listed payment to a tutor for the Townes' youngest child, Joseph Townes. The tutor's name was not given, but it did show payment sent for passage paid in advance to cover travel arrangement for the tutor. Ellie wasn't sure why this particular page intrigued her. She hadn't given much thought to the youngest Townes child. She knew from the family Bible that this youngest son of Daniel and Camille Townes had died in 1864.

She would go back to the cemetery and look for dates on the headstones. Ellie placed the ledger with Camille's dairy to continue reading. Enjoying her quest, she discovered many books that would have been useful to a farmer or plantation owner, but there were books on every interest. Several books were undoubtedly schoolbooks that were used by the Townes children, and later the children of Hattie Townes and their heirs. The portrait over the fireplace was clearly the owner of the home. He must have had the sitting for the portrait not long after settling in at Mimosa Grove, for he was young.

His dark eyes had the wisdom of a successful planter and businessman. Ellie wondered what kind of a father Daniel was to Caroline, Hattie and Joseph. She finished dusting the furniture in the room and walked back into the entry hall. Before it got too late, she would take Jack out to do his business, and then she would walk back to the cemetery to try and find the graves of Joseph, Daniel and Camille Townes.

Ellie stood on the wide back porch looking out towards the river. She took Jack's little chain and collar and walked silently through the grove of mimosa trees. The cemetery needed someone to take a weed eater through it, and then she would set about cleaning the headstones. Maybe Mrs. Eubanks at Resthaven, had a good recipe for that.

Ellie made her way through the overgrown cemetery. She could hear a mockingbird sitting in the tree nearby. The sun's rays were casting sunbeams down on two gravestones near the back of the cemetery, and Ellie was able to read the names: *Cpt. Daniel Townes-Camille Burnell Townes.* Below the names were dates that were also hard to read, but as Ellie felt inside the grooves of the numbers, she was able to make out the year 1880 as a date of death for Daniel, and 1864 for the death of Camille. Ellie read the date of Camille's death and wondered what the connection was to the youngest child, Joseph. She looked around to the headstones beside the parents of Hattie Townes, and noticed the two small stones she'd seen earlier.

She walked farther down the row of headstones and then she saw it, *Joseph Burnell Townes, July 8th 1864.* She assumed that mother and son died within weeks of one another, but would have to work on the large headstone. Ellie walked along the last row of headstones. The names were weathered, and it would take Ellie's making a gravestone rubbing to read them more clearly, but she would have a harder time deciphering the dates. Getting the cemetery into a respectable state would be another 'must do' this summer. Riley had left Ellie with a phone book and numbers that his father had contacted over the last ten years for work around Mimosa Grove. She would wait until Monday for the cashiers' check, and then she could start delegating work on the property. She and Jack walked back through the two rows of headstones. Ellie would make sure that her people were not forgotten.

She decided that she would walk down to the river, something she had wanted to do since she got back to Mimosa Grove. Putting Jack's leash on, she crooned, "Come on, little fella, let's take walk." Ellie was anxious to see the river up close, but wasn't about to get too close with Jack. The Cumberland River made a snake-like path through Hendersonville and the Southern portion of Sumner County. Million dollar homes dotted the shoreline up the river. She felt very blessed to have such a beautiful area to call home. How this plantation and all of its acreage had not been sold to developers was a mystery to her. Moving a little closer to the river's edge, she could see the remains of what appeared to be stone pylons in the water. Ellie imagined that this was the very spot where Daniel Townes welcomed his bride, Camille, to Mimosa Grove.

When Ellie turned to walk back to the house, the sun was sitting behind her, bathing the rear of the plantation in warm orange light. Seeing a figure standing on the second floor porch, she knew it was Rafe. The grove of trees that he and Hattie had walked through was still to the left of the house. As Rafe began to fade from view, Ellie had to wonder how many years he had repeated this action and pondered if her aunt Lavina had met Rafe.

Making her way into the kitchen, she poured a bowl of puppy chow for Jack. Grabbing a bottle of water from the fridge, she poured it into Jack's water dish. His silky black ears dipped into the bowl as he lapped the water. "Oh Jack, you're getting your ears wet!" Ellie whined, as she took a kitchen towel to the hardwood floor. Ellie poured a bowl of cereal and sat at the counter to eat. A small kitchen table would be a good investment. Somewhere in storage, there would be furniture from the home on Forest Drive. She would need to see what was worth keeping. The house on Forest Drive would be sold. Just as she was thinking about the surmounting list of things she had to do, the phone rang.

"Hey Girlie, I was beginning to think you'd forgotten about me! How are things going?" Char asked.

Ellie felt as though she were about to be scolded for not checking in, just like with her dad.

"Char, I'm so sorry. I've really been up to my eyes in dust and cobwebs. This house is a museum, and it takes forever to get it back in living order."

"I understand, Ellie. Is there anything I can do? Everything back here is just fine. I checked on the condo last night, and everything is in place, just as you left it."

Ellie was relieved to hear that, and said," No, I think I can take care of it all. I just need to get all the legal matters squared away. Thank you, and I appreciate you being there for me, Girlfriend."

"I'll try to do better about keeping you in the loop, I promise, *Dad*."

Ellie had a way of adding that in when she wanted Char to stop treating her like a child. It had been something the two had shared since they were in high school.

"I just wanted to check on you. I saw Sean at Pizza King tonight. He was picking up an order to go, and I was in there eating alone, as usual. He remembered me, so we stood and talked for a few minutes. I think he really is taken with you, Ellie. Are you two serious?" Char asked.

Ellie had been wondering herself about her feelings for Sean.

"Char, I really enjoyed the date we had the other night, but I don't know if I want to get in a serious relationship right now."

Ellie wasn't sure why she wasn't more into Sean.

"Ellie, if you aren't ready, you're not ready. Just take things slow. You've had a bad divorce and you lost your dad. You haven't had time to really relax and not worry about everyone else."

Char knew the stress that Ellie had been living under, so she was trying to be supportive.

Ellie let out a sigh, "Char, right now, I just want to enjoy the summer here. I have more to tell you, but I want to see what happens first."

Char wasn't sure what that meant, and she wasn't used to being out of the loop where Ellie's life was concerned. It was enough that Ellie was happy, so she didn't push any further.

"Ellie, I'm here for you, whatever and whenever you want to tell me."

Ellie was relieved that Char was such a good friend.

"Do you think you can come down for the Fourth of July? I was thinking about having the house and grounds in better shape by then."

For the first time, Char was getting the feeling that the adventure Ellie was on wasn't just a summer vacation. Her best friend might be considering a more permanent move. The conversation soon ended, with a promise of a possible visit over the Fourth of July weekend.

Ellie laid the cell phone on the table in the hallway, and decided to take a bubble bath in the big iron tub upstairs. Making sure the deadbolt at the front door was latched; she took her cell phone and walked up the stairs to the first landing.

"Jack, come on, boy," Ellie called.

In just a few seconds, the puppy came bounding around the corner from his crate in the kitchen. His little legs were almost too short to make the first step, but once he got the hang of it, started climbing the stairs easily behind Ellie.

She stood at the top of the second floor, listening to quiet all around her. The sun had set, and the downstairs had gotten dark except for the glow of the chandelier hanging in the entry hall. Ellie walked to the room in the front of the hall, and looked around the now empty space. She tried to imagine what it could have been when Daniel Townes had the house built. There was a row of shelves that spanned the width of one wall, and across the front wall was a large window that looked down onto the roof of the front porch. She could see that at one time, the window had actually been a door to another porch. Other than those features, the room was plain and without decoration.

Ellie had carried all of her luggage and trunks from the attic and placed them on the floor in this room. She also kept the vacuum cleaner and other comfort items from home in this room to keep the clutter from the other bedrooms. As she turned to take her pajamas and toiletries into the bathroom, she suddenly thought about the soldier. Surely he wouldn't just show up while I'm bathing! She hoped that her privacy wouldn't be invaded, and she made a request out loud.

"Raford Collins, if you can hear me, I would appreciate you not just showing up without warning. It is neither fitting nor proper for you to just wander about unannounced."

Ellie thought as silly as it was, it couldn't hurt making her petition known. She walked into the large bathroom, called for Jack, and closed and locked the door. The huge iron tub began to fill, and Ellie sank into the luxurious warm bubbles.

While she soaked away the day's cleaning and meeting with Rafe, her mind wandered to Riley Langley. His handsome looks and Southern charm had caught her eye more than once. She couldn't get his deceased wife and child out of her mind. She wasn't sure if he would ever share that part of his life with a stranger, but she knew a little something about losing a loved one. He had asked her to go with him to meet his folks. What was that all about? She would like to see more of Riley and would enjoy a social call whenever he decided to stop by. Ellie wanted to convince Rafe about getting her back to his time. She felt that would be the only way she could find out why Hattie hid the letters in the attic and married someone else when it was evident she loved Rafe.

Ellie loved the large tub and the spacious bathroom, an obvious addition to the upstairs in the last century. She quickly dressed and took her dirty clothes back to the small room. She decided to take the front room with the large four-poster bed. Thanks to Rafe, she now knew that she had chosen Hattie's room. She took the new sheets, mattress pad and blankets into the room and quickly began making the bed. The walls were painted pale blue and the woodwork remained in its original condition throughout the home. Ellie was thankful the later Townes descendants hadn't painted over the lovely woodwork. The small rocking chair in the corner of the room must have seen many a Townes rocked and put to sleep.

Ellie finished making the bed and walked back downstairs to get a cup of hot chocolate and let Jack out before bed. As she walked down to the entry hall, she remembered she wanted to read more from Camille's diary and wanted to get the two samplers out of the trunk and place them in the frames she found inside the drawers of the sideboard in the dining room. She wanted to put them up in the blue bedroom, her bedroom.

After Jack had quickly done his business, Ellie came back inside and locked the back door. She found the cocoa in the cupboard and made herself a cup while she tried not to think about being all alone this first night in Mimosa Grove. She took a leisurely walk through each of the rooms downstairs, admiring all the antiques and furnishings that were lovingly preserved. Turning off the downstairs lights, and bringing her cocoa and the diary, she began making her ascent to the second story. Jack bounded up the stairs now, racing to the top before Ellie. When he reached the top, he began to sniff the floor, as if he were tracking something. He went from room to room, sniffing as he went first one way then another. Ellie had never let herself imagine more than one ghost haunted the home. One ghost in any house was one too many, or that is what she told herself.

"I promise that if you will keep your journals and records, they will indeed be a source of great inspirations to your families, to your children your grandchildren . . .and in that glorious day when our families are together in the eternities, we will already be acquainted."
-Spencer Kimball

Chapter 8

Riley had finished his beer and tossed the can into the trash. He had gotten accustomed to the quiet; though he would have to admit, he wouldn't mind hearing the sounds of a teenager in the house. Taylor would have been thirteen this summer. Riley missed his girls. He had avoided relationships until a respectable time had passed. In the last two years, he addressed his baser needs with Jamie. She was attractive, had a body to make any man look twice, and was independent. She was a substitute for the part of his life that was lacking attention.

Relaxing on his covered patio in the warm June evening, he began to think about the shallowness of his arrangement with Jamie. He would need to end the arrangement. Hearing the sound of a police siren, he felt his pulse race as he recalled the horror of his girls' accident. He only momentarily gave the siren his attention, centering instead on the reading of Lavina George's will when he met Ellie Morgan. She was someone he wanted to protect, even though she was independent. His Southern upbringing naturally caused him to offer help and hospitality to her. Ellie was a breath of fresh air to Riley's monotonous life.

He had poured all his energy into the law firm. When his father retired to enjoy life with his wife of fifty years, Riley was given his father's portion of Langley and Murdock. Mr. Murdock had been Donovan Langley's partner since 1965. The two had graduated law school together and started their own firm. William Murdock would soon retire as well, and at the present, had no one in line to take over his share of the firm. Riley's father thought well of Shelby and Lavina George. Shelby had given Donovan his first loan, and the two had remained friends over the years. Shelby George was a respected citizen of Hendersonville, Tennessee.

His family had been in Sumner Co. since the early 1800's. His family was what Riley's father had called *old money*. He and Lavina had lived a comfortable life between their two inheritances. Shelby had worked for many years as a loan officer, then the bank's president. He had been a member of the Sons of Confederate Veterans, and Lavina had spent her life volunteering to the various Civil War affiliations such as the United Daughters of the Confederacy and cemetery preservation. Although their lives were full, they were childless. Adoption was never mentioned, spending their lives helping the needy children in the community instead.

Riley had liked the Georges, and his father would look in on the couple regularly. After Shelby passed away, Donovan Langley began helping Lavina get her affairs in order for the day when she couldn't care for herself. It was then that she began to search out an heir for her large estate. Donovan had located a niece and nephew who lived in Indiana and it was decided that the heir to the Townes estate should be a female, as it had been that way since the beginning. When Lavina learned of the death of her niece, Elizabeth, she quickly changed her will to leave the estate to the daughter surviving Elizabeth Camden.

It was Riley's duty, upon the death of Lavina George, to make contact with her great niece. He had never thought about Ella Camden until his meeting with her that last week in May. He didn't want to be interested in her. His casual arrangement with Jamie had worked in the past. In fact, she had contacted him prior to his taking Ellie to Mimosa Grove. Jamie had been waiting for him at his apartment above the offices. He never brought her back to his house, his bed that he had shared with Katie. He would never be able to do that.

When he had arrived back at the apartment, she was waiting for him in the large bed, with two glasses of cognac. Her appetite for Riley was quite healthy, and he was satiated until the next time she would fly into Nashville. The morning after her layover, Jamie had overslept. She usually went down the back stairs and out to her taxi, not causing any embarrassing stares from Carol, his secretary. That morning, Jamie hadn't cared. She walked into the entry to leave the key, as if making a statement to the two women, one of which was Ellie. Riley had gone downstairs to get an early start to the day before his morning appointments, so was unaware of Jamie's theatrics.

Riley had been trying to keep his mind on his court schedule for the week, but he couldn't stop thinking about Ellie. He had given in to his thoughts and driven out to Mimosa Grove. Ellie wasn't upset with his dropping by, even welcoming him. He had been thinking about her comment, *she's all I have left*. He never thought about her having a loss in her life. He wanted to learn personal facts about her, which would involve more than just being her lawyer. If he pursued a personal relationship, he feared Ellie would think her inheritance was the motivation. He would have to try to convince her otherwise.

He wanted to call her tonight, but it was already ten o' clock, and he figured she would be worn out from her day of cleaning. He had an open invitation each Sunday to the family dinner, a tradition in the Langley family, and he would officially invite Ellie to come too.

He knew his mother would be awake, so he quickly dialed the number. Portia Langley answered the telephone, half-awake.

"Mom, did I wake you?"

He suddenly felt ashamed for calling so late.

"No, Dad and I fell asleep watching a movie on HBO. It's a free weekend, and he thinks he has to watch it non-stop." Portia laughed.

Noticing the time on the bedside clock, her jovial mood changed.

"Is everything okay, Honey?"

Riley heard the concern in his mother's voice and wanted to ease her mind.

"Everything's fine Mom. I just wanted to see if you would mind if I brought a guest tomorrow for lunch after church?"

Riley waited for moment, then continued, "I thought you and Dad would like to meet Mrs. George's niece, Ellie Morgan. She is staying in the plantation house this summer."

Portia was caught off guard. Riley hadn't brought a friend home for Sunday dinner in years.

"Riley, you just bring your friend along. Dad and I would love to meet her."

Riley was glad for his mother's approval.

"Ellie might have to bring her puppy along, do you mind?"

Portia was so glad that Riley was showing an interest in someone. He hadn't done that since he brought Katie Jacobs home from college.

"You just bring Ellie right along. Renae and Brent will be here with the kids, so it will be nice having a full table."

Riley smiled at that thought.

"Okay then, tell Dad 'Hi', for me, and I'll see you tomorrow around one o'clock. Love you, Mom."

Portia felt her eyes tear up as she said, "I love you, Honey. It will be good to see you tomorrow."

Portia set the phone back on the night table. *Well I'll be.*

Riley went back into the house, changing his mind and calling Ellie now. He hoped she'd still be up. She'd have to say 'Yes' now; he already told his mother he was bringing her.

Jack was smuggled into the bed beside Ellie while she read the diary. The curtains in the bedroom were blowing toward her, and a warm breeze drifted into the upstairs. She was reading the page prior to the birth of the baby entry. Gifts had been sent before the freezing waters would make river travel slow, if not impossible. The large dining room table, chairs, and sideboard were the most impressive pieces that came by flatboat down the Cumberland River. These were gifts from Camille's mother. Also delivered to Mimosa Grove that season was a beautifully carved pianoforte and stool from New York City. Camille had spent many hours playing into the evening, something that her husband very much enjoyed. Several more baby gifts would be coming any time.

Ellie turned the next pages beyond the entry she read about the sadness of losing Baby Daniel. She put her head back on the pillow and let out a sigh. *How sad for a young mother to have to bury her child without the help and ministrations of family.* Camille was only attended to by her husband and the neighbors who lived on the adjoining plantation, Hade and Sally Flynn. Life during the 1800's was not a long one. There were no guarantees for the survival of the youngest of the family. Ellie assumed it might be a reason for cemeteries to be a necessity on the family's property.

Ellie was about to turn the page when the sound of her cellphone snapped her back into the present. She looked down at the display. *Riley? What's he doing calling at this hour?* Ellie sat the book down and answered.

"Hello. Riley, is something wrong?"

"Hi Ellie, please forgive my calling so late. I have let the weekend get passed me, and I wanted to invite you to join me for dinner at my parent's home tomorrow. It's last minute, I know, but my mom extends her welcome too."

Ellie brushed his litany of apologies aside and accepted, "I'd enjoy that. Thanks for inviting me, Riley."

Riley wasn't sure he had heard her correctly.

"You will? That's excellent! I can be over around noon. My folks have a long-standing tradition that we have Sunday dinner at their home. My sister, Renae, and her husband and kids will be there too. I am usually the odd man out. It'll be nice bringing a pretty lady along."

Ellie could feel herself blushing at the compliment.

"Is there something I can bring, to help your mom with the cooking?" she offered.

Riley liked her willingness to pitch in, but said, "Oh no, that isn't necessary. I mean, she would appreciate the offer, but she feels like it is her duty as a Southern woman and mother to make the Sunday meal," Riley explained.

Ellie laughingly replied, "Well far be it from me to take that honor from her. I'll enjoy a good Southern home-cooked meal, and I'm looking forward to meeting your family."

Riley liked the way the conversation was going.

"Thanks, Ellie. I'm looking forward to seeing you again. This time, it won't be about legal things. It will be nice to just spend a day getting to know you better."

Riley hoped his forwardness wasn't a put-off to Ellie.

Ellie was excited about spending time with Riley, too.

"Oh, before I forget, you can bring Jack along too. Don't want him to be left out; besides, Mom is a dog lover, and the kids will truly enjoy him to the point of exhausting him!"

Ellie hadn't even thought about what she would do with Jack.

"It's very gracious of your mom to let me bring Jack along. I appreciate that."

Riley was just glad that she agreed to come.

"Well, I'll let you get some sleep. You have a big day tomorrow!" Riley said.

"Okay, thanks again for the invite. Jack and I are looking forward to it. Good night."

"Night, Ellie."

Several times a day, Riley would wander into Ellie's thoughts. It touched her how nervous he sounded asking her to the family dinner. Maybe this summer wouldn't be boring after all!

Ellie turned her thoughts back to the journal. She'd read a bit more before she called it a night. Flipping passed the pages she'd read about the death of Camille's first baby, the next entry was almost two years later, announcing the birth of a daughter, Caroline, in 1838.

> *13, February, 1838–*
> *My soul doeth magnify the Lord. We have been blessed with a wee little sprite, not more than 6 and ½ pounds. Lucy says she is no larger than a bag of spring apples. Her hair is fair, like my own mother. Her eyes are dark, like her papa's. The veil covering my joy has been lifted. She is named Caroline Isabel, after my mother.*

Ellie wondered about her grandmother, Camille, and her mother Isabel Burnell. Both were strong women; it was demanded of them in the period in which they lived. Modern medicine was a chest full of roots and poultices, Indian medicines passed from mother to daughter. Every woman during this time would have doctored their own families, and the high mortality rate of infants and women in childbirth were staggeringly high.

Not long after the birth entry of Caroline Townes, Daniel and Camille welcomed another child, a son born on August 17, 1840. This child, Jacob Washington Burnell, would be his father's shadow for his short time on Earth. Two years later, another daughter would be born into the family circle, Harriett Colbert Townes on May 9, 1842.

> *15, May, 1842–*
> *Through Providence's loving kindness, I have been brought through the valley of the shadow of death. Six days have passed since little Harriett made her entrance into this world of woe. Lucy and Mrs. Flynn have taken care of the wee babe, as her own mother couldn't even raise her head from her pillow. Dr. Thompson tells me today that I should be back to health, but there should be no more lambs in our little nursery. Caroline calls her new sister, Hattie.*

Ellie could only imagine the ordeal that Camille endured bringing Hattie into the world.

An entry into the journal would describe an outbreak of typhoid in the Townes' nursery.

3, June, 1844-

Awoke early to the fever in our nursery. Mose brought up several chunks of ice from the spring house. The heat in the upstairs only aggravated the affliction. Lucy made a nice pallet on the porch, only to come back and find Jacob burning with it in his own crib. I pray to the ever-loving Father, who hears all our petitions, to heal the children.

10, June, 1844

Mose went to the Choctaw medicine woman from over the ridge who sent a poultice to be applied three times a day to each of the ill. Praise be to God for his ever-loving kindness. Caroline has started to show signs of her health returning. Daniel sat with Jacob throughout the night, ministering to his needs, wiping his fevered little brow. I have applied the poultice to Hattie, who seems to have the fever the least of the three. Mrs. Flynn's daughter, Sarah, passed yesterday. I sent Lucy to help with the laying the body out for burial. I will call on them tomorrow, if the children's health gives me leave.

16, June, 1844

The sorrows of this life pale to the rejoicing in the presence of the One who shines brighter than the morning sun. A tender, precious life has been taken from us, only to live forever with his Heavenly Father. Jacob breathed his last yesterday-a fitful night of agony that no one could take from him. Daniel lay prostrate on the child's bed, begging for his life to be spared. God makes no mistakes.

Ellie was saddened to read the pain of this young mother. Death was commonplace in Victorian times, but the death of a child was the most difficult to accept. Camille described the day following Jacob's death. The servants put a large boiling pot in the yard for dying the clothes. Mourning customs dictated that the household would be dressed for deep mourning. At the hour of Jacob's death, the clocks were stopped, as well as all mirrors covered. Lucy washed the child's body and dressed him in his breeches and finest shirt. Camille then lovingly trimmed several curls from the back of the young child's head. She sadly tied the black satin ribbon around the little curls and placed them inside a wooden box. Next to the curls, she placed the tin type photograph, made by the traveling photographer earlier that spring. *A succession of tears dropped into the box as the lid was closed, forever sealed.*

For the next twenty-four hours, Hade and Sally Flynn would take turns sitting up with the young child. The house would be draped in black, except for the white wreath that adorned the massive front door to Mimosa Grove. Friends from around the area would make their way to the Townes' home to pay their final respects to the young son of Daniel and Camille Townes. He would be in the front parlor, lying in repose inside the small, ornately carved wooden box lined with a piece of muslin cloth. The following day, another sleeping child would be laid to rest under the shade of the mimosa trees.

The following entries were short and made mention of the tornado that struck the plantation one spring afternoon in 1847. Several entries told of family gatherings at Mimosa Grove and additions of outbuildings and successful harvests over the next few years. It was in the winter of 1850 that a surprise would be visited upon Camille Townes. Her thought was that she was barren after the difficult birth of Hattie, as well as the deaths of the Townes' two young namesakes. She felt that somehow, she would not be entrusted with another baby.

However, she would give birth to a robust nine-pound baby boy, Joseph Burnell Townes. Caroline, twelve, and Hattie, eight, were quite the proud sisters. This would be the end of Camille's childbearing. She almost bled to death after Joseph's birth, and her health never fully came back to itself. Ellie once again marveled at the fortitude her ancestor had. Maybe it was from her that Ellie would acquire her strength. Drifting asleep with Jack curled in a ball beside her, she never heard the hobnail brogans walking down the attic stairs, nor did she stir when Rafe came into the room and sat in the rocker watching her sleep. She was oblivious to it all.

Ellie awoke from a deep sleep to feel the warm breath of Jack licking her nose. He was too afraid to jump down from the tall bed, and he needed to be taken outside. Ellie would be glad when he was able to go all night without a trip to the backyard. She hurriedly crossed the room to close the window against the chilly breeze. Grabbing her robe and slippers, she turned on the bedside lamp. For a moment, she imagined something moved from the chair in the corner. When she looked back to see, there was nothing there.

Ellie had grown accustomed to seeing Rafe appear and disappear before her eyes. She was anxious for him to return and talk with her. Carrying Jack down the flight of stairs and placing him on the carpet, she snapped his leash to the collar. She let him pull her down the hallway to the kitchen, where she unlocked the deadbolt and turned on the outside spotlight.

Jack sniffed the air and hurriedly scampered across the porch and down the large granite steps. He wouldn't take long, as he was becoming used to having the run of the house. To his credit, Jack had only had two accidents, and Ellie felt he would do much better when she had a set schedule. Smelling the honeysuckle and the river's aroma reminded her of the date she and Sean had shared down by the Ohio River back in Indiana.

She wished that her love life wasn't so complicated. *Listen, to me! I have a love life!* There was a promise of a relationship with Sean, but she really enjoyed the newness of her friendship with Riley. Unexplainably, Ellie was drawn to Riley. She suddenly felt a little twinge of panic at the thought of meeting Donovan and Portia Langley. She wasn't used to being around big families. Wondering if they would compare her to the fine character of her aunt Lavina, she called Jack, put him back inside his crate, and settled back into her bed.

Riley had turned off the lights in the living room and headed for bed. He was excited about seeing Ellie in the midst of his family. As he walked down the hallway, he stopped outside of Taylor's bedroom. For several years, it had been left as if was. Finally, his sister had convinced him that she would only dust and vacuum the room, not disturbing the toys or clothes.

In time, he saw that keeping her room the same wasn't going to bring her back. He slowly relented and Renae put her niece's things into the closet. As he looked in the bedroom, he imagined what the room would look like if Taylor were living. Since he had grown up with a sister, he had no doubt the floor would be cluttered.

"Taylor, I will never stop loving or missing you and Mommy, but I think I need to have someone in my life again. I know you and Mommy are okay now."

Riley had wiped his eyes and closed the door. It took him a long time to fall asleep, as his thoughts went from Kate to Ellie. When he finally drifted off to sleep, he was dreaming about Ellie. When he awakened, he found a cold shower was necessary to start his day.

Ellie was slow to get up; she had gotten out of the habit of going to church on Sunday. It had been instilled in her since she was old enough to remember, and she'd made sure Cassie had a religious background. What a comfort the memories of the Bible had been when she lost her mother, father, and her marriage ended. Feeling she had backslidden, guilt reared its head. So, major on her list of things to do would be finding a church home. Maybe she could better understand what was happening between her and Rafe if she talked to God about it. She had prayed for safety, that this spirit wouldn't do her harm, and she felt her prayers had been answered. She would consult with Riley about churches today.

Going downstairs to eat her breakfast, Ellie remembered Camille's diary and retraced her steps to retrieve it. Lying on the floor by the rocking chair in her room sat the hatbox, with the lid lying beside it. Convinced she hadn't removed the hatbox from inside the trunk, and knowing she didn't sleepwalk, she determined Rafe had taken them.

Ellie let out a sigh, "Okay, Rafe. I get it. I will open the letters tonight, and I'll start reading them."

Ellie didn't even find it strange that she was speaking aloud to a ghost. She just accepted it. It was becoming clearer to her that somehow her being at Mimosa Grove wasn't just the luck of the draw. The fact she was chosen to inherit Mimosa Grove was more than just keeping a house in the family. She was brought here to help this poor soul find rest.

Returning downstairs with the journal, she laid it on the spot on the large mahogany table in the entry hall. Mentally noting the evening would be for concentrating on Hattie and Rafe, she spent the rest of the morning taking care of Jack and getting herself ready for Riley. Showered, she dried her hair and used the flat iron to straighten out the waves that plagued her long locks. Choosing a nice pair of Capri pants and a peasant style top, she slid her feet into a pair of sandals, and walked into the large bathroom to finish putting on her makeup.

Ellie wondered what Riley would think of her if she told him about Raford Collins. It probably wasn't a good idea to share such things before they had even had a first date, and something made her feel she was betraying Sean. Ellie made up her mind she wasn't going to feel any guilt for enjoying this day with Riley and his family. Thinking of Riley Langley, her pulse quickened, and she recalled he sounded excited about today too, personally, not lawyerly.

Ellie viewed Riley's black Lexus driving up the long driveway. He put the SUV in park, unlatched his seat belt, and walked toward the front door. He seemed more handsome than when she first met him, his dark hair and mustache reminding her of Rhett Butler. She laughed at herself for the way she always came back to that movie. She hurried down the stairway and into the entry hall, checking herself in the large hall mirror before answering the door.

Riley gave her a hug as he came inside, "Thanks for agreeing to lunch on such short notice."

Ellie smiled, "I'm looking forward to seeing your parents and sister. I also appreciate you inviting Jack!"

Riley stood in the hallway, not noticing the apparition that stood in the hallway above. Ellie felt his presence, but said nothing. Grabbing her purse, she called for Jack.

"I have a small crate that he can ride in, to keep the puppy hair off the seats. We can switch it from my truck to your SUV if you don't mind," Ellie suggested, walking down the large granite steps.

Riley was already walking to her truck as she locked the door behind her. Turning to glance back at the bedroom window, she left Rafe, peering down, once again alone in the house.

The ride to Riley's folks' home, in an upscale neighborhood near Rock Castle, took less than twenty-five minutes. Riley thought it was a bit much for two people in their early seventies, but he also knew both were physically in as good shape as most fifty year olds. Their home was beautiful, Ellie thought, and she suddenly felt underdressed. Riley pulled into the drive, and two young children ran outside to greet him. Ten year old Braden was a blonde headed, blue-eyed boy, and his sister, 8 year old Sophie, was dark haired and dark eyed.

"Uncle Riley!" they both yelled in unison.

Riley opened the door and both latched on to an arm. While he hugged them, Ellie went around to the back seat to leash Jack. The kids made a beeline for the pretty lady with the cute puppy.

"Guys, this is Miss Ellie, a friend of mine."

Ellie smiled at both of the children and introduced Jack.

Busy petting Jack, Riley corralled them with, "Come on, guys. Let's go inside. Meme will be mad if her food gets congealed!"

Riley had heard that from his father for as long as he could remember.

As they walked into the formal entry of the home, Ellie felt like a tourist. She noticed the beautiful wood flooring throughout the downstairs, with lovely rugs covering the floors. Portia Langley came from the kitchen, wiping her hands on a dishtowel.

"Ellie, please come in. We're so happy to have you join us today," she said with a slow, Southern accent.

She leaned over, giving Ellie a hug. Ellie could see where Riley inherited his long, lean form. Portia was above average height, and it was obvious she belonged to a gym, as she had no extra weight anywhere to be seen. Her hair was short, but cut in a trendy, fashionable style. Ellie noticed the scent of her perfume as they embraced. *Chanel, very nice.*

From the living room came Donovan Langley, Renae and Brent. Smiling, everyone made their introductions. Donovan came over and hugged Riley and Ellie.

"Your aunt was a kind soul, Ellie. We are so happy to have you living at Mimosa Grove."

Immediately liking Mr. Langley, Ellie returned, "Thank you, Mr. Langley."

Donovan and Portia smiled, "You can call us Portia and Donovan. No sense in being too formal with this group!"

Ellie was glad that Portia wasn't pretentious. She had a sweet smile, and Ellie felt that she would have been about the age of her mother, had she lived.

"Thank you, Portia. I appreciate your invitation for lunch; it smells delicious."

Everyone noticed the small puppy that was being taken from her grasp by Braden and Sophie.

"Memes, can we take the puppy outside?" the two chimed.

"Ellie, do you care if they play outside? We have a fenced yard," Portia said.

"I don't mind, he seems to be ready for some fun. Is there anything I can do to help you?" Ellie asked.

Portia smiled, "No, but thanks for offering. Riley, why don't you and Ellie go on out to the sunroom and catch up with Brent and Renae. I have it all under control."

Obeying, Riley took Ellie to visit for a few moments with his sister and brother-in-law. In a few moments, Portia and Donovan came to the door to tell everyone it was time to eat. After much cajoling, the two youngsters brought Jack back into the house. Jack stretched out on the large rug in front of the glass window, closed his eyes, and went to sleep.

The large table seated the eight family members comfortably. Ellie watched Riley as he talked with his nephew about sports and how his little league team was doing.

Portia sat next to Ellie and said, "If you need anything while you are staying at Mimosa Grove, please call. Don and I can give you recommendations and names of the people who have worked on the house and grounds since Mrs. George passed on."

Ellie smiled, "That would be very nice, thank you. I know I am going to need a lawn service to come and do some mowing and trimming around the cemetery."

Braden and Sophie's eyes widened at that mention of cemetery.

"You have graves at your house?"

Riley spoke up, "They have been there for over a hundred years, Bub. I doubt anyone is hanging around the cemetery these days."

Ellie hoped her expression didn't give a hint otherwise.

"My great aunt Lavina specifically asked that I take care of those graves as well as the Confederate graves in Resthaven Cemetery."

Donovan sat his sweet tea down on the table, adding, "I remember Mrs. George took flowers two or three times a year and placed them on the Confederate gravestones. She was in the United Daughters of the Confederacy, and she made sure those graves were always 'decorated' as she called it. She mentioned when she was writing her will that it had been a tradition since the Civil War to tend to those graves. I thought she said her great-grandmother started tending the soldiers' graves right after the War Between the States."

Renae smiled and added, "Ellie, you don't want to get Dad started on the War; he dragged us all over the state when we were kids looking at battleground sites."

Portia glanced across the table at Renae, lowering her eyes twinkling eyes.

"Well, I actually teach history, so it all interests me. I feel like I live in a museum," Ellie chuckled.

Talk continued about the house and Ellie's stay over the summer. As she spoke of her plans, Riley caught himself staring at her as if she held a spell over him. He didn't notice the other family members had seen it too, and each was giving one another smiles across the table. Later, when Ellie went outside with Sophie and Braden, to take Jack for a potty break, Riley's mother and sister started in with their own observations.

"Riley, she is such a nice girl. Have you two been seeing one another long?" Portia inquired.

Riley slid his hand through his dark hair, acting as if he were about to start a litany of denial. He thought better of it, since there was no fooling his very perceptive mother and equally keen sister.

"Look, we saw how you were looking at her. You looked like a moon calf, Riley!" Renae teased.

"We haven't dated, actually. I haven't had the chance. We went to Miss Nell's for bar-b-que the week she came down for the reading of Mrs. George's will, but that is pretty much it. I would love to take her out, but you need to just back off the subject of anything serious. I don't want to get serious about someone who's just here for a few months."

Portia and Renae were crestfallen.

"Now son, you can't go shutting a door on Ellie just because you feel she might not be around after the summer's end. Maybe you should start thinking about a reason for her to want to stay. Just let things happen if they are meant to be. We just want you to be happy."

Riley looked to his dad to save him.

Donovan spoke up finally, "Son, I think your mother is right. I set quite a store on Miss Lavina, and I think Ellie is a lot like her. You might want to give it some thought."

Just then, the kids came in with Jack. As Ellie closed the door behind them, she sensed she had interrupted a serious discussion.

Riley walked over to her and said, "Are you okay on the time?"

Ellie wasn't sure what he meant.

"I'm good with staying for a while. I think Sophie and Braden are giving Jack a good dose of socialization," she laughed.

Portia ushered the family into the den, and everyone sat around the room in a variety of couches and chairs. Ellie sat on the love seat, which was one of the last seats available. She figured that was planned, but didn't mind.

Riley walked over and sat beside her, whispering in her ear, "I think we were set up; I hope you don't mind."

Ellie whispered back, "Not at all."

Her breath fanning his ear sent a surge of heat through his body. Obviously, Ellie had an instant, very pleasant effect on him.

Ellie and Riley spent the rest of the afternoon enjoying the time with the Langley clan. Ellie missed being part of a family, and she was aware of how much she missed having Cassie nearby. She tried not to let those thoughts ruin the moment. She was actually hoping this would be the first of many Sunday dinners. Sitting close to Riley, and listening to the sound of his voice, gave Ellie a warm, cozy feeling, and she treasured it. She had been daydreaming and didn't hear the question Brent asked her.

"Ellie, did you say you found a lot of interesting things in the house?"

Ellie felt embarrassed for not being more attentive to the conversation around her.

"Yes, there were trunks full of heirlooms and photographs. I've been reading a journal and a ledger from the 1830's, and a cache of letters from the Civil War, it's all very interesting," Ellie beamed.

The grandfather clock in the hallway chimed four o'clock.

Riley leaned in to Ellie and said, "How about we take off in a few? I would say Jack is getting hungry, and I'd like to take a look around the house, just to be sure everything is okay."

Ellie was glad to be able to spend some time with Riley alone. She liked knowing that someone had her back, if she needed it. Everyone started leaving at the same time, and Portia walked to the door with her hand in Ellie's, a very loving gesture for someone she'd just met. Ellie had missed having a mother to share her life with, and she felt that Portia must be a loving mother to both Riley and Renae. They were fortunate to still have her with them.

As they got to the front door, Portia hugged Ellie and said in her ear, "You're good for Riley; I am so glad you're here, Honey."

Ellie hugged her back saying, "Thank you, Portia. I think Riley is good for me, too."

After they had driven down the highway a little ways, Riley turned to Ellie.

Smiling, he asked, "Now what was my mom whispering about to you?"

Ellie could feel her face flushing, and decided to play dumb.

"I don't know what you're talking about. Your mom just gave me a big hug."

Riley didn't buy it, for he knew his mom would like nothing more than having him married off again.

"She means well, but she tends to think I am still her little boy," Riley offered.

Ellie stared out the window to avoid his gaze.

"I remember how my dad was with me, being an only child. I still miss him being my best supporter."

Ellie missing her father so much caused Riley to reflect on the blessing of his own parents.

"Ellie, I'm fortunate to have my folks in good health and living close by, and I'm really sorry for your loss."

Ellie turned and gave Riley a smile, "Thank you, I know you are."

Before long, they were pulling into the long driveway at Mimosa Grove. Riley pulled up to the house, near the large granite stone where the women would step out of the buggies or carriages. Jack was in need of a walk in the yard, and he was pawing to be down and out of the car. As she watched him sniff for a good spot, she got his crate out of the car and closed the door. Riley was around to the side to help her carry it over to her truck.

"Thanks again for coming with me today. I think you were a hit!" Riley admired.

"Well, I felt very comfortable with your family. Your sister, Renae, reminded me of my best friend, Char. They seem to have similar personalities. Your folks are great, Riley. They were very kind to me."

After Ellie snapped the leash on Jack, the two made their way to the house.

"Hey, do you want to show me the graveyard? Maybe I can do the work and save you some money."

Ellie wasn't sure Riley knew what he was getting himself into. He hadn't seen the overgrown cemetery.

"Why don't you look at it first, and then decide. I think it would be great if I can get the headstones cleaned as well. Aunt Lavina really wanted me to try and preserve the graveyard if possible. She seemed to have a preoccupation with death! Decorating for all the soldiers at Resthaven and this graveyard are quite a lot," Ellie said, sardonically.

As the two walked towards the back yard, they walked closer to one another. The sun was on its descent, making the limbs of the mimosa trees a canopy of shade. The mockingbird that Ellie heard the night before was making a chatter in the limbs above them. Ellie couldn't help but think about Rafe and Hattie walking through the grove together. She remembered that she had promised to read the letters.

Riley didn't notice the unseen apparition that stood just beyond the mimosa trees as they approached the gate to the cemetery.

Riley commented, "Wow. I had no idea this was back here. There must be ten gravestones, maybe more. I doubt we'll ever know for sure."

Ellie was watching her step, afraid a snake would slither across her feet as they stepped through the weeds in between the rows of graves. Riley watched his step to keep from stepping on a headstone, since one had fallen over.

"I can try and set this stone again if you'd like. I can bring out a few tools and try to set the stone in concrete at the base. I'd say it just fell over from the ground settling over the years."

"Thank you; I don't have any tools with me. I also think I will call Mrs. Eubanks at the cemetery to find out what would work well on the stones. They are really hard to read because of the moss and weathering."

Riley was reading one of the headstones, rubbing his finger across the moss-covered letters.

"I can't see what this says, but the year was 1863 or '64."

Ellie walked over, inspecting the headstone.

"I think that one is Joseph Townes' grave. He died in 1864," she said.

Riley had moved to another grave; the name was one that he couldn't make out.

"Ellie, can you decipher this one?" he asked, as he rubbed some dried moss out of the grooves inside the letters.

Ellie stepped across the stones that were piled next to the headstone. She tried to make out the letters, but they had been filled in with a type of gritty fungus that was growing on most of the stone.

"I can only make out the sixty-four. I wonder what happened in 1864." Ellie said, "I know that Camille and Joseph both died around that time."

Riley walked around the perimeter of the cemetery, looking at the rock wall that would need to be reset.

"Do you want to just redo the stone around the cemetery? I have a friend that could probably reset the wall and replace some of the missing stones for you."

Ellie was excited about the prospect of getting the cemetery in a respectable condition.

"Oh that would be great. I really want to get the cemetery in shape. Thank you," Ellie said.

Riley smiled, "Sure thing. I think it is neat that you have it on the property."

After a few more minutes of walking through the cemetery, the two made their way back to the house. Just as they were about to walk out of the grove, Riley slowed down, feeling an overpowering urge to kiss Ellie. Not wanting to make a move too quickly, he dismissed it. Ellie felt his pace change.

"Is something wrong?"

Riley kept walking.

"No, I'm fine. Just pondering."

Ellie dug in her bag for the keys while Riley held the screen door open. She turned the deadbolt and walked into the house. As soon as she set a bowl of food and clean water on the floor, Jack dove into it, lapping up the water between bites.

"Would you like something to eat? I could throw something together for us," Ellie offered.

Riley was enjoying having Ellie all to himself.

"Sure, whatever you fix is fine. I would be eating a Lean Cuisine if I were home."

Ellie pulled out a pizza.

"I know it isn't a home cooked meal, but after that delicious four course lunch, I don't need much!"

Riley was agreeable as he walked over to the pantry door.

"I guess I forgot about the mudroom and pantry."

Ellie turned from her task of turning on the oven.

"I'm thinking that at one time, this was a butler's pantry, a walk through to the stairs. I believe, when Aunt Lavina lived here, it was closed."

Ellie walked into the entry hall to turn on the chandelier for more light. She stopped dead in her tracks. Lying on the table, next to the journal, were the letters, still wrapped in the faded red satin ribbon. Ellie gasped, and the sound brought Riley into the entry hall.

"What's wrong?" Riley asked.

Ellie wasn't thinking, and said, "He moved them."

Riley was confused.

"Who moved what?" he asked.

Ellie caught herself; she didn't want Riley to know that she had been conversing with a ghost. *What would he think if he knew I have seen a ghost, just as real as he is?* She decided to play it down.

"Oh, when something odd happens, I just blame it on the ghost. You know, it's easier than admitting I am forgetful."

Riley wasn't convinced, but he went along with her.

"I guess the mind is the first thing to go, right?"

Together, they returned to the kitchen, unaware of the soldier standing beside the table. Rafe was now convinced if Ellie was to help him find Hattie and the reason she didn't answer the letters, he would have to take her with him.

"It is indeed a desirable thing to be well descended, but the glory belongs to our ancestors."
- Plutarch

Chapter 9

Ellie and Riley sat in the kitchen eating a supper of pizza and chips. She was a little embarrassed that she didn't fix him a more nutritious meal for their first dinner together, but she hadn't had much time to cook since arriving at Mimosa Grove.

The evening was a pleasant one. They talked about the house and grounds, and what Ellie had decided to do with her unexpected wealth. They even talked about Indiana and Ellie's school. The conversation never delved into the deeper recesses of Ellie's life, only the superficial and safe topics. Riley avoided his personal life as well, just talking about his life since the accident, not divulging anything prior to that time.

After dinner, Ellie took Riley on a tour of the house. He had not seen the fruits of her labors: cleaning and removing coverings. Ellie took Riley into the formal dining room where he played the pianoforte. Ellie was pleasantly surprised that he could play and was impressed with his version of *Amazing Grace*.

"You've been holding out on me, Riley! Where did you learn to play the piano like that?"

"My grandmamma Langley had a large grand piano sitting in her formal calling room. Every Sunday after dinner, she would gather everyone around to sing while she played. I would stay with her during the summer, and she taught me to play. I never had more than few lessons, but it just came naturally. I play mostly by ear."

Ellie sat on the chair beside him. She was learning that Riley Langley was not only a lawyer, but also a Southern gentleman to the core with hidden talents. Ellie couldn't help but wonder what other talents he was hiding.

"I always loved that song," Ellie said.

Riley turned to her and smiled, "I'm glad you decided to stay this summer. I'd like to get to know you better."

Ellie could feel her heart racing. She had been thinking the very same thing earlier.

"I'd like to get to know you better, too, Riley. You've been such a big help to me."

Riley wasn't fishing for compliments. He wanted to ask her out again, but he was starting to feel like an awkward teenager, laughing at himself for being so nervous.

Turning toward Riley, Ellie ventured, "Do you want to see the upstairs?"

"Sure, I didn't really pay much attention when I was here last. Seems like you had me packing large trunks down the stairs all night," Riley teased.

"Oh please, you only carried two, and one was as light as a feather!" Ellie retorted.

"Did you ever get the little trunk opened?" Riley asked.

"Nope. I tried after I got home, but it wouldn't budge. Sean suggested I call a locksmith."

"Who's Sean?" he asked.

Ellie shared truthfully, "He's someone I work with. We've gone out a time or two," Ellie said, feeling a bit defensive.

"Hey, you don't owe me an explanation."

Ellie hadn't really given Sean much thought with Riley around. That should have made her feel badly, since Sean was starting to take a real interest in her.

"Riley, I'm not in a serious relationship; I've only had one date since my divorce," Ellie explained.

Riley took a chance and shared his heart, "I would really like to take you out, on a real date, without talking about a will or legal matters. Would you like to go out sometime?"

Ellie smiled, and the dimple in her cheek was more evident than usual.

"I would love to!"

Curious about Riley's relationship status, she timidly moved ahead.

"Is there anyone special in your life? I'd be willing to bet you're quite popular with the single ladies of Hendersonville."

Riley wasn't smiling now, and his tone was more serious.

"I really haven't had much interest in dating, Ellie. I suppose I should tell you everything up front, if we're going to get off on the right foot. I'm a widower."

Ellie put her hand on Riley's.

"I know, Riley. I saw you at Resthaven the day I left. I'm sorry about your wife and daughter."

Riley wasn't sure he should be thankful he didn't have to go into the accident, or be angry that Ellie saw him grieving and didn't' tell him.

"Why didn't you let me know you were there?" Riley asked.

Ellie started walking up the stairs, and Riley following.

"I didn't want to intrude on your privacy. I was at the cemetery to talk to Mrs. Eubanks, and I only saw you as I was leaving. I found out from Miss Nell. I guess she just wanted to protect you," Ellie said.

Riley's mood softened, knowing that Miss Nell wasn't one to gossip. He squeezed her warm, soft fingers in his.

"It's okay; I don't talk about that period in my life with everyone. I'm glad you know now."

As they reached the top of the stairs, Ellie noticed that the attic door was ajar, and she knew that she hadn't been up there.

"You have been busy up here," Riley said.

He admired the work she had done on making the house look homier. Sticking his head inside the blue room, he asked if it was hers. Ellie peered inside; almost afraid she would see Rafe stretched out on the bed or something.

"Well, it is for now. I haven't had time to hit that back room and clean it from top to bottom. Eventually, that is going to be my suite," Ellie teased.

Admiring the antiques that filled the space, he commented, "I still find it hard to believe that all of this is the same as when your aunt left."

The two stood admiring the furnishings; then Ellie led him out to the room she was using as a closet space. Riley saw the two trunks sitting on the floor and went over to the smaller of the two.

"Do you want me to see if I can get this one opened up for you?" Riley asked, looking up at her.

Ellie wasn't sure why, but she decided not to tamper with it just yet.

"I think I like not knowing what's in it, if that makes any sense. It's as if I'm unraveling a mystery. I don't think it's time yet for me to know what's in there."

Riley had a quizzical look on his face.

"Well, if you change your mind, I know a good locksmith."

Ellie smiled at Riley's offer, then added, "You know, this room has baffled me since the first time we toured the house. But I think I might have an idea what it was used for."

Riley's eyebrow rose, wanting to hear more.

Ellie continued, "When I was looking through Daniel Townes' secretary, I found his accounts ledger for the plantation. On one of the pages, it showed where a tutor was hired for the youngest child, Joseph. It even showed where he had paid in advance for her salary and passage to the town."

Riley added, "Wasn't it usually men who were teachers during that time?"

Ellie wasn't sure about Southern communities, but she knew that most teachers during the time period were men, or unmarried females. Most of the women taught in the boarding schools, such as the one where Caroline and Hattie Townes attended in Gallatin.

"The name is in the ledger, but it appears to have been erased, or faded with the age of the book. It's in pencil, so that makes it even harder to read," Ellie said.

They walked through the next two bedrooms, Riley giving his thumbs-up to Ellie's quick turn-around on the cleaning.

Noticing the attic door, he asked, "Have you done anything more to the attic since we were last up there?"

Ellie didn't want to go back up there just now, afraid that Rafe might be lurking in the shadows.

"No, I plan on going back up there later. I still don't know what I am looking for!" Ellie remarked.

As they started down the stairs, Ellie looked back over her shoulder. She had that uncanny feeling that eyes were watching her. For a moment, she saw the apparition of Rafe Collins standing in the doorway to the attic, and it was as if he was unable to cross the threshold into the hallway.

"Is everything okay, Ellie?" Riley asked.

He had stopped on the landing before going the rest of the way to the first floor.

Ellie twisted around to answer Riley, "Yeah, I just thought I heard something. It's nothing though."

She hurried to catch up with him. When they reached the bottom of the stairs, Ellie saw the letters lying on the table. She would have to remember her promise to read them.

Riley said, "You have done a great job on spiffing up everything. I enjoyed the tour."

Ellie beamed, "Glad you approve! You're welcome to come back anytime!"

Smiling, Riley decided to throw caution to the wind and ask Ellie out for dinner.

"How about coming to dinner with me this week? I promise I have something more upscale in mind than the Fillin' Station."

Ellie looked crestfallen.

"But I *love* the Fillin' Station. You can't beat Miss Nell's barbeque! I'm just joking, Riley. I would be honored to join you for dinner."

Riley wasn't sure where he would be taking Ellie, but that was of little importance at this point. He would make sure their first date was one that she would remember. Maybe she would forget about the friend she had back in Indiana. He would contact Jamie before she had another layover too. As he made his way to the door, he reminded Ellie about their meeting at the courthouse to take care of the legal matters first thing in the morning.

"I'll be there. Do I need to bring anything special?" Ellie inquired

"Just bring your copy of the papers I gave you in the envelope, and of course you'll need a driver's license for identification. Did you get an account at the bank yet?" Riley asked.

Ellie explained that she spent the better part of Saturday morning getting her bank account opened and getting an address for mail to be sent from Indiana. She was able to take care of those important matters in a couple of hours.

"Well, I guess I'll see you tomorrow, Ellie."

Before walking out the door, Riley pulled her toward him for a hug. Ellie was surprised and elated as she returned the gesture.

"I had a wonderful time with your family today, Riley, and I'm glad we were able to get some things out in the open."

"Me too," Riley agreed.

He was glad that Ellie hadn't asked more about Katie and Taylor. Ellie held the door as he stepped onto the front porch.

He turned and yelled back towards the kitchen, "See ya later, Jack. You watch out for any ghosts, you hear?"

Ellie wished he hadn't said that, but she smiled and laughed.

"I'll be at the court house by nine."

Thinking Ellie might not remember the way, Riley asked, "Do you need directions?"

Ellie had her security blanket, her GPS, so she felt confident driving around town.

"No, I can find it."

Riley walked around to get into this car. He thought for a moment that he saw something move across one of the upstairs windows, but accused his eyes of playing tricks. The mimosa tree near the house appeared to be waving goodbye as he started the car. Ellie was standing on the porch, waving, as Riley smiled into the rearview mirror. He grinned all the way home that night.

The clock in the entry hall started running again, unbeknownst to Ellie. How it just started on its own, she couldn't explain. That was one less thing that needed fixing. As the chime struck eight, she carried her reading material, retiring to the front parlor. Ellie had started giving names to the rooms of the house. The front parlor was *Camille's parlor,* and the room directly across the wide entry hall was *Captain Townes' library.* Both rooms were decorated in the style that would be befitting for a ladies' visiting room as well as a gentlemen's smoking room.

Ellie thought she could faintly detect the smell of tobacco in the library, giving her the impression that it was a gentlemen's room. She liked the size of the front parlor in which she was sitting now. The lovely settee and matching chairs were original to the house. The style appeared to be more towards the late 1800's. Ellie assumed; she decided that Camille Townes' original furniture during those early years at Mimosa Grove had undoubtedly worn out with the children and constant use.

She sat admiring the French Vase and Louis XVII figurine on the mantle. Sitting beside the figurine was a photograph of an unknown relative from the late 1800's. Ellie imagined this was a child of Hattie or Caroline's. There were so many treasures to be discovered and labeled in the house. Ellie didn't know how she would have time to catalog it all. She would be taking digital photographs throughout the house for insurance purposes. The large table that sat in front of the window was covered with a lace tablecloth. This must have been an old piece from Camille's possessions. There was large crystal compote that sat in the center of the table that now held wooden fruit--the colors faded from years of the sun's rays. Another small trinket, a small silver bell, sat next to the compote.

Ellie picked up the bell and admired its delicate features. She had seen similar bells at other plantation homes; it was common for the servants to be summoned by their mistress with a bell. Ellie was not aware the Townes family *owned slaves*. As Ellie turned the bell in her hand, she saw the tiny words engraved on one side: *With gratitude and appreciation, Christmas 1860.* How lovely, Ellie thought. It must have been a gift to one of the family. The silver had turned a dark gray, tarnished from years of sitting on the table.

Ellie replaced the bell, hearing it tinkle as she set it down. She had placed Camille's journal on the table. Retrieving the letters, she carefully untied the satin ribbon, taking the next envelope from the stack. The script was identical to the first, the formation of the letters purposeful and plain to see: *Miss Hattie Townes, Mimosa Grove, Hendersonville, Tennessee.* Ellie turned the envelope over to see the sender's name written across the back: *Pvt. Raford Collins, 11th Tennessee Infantry, Vaughn's Brigade.* When she opened the letter, a small four-leaf clover fell out of the fold, preserved for almost 150 years. Ellie felt a chill go down her spine and wondered if Rafe carried one for good luck. She opened the delicate paper and began to read.

> *Dearest Hattie,*
> *I have waited for a few weeks to receve word from you. I hope you are well, we have had much sickness in the camp. Several of the boys from Davidson County came down with the measels. They were sent on to a camp north of here. Our rachons didn't come today, so lots of the boys are going from tent to tent looking for anything extra to eat. I'm not too hungry. I was hoping Mama would send some of the bacon from the smoke house. What a feast we'd have. I hope yor getting along, Hattie. Tell me stories from Mimosa Grove. Is Joseph still studing with the teachr? He gives the poor woman a greevous time, but I think he is sweet on her just the same. The colnel says we are moving out in a day or two, so I may not be able to write for a wile. I have your lace hankie near my heart; I sewed it to my shirt on the inside. I think about you when our company marches and drills. I can't recall the number of the times I have wished to be walking along the mimosa grove with your hand in mine. Ellie, I need to know you still feel the same. Send a letter soon, so that our regiment won't be too far from the*

> *railroad. I heard the Yankees aren't holding the rail. Pray for my soul, Ellie, should a minie ball take me from this world to the place where the immortal walk in blameless white. I'll forever be yours, Rafe.*

Rafe doesn't divulge his whereabouts. Ellie assumed that he wasn't trusting of the mail reaching the enemy's daughter without being opened. Even though Tennessee was in the South, there were those who decided to support the Union. The eastern portion of the state had remained a holdout for the Union, and the west and south were clearly aligned with the Confederacy. The area near Hendersonville was a hot bed of dissention. While most folks in Middle Tennessee owned plantations and farms, not all supported the use of slavery to work their large sums of land. Many slave-owning residents of the area couldn't understand how their neighbors could remain loyal to a government that had invaded their land. Ellie's great-great-great-great grandfather was such an anomaly.

Ellie wasn't sure why Hattie didn't answer the letters. Maybe she did, and Rafe had moved away from Camp Cheatham. Ellie picked up the next letter. It was still sealed, although the small portion of adhesive was all but disintegrated. She carefully removed the thin paper from the fragile envelope. A sound took her attention away from her task momentarily. It was Jack, whimpering in his crate.

Ellie walked to the kitchen saying, "Coming little guy. Mamma will take you out for a potty break."

Ellie walked past the clock, noting it was almost ten o'clock. She opened the crate and hooked his little leash to the collar.

"Come on, let's go outside!"

As she let him walk around the yard, she could hear the bullfrogs croaking down by the river. There was a distant sound of music coming from the river, and Ellie could see a houseboat just beyond her house. She needed to get a motion detector anchored near the back of the house. Without using her porch light, it was pitch black out there.

In a few moments, Jack was back on the top step. Ellie wiped the dew off his paws and sat him down. Teething a chew toy from his crate, he proudly followed his master into the entry hall. When she got to the doorway into the parlor, Ellie half expected to see Rafe sitting on the settee, but nothing out of the ordinary was there. Jack on her lap, he settled himself into a warm little ball and Ellie reached for the next letter.

Riley walked in the house and laid his keys on the hook by the door. In the kitchen, he took out a can of diet soda, reaching up in the cabinet for the bag of chips; he carried them out to his lounge chair on the back porch. He reviewed his day with Ellie. She hit it off wonderfully with his sister, her family, and his parents. It had been such a long time since he wanted to include another woman in his close-knit family circle. He had spent the whole day with his thoughts centered on Ellie, and was looking forward to their date, hoping there would be more to follow. He wished Ellie weren't staying at Mimosa Grove alone, but was thankful she didn't bring her friend, Sean, along.

The summer would go by quickly, and then she would be going back to her job. Surely he could call in a favor or two from one of his friends on the school board, maybe finding her a teaching job here. She didn't need a job with the money she had inherited, but Riley just wanted to cover his bases. *Cover his bases?* Why was he feeling this way about her? He had been coasting along just fine with his arrangement with Jamie. Now, since meeting Ellie three weeks ago, his whole moral compass had changed. He actually felt sleazy for his *layover dates* with her.

He couldn't quite understand why Ellie Morgan was able to touch a part of him that he didn't think another soul hadn't in so long. At least he wasn't feeling guilty for wanting to see Ellie romantically. Katie wouldn't have wanted him to be alone, and that was exactly what he was. His arrangement with Jamie Willard had done nothing to change that. He was glad that he would be ending it. Happy Lavina had brought Ellie to Mimosa Grove, he was going to do his best to keep her there.

The second letter was longer than the first. Rafe described the camp in which he had been staying. The unit contained over eight hundred men, and this letter, dated July 1861, described a skirmish near the Cumberland Gap and Tazewell. He mentioned an outbreak of measles that had killed a good number of men already, and they had been taken north somewhere near Lexington. Ellie remembered that Camille Townes' parents had a large plantation and horse farm near there, with several slaves. Rafe asked if Hattie had gotten the picture he had sent her. He and a friend had gotten their photograph made near Nashville when they mustered. Ellie remembered the picture inside the wooden box of tin types. The Confederate soldier's photograph was that of Rafe. Ellie had forgotten about it being in the trunk. He also mentioned Camp Jackson, a Confederate camp near Hendersonville.

He told Ellie that her mother, she and Joseph should be careful, but expect to have soldiers in the area. He asked about Caroline and the new little one. He mentioned seeing her husband at camp. It was obvious from his tone that he was worried about their safety. Just writing such letters could be dangerous in itself. Rafe reminded Hattie of the hankie that he was carrying, that it was his good luck charm.

The rest of the letter asked about life on Mimosa Grove and how much he looked forward to the end of this war. Rafe spared Hattie the details of battle: his letters only spoke of the general news in the camp. He asked that she send a letter to his mother near Goodlettsville, to let her know that she and Mimosa Grove were well.

Ellie wanted to know why Hattie didn't write him back. Had she found another beau so soon after her courtship with Rafe had ended? Jack was restless and Ellie felt the room become drafty. She reached behind her and pulled the crocheted throw over her shoulders. Before she could reach for another letter, the temperature change became apparent: standing in the doorway was a vapor that began to take form.

She watched as the figure of Rafe Collins became flesh and walked over to the settee.

"Who was with you today? I tried to talk to you, but couldn't."

Ellie was getting used to Rafe's sudden appearances.

"I saw you, but I was afraid to say anything. You really must be careful when you decide to *show up*, Rafe. Some people wouldn't understand your being here," Ellie tried to explain.

"Was that your man? I mean, are you two married?" Rafe shyly asked.

Ellie smiled, "No, I'm not married. I was, but he was unfaithful. I'm divorced."

Rafe looked embarrassed for asking a lady such a forward question.

"I never knew a divorced woman."

Now it was Ellie who felt embarrassed.

"Well, the gentleman you saw is a friend of mine, and I don't want him seeing you. He wouldn't understand such things," Ellie said.

Rafe wasn't sure he even understood what was happening.

Ellie wanted to know what it was like, his fleeting between the here and the hereafter.

"I saw your picture, Rafe, the one you had taken in Nashville. You looked very handsome. I wanted you to know that Hattie received it."

Rafe looked as though the memory of that day was coming back to him.

"Yeah, I sent that to Hattie when we left for Camp Cheatham. I didn't know if she got it or not."

Rafe sounded sad as he looked down at the stack of letters. Ellie tried to get his attention away from the letters.

"Rafe, I have thought of a way to help you. I found Captain Townes' account ledger in the library."

Rafe looked across the hallway, recollecting another memory from a happier time.

She continued, "The ledger shows an entry for payment and passage to a tutor that was hired for Hattie's brother, Joseph. Do you remember that?"

"Yes, I remember a teacher who came to stay with the Townes family. She lived with them before the war broke out. I don't remember where she went after that."

Ellie was excited that she would have a way to fit in at Mimosa Grove should she go back to help Rafe. She would have to get there before the other tutor would arrive. She could settle that once she talked Rafe into taking her back with him.

"So, will you take me?" Ellie asked.

Rafe wanted to know why Hattie ended the relationship, or if something happened to her. He obviously was a troubled spirit who hadn't been able to find peace, and he needed a mortal to help his soul find rest.

"Miss Ellie, if you can find Hattie, talk to her for me, I'd be forever in your debt. I have to explain to her . . ."

Rafe didn't finish his sentence.

It was as if he were seeing things she couldn't. He looked out the window seeming to feel he was being rushed.

"It's not safe for me to be here, Ma'am. There's Yankee troops' moving up from the South; I have to make it back to my regiment. I'll come back when it's safe."

Ellie couldn't see what was beyond the window, but Rafe was caught between the two worlds. How would Ellie help Rafe without leaving those she loved? She would have to keep searching for the answers until he came back.

"Be careful, Rafe. God go with you."

Ellie walked over to him and hugged him. His wool shell jacket scratched her cheek as she placed her head on his shoulder. He wasn't sure how to respond to such a forward gesture by this woman, but let her embrace him. When she moved away from the embrace, he was gone. The only sound in the house was the ticking of the grandfather clock in the hall.

Ellie sat in the parlor trying to understand why Rafe Collins chose her to help him find out why Hattie didn't answer his letters. She felt that she wouldn't be able to understand why Hattie Townes married another man unless she could go back to his time. Something happened after Rafe enlisted, and Hattie ended up marrying another man.

It was getting late, and she knew that she had an early meeting with Riley. She took the letters and placed them inside the hatbox. Beside her was the journal that belonged to Camille Townes. She picked up the journal and turned off the lights as she walked out of the room.

"Come on Jack, let's go to bed. It's been a long day," Ellie murmured as she made her way up the flight of stairs to the second floor.

As she reached the landing, she thought for a moment there was a candle burning in the small room that was now a closet. Ellie walked closer to the room, unsure of what she was seeing. It was as if a scene from another time was being played out before her. Inside the room, she could see a shadow cast on the wall of someone sitting on the opposite side of the room. Ellie's heart began to beat faster as she slowly walked nearer to the room. Jack had already walked into the bedroom and was oblivious to the activity in the adjoining room.

"Rafe? Is that you?" Ellie softly asked.

When Ellie reached the threshold of the room, she was shocked to see a young boy sitting at a desk dipping a pen into an ink well and blotting the paper with a small sheet of blotting paper.

The boy was unaware of Ellie's presence, but kept working on his lesson. Ellie tried to enter the room, but when her foot crossed into the candle lit room, the scene vanished into darkness. If Ellie didn't believe it before, she knew it now; she was being visited by the ghost of a soldier, and sharing a house with a family in another time. She knew that she couldn't share this with another soul for fear of being seen as crazy or unstable. Ghosts were not supposed to be real. She would try to do what she could to help Rafe, but she didn't want to invite any other spirits into her home. She wanted to live in the present, and Riley was a good reason to remember that. She closed the door to the closet room and made her way back into the bedroom. She quickly changed into her pajamas. She lifted Jack up into bed and sat the journal on the night table.

"I guess I'll have to save this for another day," Ellie said as she drifted off to sleep.

Ellie awoke to Jack's barking to go outside. She checked the clock beside the bed, and saw that it was only 7 A.M. She quickly grabbed her slippers and robe, and trailed Jack downstairs to the back door. The morning dew was still glistening on the leaves of the trees as the sun's rays bathed the house in its warmth. Ellie loved watching the sun glistening on the river below. It was a sight she had grown to love. Ellie's eye moved over to the summer kitchen. She still hadn't made it inside that little building to see what treasures it held. She would do that later. It might take all summer to finish the list of things she wanted to do with the plantation. After Ellie tended to Jack, she came inside to begin her morning rituals.

Riley would be waiting at the courthouse a little before nine, and she was looking forward to seeing him again. As she walked back upstairs to get ready, her thoughts went back to the scene she witnessed in the closet room. Since coming to Mimosa Grove, she had experienced things she would never have thought possible. Rafe Collins was proof of that. Now, she was seeing a glimpse into the past, something she never expected. Ellie peered into the small room on her way to the bathroom, and she couldn't believe her eyes.

On the floor in the corner was a piece of paper. Ellie bent down to pick it up, and to her amazement, read the note that was written with a quill pen in dark blue ink.

> *Study to shew thyself approved, a workman needeth not be ashamed of his labor. Please write this repeatedly, 20 more times. Thank you, Miss Morgan.*

Ellie stared at the paper in disbelief. The writing, even though it was Victorian penmanship was unmistakably *hers*. She was even more amazed at the name, her married name. Would this be her way in to the family, when Rafe takes her back to his time? She wanted to tell someone about this incredible experience she was having, but whom could she trust to understand and not judge her as crazy? There was nothing that she couldn't tell Char. She wanted to have one of their girl talks and tell her everything about her conversing with a ghost, and how she was beginning to have feelings for someone other than Sean Barrow. She wanted to tell her that she might not want to return to Indiana after all. Ellie's head began to hurt.

She had to keep her promise to Rafe, and she had to fulfill her duties to her deceased aunt. The month of June was already starting its second week, and she would have to do a lot of reading and research if she were to help Rafe and Hattie. What if she couldn't keep her promise?

Ellie took the piece of paper and slipped it in her pocket. She went about getting ready to meet Riley. She finished putting on her makeup; then went down the stairs to the entry hall. The hatbox and letters were right where she had left them. She put them back in the parlor and pulled the wooden doors together. Next, she put Jack in his crate. It was 8:20, and she would need to leave if she were to make it on time to the courthouse. She locked the large wooden door and walked out to her car to head into town.

The morning meeting at the courthouse took less than an hour. Riley looked handsome in his dark gray suit and tie. She couldn't deny it; she was attracted to Riley.

After the paperwork was taken care of and Ellie became the legal owner of Mimosa Grove plantation, Riley walked her out to the car.

"I'd like to take you out to celebrate this momentous occasion!"

He looked at Ellie, as if he were holding his breath for an answer.

"Riley Langley, are you asking me out on a date?" Ellie teased.

Riley moved in closer to Ellie, bending his head down to within inches of her face.

"I sure am. It's been awhile since I've been on a date; I guess I'm a little rusty at this."

Ellie felt a surge of electricity charge through her body at his closeness.

"Well, I would love to go out with you. Do you want me to drive into town and meet you?" Ellie asked.

Riley seemed flustered at Ellie's suggestion.

"Ellie, you haven't lived in the South long enough, I suppose, to see how true Southern gentlemen treat their dates. Down here, a gentleman *always escorts* the lady."

Riley gave Ellie a look that implied *Yankee* gentlemen didn't hold to such rules of chivalry. The comment was lost on Ellie, as her mind was racing to thoughts of what she would wear and where were they going.

"I have to be in court later today, but can be at your place by six. Is that too late?" Riley inquired.

"I think that would be perfect. I have some things to do at the house today, and I am going to make some calls to get some work done around there before the Fourth of July. Should I dress casually or formally?" Ellie asked.

Riley flashed a devilish smirk and replied, "How about you dress in something comfortable. It's going to be warm out today, and we might be outdoors for awhile."

Riley bent down to hug Ellie.

"I'm looking forward to seeing you later. Bye now."

Ellie drove back toward Mimosa Grove. She reached for her cell and called Char to tell her about Riley. She hadn't felt like this since high school. While her date with Sean had been an awakening of sorts for her, this feeling was different. Ellie wasn't sure what the connection was to Riley, but she knew that she hadn't felt this attraction for another man before.

Ellie laid her purse and keys on the large table in the entry hall. The house seemed different. She walked into the hallway that led to the kitchen, and as she passed the formal dining room, caught a glimpse of the hem of a dress. The sight caught Ellie off guard, causing her to have a pain of fright in her chest. What if someone was in the house intending to rob her?

She stopped, got her wits about her, and walked back to the room. It was as if the room had been transformed for a very special occasion. Against the far wall, a sideboard was laden with desserts and confectionaries of all sorts. The large dining room table was set for at least ten. The table leaves were extended beyond what Ellie had seen earlier that morning. The candles on the table were lit; Ellie felt as though she had entered someone else's home.

She thought of Jack, who should have been whining to get out of the crate. In a panic, she quickly blew out the candles and ran into the kitchen. The room was not there, but instead she found herself standing in a small room with a stone floor. There were hooks along the wall, and along the floor were several baskets and boxes, which appeared to be gifts. Ellie felt as though the room was spinning; she wasn't sure if she was hallucinating. This was definitely not *her* house, and Jack was nowhere to be found.

Ellie felt she might pass out, suddenly feeling the onset of an anxiety attack. *What's happening to me? I know this can't be happening. I just left this house not more than two hours ago; I'm not crazy!*

She turned to walk back into the hallway. She saw the room around her begin to shimmer, then change back to what she knew to be her house.

She made her way into the entry hall and sat on the wooden bench that was placed on the short wall under the stairs. Her knees were like jelly, about to give way. She closed her eyes and tried to calm herself.

The scene, in which she had walked, was similar to the glimpse into the past upstairs the night before. Were the souls who lived in the house trying to make their presence known, or was her time to join Rafe in the past fast approaching? How she wished she could open up to someone with what was going on. Had her aunt Lavina experience similar events in the house?

She decided to write down everything she could about the Townes family. She went into Captain Townes' library and took a sheet of paper out of the secretary. She began to write down the names of all the family members who lived in the house with Hattie. Next, she made a list of questions that needed to be answered before she could help Rafe. She would have to read the letters and try to decipher more of Camille's journal. Ellie listened as she stood in the hallway. No footsteps today. Could something have happened to Rafe after his visit? The letters and journal were in the exact spot in which she left them. Something wasn't right.

As she made her way back into the entry hall, she remembered Jack. "Poor baby, I forgot to come back to find you," Ellie said aloud as she sat the items on the table and walked back to the kitchen. Jack was jumping up and down in the crate, obviously ready to take stroll outdoors. She quickly took him out, and then returned to her task. Jack followed her back into the library where he went sniffing about the room as if stalking an unseen prey. Ellie opened the next letters, one after the other. Each letter described the movements of the regiment in which Rafe was assigned.

Ellie was becoming aware of the urgency in the letters to Hattie. As Rafe moved to engage the enemy at Cumberland Gap, then on to battles near and around Nashville, he began to tell Hattie of his love for her. Ellie wondered what had caused Hattie to no longer have feelings for Rafe. The last letter was from a field hospital near Murfreesboro, Tennessee. The envelope had a United States postage stamp in the upper corner, signifying that Rafe had not sent the letter in Southern occupied Tennessee. She opened the letter, reading the handwriting of a Martha Elkins. Ellie could see that this letter was much different from the previous ones.

> *December 31, 1862.*
>
> *Dear Hattie, I hope these lines find you well. I fear this will be my last letter, having been shot last evening with a minie ball from a Yankee sharpshooter. The Yankees brought us to this house where many of my regiment is waiting to see the surgeons. I have been waiting for a few hours. Don't worry, Hattie, I am not in much pain. I don't think I'll be able to get the stain from the hankie that you sent me. I have asked the kind Yankee nurse to pen these words for me, as I fear I am too weak to perform the task myself. It is my hope that you will forgive me and remember me in your prayers as I make peace with my Maker. Hattie, it pains me to tell you what I must. I have a son, only a few weeks old. I found myself in a delicate situation after a night of drinking after mustering in. I haven't even seen the child, Hattie, but I received word from her that I am the baby's daddy. I only did this to do what is right and proper for the child. I had planned to get back to make things right with the child's mother, marrying her so that no blemish would stain the child's station in life. I may not make it back to do the right and proper thing, Hattie. I am told the child, a boy, has been given my name. I am sorry Hattie, and I have asked God to forgive me for this hurt that I have brought upon you. I will always love you, no matter what happens to this mortal body. If mortal eyes could glimpse into the future, it would give me great pleasure to see you again in the grove of mimosa trees, your sweet kiss to last me through all eternity. I will love you forever, Rafe.*

Ellie looked further at the letter, and below the name "Rafe" was a scrawled attempt at Rafe signing his own name. Below this was an added note:

> *Dear Miss Townes, Raford wanted you to know that he is sorry for the hurt he has caused you. His wound appears to be mortal. I have been tending to him throughout the night. Please know that I will do all I can to make him comfortable and attend to his needs as I would my own son. Mrs. Martha Elkins.*

Ellie wiped her eyes with a tissue from the box, which sat on the secretary. She began to piece things together in her mind. *The letter could possibly have been the last correspondence from Rafe. Maybe now things make more sense. Hattie found out that Rafe had a child with another girl, so she broke off their engagement? But how did she know, since the letters were never opened? Could Rafe's family have told her?*

There were no other letters. The letter was dated 1862, so she imagined that he had waited almost a year to hear from his beloved Hattie. The plot definitely thickened where Rafe and Hattie were concerned. Ellie was fairly certain that Hattie put the letters away, but why not write to Rafe and just tell him that she wanted to end the relationship? Ellie began to feel that Rafe wasn't able to rest because he feels he has to right the wrong that was done to Hattie. It didn't make sense to Ellie.

As a mother, she felt the sadness Martha Elkins must have felt writing so many letters to sweethearts, mothers and wives. Her letter to Hattie was no doubt a nightly task following the battle near Murfreesboro. Ellie folded the letter and placed it carefully back in the envelope. She looked down at the stack of letters that she had read. *So now I know that Rafe had a child with a girl he didn't even love. It would make sense for Hattie to feel she couldn't marry Rafe.*

Ellie knew a little something about a child conceived out of wedlock. She knew that a child without a father during Victorian times was something looked down upon, unlike the times in which Ellie were living. Ellie picked up the notebook and wrote down the date of the letter. How in the world would she find out the name of the child's mother, much less the name of the child that was Rafe's son? The journal was another avenue for Ellie, but due to the condition of some of the pages, it was hard to read several entries.

Ellie had left a small piece of paper marking the page where she had finished reading the night before. The birth of Joseph Townes was the next entry that she read.

As she turned the next page, Ellie could only make out a few lines on the page. There was mention of a visit from Camille's in-laws. It had been several years since Jacob and Mary Anna Townes had seen their son. They had brought with them three slaves, along with a young mare. Daniel was adding a mare to his stable of thoroughbred horses. The visit wasn't a long one; Mrs. Townes, matriarch of the family, had taken ill. Camille didn't elaborate on the nature of her affliction, only that her father-in-law felt it best to take her back to their home, Twin Ponds. The Townes family returned to North Carolina, but left two male slaves and one female slave to help Daniel and Camille with their farm.

Daniel Townes did not own slaves, but used their labor on more than one occasion. These three slaves would be living with the Townes family the summer of 1857, but would soon be sent to live with his brother, Matthew, at his plantation. Ellie read another entry about the wedding of Caroline Townes. This grand event took place in the spring of 1859. Ellie wondered if that was why the table was set so beautifully in the formal dining room. Camille had enlisted the help of her family in Kentucky for the marriage of the oldest Townes daughter. Mrs. Burnell had brought a wedding gown for her granddaughter, purchased from the sale of a young colt to horse farm near Bardstown, Kentucky. Ellie flipped through the pages of the journal to 1860. It was here that she began to read about Hattie.

> *1, March, 1860-Hattie comes home tomorrow from her education at the Female Academy. The times we have been able to have visits do not do justice to the pangs of longing to see her. Papa will meet the train at the depot early tomorrow. Her penmanship is quite lovely, much better than Caroline's. I expect she will want to take a trip to Lexington to visit her grandparents, or perhaps a long trip to visit her father's family in North Carolina. I'm concerned for her traveling without an escort, especially now that her sister is married and living near Nashville. How the sands have flowed quickly in her hourglass.*

Ellie could imagine Camille Townes penning the words into her journal; a mother's private thoughts shared with no other. Such thoughts were brought to her own mind of Cassie. The two mothers' were not so different in their dreams and aspirations for their daughters. Ellie had longed to see Cassie weeks before, now she wasn't sure a trip would happen if she were to find a way to help Rafe. Ellie looked at the large mantel clock; its chiming of five o'clock told her that she would have to hurry to get dressed if she were to receive Riley by six.

Riley pulled into the long driveway promptly at six. He shoved his sunglasses atop his dark hair as he made his way up to the covered front porch. Ellie watched from the sidelight as he glanced out towards the grove of trees near the cemetery.

"Well you are right on time!" Ellie said happily, "come on in, I'll just be a minute."

Riley smiled, "You look great, Ellie. I hope you're hungry!"

After locking the house, the two made their way back into Hendersonville to *Barefoot Charlie's,* a popular restaurant.

It was obvious to Ellie that Riley was interested in her, and she was enjoying the heady feelings that being around him brought. They talked about the house and the phone calls that Ellie had made in regards to painting the house. Riley also had made a few calls to get a landscaping company out to mow the large lawn and cemetery. Following a nice dinner and conversation, they headed back to the car.

"I would like to take you to Nashville sometime, if you'd be interested. Have you been to the Grand Ole Opry?" Riley inquired.

Ellie was surprised that Riley was interested in country music. He seemed more like a Van Halen kind of guy.

"Actually, I've never toured Nashville, just driven through on the way to Florida. I think that would be a fun trip! I like country music," Ellie confessed.

Riley flashed a smile that Ellie was growing fond of.

"Great! I'll work on that. How about a movie?"

Ellie wasn't really interested in seeing anything that was out, but tried to act interested.

"I'm not really up on the latest releases. Is there one you had in mind?"

Riley wasn't sure of the latest movie releases either.

"I guess we aren't Siskel and Ebert. I don't know if you have any room left, but I could go for some ice cream."

Now *that* interested Ellie.

Ellie and Char made it a ritual after a day of shopping or just having their girl time, to stop at Dairy Queen for ice cream. She missed her closeness with Char; she felt a pang of homesickness for her best friend.

Riley made his way through the main drag of town, pulling into the Dairy Queen parking lot. The two walked in and made their way to the counter. The young girl who waited on them was about sixteen. Ellie was unaware of Riley staring at the girl as she took their order. Whenever he was around young children and now teenagers, Riley reflected on what Taylor might have been like.

The rest of the evening was enjoyable to both Ellie and Riley. They had a chemistry that was apparently growing with each visit. Ellie wanted to share her secrets of Mimosa Grove with Riley, but once again, kept quiet for fear of what he would think of her. Riley was thinking about Ellie and the time that they had shared in just a week. He didn't want to jump into anything, but for whatever the reason, he was feeling a sense of urgency not to let Ellie get away. Even if their dating had just begun, he knew he wanted more with Ellie than the casual relationship he had with Jamie.

Riley and Ellie headed back for Mimosa Grove as the stars were beginning to sparkle in the night sky. As they drove into the canopied driveway, Ellie decided to ask Riley about coming in for coffee. After parking next to the large stone hitching post and step, he came around to open the door for Ellie. They walked up to the large front porch.

"Would you like to come in for awhile? I can put a pot of coffee on in a jiffy," she said, hoping to share just a little more time with him.

Riley was glad for the invitation. He wasn't ready to say goodnight just yet.

"Sure, I would love to. I am starting to get attached to Jack."

His comment was lost on Ellie as she walked into the entry hall, turning on the large chandelier. The light threw a shadow of the two as they stood in the center of the hall. Ellie looked up into the upstairs landing, thinking she saw the outline of a figure.

"What's wrong, Ellie?" Riley asked.

"Oh, it's probably just the ghost." Ellie said warily.

Riley looked at Ellie, not sure if she was trying to make a joke.

"I think I have an old house that is settling and creaking, that's all," Ellie lied.

Down the hallway into the kitchen, they found Jack trying to get his kennel door open.

"Hey Jack. You wanna go out?" Riley asked as he bent down to get the little cocker spaniel out of his cage.

The puppy showered his face with appreciation, as if a convict being paroled.

He turned to Ellie, who was making the coffee, "May I take him out?"

Ellie happily agreed, "Sure, thank you!"

Ellie watched as Riley snapped the leash onto Jack and walked him out the back door. She could his shoes as he walked across the porch and down the granite steps. She also heard another set of footsteps, this time overhead. Ellie felt her heart lurch into her throat, not wanting Rafe showing up with Riley here. It sounded as if he were pacing the floor, like a father waiting for the birth of a child. Maybe it wasn't Rafe this time. She had already seen glimpses of Camille Townes and the young son, Joseph. Living with the knowledge that she wasn't alone didn't frighten her as she thought it would.

Her first few encounters with Rafe had left her quite rattled, but Ellie had compassion for this lost soul. She knew that all the ghostly images that she had been brought up with in movies and television were nothing like what she had experienced here. Maybe it was her compassionate side that allowed such visits to become less unnerving. She liked Rafe. Ellie snapped back into the present when Riley accidently let the screen door slam closed.

"Sorry about that. Jack was ready to come back in."

Riley took a deep breath, inhaling the aroma of the coffee that was just finishing brewing. Ellie took down two large mugs from the cabinet.

"You've really added some nice touches to the house. Have you given any thought to modernizing the kitchen and baths?" Riley asked.

Ellie poured the coffee into the mugs, adding, "Well, I think I am going to, but I haven't had time to check into prices. I don't want to start spending like I have an endless supply of money."

Riley nodded, "I totally understand. You're quite wealthy now, Ellie, but you're wise to be frugal with your funds. Oh, that reminds me; I sent the check to your uncle Loren this morning. I also sent a letter explaining your aunt Lavina's wishes. I'm sure he'll be pleasantly surprised!" Riley said, smiling.

Ellie said sadly, "I'm sure it will be used in his care at the nursing home. He has a son; I'm sure he will appreciate the gift as well."

Ellie and Riley spent the rest of the evening talking about the house and the plans Ellie had for it. She wanted to have it in tip-top condition before guests arrived later in the summer.

Riley looked down at his watch and said, "Well, I'd love to stay and visit longer, but I have an early day tomorrow. I need to swing by the office and pick up some files, then head home."

Ellie sat her mug down and started to walk with Riley to the door.

"I had a wonderful time tonight."

As they got to the door, Riley bent down and gave Ellie a hug. He thought about a kiss, but wasn't sure if she would think it was too soon. Ellie wondered if he would kiss her, thinking that wouldn't be too forward of him. They both spent an awkward moment before Riley turned for the door.

"I'll call you tomorrow, if that's okay?"

Ellie smiled and said, "I'd like that. Drive safe."

Riley closed the door, and Ellie listened as his footsteps faded into the night. She peered out the sidelight as she watched Riley saunter out to his car. *A kiss would have been a nice end to a nice evening*, she thought.

The next two weeks were full ones for Ellie. She finished cleaning the upstairs rooms, moving her bedroom permanently into the room facing the river. She made contact with Helen Eubanks and purchased flowers for Confederate Memorial Day. She and Helen placed roses on each of the Confederate's graves, as well as a large arrangement for Shelby and Lavina George. The painters were contacted and arrangements were made for them to come the week following the Fourth of July holiday, just two weeks away. Riley was a frequent caller as well. It seemed that he was unable to stay away and Ellie certainly didn't mind his occasional calls either.

Ellie and Cassie had also had a chance to talk, and it was decided that Ellie would drive to Maryland after the painters were finished. She would have a few weeks before having to contact the school about taking a sabbatical. Char had given her a definite 'yes' for a visit over the holiday. She would be driving down for the Fourth of July; and return the next week when Ellie would be visiting Cassie.

She walked with Jack upstairs to retire for the night. The large windows were opened to allow the breeze from the Cumberland River to cool down the upstairs. As she prepared for bed, her thoughts were once again on Rafe and his promise to come back for her. She wanted to end his wandering through eternity, a soul who could not find rest.

This evening, the sounds of frogs croaking near the bank of the river and the Mourning Dove's sorrowful call from the willow tree by the corner of the house, were just two reasons for Ellie's bout with insomnia. She decided that reading might help her to relax and fall asleep. She hadn't read the journal for more than a week. The bookmark was just where she left it.

> *June 1859,*
>
> *Hattie has met a young man from Goodlettsville. Hattie confided in me that Raford is the brother of Miss Maggie Collins, her dear friend from the Female Academy. Raford Collins and his father, Isaac, visited Mimosa Grove Tuesday last in regards to purchasing a horse from the stables. They brought a servant with them, and he appeared to be the property of young mister*

Collins. The evening was filled with much laughter and music by Hattie on the pianoforte. Daniel and Mr. Collins retired to the library to share brandy and cigars, while Mr. Collins and Hattie walked the grounds. To be a young belle again. Joseph shared his time with the young Negro, who sat on the front steps waiting for his master to take his leave. I fear that he might see the folly of a planter's right to own another. His grandfather's both feel this is just the way the Maker set forth the world back in the days of the Patriarchs. I could hear Mr. Collins and Daniel talking about such things, and it was clear that such talks would no doubt be happening all over the nation. We, of the fairer sex, are not to discuss such things as politics. We are to remain silent and take care of the affairs on our plantations. How I hope the nation doesn't come to blows over it. I will do what I must to protect our family from the evils of slavery.

Ellie was surprised at the length of the entry, but could imagine Camille sitting alone in the house, no other females to share her concerns and thoughts. She flipped pages trying to learn something more about Hattie's courtship with Rafe. She found the next entry dated December 1860. Ellie read the entry about Hattie spending time with the young Collins boy. Camille feared their relationship was moving towards an engagement, and she wasn't happy about that. With war looming and dissention in the town around them raging, she feared Hattie would be taken further south and she would lose both daughters to slave owners. Camille had seen the two walking through the mimosa grove, and she saw the kiss they shared. Ellie was beginning to wonder if Camille had something to do with Hattie ending her relationship with Rafe. It was clear that the country's rising gulf of anti-slavery sentiments and states' rights had visited itself upon the family who inhabited Mimosa Grove. If Ellie were to help Rafe, it would need to be soon.

Ellie decided to make her way back into the attic, to retrace her steps to the day she saw Rafe for the first time. As she climbed the stairs from the second floor hallway, Jack's stubby legs raced on ahead of her to the top of the stairs. Ellie felt a change in the temperature as she ascended from one step to another. Her head began to feel the pressure of a vice that tightened with each move to the top of the stairs. She grabbed on to the thin railing that was placed along the narrow stairway. When she reached the top, she felt herself sway from the lightheaded feeling she was experiencing. A rush of cold air rushed past her from out of nowhere, causing a chill to run from the back of her neck down through her very soul.

She crossed her arms, rubbing them to increase the warmth. It was then that she suddenly felt that she was not alone. Jack began to sniff from one box to the next, picking up dust and cobwebs on his long, silky black ears.

"Come 'ere, Jack. I don't need you getting yourself hurt on something up here."

She reached for the long chain that turned on the two large lights, only to watch one of the lights flicker, then burn out. The attic was only half lit, but she could still see what lay in the far end of the room. She felt her way to the side of the attic where she had first found the hatbox and letters; she could see a flicker of light, almost a faint stream of sunlight, which was barely visible coming from a crack in the wall.

Ellie moved gingerly through the semi-darkness of the attic. She wasn't sure where the sunlight could be coming from, since it had been a cloudy, dreary sort of morning. Ellie climbed over a box of fishing tackle and ice fishing poles that had seen many a frigid winter on the Cumberland. Ellie ran her knee into the corner of a metal trunk. The pain caused her to wince, but she held her tongue from the words that came to mind. She bent down to check for any signs of blood, but instead felt the knot that was rising on her shin. *Good grief. Now I'll have to wear slacks tomorrow to cover the bruise I'll have on my knee!* Ellie continued on, careful now to watch for hidden obstacles. She wasn't sure where the light was coming from, but it was definitely becoming brighter with each step she took.

A large chest of drawers was pushed against the wall where she had found the hatbox, and it was behind it that the strange light was beckoning to Ellie. Ellie tried moving the chest away from the wall, having to first move a smaller trunk that had been wedged beside it. Feeling the weight of the trunk, she decided to just try and climb onto it for a better view. As she peered through the sliver of space between the ancient wall boards, she was amazed to see a light so bright she felt she should look away or fear the illumination would rob her of sight. She put her hand on the wall to steady herself, just as Jack came to sniff the area before her. She wasn't sure what happened next; her knee began to sway with the top of the trunk lid as it gave way. Ellie had a feeling of an overwhelming need to take in as much air as she could. The pressure within her ears became so intense she was sure her head would explode; then, as suddenly as the frightening experience began, it ended.

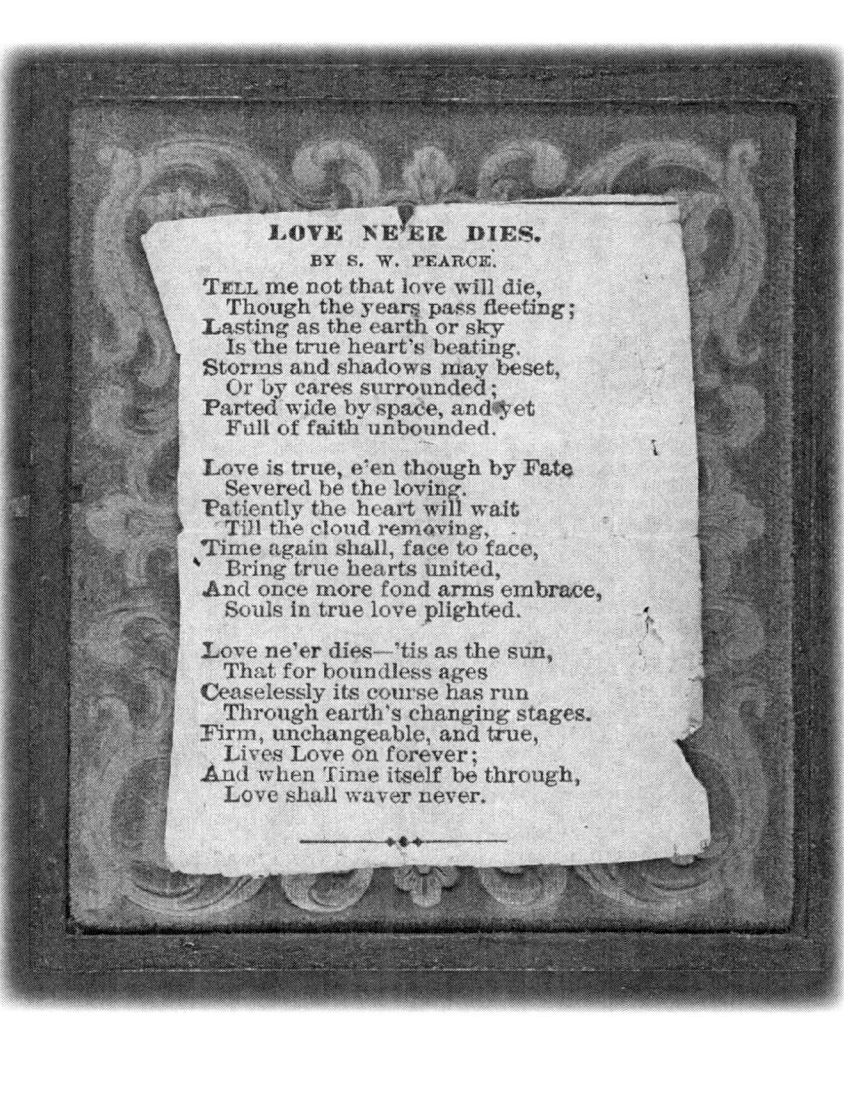

LOVE NE'ER DIES.

BY S. W. PEARCE.

TELL me not that love will die,
   Though the years pass fleeting;
Lasting as the earth or sky
   Is the true heart's beating.
Storms and shadows may beset,
   Or by cares surrounded;
Parted wide by space, and yet
   Full of faith unbounded.

Love is true, e'en though by Fate
   Severed be the loving.
Patiently the heart will wait
   Till the cloud removing,
Time again shall, face to face,
   Bring true hearts united,
And once more fond arms embrace,
   Souls in true love plighted.

Love ne'er dies—'tis as the sun,
   That for boundless ages
Ceaselessly its course has run
   Through earth's changing stages.
Firm, unchangeable, and true,
   Lives Love on forever;
And when Time itself be through,
   Love shall waver never.

BOOK II

"Mimosa Grove, Hendersonville, TN - October 23, 1860

"Generations pass like leaves fall from our family tree. Each season new life blossoms and grows benefiting from the strength and experience of those who went before."
-Heidi Swapp

Chapter 10

Ellie looked around to the scene in which she was now a part. The train station depot was a busy place on this chilly morning. She looked around at the people sitting near her on the passenger car of the locomotive. The conductor walked down the aisle of the car in which Ellie was sitting.

"Next stop, Hendersonville. Train departs in ten minutes."

He moved on down the aisle, stopping to take tickets from those who boarded from the depot. She looked out her window at the building adjacent to the track. Ladies were being escorted by their spouses or escorts in lovely dresses with hoops, covered with capes and mantillas of wool.

There was an American flag flying over the depot, the wind causing it to appear stiff as a board. The weather appeared raw, as she noticed the ladies were hurrying from the depot station into the railcars, many with muffs or woolen gloves on their hands. Ellie knew the temperature was quite cold; she could see their breath visible in the raw air. Ellie was suddenly aware of her own clothing. She wore a lovely plaid flannel dress of tan, rust and brown. Thankfully, her brown wool cloak was lined with flannel. From the feel of her bodice, she could tell she had on a corset, and it was presently cutting into her ribs. She also could feel from the front of her dress that she had on many layers of coverings besides a hoop. Her dress appeared to have been expensive, looking around at the attire of the passengers within her railcar. The bonnet on her head must have been small; it felt dainty. She longed for a hand mirror to see if she was presentable. Even though she didn't *feel* dirty, she knew she needed to freshen up; she had been on the train for hours.

She felt behind the nape of her neck, her hair was in a tight braid around the back, as well as confined to a hairnet. Her gaze was drawn down to her feet, which were feeling very confined within her leather boots. She didn't want to raise her skirts, but she could tell her stockings went up to her thighs. The gloves on her hands appeared to be dainty leather gloves of goat kid. A lovely pocket watch hung from a chain attached to her waist, suspended from the button on her bodice. Ellie tried to remember who had given her the watch. It was quite lovely with the gold engraving on the front cover. She felt the earrings dangling from her ears; they were very small shepherd hooks with some type of stone attached. Beside her was a carpetbag of sorts, and it appeared to be full of all sorts of papers. She peered inside, and there were several folders and a book within. She noticed that she had a small leather wallet, and inside were quite a few bills.

Ellie couldn't imagine why she would be traveling with such a large amount of cash. Inside the bag was a folder containing her teaching certificate from the Central Normal College, Danville, Indiana. The name appeared in very stylish script typical of the 1800's. Ella Camden, March 22nd, 1850. She had been teaching for some time now. She hadn't been Ella Camden for many years. Her name was Ella Morgan. She had no wedding band on her left hand, no longer needed to wear it. At present, she had no idea how she was to get to Mimosa Grove, if that was her destination. Presently, she was trying to get her thoughts clear in her head. Maybe the lack of a good meal for quite some time could be the cause for her memory to be so addled. It worried her, but she tried to put her thoughts towards her destination.

Suddenly, her thoughts were interrupted with the sound of the Conductor calling out to the cold, chilling morning.

"All aboard! Last call for Hendersonville."

The final passengers boarded the train, and the conductor quickly pulled up the steps from outside the car. The train began its lurch forward, and Ellie felt her stomach do the same.

Ellie tried to remember the day before, but at the present, didn't have a memory of anything related to Ella Morgan, teacher. 'GALLATIN' was written on the signpost, and Ellie caught sight of it as the train moved forward down the track. She had been riding the train through Kentucky, and now into Tennessee. As she sat in silence looking at the scenery from her window seat, she began thinking of a formal introduction, should she be asked. She would be a widow, which would explain why she needed employment. If anyone asked, she would tell them about her daughter.

She was staying with Ella's family. Charlotte was family; she was all that Ella had in the way of a sister.

Ellie was aware of the young woman sitting across the aisle from her, now staring at her. Next to her sat a young black woman. The Negro woman did not make eye contact, but sat rail straight in the seat.

"Where are you heading, Ma'am?" the young woman asked.

Ellie wasn't sure how to answer, but decided to try out her story for the first time.

"I'm traveling to a plantation, Mimosa Grove," Ellie answered politely.

She didn't give more information than was needed.

The pretty young woman smiled at Ellie, saying, "Well it is a lovely home. I've only been there once, when Miss Caroline was married last spring. Such a lovely affair, it was. Are you relation to the Townes?" the lady asked.

Ellie remembered her manners, "I'm Ella Morgan, pleased to meet you, Miss."

"Oh my, I am forgetting my manners. I'm Eliza Collins. Pleased to meet you. I've been at the Female Academy visiting my youngest sister, Maggie. She just graduated, and in just a couple of weeks will be returning home."

Ellie smiled at the young girl, and looking past her, waited for her to introduce the young black woman sitting beside her. Ellie assumed this was her slave. She didn't bother including the young slave in her conversation.

"Well it is a pleasure meeting you, Miss Collins."

Collins. Why is that name important to me? She tried to scan her memory for a face to go with that name, but at the present nothing appeared.

"I have been hired by Mr. and Mrs. Townes to be a teacher for their young son, Joseph," Ellie shared.

Eliza Collins smiled warmly at Ellie, and went on to say, "Well I wish you well in your new employment. Mrs. Townes and her daughters are known for their beauty and grace. My girl, Polly, and I are heading to Goodlettsville where my papa has his plantation, Elmwood. Do plan a visit, once you're settled in. My mother and father would be pleased to meet you."

Ellie liked this young girl already; her bubbly personality was contagious.

"Yes, I would like that."

Ellie had passed the first test. As the train moved along down the track, she began to feel a bit of anxiety for what would happen next. She didn't know what the owner of Mimosa Grove even looked like. Would he be meeting her at the train station? It wouldn't be long before her question would be answered.

The conductor made his way to the front of their car.

"Hendersonville ahead. Please wait for your baggage once you are outside the train."

Ellie didn't even know what baggage she brought, but she assumed it would be several trunks. She hoped something would jar her memory. She remembered once when she had the fever; it took her several hours to regain her faculties after being in and out of consciousness. Perhaps she has recently had a bout with the fever. Soon the depot appeared in her sights; she noticed it was not as large as the one in Gallatin. In fact, it was quite a bit smaller. The area in and around the depot was clearly a small, rural community. Ellie could see several wagons and buggies tied to several hitching posts near the depot station. She scanned the faces of the people waiting on the walkway in front of the depot.

As the train came to a stop, the conductor put the small step back down for the passengers to depart.

Ellie stood, turning toward Eliza Collins, "It was nice talking with you, Miss Collins. I hope you have safe travels to your destination."

Eliza returned her smile and thanked Ellie. It was then that she made eye contact with Polly.

"Good bye, Polly," Ellie said.

Eliza looked at Ellie as if she had suddenly grown two heads.

Polly appeared to be stunned, but spoke, "Goodbye, Miss."

Ellie realized she must have done something that wasn't considered proper. She kept walking to the front of the railcar, smiling at the conductor and stepping down onto the platform. She waited as a colored boy climbed to the railcar behind where Ellie had been riding, and brought trunk after trunk, setting them on the platform. Several passengers took their trunks or had their slaves carry them to awaiting carriages and wagons. Ellie thanked the boy and checked the trunks over for any damage. There were three very substantial looking steamer trunks and one small travel trunk.

A middle-aged man approached Ellie, taking his cap off as he walked closer.

"Miss Morgan?" he asked.

Ellie positioned her carpetbag higher on her shoulder.

"Yes, I'm Ella Morgan."

The man went on to make his introduction.

"Ma'am, my name is Hade Flynn. Mr. Townes and I own land next to one another. He wasn't able to get away from his plantation this morning, but I've come to fetch you back to their place."

He looked down at the trunks sitting in front of her, suddenly realizing the load he would be carrying.

"I'll start loading your trunks, Ma'am. If you'd like to follow me, I'll take you to the buggy."

Ellie extended her gloved hand, "Oh, thank you, Mr. Flynn. It is nice to meet you."

Hade Flynn was of German descent. He still carried a thick accent; one that Ellie had a hard time understanding. He had a kindly expression on his tanned face. He smiled respectfully as he moved around Ellie. Ellie was reminded of her own father when she studied the characteristics of Mr. Flynn. Hade had lived in these parts since his family settled here after Daniel Boone took several of his relatives through the Cumberland Gap. He and Daniel Townes had been neighbors for over 25 years.

Ellie walked to the buggy. Next to the nice buggy was a buckboard wagon. Sitting atop the wagon was a young man.

"This here is Jonas Dowell, my hired hand."

Ellie smiled, saying, "Pleased to meet you, Mr. Dowell."

Jonas Dowell tipped his cap and smiled at Ellie, and then hopped down to help Ellie into the buggy. He moved on to help Hade carry the large trunks back to the wagon.

"Good thing we brought the buckboard, Jonas," Hade remarked, "looks like she is coming to stay."

Jonas chuckled, "She's a right handsome woman, Mr. Flynn. Don't reckon it would hurt none if she did stay on awhile."

Hade gave Jonas a look, giving him a piece of advice.

"You won't have time to notice, Jonas. You got a barn to roof before winter," Hade said in his quiet, determined way.

Jonas smiled at his employer, knowing he was all bark and no bite.

"Yes sir, Mr. Flynn."

As Ellie sat in the buggy waiting for Mr. Flynn to come back, a young colored boy came bounding down the hill carrying a small basket. He seemed to be holding it carefully, but the basket bounced with its contents jostling inside.

"Miss, you left yur basket!" the boy called as he came running up to the buggy.

Ellie turned to see what the young boy was carrying.

"Miss, you run off from the depot without yur dog."

The boy had large brown eyes that had a tinge of yellow flecks shining in the sunlight. He was wearing breeches, and the legs were well above his skinny ankles; the rope, which held them tight around his waist, was frayed on the ends. His homespun shirt was almost threadbare, and Ellie wanted to offer him her cape, but thought better of it. Ellie reached into her bag and gave him a piece of licorice rope. His eyes grew wide to match the toothless grin he was sporting. His grubby little finger reached out to take the offering from Ellie.

"Lawd, Miss, you shore is nice."

Ellie blushed.

"Well, I'm such a silly goose. How could I forget my little Jack?" Ellie said, as she took the basket from the boy.

"Thank you, young man."

The boy smiled, feeling quite proud of himself for bringing the small dog to the pretty lady.

Hade Flynn walked up with the smaller trunk, sitting it on the back of the wagon.

"Boy, what's your business with Ms. Morgan?"

The small boy looked down at his feet, which were absent of socks and attired in old brogans that were too big.

"Nuthin', Mister. I's just fetchin' her dog."

Ellie spoke on his behalf, "And I am very thankful for his quick actions to get my dog to me before we left."

Hade patted the boy on the top of the nappy curls that covered his head.

"All right then, get on back to the depot," He said, smiling at the boy.

Hade looked at Jack who was sitting in the basket, panting, and back at Ellie. He smiled and shook his head. They headed back to the wagon. Once again, Jonas Dowell helped Ellie up into the buggy. Then the rest of Ellie's trunks were loaded onto the buckboard, and the three headed out of town towards Mimosa Grove.

"About how long will it take to reach Mimosa Grove, Mr. Flynn?" Ellie asked, pulling the wool blanket up over her legs.

"You're doing a bit of backtracking, Ma'am. Mimosa Grove was back on the hill before you ever got to the station. Takes about an hour to get there. You best sit back and try to stay warm. Looks like we're in for a snow."

Ellie was feeling the effects of the weather, so she snuggled down into the seat and pulled the blanket up closer to her chest, covering the top of the basket. She and Jack had made it, now to remember what it was that she was supposed to be doing here.

The ride in the buggy wasn't too bad, considering the road from the Louisville and Nashville Railroad station depot was dirt, but packed tight from the wagons coming and going into the town. Ellie looked at the trees, now barren of leaves except for the oak trees, which blew in the winter air. Their rustling was the only sound along the ride. Ellie noticed many large farms along the road to Mimosa Grove.

As they passed one large farm, Hade finally spoke.

"That there's my place. Got about three hundred acres, the house sits just over the rise. My wife, Sally, is all that is home now. Our boy Joshua and his wife and family have moved down to Franklin. Got farmland from the wife's kinfolk. Don't see much of him these days; takes all from daylight to dark keeping up with that piece of land. The hired hand, Jonas, came to us a few years back. Doesn't have a wife or family, but is a good hand for me. I 'spect the wife will come calling later in the week to visit with you and the Townes'."

Ellie smiled, "I would like that. Please tell her that I'll be looking forward to her visit." Hade smiled.

Ellie looked at the farm that was coming into view from the road. The fence that surrounded the farm was a split rail fence. Ellie had seen this type of fence before, but where she couldn't remember. The fences around her home were board and post. The large tobacco barn was the first outbuilding that Ellie saw as the wagon and buggy made their way up the drive. The trees that lined the drive were small cedar trees, the only green to be seen on this raw winter day. In the fields were the remains of the crops that had been cultivated earlier in the season. There were a few head of cattle that were roaming in the field adjacent to the tobacco barn.

Ellie wasn't sure if they were beef cattle or dairy, she assumed both. On around the curve of the drive, Ellie saw another large barn. The white stone structure had a curved, mansard style roof. *Very nice for a barn.* In a large pasture beyond the barn were several horses, obviously thoroughbred and very expensive stock.

Hade noticed her interest and said, "Those are Daniel Townes' pride and joy. Brought the original stock from Kentucky. He has quite a business."

Ellie nodded, "They're beautiful. I remember that Mrs. Townes' family raises horses in Kentucky." Some things were coming back to Ellie's memory now.

Before more conversation could continue, Ellie saw the house before her. It was beautiful; red brick with gleaming white columns and deep green shutters. The porch across the front of the house was painted a shade of grey, and the large limestone steps that led up to the porch from the drive were massive. The windows were adorned on the inside with French damask draperies, while there were also shutters to give added privacy in rooms facing the porch. Ellie scanned the house from top to bottom, thinking it was the loveliest home she had ever seen. The yard around the house was now brown from the coming on of winter, but she could imagine how lush and green it would be come spring. The trees around the house were bare now, but she could see how their limbs would be full of leaves, offering the house an abundance of shade.

Jonas walked around to the side of the buggy, "If you hand me your dog, I can help you out, Ms. Morgan."

Ellie removed the wool blanket that was keeping the chill from penetrating into her bones. She handed Jonas the small basket holding Jack. When he sat the basket down, Jack jumped out. He took off around the house.

Ellie exclaimed, "You'd think that dog had been here before, the way he is making himself right at home!"

Ellie stood carefully, placing her foot onto the high stone rock that served as a stepping-stone for disembarking from the buggy. She carefully maneuvered down the stairs onto the grass. Her slick soles made her walking slower than usual. Her hoop skirt swayed as she walked.

Hade was busy getting the trunks unloaded, waiting for his hired hand to help fetch them up to the porch. Ellie made it safely to the front porch, and Jonas hurried back to grab the handle of the large trunk.

Before Ellie could bang the large gold door knocker, Camille Townes opened the door. She was much prettier than Ellie had imagined; her dark black hair was parted down the middle of her head and pulled back severely into a knot at the back of her neck. She wore a simple hair adornment of lace, and her dress was of green and black checked wool. She wasn't much older than Ellie. Her dark blue eyes were framed by a dark row of lashes. Ellie noticed she had skin that reminded her of a porcelain doll. She smiled warmly and held out her small hand.

Ellie extended her gloved hand, "Mrs. Townes, I'm so pleased to meet you. I'm Ella Morgan."

Camille took her hand and guided her into the large entry hall.

"Please come in and get out of the cold." She stuck her head out of the door and said, "Mr. Flynn, would you mind bringing those trunks in, please?"

Hade and Jonas wiped their shoes on the large rug in the front hall.

"Joseph, could you come down here?" Camille asked loudly.

Ellie looked all around, peering into the rooms that flanked the sides of the hall. She had a strange feeling come over her, as if she had been here before. But that couldn't be. She had never been south of Louisville, Kentucky.

Just then, a young boy, about the same age as the Negro boy who had been at the depot, came bounding down the stairs.

"Joseph, please remember yourself!" Camille admonished. "I want you to meet your new teacher, Miss Morgan."

Joseph gave Ellie an impish grin, "Hello, Ms. Morgan."

Ellie smiled, "Good to meet you, Joseph. I'm sure we will get along famously."

Ellie was now aware that her accent was not southern at all, but the accents of the people she had met so far had a warm, soothing sound.

"Joseph, please take Mr. Flynn up to the closet room so that they can deposit the trunks."

Joseph turned to the two men, motioning for them to follow him. As they made their way up the stairs, Ellie could hear the boy and trio chattering away.

Turning to Ellie, Camille said, "You must be famished from your trip. Here, let me take your wrap."

Camille had a motherly smile; one that Ellie felt was familiar.

"Thank you, Mrs. Townes. I expect I am a little hungry."

Ellie couldn't remember when she had eaten last. The two walked into the large parlor on the left of the hall.

"Please, come in and have a seat. I'll have Lucy make you something to eat."

Ellie wasn't sure who that was, but she was glad to have a meal prepared for her. The trip and all the excitement had left her lightheaded. Ellie spent the time alone to admire the beautiful furnishings in the parlor. The wall coverings and damask draperies were done in a soft rose. The pattern was similar to what was in the hallway, but there were several different varieties of flowers mingled into the pattern.

Camille soon returned, sitting beside Ellie.

"I hope your trip was pleasant. Since the new railroad has come through town, it makes travel so much more accommodating. Why, my parents came from Lexington just last year, and it took them almost two weeks to make the trip," Camille shared.

"It wasn't as difficult as I had expected. I brought my companion, a cocker spaniel. His name is Jack. I hope that wasn't presumptuous of me." Ellie replied.

Camille didn't seem to mind Ellie's traveling companion.

"It's quite all right. Joseph has been begging for a dog since two summers past. His own dog, a rabbit dog from my father's lot, finally died of old age. I expect he will make quite a nuisance of himself with your dog."

Ellie was glad that Jack wouldn't be a problem.

"You are welcome to keep him with you in your room, if you are accustomed to having him indoors. While Ms. Lucy prepares your dinner, let's go upstairs and see your room and the classroom."

Ellie was anxious to rest before dinner. Just as the two were coming back into the entry hall, Jonas and Hade were reaching the bottom of the stairway.

"I think that is the last of them, Mrs. Townes," Hade said.

"Thank you again, Mr. Flynn. Thank you, Jonas. Please give Sally my regards. Tell her that she must come and meet our Miss Morgan as soon as she is able."

Ellie smiled, and said her goodbye's as well.

"I'll tell her, Mrs. Townes." Hade and Jonas tipped their caps to the women and walked toward the door.

Camille saw the two men out, and then turned to walk Ellie up to her living quarters. The upstairs was quite large; the sun was streaming into the hallway, giving it warmth that radiated through to Ellie's chilled bones. To the left of the stairway was Daniel and Camille's bedroom. She noticed there was a fire in the fireplace, and on the mantel were several small tin types. Hanging above the mantle was a golden oval frame. Inside was a portrait of three small children. To the right of the stairs was Joseph's room. Ellie could see the young boy lying on the floor in front of his fireplace playing with a set of dominoes. He seemed unconcerned with the new teacher who would be living in their home.

To the front of the house, there were two large bedrooms on either side of the hallway. Both were painted in feminine shades. The one to the left was Hattie's room. Camille explained that Hattie was their youngest daughter. Hattie would be returning home from the Female Academy in a week.

Across the hall from Hattie's room was Ellie's room. This had been Caroline's room, their oldest daughter. She married almost two years before, and it had remained empty since she moved out of Mimosa Grove. The small room to the front of the hallway was actually two rooms that were made into one. This room was the classroom that Ellie would be using to teach Joseph during the day. Another porch, above the downstairs porch, went out from this small classroom.

"Your home is just lovely, Mrs. Townes. It is so spacious."

Camille pointed to the stairway that was much narrower and said, "That stairway leads up to the attic."

Ellie replied, "How nice that you have added storage."

Camille pointed to the right, "Ms. Morgan, this will be your room for however long you choose to stay with us. Joseph has not had proper schooling for some time. He was quite sick last year, but has made a miraculous recovery. One would never know he had been ill."

Ellie walked into her room, which was painted a pleasant shade of lavender. There were white lace curtains that hung to the floor, and a bed cover that was crocheted lace. The furniture was a deep mahogany, which included a four-poster bed, large wash stand with white pitcher and bowl, and a very ornate dresser with mirror. The accommodations were much nicer than she could have imagined.

"This is just lovely, Mrs. Townes."

Camille was about to say something when she was interrupted by Lucy down below,

"Miz Camille, dinner's ready for Miss Morgan."

"Thank you, Lucy. We'll be right down."

Camille smiled and said, "Let's go downstairs while your food is still hot."

She turned and the sound of her skirt brushing against the door facing on her way out broke the silence in the rest of the upstairs. They went into the dining room where an older Negro was waiting to serve the two ladies.

"Lucy, this will be just fine, thank you."

Camille made the formal introductions between Lucy and Ellie.

"Miss Morgan, this is Lucy, our housekeeper and cook."

Ellie smiled and said, "I'm pleased to meet you, Miss Lucy."

Lucy's smile all but squeezed her eyes completely shut. She was not a large woman, but had a very round, full face. She wore a cotton dress with a starched white apron that was pinned to the front of her gown. Ellie sat down at the large dining room table to meal of cooked chicken with dumplings and cold milk. Ellie thanked the women and began to eat. As she ate her meal, she noticed the portraits around the room and the furnishings of fine mahogany.

It didn't take Ellie long to finish her meal, and before she could clean up her plate, Lucy appeared. She cleared the table, asking Ellie if she could be of further service. Ellie wasn't sure if Lucy was a servant or a slave. Ellie thanked Lucy and made her way into the hallway. As she was going to the parlor to speak with Camille, the front door opened and a middle-aged man walked into the house.

Daniel Townes was a handsome man, having a dark complexion and dark wavy hair. His dark brown eyes gave him a stern look, but he wasn't any more so than Ellie's own father. Daniel Townes was tall; Ellie imagined he was over six feet in height. Hearing her husband enter the house, Camille gracefully moved into the entry hall.

"Daniel, I want you to meet Miss Ella Morgan, Joseph's teacher."

Ellie smiled and extended her hand to him.

"Ms. Morgan, we are so happy to have you here with us," Daniel said.

Ellie shook Daniel's hand and said, "Thank you. I'm anxious to get started with Joseph's schooling."

Ellie liked the Townes family already. She decided that whatever reason they selected a Northerner to educate their son, she would do her best to make them happy with their choice.

The rest of the day was spent meeting the servants at the Townes' plantation. Lucy, she later learned, came to the Townes home twenty-five years earlier as a slave. She was a gift to Camille from Daniel's mother. Daniel Townes' parents had come to visit their son from North Carolina. With them came five slaves, part of Daniel's inheritance given early. They also felt that Daniel would need a work force to help build the barns and stables that would be needed to run a successful plantation and horse farm. Daniel was not in agreement with owning slaves. He had promised all five of the Negroes that they would be given employment if they would stay on, if not, they would have to return to his father's home. He would not sell them, but he didn't feel he could turn them out with no means of supporting themselves. All five decided to remain in the household. It was agreed that they would enter into a period of indentured servitude to Daniel, the customary seven years of indenture, and then, given their freedom.

Camille's family had also owned slaves, but she felt that slavery was something she didn't want to carry with her into this new marriage. Slaves would be brought into their lives as workers for a time, but they would never buy or take part in the selling of another human. The rest of the servants were Mose, a horse groom and blacksmith; Abraham, the tanner and carpenter; and the field hands, Josiah and Hiram. Ellie saw the pride in their faces as she was shown samples of their work around the plantation. She also learned of an older slave, Old Thomas, who had run away from his master south of Nashville. He stayed for a time with the Townes family, but was returned to his owner when a bounty hunter showed up at Mimosa Grove to claim the fugitive.

Daniel Townes had fulfilled his agreement to all five of his servants. They remained on the property, living in a small section of land between the plantation and the home of Ben and Elizabeth Ewers. The area in and around Hendersonville was a mix of slaveholders and those who tolerated the existence of the institution. Daniel Townes was one who was respected in the town for his beliefs, but others felt he was going to regret having free blacks living on his plantation, if there was to be a war.

Ellie enjoyed talking to Camille Townes. She was educated, graceful, and very pretty for someone of her age. Ellie felt that she longed to have a friend; life on a plantation could be very lonely for a woman. They spent the first afternoon talking and learning about the family, and what

Ellie's responsibilities would entail. Afterwards, Camille brought down the small tin type photographs from her bedroom. She shared with Ellie the faces of her children. Her oldest daughter, Caroline, had moved to nearby Nashville; she would not have a chance to make her acquaintance. Hattie, their youngest daughter, would be returning to Mimosa Grove the following day. *They all seem so familiar; it's as if I have been here before.*

Ellie spent the first evening at Mimosa Grove unpacking her belongings from her trunks and putting her things into the two large chifferobes that were in her bedroom. One trunk, a small version of the larger two, would not open. She searched throughout her reticule and within the carpetbag that carried her supplies and credentials; however, none of the keys would open the lock. She decided not to worry herself with that now. Everything she needed was unpacked. She was angry with herself for the addled state she was in since arriving in Hendersonville. There were parts of her memory that seemed foggy, almost erased. Ellie decided to keep quiet about such things. No sense giving her employers reason to think she wasn't stable.

She looked out the window in her room. The pastures were long ago harvested, and gave a sorrowful look to the once vibrant fields. Hiram, Josiah and Abram were walking back through the field; she assumed their work for the day was over. It was nearing seven o'clock and the day's light was nearly gone. Their lanterns swung back and forth as they made their way behind the barn. She reached for the matches that were in a small crystal bottle on the bedside table. She quickly lit the candles in the room.

She felt a chill that seemed to start from within. Her shawl had been placed across the bed, she assumed by Lucy. It was then that she noticed the fire in her fireplace was almost out. Just then, Joseph appeared in the doorway.

"You want me to fetch you more wood, Ma'am?"

Ellie looked down at the small wood box that sat beside the hearth.

"Oh, that would be very nice, Joseph. I guess in my excitement of unpacking, I've let my fire go down."

Joseph took the small box and turned to go downstairs. Ellie smiled, thinking he looked very much like a smaller version of Mr. Townes.

Ellie had her books and slate lying on the bed. She wanted to look at the classroom Camille had created in the small room at the front of the hallway. She gathered her things and walked into the classroom.

It was furnished very plainly, a small table and chair for Joseph, and small desk for her. There was a large map of the world hanging on the wall, as well as a map of the state of Tennessee. There was also a smaller picture of George Washington that Ellie thought looked very familiar. Perhaps she had a similar one in the schoolhouse where she had been employed.

Ellie was busy looking around at the textbooks that had been placed on one of two shelves in the room. She jumped when she heard two sets of footsteps coming up the large stairway.

"Just put the wood in the hearth, son, and then go fill the box again so that Ms. Morgan won't lose heat tonight."

"Yes, Papa," Joseph said.

Ellie came out of the classroom to see Daniel Townes walking into the bedroom he shared with his wife. She could hear their conversation and closed her bedroom door, not wanting to eavesdrop. She could hear them despite her efforts. The conversation had apparently been about a meeting Daniel Townes had attended earlier in the week. Talk of the election had everyone in town up in arms. It was a short four days until the election of the sixteenth president. If Lincoln was to be elected, Ellie knew the country would be ripped apart if southerners kept their promise about leaving the Union.

"I wrote to Father earlier this month; he thinks that the Union should be spared, whatever the cost. You know how Father feels. His memory of the War with England is still strong, Camille. I worry that he will have to choose, should that come to blows."

Camille walked from the chifferobe, bringing her nightgown to the bed. As she turned to Daniel, she lifted her chignon for him to remove her necklace, before she undressed. He helped her with her undressing each evening, a ritual that had been in place since the early days of their marriage. She stepped out of the hoop and petticoats that were tied about her waist. The stays of her corset being untied was the most liberating event she experienced during her day's work. She kept her stays tight; too tight according to her husband, so that she was most often out of breath when ascending the large stairway.

As she pulled the long cotton gown over her head, she said, "Daniel, you know your father is still of the way of thinking that my father is. I'm sure they are both backing Mr. Breckinridge. I know Papa will. They want to keep their rights, but don't have much compassion towards the rights of their servants. I love my family, but I'm so thankful that our servants are not bound to us by the black stain of slavery."

Daniel admired the mind of his wife. It wasn't common for men of the day to hold their female counterpart's opinion in such high regard. To the dismay of many of the other planters in and around Hendersonville, Daniel Townes was a rare breed, indeed. Women were to keep their notions to themselves; not worrying with such things as politics or anything else that men had a say.

Daniel sat down on the settee at the end of the large four-poster bed. He began removing his boot.

"Hade Flynn told me the other day that some of the other plantation owners were thinking of moving their slaves further south, fearing what would happen should Mr. Lincoln become President," Daniel commented, nonchalantly, "it's going to happen, Camille; the whole country is on tenterhooks. We will have to hold to the bar to see what will happen as a result of it."

Talk of war was something every gentleman in the county had been debating within his shops and social gatherings.

Ellie had heard several men on the train talking about the election. They were Southern gentleman who were very upset with the thought of Lincoln being in the White House. She heard the word secession for the first time in her life just the other day. She wasn't sure how it could happen. Her grandfather's had fought in the War for Independence, but to think that in less than eighty years it would be for aught? As a Northerner, would she be safe in the south should Lincoln's election happen? The election would be held November 6, 1860. Coming to the south now might be a dangerous decision for the Northern teacher to have made.

The following day Daniel Townes awoke early. He asked Hiram to hitch the team up to the buggy and Josiah to hitch the two mules to the wagon. Camille had been looking forward for quite some time to the day when Hattie would be back to Mimosa Grove. Hattie was coming home from her two years at the Female Academy in Gallatin. Lucy would be preparing her favorite meal of fried chicken and dumplings. Ellie could already hear much commotion going on downstairs as Lucy been making trips in and out of the house from the summer kitchen. Camille had been in Hattie's bedroom changing the bed linens and airing out her room. The window curtains were slightly blowing in from the chilly breeze; Ellie felt excited for the family having their daughter home again. She was also excited to have another female with whom she could share her secrets.

Daniel, Hiram and Josiah set off for the train depot in Gallatin. The trip would take them until afternoon before they would be back to the plantation. It was later that morning when Ellie was beginning her first lesson with Joseph, that she noticed a wagon coming up the long curving driveway. Joseph hopped up from his studies to peer through the curtain on the door that led out to the upper porch.

"That's Mr. Flynn and his wife. I guess they wanted to see you," Joseph said, almost disappointed in all the fuss folks were making.

Joseph didn't seem excited to have another adult in the house today. He would much rather be out in the barn with Mose. He enjoyed being around him and working the horses. He loved fishing from the steep banks of the Cumberland, or off the dock that jutted out slightly into the river.

Ellie continued her lesson of mathematics that was planned for the day. Joseph clearly wasn't one for book learning; he was having quite a time with his multiplication figuring.

Ellie was beginning to see why Mrs. Townes had given up teaching the boy herself. She had asked her husband to place an ad in the paper for a tutor. Ellie couldn't remember reading the ad, or even having accepted the position. Funny how her mind had suddenly forgotten such things. She tried to continue the drills with Joseph, but he had gotten frustrated. She decided that two hours of drill and rote memorization was taking a toll on her patience.

"How about we take a walk outdoors? I would love for you to show me around."

Joseph's eyes brightened at the chance to be pardoned from his prison sentence.

"Yes, I think that would be a good idea, Ms. Morgan. I know just where to take you."

Ellie wasn't sure she liked the sound of that, but she hadn't seen any of the grounds, and Mimosa Grove was a beautiful plantation waiting to share its secrets with Ellie. Teacher and student walked down the stairway. Jack came bounding down the steps after them, his long ears almost tripping him as he went before them.

"Jack! You mustn't charge in front of us," Ellie admonished, "you could get crushed under my skirts!"

Joseph laughed as the pup began chewing on the laces of his shoes. Ellie bent over to pick the puppy up before one of them tumbled the rest of the way down the stairs. Camille came from the parlor just as they reached the bottom of the landing.

"Where are the two of you off on such a fine morning?" she asked.

Joseph gave his mother his best angelic expression.

"Mama, I wanted to take Miss Morgan out to the grove. She said we could take a break."

Camille couldn't bear the look her youngest child would use when wanting to get his way. She had wanted to keep him little forever; she didn't want to let this precious boy get away as his older brothers had.

She patted his blonde curly hair, "All right then, go show Miss Morgan the grounds. Put on your coat, and put your scarf about your neck."

Camille wasn't going to let this child succumb to sickness if she could prevent it.

Ellie reached for her wool cape that hung on the peg near the hallway. She wrapped a woolen scarf around her head to protect her ears from the cold.

"We won't be gone long, Mrs. Townes. I'm afraid I am not a fan of the cold," Ellie confided.

The two walked out the back of the house, down the large steps of the back porch. Ellie could see that the windows of the summer kitchen were steamed from the heat rising off the skillets and pots. The work that went into a large meal was immense. She was thankful that wasn't her job while she was with the Townes family.

They walked on passed the arbor and into a grove of mimosa trees that were growing in a neat row along the thicket beyond the house. Joseph began telling Ellie about the different trees that were around the thicket. She was impressed with his knowledge of such things. As they walked farther away from the house, she saw the object of the tour in this part of the property. A small cemetery lay just ahead of them, surrounded by a large stone fence that bordered the perimeter of the plot of land.

Ellie also noticed that to enter the solemn area, they would need to open a wrought iron gate. Joseph ran ahead and opened the latch, which broke the relative silence in the area. Ellie was mindful of the small headstones that were lined in rows. There were two headstones side by side; both of a smooth white stone. They had been carved expertly, it appeared, and both had the name TOWNES curved across the top. Below the name was a carving of a lamb and a finger pointing towards Heaven. The names of two boys were placed below the carvings. Joseph began giving an account for each of the graves in the small family cemetery.

"This one here is Daniel, and that one there is Joshua," Joseph recounted.

Ellie couldn't shake the feeling that she had been here before, listening to the crow cawing high in the mimosa tree.

"Mama says they are watching over us. Do you believe that, Miss Morgan?" Joseph looked up to Ellie, shading his eyes from the sun.

Ellie smiled at Joseph, "Yes, I believe they do watch over us, Joseph. I lost both of my parents, and I believe they are watching over me."

Joseph seemed satisfied with Ellie's response. He smiled back, standing up and brushing the dirt from his knees. Ellie touched the gravestones as if she were patting the head of a small child. There were two small markers towards the back of the cemetery.

"Who do those belong to, Joseph?" Ellie asked.

"That one is Mose's wife, Jenny. That little one beside it is his boy, Saul. They died before I was born," Joseph replied.

Ellie was sad to hear of the loss in Mose's life. The two walked back up the path to the house. The history lesson was over.

Lucy finished carrying in the last of the pots of food that she had been preparing all morning.

"Mister Joseph, you need to git in the house before you catch yer death. It's almost time for Miss Hattie to come home, and don't you be comin' to the table with dirt under your fingernails!"

Ellie put her hand over her mouth to hide the smile spreading over her face. Lucy was keeping the family in tow, and Ellie liked her already. Joseph ran through the hall and up stairs before Camille could correct him. Ellie hung up her cloak and rubbed her fingers to get the warmth circulating through her veins again.

"So where did your explorations take you?" Camille asked, raising an eyebrow.

Ellie wasn't sure if she would be upset about the trip to the graveyard, but she answered her honestly.

"He took me to the family cemetery. He wanted to show me his brothers' graves."

Ellie put her hand on Camille's.

"I'm sorry for your loss, Mrs. Townes."

She knew about losing a loved one, but not a child. She could only imagine the grief of losing two precious little boys. Camille let out a small sigh, and patted Ellie's hand.

"Thank you, Ella. It is a crown of sorrows that I bear, but I have three children that I am blessed to have still with me."

Ellie and Camille shared a moment that most women yearned to have. Female companionship in a time when there was no time for much else besides raising a family and running the plantation. Camille had longed for a close friend since coming to Mimosa Grove. The women who lived in adjoining plantations were either much older or too busy with their lives to come for a visit. Mrs. Flynn came on occasion, but Camille never developed a close friendship to her. She felt a kinship with Ellie that she couldn't quite explain, and Ellie found Camille to be kind and easy to talk to. As the two sat in the parlor, Lucy began carrying in the meal, placing the bowls on the sideboard in the dining room.

"Excuse me, Ella. I need to check on the meal."

Camille moved gracefully through the entry hall, her skirt swishing as she walked into the dining room.

Ellie looked around the room, noticing two small samplers that hung in small golden frames beside the window. Ellie marveled at the delicate handiwork, both obviously handmade by the two Townes girls. She leaned over the back of the settee to get a closer look. She was caught off guard by Camille's soft voice.

"Those were made by Caroline and Hattie when they were seven and ten years of age. I believe the embroidery is quite good for their first attempt, don't you?"

Ellie must have made a similar sampler as a child, for even the verse caused her to pause.

"The verse on Hattie's work is something I must have done as well. All we have to give our children when it is all said and done is our heritage, and hopefully an inheritance," Ellie said as she stifled a giggle.

They both shared a brief moment of gaiety before the sound of the buggy and wagon pulling up to the hitching post caught their attention.

"Excuse me, Ella, while I go help Hattie with her things."

Camille made her way to the front door just as Hattie came through the large entryway.

"Mama! I've missed you so much!" Hattie said, as she wrapped her arms around her mother and kissed her cheek.

"Hattie, you are more beautiful than I remember!" Camille said.

Ellie had walked to the parlor doorway to see Hattie Townes. She stood in the entry hall wearing a navy wool cape and dark navy crocheted hood. Her long dark eyelashes curled towards her eyebrows, accentuating her dark green eyes. The dress she wore underneath the cape was a tartan plaid wool gown. The bodice had small black glass buttons down the front with braid and tassels adorning the pagoda sleeves and hem. Her hair was pulled back into a dark net, showing only hints of the curls that her net was trying to tame. Ellie thought she was prettier than her portrait in the dining room.

"Ella, come and meet Hattie," Camille called.

Ellie made her way over to Hattie, who was taking off her cape.

"Hello, Hattie. I'm Ella Morgan. It's nice to meet you."

Hattie smiled and took the hand of Ellie in hers, "Papa told me all about you, Miss Morgan. It's so nice to have another female in the house again!"

Hattie had missed her sister Caroline very much, and now that she had started a family of her own, had little time to come for visits to Mimosa Grove.

Daniel Townes entered the house carrying a large trunk, followed by Hiram, Abram and Josiah.

"Daniel, do you need Joseph to help you carry those upstairs?" Camille questioned.

"It's all right; we can make another trip if needed." Daniel continued up the stairs to Hattie's bedroom where the trunks would be deposited.

Just then, Lucy walked into the hallway to greet the young miss.

"Miss Hattie! I shore have missed you, darlin'!"

Hattie turned from the women to hold out her arms to Lucy.

"Aunt Lucy!" Hattie squealed.

Hattie gave Lucy a warm embrace. It was a mutual affection between Hattie and Lucy, and the house seemed to have let out a sigh of relief to have the children back under one roof again.

The week with Hattie home seemed to go by quickly. Ellie and Joseph spent a good portion of each day in the classroom upstairs. Talk in Hendersonville and near hearthstones around the country was about the election on November 6, 1860. Abraham Lincoln, a Republican, had been elected the sixteenth President of the United States. Almost overnight, talk of succession was a common discussion in the South. Mose had driven Daniel Townes to the Court House in Hendersonville to cast his vote.

When he returned home to Mimosa Grove, he told his wife, "Well, we must prepare for the worst, but pray for the best."

Camille knew in her heart that this would be the beginning of many a family in Middle Tennessee choosing sides. Caroline had married only a year before, and now was living on a plantation very close to Nashville. Her husband and family owned slaves. Camille feared the family would be torn apart. She had sent word for the family to come together at Christmas, but Caroline's husband feared her condition was too fragile for travel. Camille was dismayed; it could very well be their last to celebrate as a family united under one flag.

Ellie offered her help whenever she wasn't teaching Joseph. She was able to speak with Hattie and get to know the young woman. Having no sister to confide in, she chose to share a secret or two with Ellie. As they sat in the parlor one afternoon, Hattie told Ellie of a young boy she had met earlier in the summer. Raford Collins had come up to Gallatin to visit his sister, Maggie, who had been a friend of Hattie's at the Female Academy. She talked about the young man coming to Mimosa Grove with his father to purchase a mare. Ellie could tell that Hattie Townes would like to have a beau, but her mother was none too keen on another daughter leaving the fold so soon. She had so much yet to teach her daughter. Hattie asked to have the Collins family join them for Christmas dinner, since she wanted very much to see Raford again. Daniel and Camille Townes agreed, and the necessary letters were sent to Mr. and Mrs. Collins and their children.

Christmas in Tennessee would be a first for Ellie Morgan. She had never been away from her home during the family holiday. She wasn't sure how the Townes family would celebrate this Christmas season with thoughts of war on everyone's mind. Ellie sat in her room, listening to the different family sounds throughout the large house. She sat on the couch in her room, with Jack nestled on her lap. She tried to remember her own family Christmases in the past. She faintly remembered her father's face, and the sound of her mother singing *Silent Night* after she read the Christmas story from the large family Bible. She couldn't understand what had become of her memories. She seemed to have lost a good portion of them, sadly.

"Jack, what has happened to me?" she asked, as she stroked his back and scratched the silky ears with her fingers.

She needed to make a trip to town to buy Christmas gifts for each of the family members. She would ask Josiah to drive her to town tomorrow.

As she crawled into her bed, she felt a chill that came from within. She missed her own family. She lay awake for several hours, trying to decide what special gifts she would purchase. She also was looking forward to meeting Raford Collins and his family. It would be grand to have the house full for Christmas.

The election of Abraham Lincoln had brought about a tense time for families who lived in Middle Tennessee. There were many families with strong Union ties, and Daniel Townes was one. He couldn't imagine how he could support leaving the Union, and yet that was just what family members who lived in North Carolina were deciding. The Townes family began to prepare for the holiday season, much like years before. Hattie shared with Ellie her stories of getting to meet Raford Collins when he came to get his sister from the academy for a short visit with the family. Ellie enjoyed her talks with Hattie, and she in turn enjoyed having another woman in which she could confide.

Ellie enjoyed the weekly church services in Hendersonville. The Flynns attended the United Methodist Church as well. There was a row of pews in the balcony of the church for the slaves and free Negroes to sit during the service. Ellie found it disturbing, but she accepted the way things were. Ellie soon was introduced to all the families in the area around Mimosa Grove.

Camille Townes was respected within the small circle of parishioners that were members of the Methodist Church in Hendersonville. Daniel Townes, a deacon in the church, found that other church leaders were becoming divided on the recent talk of succession by the Southern states.

"Let's not talk of such things during the Lord's day," Daniel admonished.

He could never have fathomed the events that were about to happen to his beloved country.

Preparations for the Christmas season began early in the month, as there would be guests arriving from out of town. Camille began gathering decorations to adorn the rooms of the home. Mistletoe was gathered in the trees down below the grove, and pinecones were brought up from the thicket near the Gallatin Pike. Lucy helped with the popcorn strings, and there would be bows of greenery draped on the mantles and banisters. Ellie enjoyed taking part in the decorations, and there was much lightheartedness amid the dark shadow that was ever present following the election of 1860.

Camille had read of a new tradition that was being started in many of the finer homes in the North. Families were bringing evergreens into their homes to decorate, called Christmas trees. Camille had asked Daniel to find a suitable tree from the grove, and that afternoon, a Christmas tree was cut from the choice of small cedar trees that grew near the horse pasture. Camille had received gifts from her parents in Lexington, as neither would be able to make the trip to Mimosa Grove. Adam Burnell was slowing down; it would be his last Christmas to spend on his beloved farm, Hickory Hill, nestled in the fertile valley of bluegrass, in Lexington.

Ellie and Hattie offered to help Lucy press the napkins and table linens that would be brought into the large dining room where the Christmas meal would be served. The meal was already planned, and the cooking would begin the day before Christmas Eve. The Collins family would arrive sometime the day before, bringing their servants to aid in the preparation and serving of the meal. Camille Townes was used to such practices, as her own family owned servants. She didn't want to offend her guests, so she explained to Lucy that she would have the help she needed in preparing such a large banquet. It would be customary for the house guests to remain at least a week, possibly longer should inclement weather set in. Camille had instructed her housekeeper to prepare the extra bedding for the guests.

Lucy had been brought to Twin Ponds plantation with her mother, Patsy. Daniel's father had bought them from a neighboring planter who had fallen on hard times. Lucy grew up with the Townes' children, and learned to read and write while sitting on the hardwood floor during lessons for the *master's youngin's*. When Daniel came to Tennessee to start his married life, Mary Anna Townes had given Lucy to her new daughter-in-law as a gift. She would help Camille set up her new home and be a nurse to the babies she would soon be having. Eighteen-year old Lucy would be the same age as her mistress. She cried most of the way to Tennessee, heartbroken that her mother was not allowed to join them. Daniel decided that he would no longer be the reason for another family being broken apart. He vowed to never buy or sell another human. Lucy would choose to remain with the Townes, the only family she had left.

Ellie was helping to bring in the wash from the wash house when she saw the wagons and the black carriage making its way up the long driveway. Joseph ran from the horse barn to announce their arrival as well. Daniel set the ledger he was writing in back on the shelf of the secretary. He walked from the library and put on his coat.

"Camille, come and help me receive our guests," he said in his soft manner.

Camille pulled the woolen hood up around her coifed hair. She asked Joseph to run to fetch Mose, Josiah, Hiram and Abe; they would be needed to carry in all the trunks and presents. As the first wagon pulled into the yard, two tall and able-bodied Negroes jumped off and began unloading a large, heavy trunk. Two dark-skinned women were climbing down from behind the trunks, smoothing down their dresses and pulling the blankets they had wrapped around their shoulders up and closer to their chins. Ellie peered from the window in the parlor. She noticed how finely dressed the Collinses were, compared to the scantily attired slaves that accompanied them.

Ellie counted seven slaves in all, four men and three women. Hattie had come downstairs now; quickly throwing her cape around her shoulders, her hair neatly pulled behind her head in a fancy braid.

"You look fine, Hattie. Hurry out to welcome your guests!" Ellie said.

Hattie blushed, and out the door she went. A gust of cold air blew in as she moved through the large doorway. Ellie watched the family climb out of the buggy, one by one, onto the large stone that was placed in the exact height for the ladies with large skirts. Ellie noticed how pretty the Collins' women were. Mrs. Collins appeared to be about Ellie's age. She was a fair headed, petite woman. Each of daughters was dressed in the latest fashions, like their mother. Hattie and Maggie Collins embraced when they saw one another. Ellie could see the families making their introductions as first one, and then another Collins' disembarked from the buggy. Isaac Collins stepped out of the buggy, his dark frock coat complementing his well-muscled frame. He stood nearly six foot tall, Ellie estimated. He was an attractive man; his mustache and goatee were dark with just a hint of grey. Isaac Collins was ten years his wife's senior. Ellie could see the way he cared for her, helping her from the carriage block. He stood about the same height as his son, who came around the buggy from an awaiting wagon.

Ellie could see his eyes light up like two lanterns when he caught sight of Hattie. Remembering his good breeding, he tipped his hat to the ladies and smiled at Hattie. The Townes and Collins families made their way onto the large covered front porch as the Negro women followed their masters into the house behind them. The servants of Daniel Townes began helping the three slaves of Isaac Collins unload the trunks and carry them into the house.

Once inside, Camille introduced the family to Ellie. Ellie had met Liza on the train to Hendersonville. She hugged Ellie and told her how happy she was to see her once again.

When she was introduced to Raford, Ellie had a very strange reaction to the young man. It was as if she had met him already. In fact, before she even was formally introduced, she knew he went by the name Rafe. The feeling was so odd that Ellie felt the room spin, and she reached out for the banister to steady herself.

"Are you all right, Ms. Morgan?" Rafe asked.

Everyone turned to see what was wrong with Ellie.

"Oh I'm fine, thank you," Ellie quickly replied.

As the two families went into the parlor, Lucy took to giving instructions to the three slaves who were waiting for their directions. Esther, Polly and Cordelia were on the heels of Lucy as she explained what would need to be done in her kitchen. The three women made their way back out to the brick building behind the main house; while Samuel, Jibe and George made another trip back to the wagons. Mose helped Gideon unhitch the teams and directed the others as to where they could hitch the mules and horses for the duration of their stay. He would also show the men where they would be sleeping.

The barn would not be as warm as the small cabins where the Townes' servants lived, but none felt inclined to offer the Collins' slaves a place to sleep within their own homes. The large table in the dining room was set with Camille Townes' china that had come from England. Her mother had given Camille her china as a wedding present. She was proud to have such a fine set to pass down to her daughters. Daniel's mother had also given them a set that had belonged to Daniel's mother. The Townes family had brought the fine bone china with them from England when they came to Philadelphia on the *Sarah Goode* in 1725.

The meal prepared for Christmas Eve dinner was typical for a Southern family. Ham and Turkey from the family's smoke house were cooked, as well as turnips, yams and potatoes. A procession of servants came into the large room carrying bowls and large serving dishes. The rolls that were placed in the large basket on the table were as big as Mose's hand. Ellie's mouth was watering long before the desserts were brought to the sideboard. There was mince pie, apple pie and plum pudding, not to mention the rum cake that Laura had brought along with her. A fine Madera wine was also brought up from the cellar to be shared by all the family. For the special occasion, Daniel would be allowing young Joseph just a sip.

Ellie listened to the conversations that were going on around the table, and she couldn't remember when she had enjoyed a meal more. She couldn't find any reason for her preoccupation with Rafe Collins. He didn't seem to notice her bad manners, and she tried not to be so obvious in her staring. He was too taken with Hattie for anyone else to attract his attention. In fact, the parents of both were quite aware of the two and their not including the rest of the table in their conversations. Joseph found Rafe Collins very interesting, not having an older brother to idolize. The conversation was light and no mention was made of the recent election and talk of secession. While the two families shared in the scrumptious meal, the servants stood behind the table in silence.

Following the dinner, the men took their brandy into the library, while the ladies, Joseph and Rafe, gathered around the pianoforte. Liza and Hattie took turns playing selections, and eventually began to lead the rest of the family in Christmas carols. Ellie requested *Silent Night,* her favorite. Joseph and Raford talked about the mare that would be going back home with the Collinses after their visit. The women sang and shared stories of Christmases past, while across the hallway, the men discussed politics.

Daniel Townes was a Unionist, and felt the Southern states should put aside notions of secession. Isaac Collins was a Southern Democrat, and a supporter of State's Rights. His plantation was one in which there were twenty-five slaves. He felt the election of Lincoln would mean the end to Southern rights, and was concerned with Lincoln freeing all the slaves in the south, now that he had gotten into office. The two politely disagreed with the other's political views, and, being gentleman, decided to let the matter rest on this night, the Eve of Christmas.

"I believe my son is quite taken with your daughter, Daniel. The women of Mimosa Grove are quite lovely. I wouldn't be surprised if you see much more of Raford in the future."

Daniel smiled, "Isaac, I noticed Hattie seemed quite taken with young Raford. I don't see what harm it would cause for Raford to come calling. Our home is open to you and your family anytime."

The two men walked out of the library and joined their families. The large grandfather clock began to chime ten o'clock, and the servants waited to help their masters prepare for bed.

"Lucy, you may show our guests where their rooms are, please."

Laura Collins wasn't used to Negroes having the run of the owner's home. While she was somewhat uncomfortable with Negroes being free to do as they pleased, she tried to be accepting of this arrangement while a guest in the Townes' home. The Collins family were used to being waited on by their servants, and were not about to allow such notions to enter their slaves' minds.

"Thank you, Camille for such a wonderful meal and entertainment," Laura said.

The two families climbed the stairway up to their respective rooms, as Rafe and Hattie were still in the parlor. Camille remained at the foot of the stairs.

"Hattie, it is getting late. We will retire now."

Hattie and Rafe had not had a moment alone, and seeing the families leaving the room, gave them a moment to share without supervision. It wasn't proper for two young people to be alone without another adult.

"I have to see you alone sometime, Hattie," Rafe whispered.

"Tomorrow, after we open presents, we can walk to the stables," Hattie said in hushed tones.

"Coming, Mama," Hattie said as the two young people walked into the hallway.

"Pleasant dreams, Raford," Camille said, climbing the stairs ahead of the young couple.

When they reached the top of the stairs, Hattie walked passed Raford to join Maggie and Liza in her bedroom. Rafe would join Joseph in his room. The Collinses would be sleeping in Ellie's room. Lucy had prepared a bed in the school room for Ellie.

She was not upset with the arrangement, knowing that the guests were given the best. Jack had approached Rafe as he reached the threshold to Joseph's room. He didn't bark at Rafe, but he sniffed his shoe and quickly began to wag his tail.

"He likes you, Rafe," Joseph said, as he bent down and patted Jack's little black head.

"He looks like a good dog; is he yours?" Rafe asked scratching the dog's ear.

"No, he's Miss Morgan's dog. But she says I can play with him like he was mine."

And with that, Ellie retired to her make-shift bedroom.

Ellie quickly dressed into her nightgown and crawled under the two large quilts on her bed. She could hear the soft tones of the conversations coming from the girls' room. She was suddenly homesick for her own daughter. *How odd. No one even asked me about Cassandra.*

She had a sudden pang of panic when she couldn't remember who was taking care of her daughter. She remembered Baltimore. She was quite sure she was away at boarding school. That was why Ellie must have taken on this teaching position. Ellie wasn't sure why she was having such a lapse in memory. It began to worry her, and she tried not to let the panic overtake her. She decided that she was just exhausted from the trip to Tennessee and hadn't had time to think about her life before arriving at Mimosa Grove just a month before.

As she closed her eyes, she began to see faces: a woman with long dark hair, a tall gentleman with a mustache and dark curls. Who were these people, and why were they invading her subconscious thoughts?

Before she could answer her own questions, she had fallen asleep on this peaceful Christmas Eve.

Our most treasured family heirlooms are our sweet family memories.
- Unknown

Chapter 11

Ellie was awakened that Christmas morning by the sound of the girls talking in the room beside her. They were marveling at the snowfall that had covered the trees and fences around Mimosa Grove in a soft blanket of white. Jack was already down off the bed and sniffing the floor, Ellie's cue to take him to the back the door.

"Merry Christmas, Jackson!" Ellie softly said, as she donned her robe.

She quietly opened her door and crept down the stairway to the foyer below. There was a fire burning in the parlor, and she could see Camille laying gifts under the Christmas tree.

Daniel Townes was sitting at his desk, writing into the plantation ledger. Ellie could smell bacon, and it was then that Jack made his presence known, causing Camille and Daniel both to walk from their respective rooms

"Merry Christmas, Ella." Camille softly said.

She reached out her hand to grasp Ellie's.

Ellie smiled, "Merry Christmas, Mrs. Townes."

Turning to Daniel, "Merry Christmas, Mr. Townes," Ellie said.

Daniel walked closer to Ellie and returned his greeting, "And Merry Christmas to you, Miss Morgan. We're happy to have you with us."

Ellie did feel that the Townes family had opened their home and their hearts to her during her month at Mimosa Grove. She took Jack to the front door where he only took a moment to decide he wasn't sure of the snow.

"Allow me, Miss Morgan," Daniel said. "There is no reason for you to ruin your slippers in the snow. I'll take the little imp. I need to check on Fancy. She is to foal any day."

Ellie thanked Daniel, and then moved back from the door to escape the brisk wind that was blowing into the entry hall. She quickly went upstairs to dress for breakfast.

Lucy had the three Collins' slaves following her into the dining room with large bowls of breakfast foods. Christmas breakfast at Mimosa Grove was always a special occasion. The sideboard was loaded with the likes of grits, ham, eggs, flapjacks, homemade apple butter, molasses, and rusks. These were a particular favorite of the Townes' children, and Lucy had prepared an extra batch of these lightly sweetened biscuits for the Collinses. The sound of activity and the aroma of the banquet rising to the second floor landing had brought everyone downstairs.

Ellie secured Jack in her classroom and walked back down the stairway, stopping to take in the view of the two families gathered around the large dining room table. For a moment, she felt as though she were looking through a *Currier and Ives* scene, much like she had seen in the pages of the *Harpers' Weekly*. Truth be told, she was thankful to be celebrating the holiday season with the Townes family. With her parents gone, she knew she would be very lonely this holiday season. Hattie saw Ellie and walked out into the hallway.

"Ella, please come and join us. Papa is just getting ready to ask the blessing!"

Ellie took Hattie's small hand in hers and walked into the dining room.

"Miss Ella, please sit by me," Joseph asked.

He had grown quite fond of his teacher, and Ellie had become attached to him. As everyone took their seats around the large mahogany table, the servants took their place around the room to help serve their masters. Lucy had found the Collins' slaves a help; however, she felt it was an intrusion into her domain having others messing in the area Miss Camille had entrusted to her. She would make the best of it, knowing that in a few days, all would return to normal. She also knew she was fortunate, as were Mose, Abram, Hiram, and Josiah. They were free to come and go as they pleased now.

Daniel Townes asked that everyone take the hand of the person sitting beside them, as was the custom each evening when the Towneses sat down to dinner. The Collins family were not used to this ritual, but graciously did as they were asked. Hattie grasped the hand of Maggie to her left, and felt the warm hand of Rafe seek hers. As their hands touched, Hattie could feel currents of warmth course through her veins. She blushed as Rafe smiled, obviously feeling the same effect.

Daniel began, "Let us bow our heads and offer Providence thanks for the bounty we are about to receive, and for sending us the greatest of gifts, His Son, Christ Jesus."

Everyone bowed their heads and closed their eyes as he began his prayer. Ellie quickly opened her eyes just a slit, and in doing so caught a glimpse from across the table. She could see that Rafe and Hattie were looking at one another. She quickly closed her eyes just as the *'amen'* was said. Thus began a buzz of conversations around the table.

The Townes and Collins families were getting on well, and Hattie and Rafe hadn't noticed another soul in the room. After the meal was finished, the servants began to clear the plates and dishes from the dining room.

Camille stood and said, "Let us go into the parlor and see what was left under the tree. It seems that Santa has come."

Everyone smiled, and much laughter and merriment followed as the Townes and Collins families gathered around the large tree in the next room.

"Mrs. Townes, the Christmas tree is something that we will have to incorporate into our holiday traditions. I must say, the fragrance is heavenly," Laura exclaimed.

Each person had a gift to open from the Townes family, and as was the custom, each person waited until the gift of the previous person was opened and shown to the others. When it was Ellie's turn to open her gift, she was surprised to see a small silver bell, engraved with the words, *with gratitude and appreciation, Christmas 1860.*

"Oh, it is so pretty, thank you," Ellie said, as she looked at each of the Townes family members.

Joseph was particularly pleased that the gift was acceptable. Ellie marveled at the bell, so delicate. She had seen one like it before, it must have been in the store near her home in Indiana. She couldn't decide where for sure at the moment, but she was very fond of it.

Following the exchange of gifts, the men donned boots and coats and walked to the quarters of the servants to take Christmas breakfast to them. Joseph coaxed his father into letting him go see Fancy with Rafe. Although Rafe would have rather sat beside Hattie on the settee, he didn't want to disappoint the young lad. The two bundled up and walked through the snow to the horse barn. It wouldn't be long before the mare would have her colt.

Christmas came and went, and soon the Collins family packed up their trunks and made their way out to their wagons and buggy. Camille and Laura promised to visit one another again soon, and Isaac Collins agreed to return with money for the young mare that he had chosen for his stable. Hattie, Liza and Maggie hugged one another, vowing to make a trip to Nashville in the spring to take a shopping trip for new gowns. Finally, it was Rafe's turn to bid Hattie goodbye. She walked with him to the wagon where their slaves were loading the trunks.

"I'll come back when Father comes for the mare. I'd like to start courting you, if you wouldn't mind."

Hattie smiled and said, "I'd like that very much, Rafe. I'll miss you."

As she spoke, Rafe reached down to take her hand in his.

"I'll be back, Hattie. Wild horses couldn't keep me from you."

He took her hand to his lips, and softly kissed her soft skin. Camille Townes had witnessed the intimate moment between her daughter and the Collins boy. She had to remind herself that Hattie wasn't the young girl who had left for the Female Academy three years before. She was a young woman of eighteen. It wouldn't be long until another Townes daughter would be marrying. Camille couldn't bear that thought.

Ellie spent the next few weeks working with Joseph on geography and mathematics. He seemed to have a good mind for the arithmetic, but had little interest in what lay beyond Mimosa Grove. When the family went into town the following month for shopping and supplies, they saw the newspaper article about talk of South Carolina succeeding from the Union. Daniel picked up the paper, shaking his head.

"Don't they realize that secession will only bring about ruin? Lincoln was right, a divided house cannot stand."

The effects of Lincoln's election indeed divided the nation, as well as towns, states and sadly, families. In the Townes family, Daniel's own brother was in support of the Confederacy. By the end of December, a vote was taken in the South Carolina state legislature unanimously voting for secession. Georgia and Mississippi soon followed. South Carolina would soon call on her sister states in an appeal to join them. Those who were loyal to the Union, men such as Daniel Townes, watched the newspapers for any word as to what Tennessee's position would be.

As the news of South Carolina's seceding from the Union reached the Hendersonville community, talk began about what Tennessee would do in the event more states left the Union. The topic was still very much a hotbed of debate when Isaac and Raford Collins arrived at Mimosa Grove that late February afternoon. Hattie and Camille had been sitting in the parlor by the fireplace, working on their needlepoint and listening to Ellie read from *Sonnets from the Portuguese, by Elizabeth Barrett Browning.* Lucy had been dusting the large grandfather clock in the entry hall when she heard the wagon coming up the drive.

"Miz Camille, Mr. Collins just came up the drive with his boy. They's come to get the mare."

Camille sat her embroidery down on the settee, and rose to peer out from behind the damask curtains.

"It appears he has, Lucy. Perhaps we should offer them a warm drink before they hitch the mare."

Hattie felt her heart skip a beat at the thought of seeing Rafe again. It had been nearly two months, and other than the two letters she had received since Christmas, there had been no other contact.

"Mama, would it be all right if Raford came into the parlor to visit?" Hattie asked.

Ellie had to smile, thinking to herself how proper the Townes family was.

"Well, I don't see what it would hurt, provided you have a chaperone." Camille turned to Ellie, who had put the book on the mantel.

"Would you mind, Ella?" Hattie asked as her eyes begged.

Ellie walked over to Hattie and sat beside her.

"Of course I wouldn't mind, Hattie. I have letters to write to my daughter and Miss Hobbs, my friend."

Camille seemed uneasy about something, but sat back down on the small chair near the fireplace.

"Lucy, please set some warm cider out for our guests. If you have any rusks left, you can bring them out to the sideboard."

Lucy quickly turned to Hattie and smiled at her slyly.

"Miz Hattie, would you like to help me carrying in the mugs?"

Hattie was quick to join her, as she enjoyed her time with Lucy. Lucy had been her nurse when she was a small child, and she missed the black woman's soft voice and protective arms that hugged and comforted her when she was alone or afraid.

"Ella, would you like to bring your daughter to Mimosa Grove to be with you? I know you must miss her terribly," Camille said as she continued working on the delicate embroidery on the handkerchief.

Ellie hadn't even let herself imagine having Charlotte and Cassie near her during her stay at Mimosa Grove. She would have thought it presumptuous and rude to invite her daughter without formally being invited.

"I would love to see my daughter again," Ellie sighed.

"Well then, we shall work on getting the necessary papers for her to join you in the spring," Camille said as she continued working on the small handkerchief.

Just then, Daniel Townes walked into the front hallway with Isaac and Raford Collins.

"Please make yourself at home and warm yourself by the fire."

He pointed toward the doorway into the library.

"Daniel, Lucy is bringing warm cider and rusks for our guests. When you have finished your business, you may join us in the parlor," Camille said.

Rafe peered over his father's shoulder, looking for Hattie. His eye caught a glimpse of her as she came down the hallway carrying a tray of large mugs. Her eyes danced as she saw him standing in the hallway.

"Welcome back to Mimosa Grove, Mr. Collins," Hattie sweetly said. "Hello, Raford."

"Hello, Miss Hattie," Rafe said, grinning from ear to ear.

Rafe wanted to take Hattie in his arms and hug her; she looked so beautiful with her long curls cascading down to her shoulders. She had pulled the sides back into a large tortoise shell comb. Rafe noticed how slender her waist appeared in the tight bodice of her dress. She was more beautiful than he remembered; he hoped he would get to spend some time with her alone, before he and his father had to leave again. The men walked into the library and pulled the two pocket doors closed. Rafe nervously fidgeted with his cap as he sat in the large leather chair beside the fireplace.

While Isaac and Daniel closed their deal on the mare with a handshake and the cash being put inside the secretary, Daniel walked over to Rafe.

"Your father tells me that you have wanted permission to court Hattie. Is that your wish?"

Rafe felt his palms begin to sweat, but he stood and wiped them down his pant legs. He looked Daniel Townes square in the eye, just as his father had taught him.

"Yes, sir. I wanted your permission to court Hattie," Rafe said.

Daniel smiled, and he patted the young man on his back.

"I think that would please my daughter very much."

Rafe felt a wave of relief come over him, as he thanked Daniel. He didn't even feel his feet move across the hallway to get his mug of cider from Lucy. He was floating it seemed.

Hattie looked up and saw Rafe coming in to join the ladies in the parlor.

"Hello, Raford. It's nice to see you again," Ellie said.

"Thank you, Miss Morgan. It's a pleasure to see you."

Raford came into the room and took a seat near Hattie. Camille offered him a rusk to go with his cider, noticing the close proximity of the two young people.

"How are your sisters and your mother, Raford?" Camille asked.

Ellie noticed the looks passing between Hattie and Raford, and found it amusing to watch the two.

"They are well, thank you, Mrs. Townes. My mother asked that I give you this."

Rafe got in his pocket and took out a small wooden box. On the side, engraved into the wood, C.T., and the inside was lined with a beautiful burgundy velvet material.

"Oh, it's beautiful. Please tell your mother how much I love it," Camille said, as she turned the box over to admire the workmanship.

"Samuel does a dandy job with his woodworking. Mother has said he is the best in all of Robertson County."

Camille smiled, thanked Raford again, and walked to the small marble-top table that sat beside the settee. "I appreciate the gift, it's very pretty."

Hattie and Raford walked over to the fireplace to warm their hands and talk more privately, while Camille and Ellie made room for the men to join them for a glass of cider. Hattie peered over her shoulder, and saw that the adults were engaged in conversation, not paying attention to them.

"It is so good to see you again, Rafe. I've missed you."

Rafe leaned in to Hattie, speaking softly, "I asked your father for permission to court you. He said it was all right."

Hattie looked down, her dark lashes closing for a moment.

"That makes me very happy, Rafe. I asked Mama if it would be all right, and she said it was."

The two smiled, and Rafe quickly touched her hand as it rested on the mantle. Just then, Joseph came into the house from the stable.

"Mose has the mare hitched up, Papa. He said she is fit to be tied having to leave her colt."

Joseph liked being in the stables, tending to the horses with Mose. He enjoyed the freedom of being out of his mother's and father's watchful eye, and sometimes took a draw off Mose's corncob pipe. Camille would take a hickory switch to his britches if she caught wind of his sinful habit. But for now, his secret was safe. Mose set quite a store on the boy, and it was a mutual affection that the two shared.

Ellie could faintly smell smoke on his breath as she came over to sit down on the floor next to her.

"Joseph, did you finish reading your lesson this morning?" Ellie asked.

Joseph didn't hold much stock in reading, but Ellie had found that he liked *Robinson Crusoe*. She had stuck the book inside her bag as she made preparations for her trip.

"I read some," Joseph confessed.

His mother looked over at him and said, "Well, you should make your apologies and go upstairs to finish whatever assignments you are neglecting, Joseph. We have secured a very good tutor for you."

Ellie smiled at Camille and added, "If you'll excuse us, we have lessons to do."

She reached out her hand to Isaac and said, "Mr. Collins, please give my regards to Mrs. Collins and your daughters. It was a pleasure seeing you again."

"And you, Miss Morgan," Isaac Collins answered.

She turned to Rafe, "I enjoyed seeing you again, Raford."

Rafe looked at Ellie and smiled, "Thank you, Miss Morgan."

As Rafe was finishing his sentence, Ellie had a feeling come over her, much like she felt when she was sitting on the train in Gallatin. It was a feeling she couldn't quite explain. For a moment, she felt as though she had been in this place before, but she couldn't have. She shook off the feeling, and reached down to grab the hand of Joseph.

"Come along; let's get started on *Robinson Crusoe*."

The two walked out of the parlor and up the stairs. When Ellie reached the landing, she turned to gaze down at the scene below. *Why does this all look so familiar? Rafe's expression reminds me of someone; I feel as though I knew him long before I saw him that week of Christmas.* Joseph had made his way into the classroom, rushing ahead of Ellie. Ellie dismissed her strange thoughts and walked down the hallway. Ellie and Joseph began their lessons, and she soon forgot about the odd feeling that plagued her.

A month passed, and Raford Collins had made two trips to Mimosa Grove to see Hattie. Upon each visit, Ellie was designated the chaperone when the two went in the parlor to escape the pestering of Joseph or the watchful eye of Camille Townes. Hattie was quite smitten with Rafe, and the letters she wrote to him each week described the loneliness that she felt in his absence. Rafe had been missing Hattie as well, and he hoped that later in the year he could speak to her father about marriage. His father wasn't blind to the feelings his son had for Miss Hattie Townes. He mentioned to Rafe one afternoon that he would like to deed him his portion of Elmwood when he decided to find a wife. Rafe would continue the family tradition of raising cotton, cattle, tobacco and hogs. Of course, he would be given slaves to work the farm.

Rafe had walked down to the lower pasture to survey a good spot for his own plantation. His slave, Gideon, walked along beside him.

"Someday, this will be where Hattie and I will live," he said to Gideon.

Ellie wanted to go home for a visit; she couldn't understand why her letters had not been answered. She worried about her daughter, but knew the mail was slow reaching Indiana. She tried not to worry about the possibility that something could be wrong. The winter was a harsh one, the ice skimming over the Cumberland River caused river traffic to be at a standstill, and no movement meant supplies that needed to move down river was slow to nonexistent. Ellie opened her curtains and peered out the window to the ground below.

She had been with the Townes family for three months now. She had become one of the family so it seemed. Camille had begun to open up to Ellie, and the two shared many evenings in the family parlor talking about the lives before children. Ellie found Camille to be well-educated, having been taught by a tutor who lived with the family, much like she was doing with young Joseph. Hattie had also grown fond of Ellie, sharing her hopes and dreams of one day being a wife and mother. She had shared one evening when the two were reading together out of her copy of Elizabeth Barrett Browning's sonnets.

"Ella, do you think that Rafe has intentions of asking me to marry him?" Hattie asked.

"I know he is quite smitten with you, Hattie. I see the way he looks at you, and I also have seen how you look at him."

Ellie put the strip of satin ribbon where she finished reading.

She asked Hattie, "If he asked, what would you tell him?"

Hattie's dark green eyes seemed to sparkle at the thought.

She leaned towards Ellie, speaking in soft tones, "I have thought of nothing else since his last visit. I think I would say,' Yes', if he asked me."

Ellie smiled, knowing that it would be a matter of time before the two announced their engagement.

She replied, "Rafe is a very nice young man, Hattie. I'm sure it won't be long before there is another wedding at Mimosa Grove."

Daniel walked into the house, closing the door behind him with a loud thud. Behind him came Joseph, who appeared to be a condemned prisoner being led to the gallows.

"Wait for me in the library, Joseph. I need to speak to your mother."

Ellie and Hattie heard the exchange, and Hattie raised her eyebrows.

She whispered to Ellie, "Papa is angry, I wonder what Joseph has done?"

Ellie remembered the lad often spent time in the barn with Mose, and she had smelled pipe tobacco on his breath. She wasn't sure how she knew he had been smoking a pipe, but the smell was familiar to her. Just then, Daniel appeared in the parlor.

"Good afternoon, Miss Morgan. Hattie, have you seen your mother this morning?"

Ellie smiled and said good morning to Daniel.

"No, Papa. She and Lucy were up in the attic earlier looking for the trunk with our Christening gowns. She said something about wanting to take it to Caroline. Is something wrong?"

Daniel moved over to Hattie, kissing her on the head, saying, "No, nothing to worry yourself about, Lamb."

Ellie had liked Daniel Townes from the moment she met him. He was a loving father to his children, but a father who expected his children to be obedient. He excused himself and walked up the stairway to look for his wife. In the meantime, Hattie quickly walked across the hall to the library and saw Joseph sitting on the couch. He was looking down at the floor, sullen.

"What have you done now, Joseph?"

The sound of Hattie's voice startled him, and he jerked at the sound of it. Jack was lying beside him, and he felt a sense of protection with him there.

"Papa caught me smoking one of Mose's pipes. He's going to tell Mama."

Hattie's eyes opened wide, and she looked at Joseph sternly.

"You realize that you could have burned down the stables? What would become of the horses and their foals? You know Mama and Papa have every right to take a hickory switch to you, Joseph. Now you've gotten Mose in trouble too."

Joseph knew his sister was right, but her tongue-lashing wasn't exactly what he needed at the moment. Soon, Camille and Daniel came down the stairway. Hattie walked out of the library, passing her parents in the entry way. The two walked into the room, pulling the doors together. Hattie knew her brother would be punished, and she hoped it would teach him a lesson. She saw Mose walking up to the porch, and before he could knock on the door, she opened it and walked outside.

"Mother and Father are talking to Joseph, Mose. It might not be a good idea for you to come in right now. You know how mother can be about such things."

Mose had his cap in his hand, and his eyes were gazing down to the ground.

"Miss Hattie, it's my fault the boy was smokin' that pipe. I didn't see no harm in him trying it, hoping it would make him sick and he'd not ask again. He seemed to take a shine to it, and now he asks me every time."

Hattie smiled, knowing that Joseph had the Negro wrapped around his finger.

"I know you didn't mean any harm, Mose. Now go ahead back to the horses, I'm sure it will be fine."

Mose thanked Hattie, and then walked back down towards the barn.

Hattie could hear the swat of the belt against Joseph's backside as she closed the door quietly behind her. Ellie could hear it as well. She hoped that this would deter Joseph from continuing such a nasty habit. Within a few moments, the library doors parted, and Joseph walked quietly upstairs to his room.

Camille walked out behind him, saying, "Ella, you may start your lessons for the day now. Joseph is quite ready to begin geography."

"Yes, Ma'am," Ellie said.

She lifted her skirt and walked up the stairs to begin another day of teaching.

Every man is a quotation from all his ancestors.
- Ralph Waldo Emmerson

Chapter 12

Rafe Collins came calling early in March, after the recent snows had melted. He arrived sitting in his father's carriage beside Gideon. The driver, Gideon, was his slave, presented to Raford at birth. Gideon was a handsome Negro, dark as ebony. Gideon's parents had been slaves on the plantation of Rafe's grandfather, in Mississippi. His grandparents had given Gideon's mother and father to Isaac for a gift when he and Laura moved to Tennessee years before to start their married life. Gideon and never found a mate, but was sweet on one or two of the gals on the Collins' plantation. Regardless, Gideon was what some free blacks in the area called 'uppity'. He had been given new clothes and shoes every few months, instead of the once a year Christmas gifts bestowed on the Collins' slaves by Isaac and Laura. He had been a constant companion to Rafe growing up on his father's plantation.

The drive to Mimosa Grove took a full day to accomplish. This visit was much anticipated by Hattie. Along with Rafe, came his younger sister, Maggie. Hattie and Maggie had been inseparable while at the Female Academy. She missed her dear friend terribly since they left the academy. The two would be able to visit, as well as Hattie's opportunity to spend time with Rafe. Hattie had been looking out the parlor curtains all morning.

"Hattie, you know the watched pot never boils. Come, sit and play a minuet on the pianoforte," Camille said to her daughter.

"Mama, I am just so anxious to see Maggie and Raford. I hope they didn't encounter any problems along the way. The roads are still soft."

Hattie tried to tear herself away from the window, walking over to the piano to begin playing a song by memory. The rich tones of the piano drifted throughout the house, and Lucy came into the parlor carrying a tray of tea and biscuits.

"Miz Camille, do you 'spect the Collinses here for dinner?"

Camille took the teapot and sat it on the table beside the settee.

"Yes, go ahead and plan for three more for dinner. Hattie tells me that their driver will also be staying on. I asked Abram to make a bed for him in Old Thomas' cabin. No one has been there in twenty years, but I'm sure the fireplace still draws well."

Lucy sighed, "I'll head down there 'dreckly and start sweeping out the cobwebs."

"You may take Joseph with you. He can fetch some clean sheets and blankets. And there are some candles and a lantern in the pantry he can use."

Lucy seemed perturbed.

"Yes'm, Miz Camille. I'll get on down there now."

Lucy went into the hallway and called for Joseph to come down to help her. It wasn't long until the two were on their way down the path behind the house to the cabin where Daniel Townes had lived while Mimosa Grove was being built.

Ellie saw the carriage making its way slowly up the drive. The recent thaw had caused the driveway to be a soupy mess. The wheels of the carriage slung mud as Gideon turned towards the stepping block. He set the brake, jumping down to offer Miss Maggie Collins his hand. She stepped out of the carriage and onto the large block of stone.

Ellie noticed her dress to be a lovely shade of green with black tassels. She wore a black wool cape and hood. Rafe stepped down behind her, helping his sister down to the pebble sidewalk that led up to the large, covered front porch.

"Mama, they're here!" Hattie squealed with delight.

She quickly smoothed her skirt and checked her face in the large gold mirror that hung above the fireplace. Camille walked to the door to receive their guests.

"Maggie, how lovely you look. Rafe, please, come in out of the cold."

Camille was warm and inviting, helping the two inside.

"Thank you, Mrs. Townes," Maggie said.

Camille took her wrap, and hung it on the hall tree. Rafe took off his coat, hanging it beside his sister's.

"Ma'am, our driver, Gideon, is taking the buggy to the post beside the barn. Should I have him bring our trunks to the back door?" Rafe asked.

"Yes, Rafe, that would be fine. Then he can ask Mose to take him down to where he will be sleeping."

Rafe headed out the door, catching Gideon as he was unhitching the team.

Hattie came into the hallway to see Maggie; the two embraced.

"I have missed you, Hattie!" Maggie said.

"Come into the parlor and tell me all about Nashville. Rafe said you went there last month," Hattie said.

The two girls began talking about the latest fashions and news out of Nashville, while Camille poured tea for them.

Maggie looked at Hattie and asked, "Where's your darkie? Why isn't she doing that?"

For the first time, Hattie heard an air about Maggie that she didn't like.

"Lucy isn't our *darkie*, Maggie. We don't own her."

Maggie seemed stunned by Hattie's offense at what she said.

"I didn't mean anything by it, Hattie. I'm sorry."

Camille spoke up, "Maggie, it isn't our way to own our servants. They are free to come and go, if they wish."

Maggie wasn't used to such thinking, and she didn't hold to their belief.

"I meant no disrespect, Mrs. Townes."

Camille patted her hand, "Of course you didn't, dear. We are well aware of the views and beliefs of our neighbors, even our own family. Let's not dwell on it."

With that, the three women continued discussing the latest fashions and bonnet styles that Maggie and her sister Liza had seen while shopping in Nashville. She also told of the talk on the train of other states leaving the Union. Camille was disheartened to hear of such news, as she and Daniel had feared Tennessee would be asked to do the same again.

Rafe soon joined the ladies.

"Father said that the darkies in Tennessee will run if the Yankees come down here to stir up trouble."

Camille was not happy with the tone of the conversation.

"Rafe, we believe there is only one Union, and we should do all that we can to preserve it. Slavery is a stain on our conscience."

Rafe felt the heat rise in his face, but he remembered himself.

"Mrs. Townes, it is just a matter of time. We will be part of the Confederacy. We won't let Lincoln or any Yankees tell us what to do in our own homes."

Hattie didn't like where the conversation was going, and fearing her mother would drive her guests out.

"Rafe, would you and Maggie like to see the grounds?" Hattie quickly suggested.

A look passed between mother and daughter that was colder than any winter's chill.

Camille excused herself, telling the young ones that she would be out in the kitchen if they should need anything.

Hattie turned to Rafe, "I'm sorry for Mother's outspokenness. She doesn't understand that not everyone sees things as she does."

Rafe touched Hattie's hand, which sent a burst of sparks up through every nerve ending in her body.

"It's all right, Hattie. Folks are going to be divided over the darkies and us owning them. It's what Lincoln wants. Let's not worry about such things today. I've missed you."

Maggie smiled at the two of them, walking over to the piano. She sat down and began to play. This gave Hattie and Rafe time to talk more privately.

"I've wanted to get you all to myself all day, Hattie Townes. You look so pretty."

Hattie blushed, putting her hand on top of Rafe's.

"I have thought about you every day since you were here last."

Rafe was sitting closer than was appropriate, but he couldn't help his poor manners.

"Would you walk with me?" Rafe whispered.

Hattie lost herself in Rafe's deep blue eyes.

"I'd love that, Rafe."

The two stood, and Maggie turned towards them.

"Do you want company?"

Rafe gave his sister a look.

"If you promise not to tag along too close."

The three walked to the entry hall to don their winter wear.

"How about we walk to the cemetery. It's more private there," Hattie suggested.

As they made their way out through the winter kitchen and back door, Camille could see through the summer kitchen window how closely Hattie and Rafe were walking. She knew it would be a short time until Rafe came to talk to Daniel.

The thought of Rafe being Hattie's beau didn't upset Camille at first, but hearing the two Collins' children voice their defense of owning another human as chattel was more than Camille could stand. She knew if Hattie married him, he would take her away from Mimosa Grove and her. The marriage of Caroline had meant a move to Nashville where Caroline was the mistress of a large plantation home, and twenty slaves. This had caused a rift between mother and daughter, and Caroline's new husband was not overly tolerant of his new mother-in-law's anti-slavery views. It was because of this, that Camille had not been asked to attend Caroline when she would be confined before the birth of her first child. This troubled her, and it was partly the reason Camille held on tightly to her youngest daughter. She watched as Maggie walked on ahead of the couple, and as they walked through the grove of trees, Rafe reached to take Hattie's hand in his.

"I have been talking to Father about building my own house. He offered to give me the lower half of the plantation, Hattie. I would have near 200 acres. It would make a good place to grow cotton, and tobacco grows thick there."

Hattie smiled, feeling Rafe's warm hand over hers was something that she could get used to.

"I think that sounds wonderful, Rafe. How soon will you begin?"

Rafe wasn't sure where he should go with this question, as he hadn't even talked to Hattie's father yet about marrying her.

"I expect later in the summer. But if there's a fight, I'm going."

Hattie hadn't even thought of a fight. She had been sheltered while living in Gallatin. The country's fight between abolitionist and states' rights hadn't entered into the world of the Gallatin Female Academy.

"Oh Rafe, you can't! I would cry into my pillow every night with worry about you."

She put her hands on his arms. The closeness of Hattie and the scent of the lavender sachet filled his nostrils as he leaned down and touched her lips with his.

Hattie had only been kissed once by a boy, and it was awkward and messy. Hade Flynn's nephew had come to stay one summer before Hattie went to the academy. He had asked Hattie for a kiss, and reluctantly she acquiesced. The quick assault on her lips left her thinking that the talk about kissing was much exaggerated and something she could have waited longer to experience.

But this kiss, with Rafe, was different. She felt her ears ring and the world around her began to spin. She found herself kissing him back, as if he held a lifeline and she was drowning. Rafe pulled back, not wanting to appear a cad for taking liberties with her.

"Are you all right, Hattie? I shouldn't have surprised you with the kiss."

Hattie looked up at Rafe, her expression that of love, not disdain.

"I'm quite all right, Rafe. It was very nice," Hattie said, feeling her cheeks begin to flame.

Rafe smiled, continuing their walk and holding her hand. Camille should not have been watching the two share such a private moment, but she saw it and felt that the courtship was moving too fast for her liking.

Lucy and Joseph had just finished cleaning out the cabin when Mose and Gideon walked down over the hill.

"Lucy, you remember Gideon. He's Mister Collins' driver."

Lucy seemed unimpressed with his title.

"I remember. You can bunk down in there. It ain't the likes of Elmwood, but you won't freeze to death."

Gideon peered into the cabin, which in a matter of two hours, had been transformed into a cozy place to sleep for the night.

"Thank you, Miss Lucy," Gideon said, as he smiled and tipped his cap.

Lucy gave a *humph* as she and Joseph moved passed the two men. She walked up the hill, pulling her shawl around her shoulders.

"Uppity. That's what he is."

When Hattie, Rafe and Maggie returned from their tour of the grove, Daniel was coming through the front door. His trip into town to the bank had been foreshadowed by the news he heard while at the dry goods store.

"It appears that the fort in Charleston Harbor has been given notice to surrender. Major Anderson was told to surrender the fort to the Confederacy."

Camille began to ring her hands.

"Oh no, Daniel. Do you think they will surrender the fort?"

Daniel seemed to be preoccupied with his thoughts, and family who lived in the Confederacy.

The following weeks led the country closer to war, and Daniel Townes found his neighbors were at odds with what the state of Tennessee should do. Families who supported the President and his views on preserving the Union were in the minority in Middle Tennessee. Many young men supported their fellow southerners who were living in the Deep South.

It was the morning of April 12, 1861, when the residents of Sumner County Tennessee and the rest of the United States learned of the firing upon Fort Sumter by Southern troops in Charleston Harbor. Daniel and Camille Townes had been praying that a war would be avoided. Ellie was terrified what would happen if she were not able to get back to her home in Indiana, to her daughter. She once again sent a letter to Cassie and her friend, Charlotte. The absence of any correspondence since her arrival to Tennessee caused her great anxiety. She couldn't imagine what would be keeping her daughter from sending a note.

Following the firing on and the surrender of the fort, the newspapers began carrying the story of the bombardment of the fort. The calling up of 75,000 volunteers to fight for the Union was the death nail that hastened the seceding of several states. Daniel Townes had watched the papers closely for word of the Governor's response, and Governor Isham Harris declared he *"would not furnish a single man for coercion, but 50, 0000 if necessary for the defense of 'our rights and the rights of our Southern brethren"*.

Hattie was much like other young women with beaus of fighting age. She worried about her own Rafe, and prayed for the country to find a peaceful solution. President Lincoln called for all states to provide regiments to the Union. She read a copy of the April 1861 edition of the *Harper's Weekly*, and the articles were all about the battle for Ft. Sumter and Lincoln's call for additional volunteers from all the states to put down the rebellion. It was obvious that resolutions adopted in several towns condemned the President for the calling up of troops, supporting the South instead.

Word soon spread of troops being organized all around Hendersonville. Daniel knew it was only a matter of time before he would be called upon to join with the men and boys who would answer the Confederacy's call to arms.

Spring was all around Mimosa Grove, and the blossoms on the mimosa trees framed the house in pink blooms. The honeysuckle that was growing all along the fence row leading from the house to the cemetery beyond the grove gave a sugary aroma that wafted into the upstairs bedrooms.

Ellie awoke that May morning to the sound of the mocking bird calling in the oak tree in the front lawn. As she quickly dressed, Jack was whining to be taken outside for his morning rituals. Ellie pulled her hair back in a chignon and used the water in the pitcher and bowl beside her bed to wash her face. She looked into the mirror, and for a moment, thought she saw the room changing in the reflection. She quickly turned to see what was causing her to question what she was seeing. In the doorway, she thought she saw a man, but his appearance was somewhat strange. She blinked, as if to check her eyesight, and when she opened them again, the figure was gone.

"What is causing me to have these feelings and such odd visions?" Ellie had spoken aloud.

She wasn't sure why she was experiencing so many unexplained maladies, but she didn't have time to dwell on such things.

She was late for breakfast, and for taking Jack outdoors. As she made her way to the stairway, Hattie was coming out of her bedroom across the hall.

"Ella, I overheard Papa tell Mama this morning that Sumner County was calling for troops. I'm so worried for Rafe," Hattie sobbed.

She came to Ellie and threw her arms around her for comfort.

"I know, I read the *Harper's Weekly* that your father brought home from town. I had hoped this day wouldn't come."

Ellie and Hattie walked downstairs together, talking quietly about Rafe and a letter that Hattie needed to mail.

"I have a letter to mail to my daughter, so I would be happy to have Mose or Josiah drive me to the post office if you'd like."

Hattie smiled, "Yes, I would very much like that. I have to see Rafe again."

In the dining room, Lucy was already serving Daniel and Camille their breakfast. Joseph came in behind Ellie, asking if he could take Jack outdoors for his morning walk.

"I think he will be fine; you can let him out alone today," Ellie said.

The mood at the breakfast table was a somber one. Talk of troops being raised all over Tennessee was the topic of conversation.

"Mama, would it be all right if Rafe came courting this weekend? I have a letter being sent to the post office today."

Camille remembered the last visit with Rafe and Hattie's kiss by the grove. She had hoped that the two were not as serious as the kiss had indicated. She looked at Daniel, who was oblivious to the look on Camille's face. Ellie wanted to speak on Hattie's behalf, but remembered her place.

Finally, Hattie said, "Please, I would like to see him. It has been a month and a half, Mother. We can't go on forever just writing letters."

Daniel smiled at his daughter, remembering the way Rafe had asked him permission to court his daughter.

"I think it would be fine, Hattie. You send the necessary letters for Raford to come for a visit. He can stay in Joseph's room for the duration. Now, let us talk of other things."

The following weekend, Gideon came driving up the drive in his master's buggy. Rafe was sitting inside, almost jumping out of the door when the buggy came to a stop. Hattie had been nervously pacing in her bedroom, while Joseph sat at his desk reciting his multiplication tables through twelve. The knock on the door brought Hattie down the stairs, her skirt and petticoat swishing against the spindles of the stairs.

Just as Hattie's feet reached the bottom step, Camille Townes walked to the door and was opening it to the young man.

"Raford, how nice to see you again. Please, come in."

Rafe thanked Camille, and then moved past her to Hattie. Forgetting themselves, they embraced. Camille stood in the entry way, waiting for the embrace to end.

"Hattie, why don't you and Raford go into the parlor, and I'll have Miss Lucy bring refreshments for you both."

She walked through the hallway and out the door to the summer kitchen.

"I've been thinking about you every day since you were here last. I have read your letters over and over," Hattie said.

Rafe moved closer, and took her hand in his. He was about to say something to her when Joseph came into the room. He sat down on the floor in front of the fireplace. Hattie looked at him with an icy stare.

"Aren't you supposed to be studying your lessons with Miss Ella?"

Joseph was oblivious to the couple wanting to be alone. He poked the fire with a stick.

"Yeah, but Miss Ella said I could come down to say hello to Rafe."

Rafe smiled, knowing that Hattie was not amused.

"It's good to see you again, Joseph. Maybe your folks would let you come to Elmwood this summer and see the mare we bought from you. She will have a foal later in the summer."

Joseph's smile radiated over his whole face.

"I would like that very much."

Camille came into the room carrying a small tray with a pitcher of fresh squeezed lemonade.

"Like what very much?" she asked.

"Rafe asked if I could come to his plantation to see the mare and her foal this summer."

Camille tried to hide her displeasure at the thought.

"It seems that you have the here and now to worry about, and it is time for you to finish your lessons for the day."

Joseph was sure his mother would acquiesce to his going, but would let the matter rest for now. Camille poured the glasses full of lemonade; then moved to the small chair beside the fireplace, across from Hattie and Rafe. She began to work on the small crocheted blanket that she was making for her first grandchild. She engaged in small talk about Rafe's mother and sisters, and then quietly sat as the young couple spoke quietly between themselves.

The two days that Rafe was able to visit Mimosa Grove were happy ones for Hattie. She began to think of being Rafe's wife, and hoped he would ask her to marry him before he left for Elmwood. The two took walks down to the river, watching an occasional boat go down the Cumberland River. Rafe talked about the house he would be building soon, and Hattie imagined what life would be like living with Rafe and his family. She was sure he was telling her about his plans because he wanted her to be part of them, but she couldn't say yes to a proposal if there wasn't one being offered.

The talk of a possible war also lingered over the household. Rafe had confided in Hattie the evening before he left that if Tennessee called up arms, he would gladly go. In fact, he expected there to be an announcement any day. The thought frightened Hattie.

During dinner, Daniel avoided that topic of war, sure that such talk would only upset Camille and Hattie. She would be awaiting word of the birth of their first grandchild, and as soon as it was possible, go to visit the new parents.

That evening, Ellie tried to fall asleep. She felt a panic overtake her that she couldn't explain. Jack nuzzled his wet nose under her arm. *You feel it too, don't you, fella? Something is wrong.* There were holes in her memory, plain and simple. She had tried to keep busy, settling into life at Mimosa Grove. Letters she had written had gone unanswered, and she began to feel a dark blanket of fear cover her, suffocating her. *What has happened to me? I have a daughter, a home, a life somewhere. Why can't I remember? Why doesn't Cassie respond to my letters? Could she be sick, or worse . . .?*

Ellie tried to stop the thoughts from overtaking her, but she couldn't. She got out of bed, walked to the fireplace and put another log on the hearth. It was then that she heard the voice. At first, it was just a murmur coming from the hallway outside of her room. She listened, but all she heard was the sound of her heart thumping wildly in her ears. She moved slowly towards the door, opening it very slowly. Jack stirred on the bed, but only raised his head to see where Ellie was going.

"Stay, Jack," Ellie commanded, as she walked into the hallway.

The candle's flame flickered, as if it would be extinguished. She stood, quietly, looking for the source of the sound. Then she heard it again, only this time, she could tell from where it was coming. She looked at the stairway that led to the attic. She heard it again, and the voice was clearly calling her name. She thought perhaps Joseph was playing a trick on her, but he was sound asleep. Rafe was asleep as well; she knew neither of them could be the culprit. She slowly crept up the stairway, trying not to make a sound.

When she reached the top step, a gust of air met her and moved passed her, causing her nightgown to blow about her legs. "What in the world?" she gasped. The attic was almost empty, with the exception of a few trunks and crates. She held the candle in front of her, its flame moving about. Her hand began to shake.

"Ellie, where are you?" the voice said.

Ellie tried to make sense of what she was hearing, looking into the dark attic; not seeing the source of the sound.

"Who are you?" Ellie demanded.

She suddenly was afraid. *Could the house be harboring spirits?* Just then, Ellie heard Hattie calling from the bottom step.

"Ella, are you up there?" Ellie jumped, almost dropping her candle.

"Hattie? I'm up here," Ellie replied.

Hattie hurried to see what the matter was.

"I heard you talking to someone, and I was afraid you were in danger," Hattie said, walking up the stairs.

Ellie suddenly felt ashamed of bringing Hattie upstairs from her sleep.

"I thought I heard voices calling my name. It must have been a dream," Ellie lied.

"It's all right, Ella. I'm just glad you're not hurt."

Hattie reached out and put her arm around Ellie's shoulder.

"Thank you, Hattie. I'm sorry I woke you."

Hattie smiled and replied, "It's all right. I was having trouble sleeping tonight. I don't want Rafe to leave tomorrow."

Ellie quietly walked with Hattie to her door. She turned back her coverlet as the Hattie climbed back to bed.

"Thank you again for checking on me. Try to rest; morning will be here soon enough."

Hattie pulled the covers about her neck.

"Good night, Ella."

Ellie closed the door and walked back to her room. She couldn't shake the feeling that she had been called to the attic by something or someone. This wasn't the first time she had seen something or heard someone calling for her. Maybe it would be best to let it rest.

The next morning, Lucy made two lunches for Gideon and Rafe's journey back to Elmwood. She then brought in the breakfast dishes for the Townes family. Rafe had wanted to talk to Hattie's father before asking for her hand. Until he had the blessing of her father, he would not feel right asking Hattie to marry him. Before he entered the dining room, he walked across the hall to the library.

Daniel was sitting at his secretary, writing in his ledger. Rafe knocked on the door that was partially closed.

Daniel looked up from his work.

"Come in, Rafe," Daniel said, as he stood to greet Rafe.

"Sir, could I have a moment of your time?"

Rafe was nervous, not sure how the discussion would go.

"Of course, Rafe. Sit down and tell me what's on your mind."

Daniel had some idea, but wanted to give Rafe a chance to speak his mind.

"Sir, I have been courting Hattie for a few months now, but have known her for quite some time. I have come to love her, sir. I would like to ask for your blessing in asking her for her hand."

It seemed like time stood still as Daniel took in what Rafe had asked of him. This young daughter, whom he loved more than life itself, was his last daughter to live under his roof. He and Hattie had a special bond. She was like him. As Rafe sat on the couch, unsure what was about to happen next, Daniel walked over and took his hand. He shook it with a firm grip.

"Son, I would be honored to have you ask Hattie to marry you. You have my blessing."

Rafe stood and shook Daniel's hand. He thanked him and wiped the sweat from his palms on his pant legs. He wasn't aware of the smile that had overtaken Daniel's face. He knew all too well the anxiety Rafe was feeling. He couldn't help but remember his own awkwardness when he asked Adam Burnell for Camille's hand.

The two walked out of the library and into the dining room where the ladies and Joseph were already seated. Hattie smiled, seeing her father and Rafe getting on so well. Daniel decided not to mention the discussion in the library until Rafe and Hattie announced it themselves. He would speak to Camille later, and share the conversation and his blessing on the marriage.

The talk around the large table centered on the birth of Caroline's baby. News would be arriving any day from one of the slaves from Twin Ponds announcing the arrival. As soon as the meal was finished, Hattie and Rafe walked together, leaving the watchful eyes of Camille and Daniel. Gideon carried out their trunks and loaded them into the wagon. He then led the team to the buggy to be harnessed for the trip home. Rafe could see through the branches of the mimosa trees that it would soon be time to say his goodbyes to the family.

While he had Hattie all to himself, he walked with her farther behind the grove of trees. The two shared a private goodbye, one that would remain with them for the rest of their lives. Hattie reached into the small pocket that was sewn into the side of her skirt. She brought out a small lace handkerchief.

"Rafe, I want you take my hankie with you, so that you will have something of mine until we can be together," Hattie said as she held it out to Rafe.

Rafe took the handkerchief and held it to his face; breathing in the scent of lemon verbena that Hattie wore.

"I'll keep it in my shirt pocket, next to my heart. Thank you, Hattie. I love it, and I love you," Rafe declared.

Hattie couldn't believe her ears. She had dreamed about Rafe professing his love for her in a hundred different places, but being in the mimosa grove that May morning was a perfect place and time.

"Oh, Rafe, I love you, too. I didn't know if you cared for me as much as I do you."

She put her arms around him, hugging him tightly. It seemed the perfect time for Rafe.

He pulled Hattie away from her embrace, "Hattie, will you marry me?"

Hattie had imaged this moment so many times in her daydreams. She never imagined it would be today. She was so overcome with emotion that her eyes were flooded with tears.

"Yes, Rafe. I will marry you!"

He took her in his arms and kissed her in a way that she had never been kissed before. It was as if she were the lifeline to a drowning man.

When the kiss ended, the two stood in a long embrace.

"I don't think I shall ever forget this moment, Rafe. I will love you until I die."

Rafe smiled, his blue eyes staring into her very soul.

"I will love you forever, Hattie."

That morning was one that Hattie would never forget. She couldn't have known it then, but it would be the last time that she would see Raford Collins alive.

Blue-Eyed Soldier Boy
By my window saddly sitting,
In the steady glowing gloom
Where the twilight shadows flitting,
Like hushed hands into my room,
Find me sighing, watching, weeping,
O'er the death of ev'ry joy
As I wait in vain thy greeting,
Blue Eyed Soldier Boy,
As I wait in vain thy greeting,
Blue Eyed Soldier Boy.
-Jennie Caufield

Chapter 13

It was May 1861, and Rafe Collins had no more arrived back to Elmwood when the State of Tennessee started to organize regiments, prompting a rush on men to leave their communities and join the call. There was so much to do. He hadn't even bought a ring for Hattie! He had told his parents and sisters of his proposal on the night he arrived home. Laura Collins was overjoyed to be gaining a new daughter, and Isaac thought the marriage would be a good business arrangement as well. The Collins and Townes union would be a good marriage. Isaac would give Rafe his share of the plantation so that a house could be built. But it would have to wait.

In the next two weeks, the Collins family would be caught up in the excitement of the talk of war. Officially, the state had remained in the Union, having voted that February not to leave the Union. However, that changed when another vote was taken. Rafe had learned from his friend, Jesse Taylor, that there was a Company forming near Goodlettsville, and they needed upwards of 100 men to form a regiment. Rafe had spoken to his father the night before he left for Nashville.

Within the week, Rafe sent a letter to Hattie, telling her that he would be delayed in coming to Mimosa Grove. He explained the sudden change in plans, but promised to send her word as soon as he knew where he would be going.

His father shook his hand saying, "Son, it is our right to live as we see fit, holding to the Constitutional rights we have been afforded. It is evident that the Yankees will come into our towns and free our servants; we cannot let the aggressor try to bring an end to our rights. You have my blessing, and I am proud of you today, Son."

Isaac then presented his son with a bayonet and scabbard that was made by Jonah, the smith on the plantation. Another slave, Uncle Robert, had fashioned the scabbard for Rafe. The gift was a treasured memento that Rafe would carefully guard and protect. Rafe turned to see his mother standing in the parlor doorway.

"Oh Rafe, I wish you wouldn't go," Laura said as she put her head on his chest.

"Mama, you don't have to fret. Why, this war will be over in no time. You know the war won't last more than a few weeks, and I'll be home to start building the house for Hattie and me."

Laura Collins, along with Maggie and Liza, had sewn a small flag for Rafe to take to Nashville. He carefully folded the flag and put it inside his duffle bag.

"You take care of yourself, and write to us as soon as you can."

Rafe hugged his mother tightly, giving her a kiss on her cheek. He then embraced both sisters, promising to return soon. Polly, the nursemaid to the Collins children, wiped her eyes with a dishcloth.

"Mist'r Rafe, you watch yo'self now. I be prayin' for you."

Rafe bent down and gave his old nursemaid a hug, "Thank you, Polly. Don't you be worrying yourself. I'll be back before you know it."

On the afternoon of May 14, Rafe and his friend, Jesse Taylor, were sent off from the town amid the cheers and admiration of the townspeople. The young women gave each young man leaving for Nashville a flower, and the minister of the Baptist church in Goodlettsville, Reverend Silas Duffy, gave each soldier a Testament to keep on their person.

Rafe wished Hattie could have ventured to Goodlettsville to see him off. There wasn't time. The new recruits would soon board the train and join others in Nashville, where they would take their oath and enlist. Their county had furnished three companies to join the Confederacy.

They would be joining other boys from the Robertson county area to be sworn in to service.

They made their way through town to the Court House, where there were several young men waiting in line to be sworn in and fill out the necessary paperwork. The officer began asking Rafe questions as to his age, occupation, height and weight. He was also asked his hair and eye color along with his complexion. After signing their enlistment papers, Rafe and Jesse were each given a bounty of fifty dollars for enlisting for a period of twelve months.

Rafe and Jesse were directed to enter a large building behind the Court House where local women had brought their sewing machines to make uniforms for the soldiers. Rafe stood in line waiting for his turn to receive the abundance of supplies, more than he felt he would be able to carry. Gideon walked along side of Rafe, looking at the production that was going on before him. There were at least twenty women sewing, their treadle machines humming along to match the chatter of the women operating them.

Farther down the line were young girls rolling cotton bandages and assembling the *housewives:* sewing kits for the soldiers.

"Hey Rafe, after we git our uniforms on, let's go have a picture made. My mama would want to keep it on the wall, seein' I'm her only son."

Rafe smiled at Jesse, thinking he was only signing up for the honor and glory that soldiering would bring. He was thinking of the kisses he would get from the young pretty girls in town.

"Yeah, that'll be okay. I want to get two made; one for my mama, and one for my girl, Hattie."

As they made their way down the line, they were issued medium gray, wool satinette frock coats with a blue collar signifying infantry. The jacket had eight brass buttons, as was the standard issue for Tennessee soldiers. After receiving their jacket, each was given a pair of mixed gray wool slacks with a blue stripe along the side. The shirt that was given to the soldiers was a thin wool and one undershirt. The headgear was a gray kepi hat and a brass insignia of the 11th Tennessee situated in the front.

Rafe was proud of his uniform, and told Gideon, "Wait till Mama and Daddy see me in my uniform, Gideon."

"Yes, sir. You shore do look a sight, Mist'r Rafe!" Gideon said, smiling.

Gideon looked around at the tables lined with women working, and towards the back of the large room sat the Negro slaves who were brought with their mistresses to work alongside them. Gideon noticed a woman who briefly looked up from her sewing. He smiled and tipped his cap. Lucy had called him *uppity*, but Miss Laura had expected good manners from all her slaves.

Down the next aisle, the new recruits were given their shoes. Brogans were standard issue instead of the boots the first recruits were given. Rafe was trying to keep an inventory of all the items he had so far received. He would look quite the sight for Hattie. Why, in a month or two, he'd be back home after whipping the Yankees. He'd probably not even get his uniform dirty.

The man behind the table began issuing accoutrements. Each soldier was given the following: one leather haversack, black leather belt with brass buckle, oiled blanket, wool blanket, tent, cartridge box, cap box and gun sling. In addition to these items, he was given a Springfield flintlock musket, one buck and three shot. On his side he had carried a Bowie knife. Jesse was trying to maneuver his load as best he could.

"How do they expect a fella to carry all of this?"

Rafe was loaded down as well.

"I don't know, I was thinking the same thing. I guess we'll find out soon enough."

A tall, stern officer began barking out orders to the young recruits. They were told they would be heading out in one hour. Rafe learned quickly that he would no longer be making decisions for himself.

Gideon tried his best to help his young master carry the load he was trying to balance.

"Mist'r Rafe, you goin' to git yor picture taken?" Gideon asked.

"Yeah, as soon as we find the studio," Rafe answered.

He was trying to get his supplies balanced in his hands, but neither he nor Jesse could manage walking with the load of supplies.

"Hey, let's go over to the trees there and put on our uniforms," Jesse suggested.

"I ain't strippin' nekkid for the world to see, Jesse. We can go put on our uniform at the photographer's studio," suggested Rafe.

Rafe turned to Gideon, "You stay here with our supplies, Gideon. We'll be back in two shakes of a lamb's tale."

Gideon wasn't at all happy about being left out of the excitement of the photographer's studio, but did as he was told. Rafe and Jesse walked out into the street, looking down towards the center of town.

Jesse said, "I say we head out that way, with all the soldiers in town, I'm sure someone can point us down to the photographer."

Rafe agreed, and the two young men set off to the find the studio of *CC Giers & Company*.

The mood in the city was light. All around the city, soldiers were escorting the pretty girls who had come to the city to see the newly enlisted soldiers. Rafe noticed how the men were being forward in public; something he was not used to. Ill-bred behavior would be the least of Rafe's worries as he began his duty as soldier in the 11th Tennessee Infantry. They made their way down the street, and in no time saw the photography studio. The line wasn't too long this warm afternoon. Rafe and Jesse hurried to take their place in the group of young men who were going off to protect and support the Confederacy.

It wasn't long until the gentleman came into the waiting room to get Rafe and Jesse.

"You two boys wanting a plate taken together or will it be two separate photographs?"

Rafe began, "We'd each like a photograph made. I'd like a quarter plate with this frame, the other in a carte de viste."

The photographer took the frame that Rafe had been holding.

"Very well. Whoever is going first, come over and have a seat."

With that, he began arranging the chair and scene that would be the backdrop of Rafe's photograph. Rafe reached into the breast pocket of his jacket, and pulled through the opening in his jacket the lace hanky that Hattie had given him before leaving Mimosa Grove. He arranged it so that all the buttons closed in around this area.

"I'd like to leave this out, if that'd be all right."

The photographer had already photographed several soldiers in various poses that afternoon; he didn't seem to be impressed with Rafe's request.

The photographer busied himself with the camera, first inserting one glass negative into the wooden slot of the apparatus. Next, he moved back over to where Rafe was sitting, reminding him to hold his pose. He would need to sit very still while the image was being cast on the plate, nearly thirty seconds, without blinking. The plate was then taken back behind the black curtain, where the photographer bathed the glass in a mixture of silver nitrate. Within a short time, the negative image turned to positive, and there in front of Rafe was the first photograph he had ever had taken in his life. The photographer told him to return the following day and his images would be ready.

"We're leaving tonight. Would there be any way the tin type and frame could be shipped to a plantation in Hendersonville?" Rafe inquired.

"I reckon that would be all right. Write down the address on this paper. If you pay today, we can make sure the photograph goes to the right person. Who are you sending this one to?" the photographer asked as he waited to print out the name.

"Please send that to Miss Hattie Townes, Mimosa Grove Plantation, Hendersonville. The carte de viste will be sent to Isaac Collins, Elmwood Plantation, Goodlettsville, Tennessee."

And that was the start to Raford Collins' life as a soldier in the 11th Tennessee Infantry. The merriment that existed that unseasonably warm day in May would soon cease. For many a soldier mustering in during the first few months of the war, the realization that the war would not be over in a few weeks became a startling reality.

"I wish a letter would arrive so I would know how Rafe is doing," Hattie said as she tried to continue her needlepoint.

"I would expect some news soon, Hattie. His last letter to you said he was going to head to Nashville to enlist. I know it's hard, but you'll hear something soon."

Ellie patted her shoulder as she sat down beside her. The two had become close since Ellie came to Mimosa Grove.

In just a few short months, she had grown to care very much for the pretty, upbeat young woman. She also had been privy to the secrets she might have shared with her sister, had she still lived at home. Ellie was told of the proposal, and she was also told about the kiss. As for a wedding date, none had been discussed. That was why Rafe was coming back to Mimosa Grove; they would announce the wedding date to Hattie's family.

Camille had been unusually quiet about Hattie's news. Hattie had only recently shared Rafe's proposal with her mother. She was going to wait, but Daniel had already talked to his wife after Rafe had spoken to him. Camille wasn't happy about it, but tried to keep her thoughts to herself. She worried that Hattie would become a slaveholder, like Caroline. She had wanted to keep Hattie away from such a life. She had confided in Lucy about her fear. Lucy felt the Collins girls were uppity, and they put on airs that didn't impress her one bit. She didn't want her sweet Hattie to become hardened and uncaring towards *her kind*.

The following week, Daniel accompanied Camille to Nashville so that they could be with Caroline and her daughter. The baby was named Harriet Burnell Corbin. James and Caroline were living at the home of his parents, Twin Ponds, since the birth of their daughter. Caroline had sent word that she wanted her mother to come if possible. Caroline's husband had planned to stay with his wife and new daughter, but felt he should defend his homeland. He left with his brother, Todd, to enlist at the Court House in Nashville.

The newborn would be called Rett. Camille and Daniel spent a week loving and petting their new grandchild. Caroline was relieved to have her mother near during her time of recovery from the birth. When the visit ended, the Towneses were apprehensive about leaving their daughter and new granddaughter with the Corbin family. Camille knew another visit to Doe Hill, Caroline's home, might not be safe. Camille urged Caroline to leave Twin Ponds and join the family at Mimosa Grove. Caroline declined their offer; she would remain with her husband's family and the Confederacy.

Rafe and his regiment were transported by rail to Camp Cheatham, near Springfield, Tennessee. They joined the soldiers from Robertson County who had been training in the camp for a couple of weeks. Rafe was surprised to see so many soldiers in one place. There were rows of tents that spread out before them, numbering several hundred. It had been raining for three days, and the camp appeared to be an island of white with a river of rain runoff streaming through the center of the camp.

A loud, short man in a gray coat and slacks met his company at the front of the camp.

"First thing you be doin' is strikin' yur tent over yonder. Git yur gear unpacked and commence to settin' up camp."

The laughter that had been so prevalent on the train ride down to Camp Cheatham suddenly ended. Soldiering had become more serious.

Rafe and Jesse began unloading their belonging. Gideon stepped behind the two; toting what each dropped in the slopping and sloshing through the mud. The first thing that needed to be done was striking their tents. Neither Jesse nor Rafe were seeing much success in their attempts. Finally, two seasoned privates came over to offer their assistance to the fresh fish, a name given to new recruits. A steady rain was coming down, and the rubber blanket and cape that they brought along would come in handy, it seemed.

As soon as they were finished putting their gear into the tent, the short man came back to speak to the men.

"Boys, yur now part of the 11th Tennessee, and you'll be votin' for your commandin' officer shortly. Yur the last group to muster in before we finish drillin' for battle. You got some ketchin' up to do boys," he said as he produced a tobacco-stained toothy grin.

Rafe felt a surge of excitement go through his body as he heard the word *battle*. He still had a romantic view of what war would be like. He remembered the photograph that had been taken earlier that morning; he hoped it would arrive soon, along with the letter he mailed to Hattie. Rafe and Jesse sat on a turned up stump that had been placed where they had pitched their tents. The other men from Robertson County had soon gotten their tents up, with a little help from some of the more seasoned recruits. In the distance, someone was playing the banjo to the tune of *"Dixie"*, and the men began to sing.

Hattie and spent the better part of the time since Rafe enlisted waiting for her first letter. The first letter arrived the last week of the month. Camille had returned from her visit to Nashville to be with Caroline and her new baby, Rett. Life at Mimosa Grove was very much as it was before. Lucy and Mose had taken the buckboard into Hendersonville to bring dry goods back to Mimosa Grove. Folks in town began looking at the Townes family as Union sympathizers. Lucy was suddenly aware that life as she knew it was about to change.

When Lucy carried in the items that Camille had requested, she laid the parcels from the post office on the large table in the entry hall.

"Miz Camille, I left the mail from the post office in the entry. I thought I saw a package for Miz Hattie. I saw the name of her beau, Mister Collins, on that package."

Lucy was not at all happy that Hattie had fallen in love with a slaveholder's son. Lucy had been with Camille since she arrived at Mimosa Grove. Daniel Townes' family still had several slaves in their possession; many of Lucy's family remained in bondage. Lucy was thankful for her freedom, but it was not a freedom like the white folks had.

Even though she, Mose and the others were no longer slaves, they did not enjoy the benefits that freedom brought. They were still considered the property of Daniel Townes in and around the town of Hendersonville.

The servants of Mimosa Grove were an anomaly in the area in which they lived. For that reason, Lucy remained loyal to the Townes family to a fault.

"Thank you, Lucy. I'll call Hattie down to get her package. She's been mulling about the house ever since Raford went to join up with the Confederates," Camille called from the parlor.

Lucy harrumphed to herself, putting the dry goods into the pantry. She tried to remember her place, but the airs that those uppity Collinses put on didn't make them no better than any other slave holder in the rest of the south.

Camille continued into the entry hall. She looked down at the package that was lying on the table and noticed the postmark from the Confederate States of America, Nashville, Tennessee. She drew in a breath, and then walked to the stairs.

"Hattie, could you please come downstairs?"

Hattie had been writing a letter to Maggie Collins, when she heard her mother calling to her. She placed the letter into her writing desk, and walked downstairs to her see what her mother wanted.

"Hattie, you have mail. I thought you might like to see it."

Hattie looked down and saw the package lying on the large hall table.

"Oh Mama! Is it a package from Rafe?" she asked excitedly.

In two shakes of a lamb's tail, Hattie was standing at the bottom of the stairway. She picked it up and saw the Confederate States of American stamp at the top of the package. The contents of the package were light; making it even more exciting to speculate what was inside. She took the package and went into the parlor to sit on the settee. Ellie and Joseph had finished their lessons for the morning, and Ellie came into the parlor just as Hattie was opening the box inside.

"Well, what did you get in the mail today?" Ellie asked.

"Ella, I got a package from Rafe! I can hardly keep my fingers steady to open the box!"

Ellie asked, "Would you rather be alone? I can come back later."

Hattie was just getting the string cut and had made her way into the box.

"Oh no, I want you to stay."

Ellie came into the room and sat beside Hattie. Inside the package was a neatly written letter on military stationery, along with a small box. It was from *C.C. Giers and Co.* of Nashville. The small box was no more than

Lost Letters

four inches by five inches, with a string tying the top and bottom together. As Hattie untied the string, she reverently opened the small frame that was wrapped in tissue.

"It's a picture! Oh look, Ella. Rafe sent me a picture in his uniform."

Ellie moved closer to see the tin type that Hattie was holding in her hand.

"Look how handsome he looks in his uniform, Ella," she said lovingly.

Hattie held the photograph closer to see the detail and image of the man she loved.

Ellie looked closely at the photograph, having an uncanny feeling that she had seen it before.

"I see a hanky in his jacket, Hattie. Did you send that to Rafe?"

Hattie smiled, remembering the afternoon that she gave him the lace handkerchief. It was also the first time he kissed her.

"Yes, I gave it to him. He said he would keep it with him always. Oh, there is a letter too! I was so excited to see Rafe's photograph, I almost missed seeing the letter!" Hattie exclaimed.

Ellie asked if she could see the picture again, while Hattie took the letter out of the envelope and began reading it.

"He says that he is mustered in today and that he and Jesse Taylor are going to Camp Cheatham, near Springfield. I wonder what day that was."

Ellie didn't hear Hattie, as she was examining the photograph of Rafe. *Why does this photograph look so familiar? I couldn't have seen it, he just had it taken. But I know I've seen this before.* As she looked at the image in her hand, she tried to think back to where she had seen it.

"Ella, did you hear what I said?" Hattie asked.

Ellie hadn't heard a word, and she quickly apologized for not being more attentive.

"It's all right; I've been a silly goose ever since Rafe proposed marriage to me. I just wish Mr. Lincoln hadn't called on the soldiers to fight, Rafe would be here to plan our wedding."

Hattie was suddenly saddened by the thought.

"I know, Hattie. I haven't heard any news from back home. It worries me so; I miss my daughter."

Hattie hadn't even thought about Ella's life prior to coming to live at Mimosa Grove. Now she felt very selfish for only emphasizing her own problems.

"Oh Ella, I'm sorry. I have been so preoccupied with my own affairs that I haven't even asked you about yours. Please forgive me."

Ellie reached her hand to clasp Hattie's.

"It shouldn't trouble me so, because I know mail from the North isn't priority, but I do worry about Cassie."

Just then, Daniel Townes came into the house. He hung his cap on the hook in the entry. Joseph heard the door and came running down the stairs to see his father.

"Papa, Mose says I can go along to shoe the mules over at Mr. Flynn's if you say I can go. Can I go?" Joseph asked in a pleading tone.

Daniel patted his son's head.

"Well, I suppose it would be fine, so long as you don't get yourselves into any trouble."

Daniel smiled and walked past Joseph, who was already out the door running towards the barn. Hattie looked up from her letter and picture to address her father.

"Hello, Papa. Come see Rafe's picture. He sent me a photograph of himself on the day he enlisted."

It was obvious that Hattie was beaming with pride, but Daniel wasn't sure she understood what the future would hold for the two of them.

Daniel came over to take a closer look at the photograph in the black case that Hattie was holding.

"Good afternoon, Miss Morgan. How is young Joseph progressing with his studies?"

Ellie felt a fond affection towards Daniel Townes, as he always seemed genuinely concerned with his son's education and was always pleasant. Hattie had gotten most of her physical characteristics from her mother, but her personality was that of her father.

"Oh yes, Mr. Townes. He is doing quite well in his mastery of arithmetic, and we're making progress with his geography."

"You are doing a splendid job, Miss Morgan. Joseph was not interested in either subject. Mrs. Townes and I feared we would have to send him to a boarding school for his education. We were so thankful to have seen your advertisement in the paper."

Ellie didn't remember putting any advertisement in the paper, but smiled as if she did.

"I am thankful as well, Mr. Townes."

Daniel looked closely at the photograph.

"He looks very much the soldier, Hattie. I hope we won't have cause to meet down the road on the battlefield."

Hattie looked up, alarmed at her father's comment.

"Papa, why would you say such a thing?"

Ellie felt a pang of dread, not knowing where it came from.

"Let's not speak of it now," he said seeing the look of fear in her eyes. "Don't fret now, Hattie."

Daniel bent down and put a kiss on top of his daughter's dark head. He put the photograph back in her hand and excused himself. He walked out of the parlor to find his wife.

Rafe and the men of the 11th Tennessee spent most of the day drilling and marching. He had finally received his first letter from Hattie, thanking him for the photograph he sent to her. The mail had taken quite a spell to reach the camp, but it seemed that everyone had a letter or package from home to enjoy. Rafe read her letter at least twenty times since receiving it. He brought the paper to his nose, taking in the scent: *Lemon verbena*. Besides the letter from Hattie, he had received a package from his mother and sisters. Inside the box had been a new shirt, of white muslin, and a pair of socks.

Jesse Taylor had written to his mother about the events during the week at Camp Cheatham. An epidemic of measles had swept through the camp, infecting nearly two hundred soldiers. The 11th lost several men to the disease. Rafe and Jesse had been spared the disease through Providence, and continued to drill with other regiments. At the end of July, the men of Camp Cheatham had been thoroughly trained and prepared for battle.

It had been almost two months since Rafe and the men from Robertson County had left for Nashville. Rafe learned from a sergeant that the regiment would soon be moving out. He sat in his tent listening to the frogs croaking by the stream that flowed near camp. He began to light a candle just as the last of the sun's rays were filtering through the tent flap.

"Rafe, you think we'll kill us some Yanks on the way to wherever it is they're marching us to?" Jesse asked, breaking the relative silence.

Rafe turned to Jesse, who had been writing a letter to his mother.

"I reckon we could, Jess. The colonel said he figures they're gettin' close, probably already into Kentucky. I would expect we'll see some fightin' before long."

The two sat in silence, contemplating a battle, neither knowing how it would feel killing another human. Rafe tried to put the thought out of his mind. He sat about writing two letters that evening. The first letter would be to Hattie, telling her of the troop's movement to East Tennessee. He also talked about the house he wanted to build for her, just as soon as this war ended. In the midst of his break from the monotonous day of drilling, the realization that he was about to face the enemy and possibly the end of his life suddenly became very real to him.

The morale in the camp was high, and most of the young soldiers were bragging of their military prowess. Rafe tried to get his mind back to Hattie and the thought of marrying her.

"Jesse, when we head back to Goodlettsville after the battle, I want to stop at Mimosa Grove. I want you to meet my Hattie. I'll be needing a best man for the wedding, you know."

Jesse sat up on his bedroll, smiling at Rafe.

"You sure she wants to marry you? What if she finds another fella while you're gone?"

Rafe hadn't even let that thought enter his mind since proposing to Hattie. He would soon be marching to battle, and he wanted to be sure his letter reached her and his folks before he left camp.

The days at Camp Cheatham were long and monotonous for Rafe and his regiment. No more letters came during the month of July. Rafe had received a letter from his mother, but no word had come from Hattie. On the twentieth of July, the 11th Tennessee would be marched to East Tennessee to garrison a strategic location where Kentucky, Tennessee, and the Virginia borders converged. It was an area where the Union was expected to invade into the South. Colonel James Raines gave the orders for the men to begin movements towards Nashville.

Once reaching Nashville, the men came upon a great concourse of people who had gathered to send the Confederacy on to battle. The Mayor and other officials offered speeches for the brave boys who would defeat the Yankees. The local citizens had come out to send the brave Rebel soldiers on to victory. Rafe looked amongst the crowd that day, searching for a face that looked familiar. He half-heartedly expected to see Hattie in the crowd as he looked for her. The regiment was given its orders to report at Cumberland Gap, Tennessee where they would become part of Brigadier General Felix Zollicoffer's Brigade. As the army marched out of Nashville, another battle had just taken place in a Virginia town called Manassas.

"There is no king who has not had a slave among his ancestors, and no slave who has not had a king among his"
~ Helen Keller

Chapter 14

Ellie had been given the rest of the summer to enjoy a respite from her teaching duties. She offered her assistance wherever it was needed around the plantation. As soon as it was safe, she would be taking a train north back to Indiana to see her daughter. The Towneses knew that it would not be safe for her to travel in a few weeks, so she would have to be ready to leave as soon as the railroads were free of soldiers being transported. Ellie had been helping in the garden with Lucy, as the harvest was in full production.

Sally Flynn had come for a visit, bringing news that the boys from the area had marched through Nashville. Their son, Josh, had joined up with the brigade that left for East Tennessee. Ellie also knew that the Townes' oldest daughter, Caroline, had a husband in that regiment as well. So many men had left the community to defend the state. Ellie wondered why Hattie had not received word from Rafe. She had come to like the young man, and now with Hattie being so worried about his safety, she couldn't help but feel a sense of dread where he was concerned.

The women had begun bringing the vegetables into the root cellar by the bushel baskets. The turnips and potatoes would be a welcome addition to the table when the cold of winter had set in. Lucy was putting corn and beans into the glass jars, while Joseph was busy stacking the jars down in the cellar as they were cool enough to move. Hattie came back into the kitchen to carry the jars of tomatoes.

"Lucy, will you please take my letter to the post office when you and Mose go into town today? I haven't heard from Rafe, so I wanted to write to Maggie to see if she had received word from him."

Lucy put down her jar, wiping the lid with a clean cloth.

"Of course, Miz Hattie. Wouldn't be a bother at all."

"Thank you, Lucy," Hattie said sweetly.

Hattie took the jars out of the kitchen, and Ellie overheard Lucy mutter something under her breath. She wasn't sure what she said, but her demeanor had changed after Hattie walked away.

Camille confided to Ellie, "I know the wedding is just a matter of time. Once the war is over, I suppose Hattie will be leaving Mimosa Grove just as Caroline did."

Camille tried not to show her sadness, but Ellie knew her heart was breaking at the thought of Hattie leaving her. She had just returned from the Female Academy where she'd lived for two years. Lucy came back to the kitchen for more jars.

Camille said, "Oh, I have a package for Caroline and Rett, could you please see that it gets to the post as well, Lucy?"

"Yes'm. I'll gather the mail dreckly, and Mose can take me into town, Miz Camille," Lucy replied.

Lucy finished wiping off the jars; then took the large pot off the fire.

"Joseph, go fetch Mose and Abe. I need this pot dumped. We got to head to town for your mama."

Joseph hopped down from the slab of wood that was used for a counter, grabbed an apple and ran out the door. Ellie watched as he hurried down the path behind the large house to the barn.

"He surely does enjoy being with Mose, doesn't he, Camille?"

Camille walked to the doorway, watching her son until he was out of sight.

"He does for a fact, Ella. I expect he enjoys the company of Mose more than his mother."

Ellie remembered the punishment Joseph had been given for smoking Mose's corncob pipe weeks before.

"Well, he is a good boy. I'm thankful he is too young to run off with some of the other boys to fight the Yankees," Ellie remarked.

Camille seemed shocked at Ellie's comment.

"Miss Morgan, our family will not be running off to *kill any Yankees*. We have chosen to remain loyal to our country; Daniel will not raise arms against the North," Camille declared.

Ellie had felt that the Townes family would be neutral from comments she had overheard Daniel make since coming to Mimosa Grove.

She also worried that she might be dismissed. Many of the nearby towns were putting pressure on their neighbors to side with the Confederacy and Northerners were seen as potential spies or sympathizers.

Ellie walked over to Camille and took her hand, "I didn't mean to be disrespectful, Mrs. Townes. It appears we are both in the midst of trying to uphold what we believe is right, and we will have those who don't agree with us."

Camille's tone softened and she backed away from her defensive stance.

"I am just so worried, Ella. What if Rafe comes for Hattie and takes her with him to his plantation? What will happen then?"

Lucy came back to tell Camille that she, Mose and Joseph would be going into Hendersonville.

"Thank you, Lucy. I believe Hattie has a letter on the table, and my package is lying there beside it."

Lucy walked into the house, leaving the two women again.

"I don't know how long this war will last, but I don't see Hattie leaving Mimosa Grove. She loves it here, and I believe family is very important to her," Ellie said.

The two walked out of the summer kitchen and entered the back door to the house.

That evening, Daniel had gone into the library to work on the account ledger. Profits had been very good for Mimosa Grove. The horses that he had sold that year brought a good price, and the sale the previous year of his parent's plantation had been divided between the remaining children. His brother had left North Carolina for Maryland once his father had passed away. Daniel had toyed with the idea of taking the plantation himself, but with talk of secession, he agreed with his brother that selling the plantation while he could get a profit was best. The matter of the slaves had been the greatest point of contention between Daniel and his brother, Matthew. Daniel wanted no part of the ownership of the fifteen slaves who were deeded to him.

His brother had sold off his share, making enough to put with his inheritance to buy a large farm near Hagerstown, Maryland. That summer, a neighbor of Joshua Townes loaded the slaves on a buckboard wagon for Tennessee. Fearing the Northern soldiers might take them for digging fortifications, they were sent further south before coming up through Nashville to Mimosa Grove.

The band of slaves, ten men and four women arrived at the plantation in late July. Seeing the ordeal that they had already been through in their travels, they were given clean clothes and food immediately. Next, Daniel gave each of the slaves their manumission papers and ten dollars out of his inheritance: a nice sum, to begin their lives with as they wished. Many of these slaves had been the offspring of those on the plantation when he was a boy. None, however, were relatives of Lucy. He urged them to go north, but to be sure to have their papers with them. He reminded them that there were bounty hunters who would be patrolling the river banks and train stations for runaways. It was decided that they would be taken to the cabin of the Choctaw medicine man, and from there, they would be taken across the river into Kentucky. Daniel knew of several families that had strong ties to the Underground Railroad. He hoped they would be able to help them.

Now, sitting in the library that August evening, he wondered what had become of the fifteen souls he had set free. He wondered if they had made it safely to the North. He also wondered what had become of his brother. He hadn't heard from him since he left that September day last year. He sat at the secretary desk writing a letter to his daughter . . . He asked her to come back to Mimosa Grove with her daughter, to have the family under one roof while her husband was fighting in the war. After sealing the envelope, his thoughts went to Raford Collins, the young man who had asked for his daughter's hand just three months before. He couldn't help but wonder if Hattie and Rafe would be married.

Ellie had heard the rustle of a skirt outside in the hallway, but she wasn't sure if it was just Hattie going down to the privy outside. Half asleep, she took the candle and walked quietly over to the doorway. As she peered out the small crack, she saw Lucy carrying something in her hand, walking up to the attic stairs. *What in the world is she doing at this time of night?* Ellie watched quietly as Lucy walked up the stairs as quiet as a mouse. Not wanting to spy, Ellie closed the door to her bedroom. *It isn't any of my business, but why is Lucy in the attic this late at night?*

Ellie began to think of the strange occurrences that she had experienced since coming to Mimosa Grove: the loss of memory, hearing voices and seeing a strange apparition of a man in the hallway. All of these events had been pushed farther and farther back into her mind. She couldn't explain them, so why worry and fret about it now? But it was strange, nonetheless.

That night, Ellie dreamed the most perplexing dream. In a different time, she and Jack were sitting with a gentleman on the steps of Mimosa Grove. Ellie had always sensed that she had been to Mimosa Grove before working for the Towneses. Ellie tossed and turned, and when she awoke the next morning, felt as though she were rising from a fog.

During the following weeks, Ellie made preparations for her trip back to Indiana. She had planned to leave the end of the month, and even though Daniel wasn't sure traveling the railroad would be safe, he promised he would see her safely to the train station in Gallatin. All was going according to plan until word came that travel to the north would not be possible. The Union had moved closer into the Northern portion of the state, and civilians were urged not to travel north from Tennessee into Kentucky. There had been several skirmishes in and around the Kentucky-Tennessee border, and it was looking doubtful that she would be able to leave.

News of the Southern victory in Manassas quickly reached the Southern towns in and around Nashville, and it was becoming clear that this war would not be over in a few weeks. Jesse and Rafe had volunteered for one year of service, never thinking it would be more than a few weeks.

As they marched along the dirt roads in the sweltering heat of July, Rafe's thoughts began to wander back to Elmwood, the breeze blowing through the windows of his parent's home, and the lazy evenings sitting under the large willow trees that shaded the porch in the summer. His pleasant thoughts were interrupted by the biting and buzzing of a mosquito. The incessant buzzing drove him to perdition as he tried to swat at the pest and continue the march.

The load that he carried became quite cumbersome as the march continued along the dusty road. The sweat ran down into his eyes, and he wished he could shed the heavy wool jacket that was now feeling like a lead weight on his body. He began to think about Hattie now. When would he hear from her again? It had been almost a month since his last letter. For the life of him, he couldn't understand why she stopped writing.

On they marched, until finally the Colonel gave the orders to beauvac for the night. It was a welcome relief to take the pack from his shoulder, the gun wearing down on his other shoulder. The men would only have time to rest for the night, so no tents would be raised. The men found a spot under the trees and spread out their bedroll. Rafe's canteen was dry, and he walked to the stream near which they had the good fortune of camping.

Several of the men had walked down to the stream to fill their canteens for the next day's march. Talk of the Battle of Manassas seemed to be the conversation that was most common that evening. Rafe joined in with the usual summation of the Yankee army. The Tennessee boys would give them their comeuppance, and it was only a matter of time before they sent them skedaddling back across the Mason-Dixon Line.

That night, the excitement was running high among the young recruits. The sounds coming from the camp was a mingling of raucous laughter, boasting and the lonesome contrast of the mourning dove. As if it were a premonition of what was to come, the sorrowful sound seemed to overshadow the jovial mood that had infected the 11th Tennessee.

"My mammy used to say that someone was about to die when the mourning dove settled outside their window. You ever hear tell of that, Rafe?" Jesse asked.

Rafe had been listening to the sound of someone playing a tune on the harmonica somewhere nearby, and the sound of Jesse's voice jostled him back to the conversation.

"I heard something similar, I suppose. What'd ya have to go and bring that up for? We aren't going to the by and by just yet," Rafe said as he playfully swiped his hand back and forth through Jesse's thick blonde hair.

The two shared a brief tussle, and then moved back to their bedrolls.

"Jesse, just in case I was to meet my maker on the battlefield, would you swear an oath that you'll find Hattie and give her the hanky she gave me? I want her to have it back if something were to happen."

Jesse felt uncomfortable with Rafe's change of demeanor.

"Oh shoot, Rafe. Ain't nothin' going to happen to your lacey hanky, you paper-collard dandy!"

With that, Rafe relaxed.

"Just the same, I want you to promise that if something were to happen to me, you'd make sure my daddy and mama get my things."

Jesse asked the same of Rafe, seeing that he was dead serious this time.

"You know I will, Rafe. I swear it."

The two shook hands, and Rafe reached inside his haversack to draw out the small testament that the preacher had given him almost two months before. He wasn't sure where to read, but his hand turned to the book of Psalms. It was there that he found the 23rd chapter and began to read it to himself. Just as David must have prayed before meeting the mighty Philistine, Goliath, Rafe began to pray for his and Jesse's safety as well.

Hattie and Camille had been making gifts to send to Caroline and Rett. After the church service, a call had gone out for all able-bodied women to come for a time of sewing for the soldiers and *The Cause*. Camille had decided it best not to go. Daniel had finally received word from his brother, Matthew. He had gone to volunteer with the Confederacy, even though he was living in Maryland. Being a border state, not seceding from the Union, there was many a Southern supporter living in the area. Matthew wanted to send a letter to his brother, mending the rift that had befallen them after the selling of the family plantation.

Now Daniel was feeling the sadness of his own brother being a soldier for the Confederacy, while he still remained loyal to the Union. It was decided that the family would not openly support either side. Hattie could not abide by her family's turning their back on their neighbors and friends. She would have to support the Confederacy and the man she loved.

She began attending the weekly sewing circles to knit socks and makes shirts to be sent to the soldiers. She also rolled bandages to be sent to the battlefields, not sure if her own love, Rafe, would be somewhere on the battlefield injured or worse. The thought was almost too much for her to dwell on. For that reason, she continued to write to Rafe, not sure if her letters would reach him. On her way to the sewing circle, she would have Lucy mail a letter to the last camp address that Rafe had sent to her. She prayed for his safety nightly, and continued to ask Lucy to carry her letters to town when she went with Mose to get supplies.

Ellie had come upon a conversation between Daniel and Camille one afternoon regarding Hattie's weekly sewing circle trips. She was sure that Daniel would put an end to it, fearing that she would be turned on for being part of a Union supporting family.

"How can we tell her that she can't support the man she loves, Daniel? She is only doing what any woman would do for the man she is about to marry. You know it pains me to say it, knowing what his family stands for," Camille said.

Daniel was thinking of his family's safety at the moment, and it was clear that feelings were being worn on the sleeves of many a southerner. Many slave owners in the area were fearful of what would happen to their property should the Yankee invaders come into Tennessee. The townspeople of Hendersonville would not take kindly to a Yankee supporter amongst their small circle. It was clear to Daniel that he would no doubt face much ridicule and possible violence for remaining loyal to the Union.

"Camille, it might be best if we send Miss Morgan home as soon as possible. If she wants to make safe passage, I'm not sure how safe the rail will be, much less the roads. The army is moving up from the south to protect Fort Donelson; it is only a matter of time before the Northern Army will be near Hendersonville. We have to prepare for what is to come."

Camille began to pace as she let what her husband said sink in. Her thoughts for Ella were those of compassion, knowing that she had not seeing her daughter in months. Camille worried for her daughter and granddaughter as well.

"Well then, we must do all we can to help Miss Morgan leave while she is able. Do you think we can have her safely transported by the week's end?"

Daniel closed the parlor doors, and Ellie was unable further hear the conversation.

Ellie made her way back up the stairs, and upon reaching the landing, met Lucy coming down from the attic. Lucy was surprised to see Ellie, thinking she was outside with Hattie on the back porch. Jack had scurried up the stairs behind her, going to Joseph's room where a small treat or morsel of food could be found.

"Oh, Lucy, you startled me!" Ellie said as she came face to face with the Townes' servant.

"Excuse me, Miz Ella," Lucy said, as she quickly made her way back downstairs.

Now what was she doing up in that hot attic on a day like today? Ellie couldn't imagine what had drawn her to hot attic on this August afternoon, but it wasn't the first time she had seen her rushing down from there.

Ellie dismissed the thought and continued on to her room. She closed the shade that had been left open to allow the breeze of the morning to cool the upstairs. She was about to write another letter to her daughter to tell her of her plans to return home, when Hattie came to the top of the stairs. She walked into her room and sat on the bed, holding the small tin type photograph of Rafe. Ellie walked across the hallway, knocking softly on the door to Hattie's room.

"Hattie, may I come in?"

Hattie looked up from the picture, and it was then that Ellie could see a tear that had began to run down Hattie's smooth, pale cheek.

"Oh Hattie, what's wrong?"

Ellie walked over and sat beside the young girl. Hattie began to cry, and it was obvious that she was trying to talk while uncontrollable sobs escaped her. Ellie put her arms around her, much like she did her own daughter, and tried her best to console her. She handed her a handkerchief to wipe her eyes.

When she had composed herself once again, Hattie looked up and began to tell Ellie what had caused her to lose her composure.

"Ella, I haven't received word from Rafe in over a month. I am so afraid something has happened to him. I wrote to Maggie, and I haven't heard from her either. Do you think Rafe could have, well, could something have happened and they won't tell me?"

Ellie could see the look of panic that had overtaken Hattie.

"I don't know why you haven't heard from him, but I'm sure we would have heard something if he would have taken ill."

Ellie wasn't sure she believed her own words, but she felt affection for Rafe, and hoped he was safe.

"I'm going to be writing my daughter, it looks as though I will be leaving possibly by week's end."

Hattie looked surprised at Ellie's announcement.

"I want to see my daughter, and I haven't heard from her either. Your parents think it best that I leave before the Yankees get into Tennessee. I'm not even sure I can get out safely."

Hattie touched Ellie's hand in a sympathetic gesture.

"How will you get home? If the Yankees are between Mimosa Grove and Indiana, you would be in danger, Ella. Please, don't leave us," Hattie begged.

Ellie smiled and patted her hand.

"If I am traveling North, I'll be fine. I'm sure your father can arrange safe passage for me. If you'd like, I can take your letter to Rafe when I take mine to mail to Cassandra. Would you like that?"

Hattie wiped her eyes and smiled, "Yes, I would. I'll write him tonight. Thank you, Ella. I love you for helping me!"

Ellie felt a rush of emotion overtake her, as she felt a pang of sadness being away from her own child.

"I love you, Hattie," Ellie said, as she gave her a hug.

She left Hattie sitting on her bed, writing a letter to Rafe. When she returned to her room, she began her own letter to Cassie. She decided that she must try to leave by week's end if she were to cross over into Kentucky, where she would be safely out of harm's way. She would need to send the letter out of Hendersonville tomorrow if it were to reach Indiana before she would arrive.

The next morning, Ellie rose early to dress and have breakfast. She hurriedly made a list of things she would need to take for her trip back home. She could feel the warm sun already making the room feel like an oven. She had written a note to the family of Rafe Collins, telling them how much she enjoyed the time during the holidays, as well as how happy she was for the engagement of Raford to Hattie. She quickly slid the note into the envelope, making sure it was addressed and ready to mail.

As she busied herself with her morning toiletries, she heard a wagon making its way up the long driveway. Ellie sat her towel down and looked out the window. Hade and Sally Flynn were making their way up to the house. Sally was carrying a large basket and Hade was carrying a large crate. She finished with her dressing and walked down the stairs. As she rounded the landing, she heard Lucy's skirt swishing down the hallway as she walked to the front door.

"Morning Miz Sally, Mist'r Hade. Come on in, Mist'r Daniel and Miz Camille is takin' their breakfast in the dining room."

Lucy stepped aside for the Flynn's to come into the entry hall.

"It sure is a hot one this morning, Lucy," Hade commented.

They followed Lucy down the hallway in to the large dining room. Hade and Sally came in, setting their baskets on the floor.

Lucy eyed Camille saying, "I'll set two more plates, Miz Camille. I'll just be a minute."

Camille smiled, "Thank you, Lucy."

She welcomed Hade and Sally, and Daniel rose from his seat as they came to the table.

"Good morning, Hade. Sally, it's so nice to see you again," Daniel politely said.

Joseph almost ran over Ellie as he hopped down steps to get to the dining room.

"Well you might say 'excuse me' young man," Ellie remarked as Joseph hurried past her.

"Sorry. Excuse me, Miss Morgan," Joseph said as he continued on his way, rounding the corner.

Ellie reached the bottom of the stairs and stopped to check herself in the large mirror that hung on the wall in the entry hall.

It was then that she noticed the Flynn's hired man, Jonas Dowell, who was sitting out on the porch steps.

Ellie quietly walked outside. When Jonas saw Ellie, he quickly removed his cap and smiled.

"Good mornin', Miss Morgan."

Ellie smiled, "Good morning, Mr. Dowell. Would you care to join us for breakfast?"

Jonas looked surprised that Ellie had invited him to come and dine with the Towneses.

"Oh, no, ma'am, thank you though. I'll just wait out here for the Flynns to come out."

Ellie couldn't imagine Jonas just sitting in the hot sun while the Flynns enjoyed a leisurely breakfast with the Towneses.

"Well, may I bring you some of Lucy's biscuits and ham?"

She could see that the thought of Lucy's biscuits and ham tempted him almost to submission, but he declined her offer once again.

"I had a bit of jerky this morning; I'm full as a tick."

Ellie smiled at Jonas' expression.

"Well, all right then. But you are more than welcome to come to the back porch if you insist on waiting outside. There is a bit of breeze coming from under the mimosa trees."

Jonas followed Ellie around the side of the house like a man in a trance. She wasn't aware of his stare as they walked around to the porch.

That sure is one handsome woman, Jonas thought to himself, as he watched the graceful way Ellie moved in her taffeta dress.

"I'll leave you here to enjoy the breeze, what there is of one. I'm going to take my breakfast now. Good day, Mr. Dowell. It was good to see you again."

Jonas tipped his cap, smiling at Ellie.

"It was good to see you again, too, Miss Morgan."

Ellie went inside the house, and could feel the sweat running down her face. She took her hanky, already damp from the humidity, from inside her sleeve, and dabbed her forehead and throat. Entering the dining room, she took her place at the table.

"Good morning, Ella. I hope you slept well," Camille said softly.

"Thank you, I did."

Ellie took the bowls of food as they were being passed around, filling her plate with ham, biscuits and gravy. As she did so, she said her 'good morning' to both Hade and Sally.

"Good morning, Ella. It's nice to see you again," Sally said.

"Mrs. Townes, I will be going into town this morning to mail letters and to purchase a few supplies for the trip back home. Is there anything I can get for you?" Ellie asked.

Camille turned to the Flynns, who were quietly eating their breakfast.

"Miss Morgan will be leaving us soon. With the war, she thought it best to go back to her home and daughter. We are distressed at her announcing to leave us so soon, but none of us know the future."

She patted Ellie's hand.

"Oh, we will hate to see you leave us, Miss Morgan. But is it safe to travel north?" Sally asked.

Ellie wasn't sure herself.

Daniel replied, "We hope that the armies aren't camped around border."

Hade didn't like the sound of Ellie leaving in such uncertain times.

"I heard tell from Tom Jessup that the troops are all over that area, coming down from the North, heading for the Gap."

Camille looked concerned.

"Daniel, isn't that where Caroline told us that Thomas was heading?"

Ellie remembered Thomas and Rafe were part of the same regiment.

"Then Rafe would be headed to that area as well," Ellie said.

This news had been weighing on Camille. She worried for the safety of her daughter and granddaughter.

"Yes, there are many boys from the county who are headed for the Gap," Hade said.

As the conversation continued, it was clear that if Ellie were to make her way north before troops began to move in and around Middle Tennessee, she would have to leave soon.

"I have enjoyed my stay very much, and it pains me to leave before seeing Hattie and Raford marry," Ellie interjected.

Daniel seemed uneasy about his daughter's impending marriage to the rebel soldier.

"I am concerned for all the boys who have gone off to enlist and fight in this war, both those who fight for the flag of Tennessee and for our country. I fear that Hattie won't be marrying anytime soon. It could be months before this war is over."

Ellie had read the accounts in the newspaper of the Battle of Manassas, so many killed and wounded.

"If the soldiers are in and around the Gap, you very well might not be safe to leave right now, Miss Morgan. It just wouldn't be safe for a woman to travel alone such a great distance," Hade said, hoping to sway her decision.

Ellie was suddenly aware that her independence meant very little when there was a war being fought. She might not be able to make it safely home to see her daughter. The thought caused a lump to close in around her.

"I think I'll excuse myself and take in some air outdoors. I'll be leaving for town as soon as Mose can hitch the team."

Ellie rose, as did Hade and Daniel.

"Miss Morgan, we will do all that we can to return you safely to your home. Please know that your safety is our utmost concern," Daniel said as he smiled sympathetically.

Ellie sighed, "I appreciate your kindness, Mr. Townes. I am going to continue praying that I will be able to secure passage to the North by the week's end."

She turned to the Flynns saying, "It was so nice seeing you, Mrs. Flynn, Mr. Flynn."

And with that, Ellie made her way out to the porch to wait for Abe.

Show pity, Lord, O Lord, forgive
Let a repenting rebel live:
Are not Thy mercies large and free?
May not a sinner trust in Thee?
- Words by Isaac Watts

Chapter 15

The days were long for Rafe and the 11th Tennessee. They had marched for weeks, and still had a ways to go before reaching the Cumberland Gap. The heat of the day made many a soldier sick, and Rafe felt he would have heat stroke from the itchy wool uniform that he wore. Gideon had kept the pace, carrying Rafe's bedroll and tent. He had even been used to cook for some of the men, once they learned he was the manservant of Rafe. The regiment had few slaves who joined their masters, but Gideon felt proud to be soldiering with Rafe.

He had been his companion since birth, and the two had been inseparable as children. Now, Gideon had been sent with Rafe to defend their homeland, their way of life: a way of life that had kept him and countless thousands in bondage on plantations across the state. Rafe had never questioned the life that he lived at Elmwood. It was all that he knew. His father had never had to raise his hand to any of his slaves, although he had to sell a young buck that had tried to steal from Isaac's cash box when he had wandered into the house.

Rafe remembered his being loaded onto the buckboard and driven away from Elmwood amidst the cries and pleas of his mother. That was only time he had seen this side to his father. He never questioned his authority when it came to the good and welfare of his sisters, mother or their home. Now Gideon stood beside Rafe as they marched on their way to battle. Jesse had tried to keep up the pace, but needed to stop. He had been battling stomach cramps since leaving Nashville, stopping every few miles to relieve himself.

"Jesse, you gonna be okay?" Rafe asked, as they followed their unit down the dusty path.

The gnats circled their faces, sticking to the sweat as it ran down into their eyes. The hot noonday sun had prompted a halt to their marching, since there was a small creek that ran parallel to the road some distance down the bank. Their commanding officer had sent word down the lines that they would stop to fill canteens, but would continue the march. Rafe pulled out an apple that he been given by one of the farmers who had passed out fruit to the passing army sometime back. Its juice tasted good as Rafe took a bite.

Gideon came back with both canteens filled full. Before long, the march was resumed. Rafe began to think about Elmwood, his father having the slaves clear the hillside where he and Hattie would build their home. He could hear the drone of men talking, some complaining, as they marched on in the heat. His thoughts went to Hattie, and their last evening together that springtime day at Mimosa Grove. Her lips touching his, the smallness of her waist as he pulled her close to him, feeling her heart beating like a scared rabbit. The thoughts of her sweet face and the memory of her kiss was something he called upon often during the long march towards the Cumberland Gap. He wondered if she had received his letter. He hoped there would be a letter for him whenever the mail finally caught up to them. How he wished for a letter from her.

The movement of troops all over the state of Tennessee became a common site in around railroad depots and along the tracks of Middle Tennessee. Hattie had watched the river, seeing steamboats traveling up and down the Cumberland. The thoughts of Rafe never were far away, but she had started keeping herself busy with volunteering her time to help with supplies for the troops. Ellie and Hattie made several trips into town to offer their time with rolling bandages and making packages to be sent off to the troops. Soon, word circled in the community that Daniel Townes had remained a Union sympathizer, and it was clear that Ellie's Union ties also made her suspicious in the eyes of the Southern ladies who sat around the large sewing tables in the Hendersonville Methodist Church.

This afternoon was like many others, she and Hattie rolled the strips of cotton cloth in balls, handing them to Lucy, who filled the crates full. Sally Flynn sat next to Hattie, doing her part for the Cause. It was Sally who spoke up in the defense of the two when a rather dour matron inquired as to why a Yankee would want to roll bandages for their Southern sons and husbands.

Ellie had not met with any unkindness for the months that she had lived among the families in Robertson County. In fact, she had taken her place at the weekly Bible meeting, paying little mind to the anti-Yankee sentiment that was spoken not only from the pew but also from the pulpit. Ellie knew that the Townes family was torn between being loyal to the state that they loved, and not draw arms against their brothers to the north.

"How's your daddy gonna side when the Yankees come to our farms and towns to steal and kill? Is he gonna turn his back on his neighbors?" Lodica Parker said as the venom seethed from each word.

Sally fidgeted in her chair, uncomfortable with the tone in the woman's voice.

"We must remember that we are to support our men, and we are here to offer our hand to support our boys from the county. Seems to me, Miss Morgan and Miss Hattie are supporting the boys from Tennessee by coming each week to offer their hand. I think we should remember to show Christian love."

The woman began to speak, but it was Hattie who interrupted.

"I'm here because somewhere the man I am going to marry could be lying sick or wounded, and it might be some Yankee woman that is given the responsibility to nurse him. I would hope that she would show Christian love towards him. It is not for you to judge whether my family sides with the Union or with the Confederacy."

The woman scrunched her nose and made a muffled snort.

"Well, soon enough you'll have to choose, and if your family has any loyalty in them, they will be siding with the Confederacy."

Ellie could see the ire rising in Hattie, and before another word was said, Hattie turned to Lucy.

"Come, Lucy. We've done all we can do here today."

Lucy stood, and put her rolls of linen on the table. She looked squarely in the eye of the woman, clearly a statement of defiance. Sally Flynn tried to lay her bandages down and gather her skirts about her without getting in the way of Hattie's angry departure. Ellie rose, placing her strips that had not been rolled back in the basket on the floor. She turned before she followed Hattie out of the church.

"Mrs. Parker, we are all sad that this war has happened. I bear no ill will towards you for being a Southerner."

With that, Ellie turned and walked straight out of the building, leaving the rest of the women with her words still stinging in their ears.

Mose turned to see the women making their way towards the carriage; he could see that something wasn't quite right.

"Miss Hattie, what's got you ladies all riled up?"

Hattie handed her bag to Lucy as she reached for Mose's hand.

"Mose, I have never been so angry in all my life! And to think we sit every week with these old hens and do every bit as much work as any of them!"

Mose wasn't sure what had caused the women to come from the sewing circle in such a snit, but it was Lucy who quietly recounted the exchange to Mose on the way back to Mimosa Grove.

As Sally, Ellie and Hattie rode in silence for most of the way, it was clear to each of them that the families who had not joined the Confederacy would be looked upon as Yankee sympathizers, and therefore not to be trusted. Hattie was still talking under her breath about the hateful Mrs. Parker when Ellie finally spoke.

"Hattie, I'll be leaving for Indiana at the end of the week. Your father and Mr. Flynn feel like now is as good a time as any to try and leave for Indiana."

Hattie turned to Ellie, clearly disturbed by her announcement.

"Oh no, you can't go! It can't be safe, with word that soldiers are moving along the railroad lines. You can't travel without a chaperone, not now!"

Ellie smiled, thinking to herself how much Hattie reminded her of her own daughter with her motherly comment.

"I'm sure that there will be other folks traveling north. I would love it if you would help me pack my trunks."

Sally had been listening to the conversation and her uneasiness for Ella traveling into possible skirmishes or being with men without a proper escort laid heavily upon her mind.

"Ella, would you like me to speak to Hade about sending our hired man with you as far as the Kentucky border? Once you're there, I'm sure Mrs. Townes' family could meet you and get you safely through to Louisville."

Ellie faced Sally, offering her her mitted hand.

"That would be very kind of you, Sally. I would feel very safe traveling with Mr. Dowell. You may speak to Mr. Flynn. Thank you."

As the three women talked amongst themselves, Lucy and Mose spoke in hushed tones as the carriage traveled over the bumpy dirt road towards Mimosa Grove. Ellie could tell they were speaking softly, as to not be overheard, and she was curious as to why the two were so secretive.

The month of July had seen the 11th Tennessee join other regiments which converged upon the Cumberland Gap. Rafe and Jesse had each been ill with a fever, but after two weeks of being kept back with others who had fallen ill with dysentery, finally were able to find their way back to their regiment. Rafe had spent hours marching in the heat, and after his bout with the fever, was still feeling the effects of his dehydrated body being forced to go without water for long periods of time. It caused his mind to wander, thinking of Hattie and what had become of her. He had received a letter from his sister, Maggie, and she hadn't heard any news from Mimosa Grove.

Rafe had spent the last night with a group of rather unsavory rebel soldiers who had stolen several kegs of whiskey from the cellar of a local farmer. Several of the boys had found the company of a group of young women who were doing the laundry for the officers from a nearby camp. Rafe and Jesse, not used to taking in spirits in such a large quantity, had found themselves in a state of drunkenness that neither had experienced in their young lives.

The next morning, the rebels had moved on, leaving Rafe, Jesse, and a handful of young men in the barnyard of the house where the ladies had been boarding. It was then that Rafe and Jesse knew they had done more than sleep their liquor-driven stupor off in the farmer's barn. Rafe looked at his disheveled state of dress, and the realization came over him. *Good lord almighty, what have I gone and done?*

He looked around for Gideon, but could not find him anywhere.

"Jesse, are you all right?" Rafe whispered.

Jesse wasn't in much better shape than Rafe, and he was still trying to put the pieces of their night of drinking and carousing into perspective.

"Yeah, but I got a thumpin' in my brain that feels like my head's about to pop."

Rafe crawled to the barn door and pulled himself up, getting his gear that was scattered around on the hay that lay strewn on the floor.

"There's about ten other fellas and an officer passed out on the ground under the tree. I gotta try and find Gideon."

Rafe made his way out of the barn, carefully surveying the yard and large farmhouse that was off in the distance. His head felt as if it was twice the size as his shoulders, and he found the world about him taking on a slant.

It was still partly dark, and there were no lights in the house.

"Gideon, where are you?" Rafe said in a loud whisper.

He walked slowly over to where the rest of the men lay sprawled out under the large oak tree. He thought he heard something, but wasn't sure. He looked all around, and then heard it again.

"Up here, Mist'r Rafe."

It was from one of the large branches overhead that the voice of his slave, Gideon, could be heard. Crouching on one of the branches in the oak tree, Gideon had taken Rafe's rifle and was guarding the men who lay on the ground.

"Good lord, Gideon. Get yourself down out of that tree. You look like Zaccheaus."

Rafe had to laugh, which caused his head to pound even worse.

"Mist'r Rafe, I took your rifle and climbed up in this here tree to guard the likes of you. You wasn't in no state of protectin' yourself. And those gals from the farmer's house wasn't interested in protectin' you either."

Hearing the sarcasm of Gideon, Rafe almost called him down to reprimand him for taking on such an uppity tone, but it was then that he realized just what he had done. His guilt made the sickening feeling in his gut and the pounding of his head seem less noticeable.

"Just git on down out of the tree, and hand me my gun."

Gideon leaned over the large branch, clinching his legs tightly to keep from losing his balance. He handed the rifle down to Rafe, carefully. It was then that two of the soldiers stirred, and Rafe motioned for them to be still. Pointing to the farmer's house, they understood. Gideon made his way down from the tree; they all began to gather their things, laughing among themselves.

They made their way towards the road; another brigade, the 4th Tennessee, was just in front of them. The soldiers marched quietly with several wagons carrying supplies and one very small cannon. It was decided they would follow along, not sharing their indiscretions from the night before; only owning up to their being kept back until their fever and other ailments were cleared to join their regiment. Rafe was feeling as if he would be sick, but kept up the pace with the others.

Sometime when he had the chance, he would find out what happened the night before.

The young women who resided in the farmhouse were busily rising to start on the day's chores. One girl, a small, dark-eyed girl of about eighteen, was still putting on her dress when the farmer knocked on the door.

"You girls get any money off those rebs? You hand it over if ya did."

The three older girls laughed, reaching for the wallets that had been lifted the night before.

"Only four, Smitty. Those are the poorest soldiers yet. It wasn't worth the whiskey we poured in them!"

"Then you best be given' me what you got, cause that whiskey ain't growing on trees."

The tall blonde put the money from the wallets under the door. The girls waited until they heard Smitty Jackson make his way back down the creaky stairs.

"How much did you get, Melinda?"

The young girl with the dark eyes took her stash from under her mattress. There was only one wallet, which was empty. There was a letter inside instead.

"Well you wasted a good night's work, didn't you?"

The other girls began to laugh, as they each had taken several wallets between them.

"I don't care. He had just sent his money to his Ma. I don't mind. He was different than the others."

One of the girls, who had been brushing her long brunette tresses, walked over to Melinda.

"Sugar, you can't fall for every one of them rebs that comes through. Do you want to get off this farm?"

Melinda looked at Lulie, smiling.

"But he was different. He talked to me, and he called me Hattie. I like that name. She must be someone mighty special."

Lulie turned to the blonde, Becky, "Don't you go ruinin' Melinda's memory. She'll get those notions out of her mind soon enough. We all did."

Melinda wasn't like the other girls who had come to stay at Smitty's farm. She had been forced to take to being hired out when her mama passed from typhoid when she was thirteen. Neighbors had helped looked after her, but she left when the old man started paying a little too much attention to the young girl. It was her only chance for a roof over her head and food in her stomach when she came to the old farmhouse starving and cold the winter before. Smitty, his given name being Herchel Smith, wasn't one to dole out charity. His farmhouse had been long known as a cat house, and it wasn't long before the farm was a popular stop over by the soldiers who were heading out of Middle Tennessee towards the eastern portion of the state.

Melinda Turner didn't much like the way things were, but it was better than nothing. She couldn't steal from Raford Collins; it wasn't in her nature to do so. Taking his wallet was something she was expected to do, but as she talked to the soldier between his swigs from the whiskey bottle, she saw he wasn't like the others. She decided she would just take his wallet to appease the other girls. When she opened the leather pouch after Rafe had passed out, she saw that he had no money, only an envelope that was neatly addressed and folded. She took the letter that had been in the wallet and opened it. It was ready to be mailed to a Miss Maggie Collins, Elmwood Plantation, Hendersonville, Tennessee.

As she read the letter, she began to dream about the young soldier who had shared the night with her. Whether he was aware of what they had done or not, it was a memory she would never forget.

"Jesse, do you still have your wallet with you?" Rafe asked, as he suddenly realized his was missing.

Jesse moved his haversack around to feel inside as they continued marching.

"Hell's bells. Mine's gone too. You suppose them tramps took our wallets after they liquored us up?"

Rafe began to feel shame for his stupidity.

"Yeah, I suppose God is punishing us for what we did. I didn't have money, just a letter I was going to mail to Maggie. How about you?"

Jesse was less fortunate. The look on his face gave Rafe the answer before he spoke.

"They took my last month's pay. Close to ten dollars. I hadn't mailed my pay out. What am I going to do now?"

Jesse was already having a hard time keeping the bile from rising in his throat, and the thought of the women taking his pay caused his stomach to wretch as he dropped to his knees alongside the road.

"Stay with him, Gideon. You can catch up when he's done."

Rafe marched on, too disgusted with himself to think of his poor friend heaving along the road in the dust.

It was a long, hot ride home in the carriage from the Methodist Church's sewing circle. Sally Flynn had promised to talk to Hade later that evening about releasing Jonas to go with Ellie as far as the Kentucky border, if needed. Camille had been working in her roses when the carriage made the turn up the long cedar-lined drive. The sultry afternoon had given way to a sticky evening. The air was thick, and the shade from the mimosa trees did little in supplying a respite from the afternoon heat. Jack was lying on the front step, trying to cool his belly on the cool limestone.

Mose jumped down from the seat to help the women from the carriage. Hattie was still fuming as she walked up the stone path to the house.

"I didn't expect you back from the sewing circle so soon," Camille said as she stood and brushed the dried grass from her skirt.

Her face was flushed from being bent over her flowers, and the sweat was starting to soak through the bodice of her cotton dress.

"Mother, I don't think I can go back there again. It was horrible the way those so-called Christian women talked about us."

Camille looked back at Ellie, who was just getting down from the carriage.

"What happened?" Camille asked.

"It was mainly Mrs. Parker who made angry, unkind comments towards you and Mr. Townes. We left when it was clear our services were no longer needed," Ellie said warily.

Camille was saddened by the display of unChristian behavior of her fellow parishioners.

"We must pray for all our friends and neighbors, Hattie, during this war."

As the three women walked up the stone steps to the front porch, Lucy and Mose stayed back, talking. Ellie looked over her shoulder as she walked into the house, and it was then that she saw Mose hand a small piece of white paper to Lucy. Not knowing she was being watched, Lucy shoved the small item into her apron pocket. Ellie continued into the house, where she could hear Hattie recounting to her mother the whole episode from the sewing circle. Ellie made her way upstairs, as Jack scampered ahead of her.

She went into her room to freshen herself from the long, hot ride from town. She decided that she would just lie down for a moment, to try and get rid of the headache that had started to plague her. She could hear the soft voices coming from the room below her, news being shared from a letter that had arrived that day from Caroline. Ellie tried not to let herself be worried that no letters had come for her since her arrival many months before.

She suddenly felt very sad, that something could have happened to her daughter or her dear friend, Charlotte. She tried not to let the depression coil around her insides and shut off the very air in her lungs. But before she could give in to the anxiety that lay beneath her calm façade, Ellie had drifted off to sleep. She dreamed of a man, a very handsome man, who was calling to her. She tried to answer him, but the words were but a whisper. She saw another person in her dream; an old lady, wrinkled and bent from age, writing at a desk. She looked up from her desk at Ellie, telling her it was time, that she would soon know. Ellie tried to understand what the old woman meant by her odd message.

She then found herself sitting in front of a trunk. She couldn't open it, although the key was sitting on the bed. She tried the key, but it wouldn't turn the lock. Then she heard the voice again, a familiar one, calling her. It was then that she opened her eyes, as if someone had shaken her from her slumber. In her half-sleep, half-awake state, she could see a man standing in the hallway, his face in a panic, calling for Ellie.

"Riley, is that you?" Ellie heard the words come from her mouth, but she had no idea what it meant.

Just then, Hattie appeared in the doorway.

"Ella, are you all right? I heard you call out."

Ellie sat up, feeling quite foolish for her being caught talking in her sleep.

"I had the oddest dream. I guess it was the heat and all the excitement of the day. I'm all right though; thank you, for your concern, Hattie."

Ellie smiled, but Hattie wasn't sure she was all right. She walked into the room and sat down on the side of the bed.

"Who is Riley?" Hattie asked.

Ellie's heart skipped a beat.

"Why did you ask that, Hattie?" Ellie asked, not realizing that she had spoken the name.

"You were calling out for someone named Riley. Was that your husband?"

Ellie looked positively mortified. It was evident that she, Hattie, had said something that had upset Ellie.

"I'm sorry; I didn't mean to hurt you."

Ellie sighed, "I don't know who that is, Hattie. I saw someone in my dream, a man. But I don't know who it is."

Hattie could see that she was clearly distressed and sat beside her, obviously intrigued.

"You dreamed about a man you don't know? That is odd, Ella."

Ellie rubbed her eyes, as if she were trying to erase the memory.

"I saw an older lady, she had to be ancient. She said that it was time, and that I'd soon know. I don't even know who she was!"

Hattie tried to offer what comfort she could.

"Well, we all dream strange things, and you have been worried about going back to Indiana. I'm sure that is all that it could be. It will be all right, Father will see to it."

Ellie was embarrassed by her strange dream, but gave the appearance that all was fine.

"Thank you, Hattie. I think I will feel much better after I start packing my things."

Hattie cast her eyes downward; her disappointment was hard to hide.

"I wish you could stay. You are the only one I can talk to about Rafe, and you have been so kind to me. You're just like my own sister, or family at the very least."

Ellie patted Hattie's leg.

"I have enjoyed getting to know you, Hattie. Your family seems like my very own. You have such a rich heritage from both of your parents. Don't ever forget where you have come from, Hattie. It's your roots, and soon you'll be setting roots with Rafe."

The mention of Rafe's name brought Hattie's fears to the surface.

"Do you think Rafe is dead, Ella?"

The question caught Ellie by surprise.

"Why would you think such a thing, Hattie?"

Hattie walked over to the window, her back to Ellie.

"I haven't heard from him since his first two letters. It has been almost two months now, and I have a sick feeling in my stomach that something is wrong."

Ellie didn't know what to say. She decided to try to say what she would want to hear.

"I haven't heard from anyone either, Hattie. I would like to think the mail has been held up due to the war. I'm sure he will write when he can," Ellie said, hoping Hattie's fears wouldn't prove true.

That evening, after the meal was served, the family spent a quiet evening around the pianoforte. Ellie enjoyed the times that she or Hattie would play the beautiful instrument and even Mr. Townes would sing along. Ellie had grown fond of young Joseph, and she could see his school work was much improved from when she arrived several months prior.

"Ella, would you like for us to send for your daughter? She would be most welcome living with us. We have more than enough room, and you would be able to continue on schooling Joseph. He loves you so."

Ellie was taken aback, not knowing how to answer such a generous offer.

"I don't know what to say, Mrs. Townes. I have truly loved my time here at Mimosa Grove with all of you. But I'm afraid for my daughter to travel without a proper escort so far from home."

Ellie now showed her fears of what might be.

"I haven't received any word from any of my family. What if something has happened to Cassandra?"

Daniel looked at his wife; clearly, Ella's concerns were reasonable.

"I don't know that it would be safe for you to send for your daughter. Is there a gentleman relative that could accompany her?"

Ellie looked down from the gaze of the Towneses.

"No, there is no one. She is staying with my friend who is taking care of my home while I'm away. Cassie is almost Hattie's age."

Camille felt the uneasy feeling that had gnawed at Ellie for months.

"Ella, we understand that you feel you must leave us," Camille said.

She turned to her husband, "Daniel, Sally Flynn wanted their hired man, Mr. Dowell, to accompany Ella as far as the border into Kentucky. They could leave from Gallatin this Friday."

Ellie's eyes rose to see what Daniel would say to her traveling with this man.

"How will Hade manage without Jonas? I don't see how he could do without him, especially with no help from his boy."

Ellie's heart sank. That was to be her way to get safely into Kentucky.

"The news I have heard is not good from Kentucky. So many towns are Confederate supporters, while Union troops are moving right through. I don't think it is a good idea for you to be traveling at all, Miss Morgan. But I won't keep you from your daughter. I'm sorry you must be placed in this position."

Ellie summoned all the courage she could call forth from her being. She stood, resolute in her decision.

"I will leave day after tomorrow. If Mr. Dowell is given his leave from Mr. Flynn, I would be most grateful for his accompanying me into Kentucky."

Hattie had been silent throughout the discussion. She spoke up only after hearing Ellie's decision.

"I do wish you would stay. With letters being so few and far between these days, how would we even know if you arrived?"

Ellie wasn't sure she could honestly answer.

"I don't know, Hattie. But if I stay much longer, I might miss my chance to get home to my daughter."

The matter was settled. Daniel took one of the thoroughbred mares from the stable and rode over to the adjoining farm of Hade Flynn. Sally and Hade were sitting under the sycamore tree that gave their large house shade from the evening sun. As Daniel hitched his horse to the post beside the house, Hade Flynn rose to meet him.

"I expected we'd be seeing you sometime today. Sally told me what happened at their sewing circle this morning. Come on over and grab a chair."

He turned to his wife, "Sally, a tall glass of apple cider would sure hit the spot about now."

Sally said hello to Daniel, then disappeared through the screened door.

Daniel pulled one of the wooden chairs over to the shade of the tree.

"Yes, the women were discussing it back at the house all afternoon. It seems our Miss Morgan has gotten herself set on leaving for Indiana come this Friday morning. I wasn't keen on her making such a dangerous trip, but then Camille shared that Sally offered the use of your hired man."

Hade wasn't a man of many words, and his thick German accent made his speech seem more purposeful and labored at times.

"If she is bound and determined, I don't think she should make the trip by way of Gallatin. Jonas was in town yesterday, heard tell of a

Confederate camp, called Boone, up on the Guthrie Road. Seems to me if we send her by way of Camp Boone, she'd be able to get to the railroad or even catch a steamer up to Paducah."

Daniel scratched his head, giving this new plan some thought.

"I could ride to Isaac Collins' plantation and see if his slave, Gideon, could get Miss Morgan through that way. He is well-known in those parts, and his son is going to marry our Hattie. I don't know how safe her travels will be once she crosses into Kentucky."

"Jonas heard the Union troops are heading down to the river; he heard tell they are starting to build fortifications along the river near Saint Bethlehem."

Sally came out just then with a tray and three glasses of apple cider.

"Thank you, Sally," Daniel said as he took a long drink of the cold cider, "this is very good."

Hade sipped his drink, while Sally took hers and went back inside the house.

"Do you think you could spare Jonas for a few days, Hade?"

Hade looked out towards his fields. The corn was ready for picking, and it was soon going to be time to make another cutting on the hay field behind his house.

"I reckon we can do without him for a few days, but that is about it, Daniel."

Daniel smiled, "You're welcome to come by and ask Mose or Abe for help. I can spare them."

Hade said, "I will talk to Jonas when he gets back from the tobacco barn. Looks like we're going to have plenty to sell this year, provided the worms stay off the plants."

Hade had a large farm, but relied on the help of hired hands to keep the farm going. His son, an officer now in the 11th Tennessee Infantry, was serving somewhere in Eastern Tennessee. He had decided that if he had to choose sides, he would go with the Confederacy. He didn't make it his business to question Daniel Townes' reasons for not going off and joining up when all the other gentleman of the county did. He hoped it wouldn't have to become an issue later.

"Well, Hade, I am much obliged for your letting Jonas escort Miss Morgan. I'll tell her to expect a hard next few days of travel north through Kentucky."

Hade smiled, "I don't think Jonas will find his task too offensive."

Daniel finished his cider, thanked Hade for his assistance, and mounted his horse for Mimosa Grove.

Ellie, Camille and Hattie sat fanning themselves in the parlor. Joseph came into the room, and sat on the floor, near Ellie.

"Is it true? Are you leaving, Miss Ella?"

The young boy appeared to be sad.

"Yes, Joseph. I'm afraid it's true. It's time I went home to check on my daughter."

Joseph seemed to be upset with her answer.

"Why can't you stay with us? You said your daughter was staying with your friend. Can't she watch her a little longer?"

Ellie reached down and patted Joseph's blonde curls.

"It makes me sad to have to leave you and your family, Joseph. I have enjoyed being your tutor very much. But I haven't heard from my daughter since I came here, and I am worried about her just like your mama would be if she didn't know about you, Caroline or Hattie."

The comparison to his mother seemed to appease the young lad.

"I wish I could bring her to Mimosa Grove, but there just isn't any way to get word to her."

Camille smiled at her son, who was too young to understand the seriousness of war and what it could mean for them. Ellie put her fan down on the table and rose, straightening her skirt from the wrinkles she had forming on the taffeta.

"If you don't mind, I think I will go up and start packing my things. Would it be all right if I asked Mose to bring my trunks down from the attic?" Ellie asked.

"Of course. Joseph, please go fetch Mose and ask him to come up to the house. I'd like for him to get Miss Morgan's trunks down from the attic," said Camille.

Joseph quickly jumped to the task. He enjoyed following Mose all about, and his cabin was always a place he enjoyed spending his time. The cabin sat down behind the row of mimosa trees, beyond the graveyard. Lucy also had a cabin nearby. Abe had taken a wife, a Cherokee squaw, who had been living near the river with a group of runaway slaves; she had set up a nice little cabin for the two of them. Soon, Mimosa Grove would have another resident. Abe's wife, Rebecca, would be giving birth sometime in the next few months.

Ellie climbed the stairway up to her room. As she reached the landing, the evening sun had warmed the second floor considerably. She pulled the curtains together, trying to keep the heat out. She opened the large chifferobe that stood against the wall opposite her large four-poster bed. She took out the dresses, petticoats and underthings that she had neatly placed inside and placed them on the bed. Next, she opened the drawers and laid her belongings from each in a neat stack on the settee beside the window.

She began to think once again about her dream. The face of the handsome man was someone she had seen before. He was standing in the hallway once before when she had heard a noise. The face of the old woman was kind, but Ellie couldn't make a sense of such a strange dream. Maybe Hattie was right. The heat and her anxiety over her situation could have been the cause. She heard Mose making his way up the stairway. He paused to open the door that led to the attic. Ellie peered out into the hallway, and soon, Mose reappeared carrying one very large trunk.

"Where would you like me to set this, Miss Ella?"

Mose waited in the doorway, the smell of sweat and smoke quite distinct in the closeness of the room.

"Right over here, Mose. Thank you. I have another, if you would be so kind."

Mose went back up to bring down the second trunk, and lay it next to the first. Ellie thanked him, and he was on his way back to his work.

As Ellie put her belongings down inside the trunk, she wondered what Mose and Lucy had been talking about earlier that day. She had also seen Lucy with something in her pocket. Those two had been acting quite secretive over the last few months, but Ellie didn't feel it was her place to say anything to the Townes. They clearly didn't treat Lucy or the others any differently from Hade and Sally Flynn. They were the exception to the rule in these parts.

In fact, Ellie was surprised with the freedom they were given to handle personal matters of the Towneses: the mail and purchases in town, for example.

Downstairs, Ellie heard Daniel come through the front door. She heard a conversation between Daniel and Camille, and then heard footsteps coming up the stairway.

"May we come in, Miss Morgan?" Daniel asked, as they stood in her doorway.

"Yes, please, come in." Ellie sat her books down on the bed.

"I spoke to Hade Flynn, and he thinks you would be safer traveling west to Saint Bethlehem, then on to Paducah, Kentucky. You could try to catch a steamer up to Evansville, or take the rail into Brandenburg. Jonas thinks it would be safer. There is too much troop movement in and around the Cumberland River near the Gap. You will have to travel without an escort for a good portion of the trip. Are you sure you want to do this?" Daniel questioned.

Camille added, "Ella, Mr. Dowell said there is a Confederate camp nearby, and that he feels you might be safe if one of the Collins' slaves drives you through. Daniel could ride tomorrow to Elmwood to ask Mr. Collins. With our families going to be related, surely he would see fit to help you."

Ellie thought perhaps Hattie could join her, just as far as the Collins' home.

"Would it be all right if Hattie came with me, just as far as Elmwood? She is so distraught over not hearing from young Mr. Collins. I think being with his sister would do her a world of good."

Ellie wasn't sure if she had spoken out of turn, but Camille didn't say no. Daniel rubbed his hand on the back of his neck, letting out a long sigh.

"I suppose it would do her some good, she hasn't been the same since he left."

"Thank you, both, for being so kind to me. I do wish I could stay on, I have loved being here at Mimosa Grove," Ellie said.

She reached out to each, and they in turn took her hand.

"You are like family now, Ella. God go with you," Daniel said.

Ellie felt that at least she could somehow help Hattie's sadness if she could be with Rafe's family for a short visit. Perhaps they had heard from him, and that would ease her mind somewhat.

After the Towneses left her room, she closed her door and began to undress for bed. She quickly took off her clothes, folding them neatly on the settee. She walked to the wash bowl, feeling the cool water bathe her face, throat and chest. The day's grime from the dusty road darkened the clean water, and Ellie quickly dried herself with the towel that hung on a peg on the wall. After putting on her nightgown, she finished packing her things. She was about to climb into bed when she remembered the small trunk she had brought with her.

Mose didn't see it, evidently, and it still lay upstairs in the attic. She would need to go up before tomorrow to get it. She put on her wrap and quietly opened her door. Just as she started to walk towards the attic with Jack in tow, Hattie's door opened.

"Ella, could you come in here please?"

Ellie turned and walked into the girl's room.

"Thank you for asking Mama and Papa if I could ride to Elmwood with you and Mr. Dowell. I have wanted to see Maggie, and I'm hopeful they've gotten word from Rafe."

"Yes, that is my hope too!" Ellie said reassuringly.

Ellie wasn't sure what caused her to say it, but she told Hattie that she too was worried about Rafe. It was good that she was going to visit his family. After the two talked for a few more moments, Ellie closed the door and continued quietly towards the stairway. The door was ajar, and Ellie was sure it had been closed before. She climbed the stairs careful not to cause the boards to creak. She bent down to pick up Jack, and carried him up the stairs.

When she reached the top of the stairs, she saw the back of someone over in the corner of the attic, the candle illuminating the shadow against the opposite wall. Ellie could see someone was putting something back behind the large chest of drawers that sat against the wall. She would have to hurry and crouch behind the large crates that were stacked to the right of the door. Quickly, she stepped off to crouch down, praying that Jack would not make a sound.

Lucy turned to face the stairs, and quickly made her way to the attic door. Ellie was thankful for being out of her taffeta dress, as it would have given her away with the rustling of the material. Ellie held in her breath, the heat in the attic almost too much to bear, until she could hear Lucy close the door behind her.

Ellie stood up, and in the dark fumbled to find the candle and matches that she had shoved into the pocket of her gown. Striking a match in the dark proved quite the challenge, as she wasted one good match on her efforts. With the second match, she found success, and the candle illuminated the small area in which she sat.

Now just what was Lucy doing up here? This was the second time she was up here in the last two months, at least that I know of. Ellie quietly made her way across the attic to where the large chest was sitting. She saw the trunk sitting on the floor. She should have just taken the trunk back down stairs with her, but her curiosity took the best of her. She sat the trunk beside her and shined the candle's light down behind the chest. It was then that she saw a section of board was sticking out from the wall.

She would have to move the corner of the dresser to see what it was, but that might wake up the Towneses below. She lifted her gown so that she could put her knee against the chest to give her stability.

The heat was almost too much, and Ellie felt she would pass out if she stayed much longer. Jack began sniffing behind the chest. He was almost to the board when Ellie started to feel herself sway as if she might faint. She reached out to steady herself, and it was then that she saw what Lucy had been doing in the attic. Lying on the floor was a hatbox; it appeared to be half in and half out of the wall.

Ellie tried to carefully get her arm to where she could steady herself and open the box. As the lid came off, her eyes strained to see what was inside. She tried to switch the candle to her other hand, and when she did, she almost lost her balance. The candle shown down inside the box, and there inside appeared to be three letters, maybe four, and each addressed to Miss Hattie Townes. Ellie tried to get a closer look, dumbfounded at what she saw. The name in the top left corner was Pvt. Raford Collins.

Ellie couldn't believe her eyes. Why in the world would Rafe's letters be inside the hatbox? It was clear that Lucy had something to do with it. It was the letter on top that she had put in her pocket today after getting the mail! She had been hiding the letters from Hattie! Ellie was about to turn and march herself down the stairs to confront Lucy, but she felt her hand slip from the perspiration that ran down her arm. She tried to catch herself, but as she fell into the wall, the room began to spin.

Ellie started to fall forward, striking her head on the corner of the chest. She tried to will herself into consciousness, but she heard a roaring in her ears that sounded like a locomotive. She surrendered into the blackness that wrapped itself all around her.

BOOK III

Mimosa Grove, July 30, 2011

Life is lived forwards, but understood backwards.
- Unknown

Chapter 16

The room was spinning when Ellie tried to open her eyes. Jack was whimpering beside her. The attic was stifling hot, but the room was nothing like it had been moments before. It was daylight for one, and she was lying on the floor in a pair of shorts and a T-shirt. For a moment, she was unsure what was happening. She remembered being in a long nightgown, and the Townes family were sleeping downstairs. It was then that she saw him, first a filmy vision, then he became a solid form. It was Rafe. Ellie tried to sit up, but she was too weak. Rafe bent down beside her.

"Hurry, there isn't much time. He's coming. Did you find Hattie?"

Ellie tried to focus on Rafe's face, the words he was saying to her.

"Rafe? Why are you here? You left months ago to join up with the 11th Tennessee," Ellie said, her voice weak.

The urgency in Rafe's voice was almost a panic.

"Ellie, did you find Hattie? Why didn't she answer my letters?"

Ellie finally began to get her memory back, or what she thought was her memory.

"It was Lucy, Rafe."

Rafe looked at Ellie, puzzled.

"It was Lucy who took the letters. She hid them up here, in the attic, Rafe. I saw her tonight!"

Ellie now remembered seeing the letters in the hatbox.

"You mean Lucy, the darkie?"

Rafe was crestfallen.

"Lucy must have wanted to keep Hattie from marrying you. She hated that your family had slaves, Rafe. I'm sure that is why. Hattie never stopped loving you. I know that."

Rafe turned, hearing someone coming.

"Ellie, did she ever know what I did?" Rafe's voice seemed to break, as if he was about to cry.

"What you did? I don't know what you're talking about," Ellie said.

Rafe looked back at the door again, then to Ellie.

"I have a boy, or at least that is what Melinda says. I wrote Hattie to explain."

Ellie was so confused now, she wasn't sure she had helped Rafe in the least. She slowly sat up and leaned her back against the wall. It was then that she felt a trickle of blood run down the side of her face. She had hit the corner of the chest when she fell. Rafe took her hand, his eyes beseeching her once again to listen.

"You did what I asked of you, and I thank you. I never knew. Thank you, Ellie."

Ellie wasn't sure of what had happened to her, which time was real and which had been a dream.

"Rafe, who is Melinda?"

Rafe wanted to tell her more, but he wasn't able. He began to fade slightly before her eyes.

"Rafe, wait. I don't understand."

Rafe stood up, feeling as if he had been somehow set free.

"It's in the trunk. Everything you need. Thank you, Ellie."

Ellie reached out to take Rafe's hand.

"Will I see you again?"

Ellie tried to make sense of it all, but her head was still spinning from the bump she had taken.

"I'm not feeling too good. I remember I got shot. I was at Murfreesboro. I remember now, Ellie."

Rafe looked down at the uniform, and it was then that he saw the small circular hole in the side of his jacket. A small, crimson stain was visible, growing darker. He reached his hand inside the shirt, his hand covered in red.

Almost in disbelief, he asked, "Did I die?"

Ellie tried to concentrate on what she could remember, and she knew it was true.

"Yes, Rafe, you died. I saw your grave. Hattie never knew why you didn't write back, and after she learned you were mortally wounded and died, she was inconsolable. She married another man some years later.

I think I had to help to you find out about Hattie so that you can rest now."

Rafe tried to say more, but it was if the life was leaving him before Ellie's eyes.

"I'll never forget you. God bless you, Raford Collins."

As she said it, his hand slipped through hers, and he began to fade before her eyes. When he finally vanished, she began to cry. It was as if she were at his graveside, like the dream. Maybe she was crying for Hattie as well.

After Rafe had left her, she noticed that the small trunk was sitting at her feet. In her pocket was the key; how it got there, she didn't know. She sat up, composed herself, and put the key into the lock that had been rusted shut. Now, miraculously, it turned.

"Well I'll be . . ." Ellie said aloud as the lock opened as easily as if she had just bought it.

Inside the trunk was an assortment of papers. One paper was addressed to Ella Morgan.

It was faded, but she could still make out the words. It was a letter from Lavina George. How in the world had it gotten into the trunk? It was as if Lavina had written a sort of family history of Raford Collins. How had she known about Rafe? It was a letter to the family of Robert Isaac Langley, applying for his application to the Sons of Confederate Veterans. His mother had been given membership into the Daughters of the Confederacy, and her son was seeking membership into the SCV.

Ellie sat and tried to understand why this paperwork would have been in the possession of Lavina George. In fact, why was the name Langley part of this letter? As she continued reading, the letter was a confirmation that Robert Langley's mother was Julia Collins Langley. Julia was the daughter of William Raford Collins, the son of Raford Collins and Melinda Turner. Ellie sat in the floor taking in the revelation of what she had read. Raford Collins was the great-great-great grandfather of Riley Langley? Lavina George had to know this.

Ellie put the letter down and continued into the trunk. Another letter was written, but this letter was much more recent. Ellie didn't notice the blood that continued to slowly trickle down her check; she wiped her cheek on the bottom of her shirt as she continued reading. The letter was handwritten, which made it harder for her to focus. The handwriting was neat, but evidently done by someone who was on in years. The letter was addressed to Ella Morgan.

> *March 11, 1990*
> *Dear Ella,*
>
> My dear, you have no doubt been confused as to why you were brought here. Now that you are reading this letter, I hope your questions have been answered. I know you were misled into thinking that you were the only heir who could own Mimosa Grove. I could have chosen your uncle, but it had to be you, Ella. Raford came to me several times while I was living in my parents' home. This home, also home to Hattie Townes, was our common ancestor. It is your heritage, Ella, to own this home. But more important, a wrong could possibly be righted by you coming into Riley Langley's life. Rafe needed to find his peace with not having Hattie as his wife. Somehow, by you meeting Riley, the love of Rafe and Hattie could continue through their ancestors. What if both of you are married to others? I am sure you're not by the time you are reading this. It was meant to be, dear one. And you have already fallen for him, haven't you? It is mutual. You will know it, if you don't already realize it, that he loves you as well. Please continue to care for Mimosa Grove as I have done. It's your destiny, Ella. It is Hattie's legacy to you. I couldn't help Rafe, but knew that someday, you would be able to. I truly hope you have been able to do what was needed to give Rafe peace. It is my hope that both Rafe and Hattie have found rest.
>
> Please give my regards to Rafe if you see him again, although I am sure he can now rest in peace. All my love and best wishes,
>
> *Aunt Lavina*

Ellie sat for a moment, too shocked to believe what she had read. How did Aunt Lavina know all those years ago that she would be here, at Mimosa Grove, able to open this trunk? It had to be that she knew all along what had to be done. She looked further into the trunk, and it was then that she saw another letter. This one was addressed to Riley. It was sealed, and Ellie decided to leave it that way. Her head had started to pound where she was cut. Her thoughts of Rafe were interrupted by a commotion somewhere off in the distance.

At first, she thought it was thunder. The banging was a deep, rhythmic sound, coming from below. She reached for the side of the chest to help steady herself as she stood. Across the way from where she stood was the mirror, the same mirror that she had first seen when she found the letters. The sound repeated, and it was then that Ellie heard her name being called.

She made her way to the window that looked out onto the yard below. It all looked so differently from what she had just seen. She wasn't sure what exactly had happened or how she had spent the past months living among her ancestors. She was beginning to remember the hatbox now, the trunks full of Hattie and Caroline's things. She remembered Riley and the date they had had only a few nights before. But how could that be?

Then she heard the sound again, this time louder, and she heard footsteps coming up the stairs.

"Ellie? Can you hear me? Ellie!" the voice was deep, that of a man.

Ellie turned to the attic door.

"Are you up here, Ellie?

Ellie slowly walked along the attic, holding on to pieces of furniture as she went.

"Riley? Is that you?"

Ellie quickly made her way towards the door, and as she reached for the knob, Riley was already pushing the door open.

"Ellie, you have had me scared out of my mind. What happened?"

Riley saw the gash above Ellie's eyebrow, the blood still oozing from the cut.

"Riley, I fell against the dresser over there; I don't know how long I've been out."

Riley took Ellie's face in his hands and kissed her on top of her head.

"You had me worried out of my mind. I have tried calling you for two days. I thought I had done something to make you uncomfortable. When I got the call from Cassie . . ." Riley was interrupted by Ellie at the mention of her daughter.

"You heard from Cassie?" Ellie almost burst into tears at the sound of her daughter's name.

"Ellie, she has been trying to call you for two solid days, and after she couldn't get you, she called your friend, Charlotte. It was then that she gave Cassie the number of my office that you had left with her."

Ellie tried to make sense of it all, but started feeling unsteady again.

"You mean I've been lying here for two days? It has been months!"

Riley looked at Ellie, not sure if she was talking out of her mind due to a concussion or if she was just being sarcastic.

"Let's go downstairs. I'm taking you in for the doctor to have a look at you."

Ellie took Riley's hand, but turned back to the trunk.

"The trunk. I need it."

Riley bent down and picked up the trunk.

"I'll be fine, Riley. Just let me hang on to you while we go down the stairs, then I'll be all right."

As they left the attic, Ellie couldn't help but wonder what the Townes family was thinking, waking to find that Ella had left. She didn't even get to tell them goodbye. Riley put the trunk on the large cherry table that sat in the upstairs foyer. He led Ellie into the bathroom where he got a wash cloth to clean the blood from her face.

"It's lucky that my father had a key to the house. Mrs. George had given it to him years ago. I hope you don't mind me taking the liberty to come in your house. I was just worried half out of my mind."

Ellie smiled now, having seen a whole different side to Riley.

"So you've said, at least twice now."

Riley had driven the ten miles from his office to Mimosa Grove in less than ten minutes.

"Thank you for coming out and checking on me, Riley."

"So what exactly were you doing in the attic on a hot July afternoon? How did you get this nasty cut on you head?"

Ellie wasn't sure how much she should say, not wanting to convince Riley further that she had a concussion.

"Riley, there is a letter for you in that trunk. Aunt Lavina wrote it to you over 20 years ago."

Riley's expression was that of utter disbelief.

"Wrote a letter to me? Are you sure?"

Ellie stood up, "If you don't believe me, I can show it to you. It is still sealed in the trunk."

Riley wasn't sure what to make of it all.

"Why would Mrs. George be writing to me so long ago?"

Ellie walked out of the bathroom and went to open the trunk.

"She wrote to me as well. Here."

Ellie handed Riley the letter, which was neatly addressed to him. If you would rather read it later, I understand."

Ellie was curious to know what could be in his letter, but took more of an interest in Riley's reaction to it.

"I can't believe all of this. It's like something in the Twilight Zone," Riley said.

Ellie sat down on the chair in the foyer.

"After what I have seen, nothing surprises me."

Riley walked over and sat beside her.

"Ellie, I've had a hard time keeping my mind on my work. I haven't felt like this in years. I guess I didn't want to feel this way, after Katie and Taylor were killed. It just was easier not to feel anything."

Ellie reached out and placed her hand on Riley's knee.

"I know what that feels like, to lose someone and feel like your life is over."

Riley looked down at the letter, then back up to Ellie.

"What I'm trying to tell you, and obviously I'm not doing a very eloquent job, is that I am falling in love with you, Ellie Morgan. I tried not to, but you have been invading my every thought since you strolled into my office wearing that very hot, pale pink suit. You had me right in the palm of your hand and didn't even notice."

Ellie wasn't sure she was hearing Riley correctly.

"I have felt something for you ever since I met you, Riley. I wasn't sure exactly what it was. I'm glad you told me how you feel. I think it was meant to be, that we meet, and even fall in love."

Riley wasn't sure what Ellie was talking about, but he didn't give her a chance to finish. He leaned over and kissed her, his lips softly touching hers.

The kiss was more than a proclamation of Riley's falling in love with Ellie; but a promise, of love over 150 years that would finally be fulfilled. It would be the legacy of Hattie Townes and Rafe Collins. Ellie would tell Riley all about Rafe, but later. She was enjoying the wonderful sensations Riley's kiss was sending throughout her body. Riley let the envelope fall to the floor as he took Ellie in his arms.

Epilogue

Riley did learn the truth about Rafe Collins. It was while reading the letter from Mrs. Lavina George that he learned his family history, and how this history brought Ellie Morgan to him. While the whole affair baffled him, he didn't question the reason Ellie was brought into his life. He would also learn about what happened to Ellie during the two days that she lay unconscious in the attic. While this was harder for him to fathom, he accepted the possibility that the paranormal was at work in helping Ellie solve a 150 year old mystery.

Ellie finished reading Camille's diary, learning of the news that young Rafe Collins had been shot and mortally wounded. The diary furnished information about a schoolteacher that had come to stay, but had passed away from a nasty fall in the attic. No mention was made about how she fell and hit her head, but Joseph told his mother that Lucy had been in the attic earlier that day. She couldn't believe such a thing about her housekeeper. Hattie was grief stricken upon learning of Rafe's death. It was her fear from the first of the war that he might not return. Hattie never learned about the letters in the attic. In fact, after the death of Rafe, her mother and brother both took sick with the typhoid. She tried to no avail to nurse them both, but neither survived.

Her father had joined a regiment of Union soldiers during the winter of 1862, but Mimosa Grove was spared during the war. The Union and Confederate armies used the home while passing through the area on their way to various battles in and around the Nashville area. Camp Jackson would use the barns and outbuildings as well. After the death of her mother and brother, a Confederate soldier made his way back through Hendersonville on his way to his plantation in Goodlettsville. He spent several weeks recuperating at Mimosa Grove.

Sometime after the war ended, a young woman and small dark-headed boy showed up at the home of Maggie Collins. The girl was sickly, but she lived long enough to tell the Collins family of the boy's father. He would be raised by the Collins family, a final tie to their beloved son, Raford.

It was after the war ended that Hattie married the young Confederate officer, Randolph Cooper Lankford. They made their home with her father at Mimosa Grove. The home was to be the legacy of each generation thereafter of Townes' descendants.

Rafe never again came back to Mimosa Grove. Ellie kept her promise to decorate the Confederate soldiers' graves in the cemetery east of town. Riley would be joining her to place flowers on all the graves, but special care was taken to keep the monument of Raford I. Collins in memorial wreaths and flowers.

Cassie came to spend time with her mother at Mimosa Grove and fell in love with the area. Her mother would not be returning to her job at the high school in Newburg. She would be living in Tennessee, soon to be married to Riley Langley. Charlotte and Sean Barrow were seen around town having dinner on more than one occasion. They would become the next pair to plan a wedding. Ellie was very happy for her friend. She would be coming to see Ellie's new plantation home over the Labor Day weekend. Ellie would finally explain it all to her then.

Birth Record

Daniel Adam Townes
Born-January 1, 1836
Died-March 3, 1836

Caroline Isabelle Townes
Born-February 13, 1838

Jacob Washington Townes
Born-August 17, 1840
Died-June 15, 1844

Harriet Colbert Townes
Born-May 9, 1842

Joseph Burnell Townes
Born-February 7, 1850
Died-July 8, 1864

Marriage Record of the Townes Family

Isabella Elizabeth Colbert-Adam Washington Burnell
12 December, 1812

Camille Sophia Burnell-Daniel Corbin Townes
16 April, 1835

Harriet Colbert Townes-Randolph Cooper Lankford
22 November, 1865

Eugenia Camille Lankford-Nathan Forrest Carrington
27 May, 1888

Susannah Francis Carrington-Jeremiah Lewis Stone
13 September, 1901

Kathleen Louise Stone-Robert Wayne Ridgeway
27 June, 1929

Elizabeth Caroline Ridgeway-Franklin Lee Camden
15 December, 1955

Ella Caroline Camden Morgan-Riley Donovan Langley
18 December, 2011

Bibliography

Ferguson, Edwin L. (1972). Sumner County, Tennessee in the Civil War. Monroe County Press, Thompkinsville, Kentucky.

Information was gathered through internet search of the 11th Tennessee. Tennesseans in the Civil War, vol.1. Copyrighted 1964 by the "Civil War centennial Commission of Tennessee".